SURRO

Even if he wasn't yet positive that they were about to be attacked, it was still possible to apply two of the most important rules of combat when ambushed: *Don't stand still* and *do the unexpected*. Reaching down suddenly, he grabbed Inge's hand and turned her sharply aside. "Come on!"

"Blake!"

But she started to run with him. Then she stumbled, and Murdock cursed. She was wearing black high heels that hobbled her as effectively as a ball and chain.

The unexpected move alone, however, had been enough. Ahead, the two utility workers broke into a run. *"Inge! Kommen Sie zurück!"* the woman behind them called out. Turning, Murdock saw the woman pulling something small and black from the depths of her canvas bag . . . a handgun. And the man beside her had a pistol tucked into his waistband, its grip visible beneath the flapping hem of his jacket as he too started running.

The ambush had just been sprung.

1319 wa

SEAL TEAM SEVEN
Nucflash

Don't miss these other explosive
SEAL TEAM SEVEN **missions:**

SEAL TEAM SEVEN
and
SPECTER

By Keith Douglass

THE CARRIER SERIES:

CARRIER
VIPER STRIKE
ARMAGEDDON MODE
FLAME-OUT
MAELSTROM
COUNTDOWN

THE SEAL TEAM SEVEN SERIES:

SEAL TEAM SEVEN
SPECTER
NUCFLASH

SEAL TEAM SEVEN
NUCFLASH

KEITH DOUGLASS

BERKLEY BOOKS, NEW YORK

SEAL TEAM SEVEN: NUCFLASH

A Berkley Book / published by arrangement with the authors

PRINTING HISTORY
Berkley edition / August 1995

ISBN: 0-425-14881-5

BERKLEY®
Berkley Books are published by The Berkley Publishing Group,
200 Madison Avenue, New York, New York 10016.
BERKLEY and the "B" design
are trademarks belonging to Berkley Publishing Corporation.

PRINTED IN THE UNITED STATES OF AMERICA

10 9 8 7 6 5 4 3 2 1

NUCFLASH

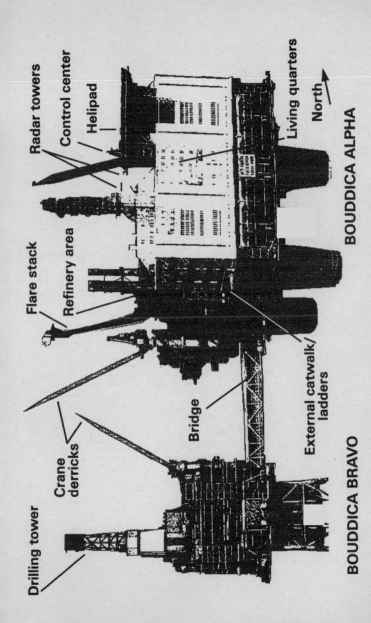

Drilling tower

Crane derricks

Flare stack

Refinery area

Radar towers

Control center

Helipad

Bridge

External catwalk/ladders

Living quarters

North

BOUDDICA BRAVO

BOUDDICA ALPHA

PROLOGUE

"Attention, attention. British Airways Flight Twenty-eight from Hong Kong, now arriving Gate Three. . . ."

Pak Chong Yong stepped off the boarding ramp, following the line of his fellow passengers into the waiting lounge in London's Heathrow International Airport. He wore an expensive three-piece suit, with five-hundred-dollar shoes, and carried a leather attaché case for the respectability it afforded him. There was respectability too in his companion, the attractive Korean woman next in line behind him. After almost fifteen hours aboard the 744, Chun Hyon Hee's pink and white business suit was rumpled, but no more so than the clothing of the others aboard Flight 28. It was not yet five in the morning, local time. The sky, visible through the big windows in one wall of the waiting lounge, was still dark, though touched by streaks of a cold, predawn light.

Filing up to the customs gate with the other disembarking passengers, both kept their faces impassive. This would be their first and possibly their most dangerous test. . . .

"Passports, please. You two traveling together?"

"Yes, sir."

His English was perfect. The passport he surrendered to the customs official at the gate gave his name as Kim Doo Ok, a vice president of marketing for the Seoul-based Daewan International Corporation. His companion's passport listed her as Madam Kim Song Hee, since their control for this operation

1

had felt they would be safer traveling together as husband and wife. Chun, like Pak, was a member of the People's Eighth Special Operations Corps.

"Business or pleasure?"

Pak allowed his face to crease in an unaccustomed smile. "A little of both, sir. I have business for my company . . . but we thought we would combine it with a small vacation."

"'At's the ticket." After a cursory inspection of their papers, Pak's briefcase, and Chun's carry-on bag, the blue-uniformed official stamped their passports, smiled brightly, and handed them back with a cheerful, "Have a nice stay in England, Mr. and Mrs. Kim!"

"Thank you. We will."

Beyond the bottleneck of the customs gate they stopped momentarily, until the jostle of people from behind forced the two of them to step aside, suddenly uncertain. Neither of them had ever been to Heathrow before, and the bustle of people was as confusing and as noisy as Hong Kong or Tokyo, and far more alien. Pak felt a shiver of xenophobia, quickly suppressed. His training in covert operations, relentless, grueling, and long, had included outings and maneuvers in several Western cities, and for a time he'd been assigned to Operation Suwi—Watchman—in New York City. He didn't like Western cities, however, and knew he would never get used to them . . . or their mongrel-yapping, contentious, and ill-disciplined people.

The corridors, coldly lit by fluorescent lighting panels overhead, were actually not that crowded. Most of the people milling about beyond the customs gate were waiting for passengers arriving on British Air 28. Their contact ought to be here somewhere. . . .

"Mr. Kim?"

Pak turned, eyes narrowed to hard slits in his round face. The man approaching him from the back of pay phones to the right had a seedy look to him, and his breath stank of too many hours in the airport's bar.

"I'm Kim."

"Long flight?"

"Not so bad. The service was good anyway."

"Glad to hear it. Things ain't what they used to be, flying." The formalities of sign and countersign concluded, the man stuck out his hand. "I'm O'Malley."

Pak ignored the hand. "Is there someplace more private? I dislike meeting in the open, like this."

"Ssst!" the man hissed. He glanced back and forth, his too-expressive face revealing his fear. "Keep it down, willya? Ain't seen no Sassmen about, but that don't mean they ain't there. C'mon."

Pak exchanged a glance with Chun. That was the problem with ops requiring cooperation with *oegugin* . . . the hated foreigners. More often than not, they were poorly trained and poorly disciplined, and they nearly always betrayed more concern for their personal safety than for the completion of the mission.

Pak would be glad when this mission was done and he could return to Pyongyang.

"That's O'Malley all right," the British airport security chief said. "But who're the two gooks?"

Colonel Wentworth glanced up from the television monitor. The Security Office was a clean, close room filled with banks of monitors and a number of security men, but the three of them—Wentworth, the security chief, and the man in the dark suit whose ID had marked him as a special agent with MI5—had this corner of the room to themselves, and no one else was within earshot.

"Their passports are for a Mr. and Mrs. Kim," Wentworth replied. "But I wouldn't place too much faith in that. Our people are checking with Daewan International now, but I expect they'll check out okay. The opposition's pretty careful about things like that."

The security chief reached for a white telephone. "So. Shall I call my people in and pick 'em up?"

"Negative," Wentworth said. He was wearing a headset and could hear the terse back-and-forth reports of the troopers on the ground, a reassuring background murmur of voices and code phrases. "My men are already on it. Let's not spook them with uniforms, okay?"

"Listen, Colonel, O'Malley's a known terr. A damned bloody Provo. If he does somethin' loopy on the concourse, it's me job, see?"

"O'Malley's not a problem," Wentworth said. "He's not carrying, and his backup stayed outside the security check zone. My guess is he just went in to pick up the two Koreans."

"Well, your *guess* had damned sure better be a good one."

1

Friday, April 27

CQB house, 23 SAS Training Center
Dorset, England

Chief Machinist's mate Tom Roselli—"Razor" to his comrades-at-arms in SEAL Team Seven—snuggled back in the deep, battered, and overstuffed sofa, working furiously at the ropes binding his wrists. His fingers were tingling; the guy who'd tied those knots had done a good, professional job of it. Roselli couldn't budge them with his fingers, and his trademark Sykes-Fairbairn commando knife had been taken from him moments ago. "Don't think you'll be needin' this, mate," his captor had said with a cheerful grin. "Wouldn't want you hurtin' yourself, y'know!"

Roselli had replied with some rather vicious curses, but neither curses nor graphically detailed threats had had the least effect. He did still have another holdout blade his captors hadn't found, but it was squirreled away in the heel of his left boot, and at this point it would take too long to work it free.

He hated being helpless, hated the feeling of not being in control of the situation. Early in his SEAL training, some years before, he and the other recruits, the tadpoles of his BUD/S class at Coronado, had been tied hand and foot and unceremoniously dumped into a twenty-foot-deep water tank. The exercise, called "drown-proofing," had required the recruits to calmly sink to the bottom, push back to the surface for a breath, then repeat the process . . . and by doing so learning to control, then subdue, the bad-ass specter of panic. Panic, his BUD/S instructors had insisted, was what killed swimmers, not drowning. Helped along by their instructors, SEAL tads were soon donning masks and even swimming underwater, still with their wrists and ankles tied.

The only way Roselli had endured it was to push through, to overcome the handicap and the sense of abject helplessness and keep on going . . . which, of course, was precisely what the instructors had intended. It was just one part of the long process by which U.S. Navy SEALs were made.

But he never did learn to *like* it.

"Face it, Razor," Jaybird Sterling said, watching his struggles from the other side of the room. "We're here for the duration."

"Screw that, Jaybird," Roselli replied. He had to lean to one side a bit to see the other man, since a terrorist hung between them, swaying slightly back and forth. Five other terrorists were scattered about the furniture-cluttered room, paying no attention to their two captives. One was sprawled in the sofa at Roselli's right side.

"How much longer, you think?" Sterling asked. "Man, I hate bein' tied down!"

Roselli looked Sterling up and down. Like Roselli, Machinist's Mate Second Class David Sterling was tightly tied hand and foot and was sitting in an overstuffed chair with his feet propped up on a low stool. "What bugs me isn't the ropes, so much," Roselli replied. He quirked a smile. "It's the fact that the sadistic bastards put us in the *comfy chairs*!"

Jaybird looked puzzled, blinking through the clear plastic goggles he was wearing. "The what?"

"The comfy chairs."

"Man, now I know you're crackin' up."

"Don't you watch Monty Python?"

"Monty who?"

"Never mind. Obviously you've never run into Monty Python, and trying to explain *that* would—"

A window at the far end of the room shattered, and a dark gray cardboard cylinder bounded into the room. "Eyes!"

Roselli yelled, interrupting himself, and both men turned their heads and squeezed their eyes shut.

The flashbang grenade had a charge reduced to training specs, but nonetheless it detonated with a rippling chain of ear-splitting cracks and a strobing pulse of light so intense that Roselli could see the flash through tightly closed eyelids. By the time he was certain that the last charge had gone off and had opened his eyes once more, the room's single door had splintered in time to the double concussion of twin shotgun blasts. The splinters were still flying as black-garbed men began spilling into the room, moving with an expert and long-practiced choreography that put a different armed man in every corner of the room in scant seconds. The harsh *chuff-chuff-chuff* of sound-suppressed Browning automatics blended together into a cacophony of hissing gunfire, and the "terrorists" began exploding in puffs of straw. Six bullets slammed in rapid succession into the straw dummy at Roselli's right, five punching through its fatigue shirt and into what would have been its center of mass . . . though one show-off round exploded the head in a whirling flurry of yellow-white fragments. The dummy hanging from the rafters between Roselli and Sterling danced on its rope for a second, then collapsed to the floor as the rope suspending it was shot through. Another one propped up on the floor to Roselli's left disintegrated, dropping a handful-sized hank of straw squarely on his head.

The gunmen were terrifying, garbed head to toe in black combat dress that included a hood tightly cinched over their heads, black gas masks and protective goggles that gave their faces the nightmarish, high-tech look of a squad of Darth Vaders with attitudes. They wore gloves and non-skid boots; two carried sound-suppressed Browning pistols, while two more wielded MP5SD3s—the H&Ks with the massive, integral silencer barrels that many SEALs preferred in close-quarters hostage-rescue scenarios. The four men of the assault team were members of the British Special Air Service, the SAS. The room, properly the CQB, or Close Quarters Battle house, was more popularly known as the Killing House, a living-room mock-up designed to allow hostage-rescue units to practice their marksmanship and their target identification.

Sitting in the sofa, covered with straw, Roselli was delighted that they were as good at target ID as they'd claimed to be.

"Clear!" the first man into the room shouted, as he pivoted back and forth, his H&K held high and deadly, his voice muffled by the gas mask.

"Clear!" his number two called from the other side of the door, as he dropped an empty mag from his H&K and slapped another home with polished and professional ease.

"Clear!" a third called from behind Roselli's sofa.

"Clear!"

For a moment the only movement in the room was the swinging of the shot-through rope, the only sound the rasp of the assault team's breathing through the gas masks, and the heavy breathing of the two rescued "hostages."

"Well, I certainly wasn't expecting the Spanish Inquisition," Roselli said loudly into the near silence.

Four masked, black-hooded heads pivoted toward the sound of his voice. "Beg your pardon, Yank?" one of the troopers said.

"Monty Python? The British comic group?"

No one said a word, and Roselli shook his head. "Damn, I though *everyone* in England would know about Monty Python!"

"Don't mind him," Jaybird told the puzzled hostage rescue team. "He never grew up. The guy specializes in obscure humor."

"I'll obscure your humor. How about getting us out of these ties, huh?"

Minutes later, Roselli and Sterling were outside in the mid-morning daylight once more, rubbing chafed wrists as they gathered with their hosts and the other two SEALs in the training exchange. Most of the U.S. Special Warfare units cross-trained occasionally with their opposite numbers in Europe, especially the German GSG9 and the world-famous British SAS, and the Navy SEALs were no exception. Four members of SEAL Seven's Third Platoon had been assigned a three-week rotation with the Special Air Service's 23rd Regiment. The other two SEALs in the program were Quartermaster First Class Martin Brown and Electrician's Mate Second Class William Higgins.

"You okay, Razor?" Brown looked worried. "We heard a lot a' shootin' and lootin' in there."

"Your turn next, Magic," Roselli favoring the big SEAL sniper with a sadistic grin. "You're just gonna *love* this."

1030 hours
BKA Headquarters
Wiesbaden, Federal Republic of Germany

"We call him Komissar," their guide said. She was a dazzling, long-legged German blonde in a severe, gray business suit, whose English contained only a trace of an accent. "And he may be our most important weapon in fighting Euroterrorism."

The two men trailing her through the gleaming corridors and warrens of the headquarters complex of the German BKA stopped and politely looked as she pointed out what was obviously, for her at least, the showpiece of the tour. Through the double-paned windows of an air-conditioned basement room, the black, white, and silver cabinets of a sprawling, mainframe computer could be seen.

Lieutenant Blake Murdock, the commanding officer of SEAL Seven's Third Platoon, along with Master Chief Engineman George MacKenzie, had arrived in Wiesbaden the previous evening, on a space-available Air Force flight out of Lakenheath. Early that morning they'd reported to the ultramodern, glass and concrete complex on a hilltop in the suburbs outside of Wiesbaden that was the headquarters of the BKA, the Bundeskriminant, Germany's Federal Investigation Department. Inge Schmidt, a BKA special agent, had been assigned by the department's liaison bureau to show the two Navy SEALs around. For a change, both men were wearing civilian suits rather than either Navy dress uniforms or the more usual fatigues or combat dress, and both carried leather attaché cases. Murdock felt distinctly uncomfortable in his monkey suit, as he called it, and was looking forward to shedding jacket and tie at the earliest possible moment.

"We've heard a lot about Komissar," Murdock said. "He's

the main reason we're here, in fact. Some of the information you have squirreled away in here about German terrorist groups may be of importance to our current investigation. Especially your Red Army faction."

"So the director told me," the woman said. With a grand sweep of her arm, she indicated the gleaming, impeccably clean and shining cabinets that housed the BKA's monster computer. "If there is information to be had anywhere on the Continent on the people you are researching, it is here, in Komissar's data banks."

"A little out of date, isn't he?" MacKenzie observed.

"Mac . . ." Murdock said, warning edging his voice.

"Komissar" was a computer, a very large computer with a mainframe occupying a small, air-conditioned room in the BKA's basement, and with terminals located throughout the office complex.

"He was installed during the late 1970s," Inge said, sounding a bit defensive, almost as though a favorite child had just been harshly and unfairly criticized. "And he has been upgraded several times since. He currently stores some tens of millions of pages of information on terrorists and terrorist groups all over the world . . . focusing particularly on those individuals operating in Europe, of course. We may not have access to your American Super-Cray computers, but Komissar is more than powerful enough to do the job expected of him."

"I'm sure the chief wasn't criticizing your machine," Murdock said diplomatically. "Or your methods."

"No, ma'am," the big SEAL added. "He's just a lot bigger than what I'm used to back home."

"And coming from a Texan," Murdock said, "that's quite an admission. In any case, we've found that the key to solving problems is never the technology. It's the people."

"That is most observant, Lieutenant," Inge said, nodding. "And you're right, of course. It is the people who make our system work. The BKA is one of the finest criminal investigation units in the world."

"We were particularly interested in your cataloguing system," Murdock said. "I was told you have a whole warehouse full of Stasi records."

"More than one, in fact. We Germans, as I'm sure you've heard, can be meticulous record keepers."

"I sometimes think record keeping will be our undoing," a new voice said at their backs.

Turning, Murdock saw a young, athletic-looking man wearing neatly pressed combat fatigues. A sharpshooter's badge was pinned to the left breast of his tunic, along with several medals that Murdock did not recognize.

"Oberleutnant Werner Hopke," the man said said, extending a hand. "Grenzschutzgruppe Nine. You must be the American SEALs, though you seem to be out of uniform. I was expecting swim fins and wet suits."

The GSG9 was German's unique answer to the terrorism that had plagued West Germany in the seventies and eighties. The face of terrorism had changed, of course, along with the changing map of Europe during the past few years, but the GSG9 had maintained its status as one of the world's elite counterterror and hostage-rescue units.

Murdock took the man's hand. Hopke had a dry, firm grip. "Lieutenant Blake Murdock, United States Navy. And this is my partner in crime, Master Chief MacKenzie. As for the uniform, well, consider this camouflage dress for urban environments."

Hopke chuckled. "GSG9 is forced to use protective coloration as well, Herr Lieutenant. My condolences. In any case, I am very pleased to meet you both. I have been assigned as your liaison with the Grenzschutzgruppe during your visit. Has our Inge been taking good care of you?"

"Our Inge?" MacKenzie asked. He turned to the woman. "You didn't say you were with the GSG9."

She laughed. "I'm not."

"Miss Schmidt works closely with the Grenzschutzgruppe, however," Hopke said. "She is, ah, I suppose a computer technician might say she is our primary interface with Komissar. Sometimes I think she *is* Komissar, which is why mere mortals like us don't have a chance to get to know her better."

"Possibly," Inge told him, with a flirtatious lift of her chin, "you simply haven't found the proper program to run on me."

"Ah, tell me about the Euro-terror groups," Murdock said

brusquely. He could sense the chemistry flowing between Schmidt and Hopke, and thought it best to get the conversation back onto strictly professional grounds.

"What did you need to know?" Hopke asked.

Murdock exchanged glances with the other SEAL, then looked Hopke in the eye. "What is your clearance, *Herr Leutnant*?"

"Blue three."

"Miss Schmidt?"

"Blue four."

"Maverick Lance," Murdock said.

Hopke's face immediately tightened. "Perhaps," he said slowly, "this should be discussed in a secure area."

Murdock nodded. "I couldn't agree more."

"Come with me."

Turning, the four of them left the BKA basement room and the glassed-in Wiesbaden computer. There were some secrets that even Komissar was not yet privy to.

2

Friday, April 27

The secure room in the BKA headquarters basement had many of the qualities of a bank vault. There was only one way in, past an armed guard and through a massive steel door that gave a muffled, pressurizing hiss when it closed and sealed shut behind them. Inside, it resembled a corporate conference room more than a vault. The soundproofing had been concealed behind rich, wood paneling, the floor was thickly carpeted, and a long table occupied the center of the room, which appeared to have been designed around it. A niche in one corner partly hid a coffee machine and a small refrigerator.

"All the comforts," MacKenzie said, pouring himself a cup of coffee. "You could live down here for days."

"There are a number of rooms such as this one in the complex," Inge told them. "It was thought back in the eighties that, should the Soviets invade, the BKA planning and command staffs could continue their work in secure conditions, despite Spetsnaz commando raids, despite even a nuclear strike on Wiesbaden."

"And speaking of nuclear strikes," Hopke said, taking a seat at the conference table, "what is this about Maverick Lance? I saw no report."

"There hasn't been one," Murdock explained. "Not yet. But

13

both the CIA and Navy Intelligence have been following a series of events, incidents if you will, here in Europe. The possibility of a Maverick Lance is very real."

"I thought your Army's Delta Force was tasked with such operations."

Murdock smiled. "You know the American military, Lieutenant. If one of the services is going to do something, they all have to have a piece of it."

"I've often wondered how Americans are able to get anything done," Hopke said, returning the smile to soften the words. "Their love of bureaucracy rivals that of the Russians."

"Or the Germans," MacKenzie said. "Who was it who invented the general staff?"

Hopke's grin broadened. "Ah, but that was *good* bureaucracy, you see," he said, bantering. "The German general staff brought the art of warfare to new heights of organization and efficiency."

"I see. Is that why Germany lost two world wars in a row?"

"Mac . . ." Murdock warned.

But Hopke only laughed. "Point taken, Master Chief. Still, this does not sound like an operation that would be of much interest to Navy SEALs. You operate in the water normally, from submarines. *Ja?*"

"SEALs is an acronym for sea, air, and land, Lieutenant," Murdock said. "We work wherever they send us, and if that means the nearest water is in our canteen . . . or in that coffeemaker over there, well, that's good enough for us.

"Seriously, though, the SEALs have been training against the possibility . . . no, the *probability* . . . of the use of a nuclear device in a terrorist attack for a long time now."

"Probability?" Hopke said, surprised.

"Look, back at the end of the 1980s, five nations acknowledged having nuclear weapons. Two more, Israel and South Africa, either had nuclear weapons or were thought to have all of the components, requiring only a simple assembly process to to have them ready to arm.

"Then the Soviet Empire collapsed, and any real hope of maintaining the fiction of non-proliferation was smashed forever. Where one nation—the Soviet Union—had maintained an arsenal of something like thirty thousand nuclear warheads, now there are fifteen nations, with more on the way if Russia's internal problems continue. Most didn't have any nukes based on their territory, or if they did, the warheads and arming codes were under firm Russian control. Other states, like Kazakhstan, inherited part of the arsenal but pledged to renounce nuclear weapons. But there were still others, like Ukraine, that felt they needed to keep the nukes based on their territory to maintain their newfound independence, just in case the Russian bear gets hungry again."

"Hell," MacKenzie said, "even if one of the new governments promises to disassemble all of the weapons it controlled, how could such a promise possibly be monitored?"

"Even more dangerous, though," Murdock continued, "you have an awful lot of very desperate people running around in a state that has collapsed to near anarchy in some areas. Much of the modern Russian economy—and that means a lot of the government—is controlled by the Russian mafia. It's an open secret that half a million hard-currency dollars will buy you a small nuke on the weapons black market. And there are generals and scientists and technicians, all of them with access to nukes and all of them knowing that pretty soon they're not going to have a job. The temptation to sell a few weapons here and there, maybe to some guy from Iran or Libya, must be overwhelming in cases like that.

"Anyway, one of the major nightmares of the people back in the Pentagon whose job it is to think about such things is the one about how easy it will be to slip a small nuclear device into a major U.S. port aboard a freighter, an oil tanker, even a pleasure boat. It wouldn't even have to be an atomic bomb. A few pounds of plutonium, stolen from a breeder reactor facility somewhere, or purchased from North Korea and scattered on the winds or the waves by a charge of conventional high explosives, could poison hundreds, even thousand of square miles. If that happened inside a major city . . ."

"Plutonium is more than a component of an atomic bomb," Inge said. "It is the single most toxic substance known to man."

"Affirmative," Murdock said. "And if you do have the wherewithal to build a bomb, you don't need a hell of a lot of the stuff. Modern nukes aren't quite small enough to fit inside a suitcase . . . but they're terrifyingly close."

"I have heard," Hopke said, "that a bright chemistry student might be able to extract the necessary radioactives to construct a small A-bomb."

"Theoretically," Murdock said, nodding. "Still, the preferred method of nuclear-club wannabe states like Libya and of terrorists worldwide is to steal the stuff . . . or to buy it from people who aren't choosy about who they sell it to. Like some rogue ex-Soviet army officer who's hard up for cold cash. Or fun states like North Korea."

"Is that what this Maverick Lance report is about?" Hopke asked. "Someone is trying to smuggle plutonium?"

"Oh, we *know* they're smuggling plutonium, Lieutenant," Murdock said. A Maverick Lance alert was part of the ongoing attempt by U.S. military and other government authorities to keep track of the world black market in stolen nuclear material and, where possible, to stop it. "In fact, it's damned scary just how many groups are involved in the traffic right now. We're here to try to find out just what it is they're planning to do with it. The Maverick Lance alert was called because the CIA has identified several North Korean agents operating in Europe, and we think they're part of the plutonium pipeline."

Inge frowned. "So you in America are of the opinion that the North Koreans and the Red Army Faction are all working together somehow? To what end?"

"That," Murdock said, "is what we would very much like to know."

"Perhaps you should tell us, Lieutenant," Hopke said quietly, "about this particular Maverick Lance."

Murdock nodded and began telling them what he knew.

For years, the U.S. Department of Defense had maintained a list of code phrases that described various types of potential nuclear accidents or incidents. A NUCFLASH alert, followed by the appropriate code word, set the forces necessary to contain the problem in motion. *Broken Arrow* referred to such nightmare possibilities as the unauthorized or accidental detonation of a nuclear device, radioactive contamination from a damaged nuclear weapon that could threaten a populated area, or the loss or theft of a nuclear warhead. *Bent Spear* covered less serious contingencies . . . a violation of the safety procedures surrounding the maintenance or installation of nuclear weapons, for instance. At the bottom of the list was *Dull Sword,* a code name for events involving nuclear material that didn't fall into the Broken Arrow or Bent Spear categories . . . a nuclear-armed aircraft struck by lightning in flight, for instance, with no apparent damage to aircraft or weapon, but with the possibility of damage to the weapons components.

Lately, a new category had been added to the NUCFLASH code phrase list, positioned between Broken Arrow and Bent Spear in terms of its seriousness. *Maverick Lance* referred to any case where it was believed that unauthorized individuals had access to nuclear weapons, weapon parts, or radioactive nuclear materials . . . such as plutonium. "Unauthorized individuals" included anyone of any nationality operating in any country who would not normally have access to such materials; a Russian Strategic Rocket Forces weapons technician would not trigger a Maverick Lance alert; an ex-Soviet general trying to sell a tactical nuclear warhead to the Russian mafia or a Libyan agent most certainly would.

Murdock reached down and opened his briefcase. Inside was a file folder containing several photographs, as well as a stack of laser-printed hard copy. He laid one of the photographs on the table before them, face up. It showed an Oriental businessman and a woman, possibly his wife, standing in what appeared to be a customs line. The angle of the photo indicated that it had been taken from up high, probably through a security camera mounted well above the customs counter.

"This is Kim Doo Ok and his wife, Madam Kim . . . at least according to their passports. Britain's MI5 picked them up at London's Heathrow Airport two days ago and placed them under surveillance.

"According to South Korean intelligence, however, the man is Major Pak Chong Yong and the woman is Captain Chun Hyon Hee, both members of North Korea's Special Operations forces."

"What are they doing in England?" Inge wanted to know.

"Meeting this man," Murdock said, sliding another photograph to the table top. It showed Pak and Chun from a different angle, speaking with a tall Occidental man with knife-thin features and dark hair. "John Patrick O'Shaughnessy. Also known as Jack Mallory or Jack O'Malley. Former member of the IRA, then of the Provos. With the new truce in force between England and the IRA, he seems to have joined one of the smaller hawk factions that's holding out for war with Great Britain to the bitter end."

"We don't often have many dealings with the Provos here," Hopke said thoughtfully. "Though there has been some crossover, we understand, among the various terrorist groups."

"The crossover is getting worse," Murdock said. "We're also interested in these two." The third photograph showed two people, a muscular blond man and a tough-looking, short-haired woman.

"I recognize the woman," Inge said. "Dierdre Müller."

"You know her?"

"Indirectly. From the data on her in Komissar. She is one of the new senior members of the RAF leadership."

"That's her," Murdock agreed. "Boss bitch of the RAF. And the man is Heinrich Adler. Also RAF, though we're not sure how high he is on the totem pole. Both of them, however, have been meeting frequently with our Irish friend O'Shaughnessy during the past few weeks . . . and now O'Shaughnessy is meeting with these two Korean Special Forces people."

"You suspect some sort of joint-unit operation?" Hopke asked, studying the photo of the two German RAF members carefully.

"To start with, we're very interested in the Koreans," Murdock said. "Point one." He held up his right forefinger. "Pak is an experienced North Korean operative. We're interested in him because the CIA identified him as one of several North Korean agents who have been operating within the Continental United States within the past few years. Point two." Murdock ticked off another fingertip. "Pak is also thought to have recently completed a stretch of 'special training' at Yongbyon."

Hopke looked up sharply. "Yongbyon? That's the People's Democratic Republic of Korea's nuclear facility."

"Like we said," MacKenzie drawled easily, "we're very interested in this guy."

"Point three," Murdock continued. "North Korea has been deeply involved with several nuclear incidents lately. It was also heavily involved in Iran's nuclear weapons program.

"Point four. The Red Army Faction has a long history of terrorist action against NATO and against U.S. military bases and personnel in Europe. Their list of attacks, usually against unarmed men and women, is too long and too bloody to go through.

"Point five. Pak and Chun are now in direct contact with O'Shaughnessy, who has been in recent contact with at least one of the RAF's new crop of leaders . . . Dierdre Müller."

Hopke shook his head, rubbing his eyes. "I think I'm getting a headache. Even Komissar couldn't follow such convolutions."

"You would be surprised at what Komissar can do," Inge said. "Please, Lieutenant. Please go on."

"I'm out of points, and fingers," Murdock said. "To put it bluntly, we want to know what the hell's going down over here. If the PDRK is dealing in nuclear material with either the IRA or the RAF, you can bet your last deutsche mark that a lot of people are going to be mighty worried, in Washington, in London, and in Berlin."

"That is something of an understatement," Hopke said. He considered Murdock carefully for a moment through narrowed eyes. "Tell me something, Lieutenant."

"If I can."

"I mean to give no offense . . . but why the two of you?"

"How do you mean?"

"I mean, why did they send the two of you, a lieutenant and a noncommissioned officer? This is no reflection on your ability, understand. But knowing your government's love of shows of power, I would have expected a delegation of a half-dozen generals and admirals at least on a mission as potentially, ah, delicate as this one . . . not to mention several of your congressmen! At the very least, this sort of information request is generally handled at a diplomatic level . . . not at the level of working people like Inge and myself."

Murdock laughed. "Don't worry, you'll probably get the brass and the congressmen too. I know for a fact that this situation is being discussed right now at high pretty high levels of NATO in Brussels. Because of the political ramifications, though, I doubt that anything concrete will be worked out. NATO still can't do much without strong UN backing, and you know what a political swamp *that* is."

"The fact of the matter is," MacKenzie put in, "that our bosses back Stateside decided to handle this on at least two levels. The generals and the politicians will be discussing the overall situation, certainly, and I imagine half a dozen of our intelligence services already have requests in to your Komissar department. But in the meantime, it happened that some SEALs were already in Europe, taking part in a cross-training exchange program with the British SAS. SEALs already have a pretty high security clearance, because so much of what they have to do is classified. So the wheels began turning back in the Pentagon, and out popped a new set of orders. Murdock and MacKenzie, go talk to the Germans."

"Often," Hopke said thoughtfully, "the best liaison work is carried out between the ordinary people who have no . . . how do you say? Political axes to mend."

"I think you mean 'grind,'" Murdock said. "But yes. You're right. The guys in the fancy uniforms at the expensive banquets are usually just putting their names to agreements that their secretaries and assistants have already hammered out."

"And what is it you need from the BKA specifically?" Inge said.

"We need anything you can give us from Komissar's files," Murdock said. "Information on these terrorists in particular, on their organizations, on any hints or rumors you may have picked up that might suggest there's some big operation pending."

An hour later, the four of them were still going over the list of names and information that Murdock was requesting. "How

soon could you run something off for us, Inge?" Murdock
asked.

"I can have a preliminary report for you on disk by late this
afternoon," she said. "A complete rundown by tomorrow.
Satisfactory?"

Murdock gave her his most dazzling smile. "No. *Not*
satisfactory. Absolutely splendid."

"Of course, it would help if I could question you further this
evening."

"Question me? About what?"

Inge gave Murdock a mischievous smile. "Well, about
whether or not SEALs like seafood, for one thing. I know an
excellent seafood restaurant in town on the Sonnenberger
Strasse. Perhaps you would care to have dinner with me
tonight?"

Murdock hesitated, glancing first at Hopke. He'd assumed
the flirtation he'd seen between these two meant that they had
a relationship that went well beyond the strictly professional.

Hopke caught his look and grinned back. "Go ahead,
Lieutenant. I knew you American Navy men had a reputation
with beautiful women, but you've made more progress with
our Inge here than a platoon of GSG9 officers in a month."
Across the table, MacKenzie rolled his eyes toward the room's
ceiling.

"Well, sure," Murdock said. "Why not? I would be honored."

Inge beamed. "Excellent! I'll need to stop at my place first,
of course, to change. Perhaps I could show you some of the
sights around town on the way."

"Whatever you say . . . Inge . . ."

Murdock felt a little out of his depth. Inge Schmidt was by
far the most direct and outspoken woman he'd ever met, as
well as one of the most beautiful. He was used to women who
let the man take the lead, and this was a new experience for
him.

Not that he minded new experiences. SEALs were well
known for their willingness to confront all types of challenges
head on.

"Wonderful!" she said. "This is going to be fun!"

"Maybe I should come along too," MacKenzie said. "You know . . . swim buddies."

"I don't think that'll be necessary, Mac. Besides, you're married."

"It looks to me, Senior Chief," Hopke said, "as though you and I will be stuck telling one another war stories, while these two investigate seafood restaurants."

"It's a dirty job," Murdock said resignedly. "But someone's got to do it."

3

Friday, April 27

1810 hours
Wiesbaden, Federal Republic of Germany
That evening, after a long day going over the data from the BKA's Komissar computer, Murdock and Inge Schmidt left the BKA complex, walking out to her sporty red Renault Alpine parked in the employees' south lot, then drove through the security gate and onto the main highway, heading toward Wiesbaden. Komissar had provided a treasure trove of data on Major Pak of North Korean Special Operations, and on the various RAF and Provo figures involved in an as yet unrevealed revival of Euro-terror, and Murdock had already arranged for a secure fax line to transmit the information back to Washington.

He and Inge had gotten to know each other a lot better during the course of the afternoon, their earlier flirtation somehow evolving into a rapidly deepening friendship. Murdock found Inge to be extremely bright and quick, with dozens of the oddest facts imaginable instantly accessible in the course of their conversation. Though she never mentioned it, a conversation with Hopke had revealed that Inge Schmidt and Komissar had been partly responsible for the chain of data that had led to the capture of the notorious Carlos the Jackal a year before.

Murdock could easily understand why Hopke had jokingly

referred to her as the BKA computer, though that statement could certainly not have been a reflection on her personality.

Murdock genuinely liked her.

It was not a completely comfortable feeling. Murdock had been engaged to be married once, but Susan had died in a car accident while on her way to attend his graduation from Annapolis. He'd tried to steer clear of romantic entanglements ever since, especially after he'd gone against his family's wishes and become a Navy SEAL. Some of the SEALs in his platoon were married—Mac and Magic, Kos and Scotty.

Splitting his life between a woman and the Navy wasn't for him, though. Not anymore.

But he couldn't deny the attraction he felt for this woman, an attraction that she seemed to echo for him. Damn it all! Where was this thing going?

"So how does the GSG9 relate to the BKA?" he wanted to know. Traffic was heavy, but Inge steered the powerful little Renault with a sure hand, guiding them safely around the slower clumpings of traffic. Soon they reached the cloverleaf winding toward the east-west Autobahn leading to Frankfurt.

"Well, the German Federal Republic was caught totally unprepared by the terrorism that began appearing in the sixties and seventies," she said. "In particular, well, there was Munich, you know. The GFR authorities did not come out of that situation looking so good."

Murdock nodded understanding. The 1972 Olympic Games in Munich, West Germany, were best remembered now for the bloody attack by seven members of the Palestinian Black September terrorist group. Two Israeli athletes had been killed by the gunmen, and nine more taken hostage. Then, at Furstenfeldbruk Airport, an ambush by Bavarian State Police police sharpshooters had gone horribly, tragically wrong. All nine hostages, along with five terrorists and one policeman, had died in the bloody, botched rescue attempt.

"Munich was the reason the Grenzschutzgruppe was created in the first place," Inge continued. "The after-action analysis indicated that the primary reasons the police failed during the attack were poor training, poor communications, and poor marksmanship. They missed their targets during the first round of firing, which gave one of the terrorists the opportunity to throw a hand grenade into the helicopter where the hostages were being held.

"GSG9 was raised out of the Federal Border Guard unit. Unlike your SEALs, the SAS, and every other elite counter-terror unit with which I am familiar, it is a *civilian* force, actually a branch of our state police, though its people do undergo extremely thorough military training."

"I've heard they're very good."

She smiled sweetly. "They are much more than *good,* Lieutenant. Tomorrow, back at the office, I will show you a trophy from the 1985 St. Augustine competition. An international and inter-service military competition, including marks-manship, hand-to-hand combat, and room clearing. The South Bavarian GSG took first place that year. The American Delta Force placed second, while your Navy SEALs took third."

"Maybe we should demand a rematch."

She tossed her head, laughing. "That might be fun. Anyway, since 1984," she went on, "the GSG9 has consisted of four combat units, each of thirty-six men. Units One and Four concentrate on surveillance duties and various operations for the BKA. They also, however, directly support the Lander units in each of our federal states."

"Wherever they're needed, huh?"

"Exactly. In addition, Unit Two has been tasked with protection of Germany's oil platforms in the North Sea and in the Baltic. Unit Three specializes in free-fall parachuting and, um, special entry. We call them for the assault when all other means of dealing with a particular threat have failed. I suppose you could say that the BKA coordinates GSG activities and operations, providing them with intelligence and, in some cases, with specific missions. We have to be extremely careful, however, because of our past history."

"The Nazis?"

"*Ja.* Exactly so. That is why the GSG9 was drawn from our *civil* police. If a military unit were so trained and so organized, there would be immediate charges that we were trying to revive the military elitism of the SS. It has led to some incredible stupidities. Not long ago, the GSG9 was brought in to help organize a sweep against terrorist targets throughout Germany, something they were uniquely qualified to take part in. At the last moment, however, the GSG was excluded from the actual operation. One of our honored members of parliament insisted that GSG9 operatives would be useless on such a mission because, his words, 'all they can do is shoot.' The sweep, needless to say, was not particularly successful."

Murdock could hear the pride Inge felt for the GSG9 in her words and in her scorn for the German bureaucracy. He had the feeling that she identified strongly with the Grenzschutzgruppe, even though she was actually employed by the BKA. A Grenzschutzgruppe groupie? Murdock grinned at the thought. "Well, I don't know about German Parliament," he said. "But I can tell you that the GSG9 has a damned fine reputation throughout the rest of the world. . . ."

His voice trailed off. Casually, he reached up and adjusted the Renault's rearview mirror.

"Something wrong?" Inge asked, glancing across at him.

"Do you normally have a BKA tail?"

"A what?" She started to laugh, and then the impact of what Murdock had just said sank home. "A tail?"

"Someone from the office who follows you home. For security purposes."

"Certainly not! Are we being followed?"

"A gray Mercedes has been trying to keep up with you ever since we turned out of the BKA parking lot. He's still there . . . about three cars back."

Inge dimpled. "Perhaps it's Lieutenant Hopke. He is—how is it you say? He has the hots for me."

"I don't blame him one bit . . . but I don't think that's Herr Hopke. Not unless he can afford a luxury car like that on a police lieutenant's salary."

"That is true. Werner drives a Hyundai."

"Hmm. It's probably nothing." But he was worried. Inge's driving had been aggressive enough that Murdock would not have expected another driver to be able to keep up with her. Germany had a "recommended" speed of 130 kilometers per hour on the Autobahn, but if Inge's driving was anything to go by, there was no law against exceeding it.

"I have a turnoff coming up soon," she told him. She grinned, and her eyes were sparkling. *Son of a bitch,* he thought. She was actually enjoying this! "Perhaps we can find out there whether or not they are following us."

"Good idea." He glanced back again. The other car was still there, third in line behind them. "Do it."

The maneuver was so sudden that it caught Murdock by surprise, even though he'd been expecting it. Inge slowed the Renault slightly. Then, without warning, without turn signals, she swerved sharply right across two lanes of traffic and into an exit ramp. As she braked with a squeal of overstressed tires into the off ramp's curve, Murdock heard horns blaring behind them . . . and then the gray Mercedes, trapped by the other cars around it, flashed past the exit and on down the Autobahn.

"Nicely done," he said. "I'm impressed."

"GSG9 training includes a special driving course."

Murdock's eyebrows raised. "I thought you worked for the BKA, Inge. You talk more like you're GSG9."

Her face colored slightly. "I suppose that's because I always wanted to be GSG9. I started off with Bavarian Lander. I took the test for GSG9, and some of the early training, but failed the physical later on. Not enough upper body strength, they said."

"They have female agents?"

"Not in the combat units," she admitted. "But in some of the others. Reconnaissance and surveillance, for instance." She wrinkled her nose. "And secretarial work, of course. But that was never what I wanted for myself. I had always wanted to be in a combat unit, since I first heard of the GSG9 when I was a girl. That must have been . . . oh, in the late seventies, sometime." She laughed. "Am I giving away my age?"

"I won't bother to add up the years," Murdock said.

"My! So gallant for an American! Anyway, I easily passed the test for BKA special agent, and when an opening came up for a liaison officer with the GSG, well, my interest in the group was well known. I am only one of quite a few agents, of course, who serve as go-betweens with the GSG9." She sighed. "I would still rather be in GSG Operations." She glanced at Murdock out of the corner of her eye, and frowned. "You're laughing at me."

"Not at all."

"Do you believe women should not be in combat?"

Murdock considered for a moment how best to answer. "I'll be honest with you, Inge, and say I really don't know. I've never for a moment doubted that a woman has every bit as much right to defend her home, her family, her country, or her ideas as a man. But integrating women fully into combat units carries a terrible price. I'm not sure we can afford it."

She frowned. "What price?"

"Training . . . and testing criteria. You said you couldn't pass the GSG9 physical. Okay, the fact is, most women have less upper body strength than most men. Most women have greater overall endurance than most men, on a long march, say, but they can't lift as much, having more trouble chinning-up into a second-story window, and they'd be at a real disadvantage in hand-to-hand combat with a male opponent."

"Not if the woman knows karate."

Murdock laughed. "What are you, black belt?"

"Brown belt, second degree."

"Good for you. Still, that doesn't have much to do with the real world."

"But if a woman has trained until she is strong enough to do what is expected of her, then she should be allowed to do anything she wants, don't you think?"

"You know, Inge, I think my only real problem with the integration of women into combat is that in too many cases, the training requirements of the various services or units have been knocked down either so that women can qualify to fill a quota, or because requirements demanding great strength, especially great upper body strength, are perceived as somehow unfair. Combat is never fair, *life* is not fair . . . and the qualifications for the people who have to depend on one another to survive combat shouldn't be fair either. If a man can do a job better, more efficiently, with less risk to himself and the other members of his team, then a man should be in that slot, and to hell with political correctness or feminist rights."

Inge was silent for a long time. "You are a very direct man," she said at last. "You don't try to put an attractive coating on what you believe."

"You asked me what I thought. . . ."

"I like honesty in a man," she said. "Even when it is misguided. Here we are. . . ."

Inge lived in an apartment complex in the town of Rüsselsheim, midway between Wiesbaden and Frankfurt-am-Main, and only about ten kilometers from Frankfurt's Rhein-Main International Airport. The two of them went up to her apartment together. Murdock waited in her living room with a Dortmunder beer while Inge vanished into the bedroom to change, and he had time to learn from her bookshelves and record cabinet that she was interested in history—especially military history—martial arts, horses, cats, detective novels, and soft rock. Periodically, the sky would roar as a big jet flew overhead on its way to or from the airport nearby, and he wondered how she was able to sleep.

When Inge emerged from the bedroom a few moments later, the businesswoman's professional look was gone. The low-cut, high-slit evening dress she was wearing now, in a dark maroon set off by earrings and a single strand of pearls, was breathtaking on her figure. Her golden hair was down now, swirling delightfully across her bare shoulders.

"So," she said as Murdock rose to his feet. "About that seafood . . ."

"SEALs generally catch their own seafood," he told her. "Now if you'd said steak . . ."

"I know just the place. And not too far from here either."

It was still light outside as they emerged from the apartment building and started walking arm-in-arm across the parking lot to the place near the street where Inge had parked the car. The sun had set, but the sky was still fully light . . . light enough for Murdock to spot the gray Mercedes parked on the far side of the street and recognize it, with near certainty, as the car that had been following them on the Autobahn. He didn't say anything to Inge, but he did let go of her arm and fall back a half step behind her.

"What's wrong?" she asked him, slowing.

"Keep walking," he said, glancing about. The Mercedes was empty. There was a lot of thick shrubbery in front of the apartment where attackers could wait unseen. There was also a panel truck parked next to Inge's car that hadn't been there before.

Murdock wasn't carrying a weapon. German gun laws were strict, and arranging for a foreigner to get a permit required so much red tape that he'd decided not to bother even trying. He was regretting that decision now.

Ahead, the back door to the panel truck banged open, and two men in utility workers' coveralls climbed out, glanced around the parking lot, then started walking directly toward Murdock and Inge. He couldn't tell if they were armed, though one was carrying something that looked like a toolbox. In fact, they could be—probably were—just what they appeared to be. *You're getting paranoid, Blake,* he told himself fiercely.

And yet there was that empty gray Mercedes parked on the street. Was it really the same car? Had it been following them earlier?

The safest move might be to simply turn around and go back to the apartment, a stronghold with a single entrance, easily defended. That might be a little difficult to explain to Inge— she would assume that he was interested in something other than a steak dinner—but Murdock was by nature a cautious man, his career in the Navy SEALs notwithstanding. And she'd seen the Mercedes too, back on the Autobahn.

But when Murdock glanced back over his shoulder, he saw two more figures, a man and a woman this time, stepping through the apartment building's front door and onto the walkway outside. The man was wearing sports clothes and a light jacket and was not obviously armed; the woman wore a T-shirt and jeans and carried a bulky, white canvas bag on an over-the-shoulder strap. Murdock and Inge had just been cut off from their retreat.

"Inge," he said softly. "I think we may have some trouble."

He felt her tense, saw her eyes flick back, then ahead, assessing the situation. "The people behind us are neighbors of mine," she said. "They live right down the hall from me."

And you're a paranoid son of a bitch, Murdock thought, but he was fully alert now, the adrenaline pumping through his system in the heady rush of imminent combat.

Even if he wasn't yet positive that they were about to be

attacked, it was still possible to apply two of the most important rules of combat when ambushed: *Don't stand still* and *do the unexpected*. Reaching down suddenly, he grabbed Inge's hand and turned her sharply aside. "Come on!"

"Blake!"

But she started to run with him. Then she stumbled, and Murdock cursed. She was wearing black high heels that hobbled her as effectively as a ball and chain.

The unexpected move alone, however, had been enough. Ahead, the two utility workers broke into a run. *"Inge! Kommen Sie zurück!"* the woman behind them called out. Turning, Murdock saw the woman pulling something small and black from the depths of her canvas bag . . . a handgun. And the man beside her had a pistol tucked into his waistband, its grip visible beneath the flapping hem of his jacket as he too started running.

The ambush had just been sprung.

4

Friday, April 27

1905 hours
Rüsselsheim, Federal Republic of Germany
The woman pointed her pistol at Murdock. "You!" she shouted
in thickly accented English. "Both of you! Stop where you
are!" A commercial jet thundered overhead, and Murdock
realized that if the woman fired the gun, few of the people in
any of the surrounding apartment buildings would even hear it.

"Lose those shoes!" Murdock snapped at Inge.

"But . . ."

"Ditch the shoes and *run,* damn it!"

If he'd been alone, he'd have had little problem avoiding the
trap. With his SEAL conditioning, he was certain that he could
outrun just about any army the opposition cared to send against
him, and that woman would have to be one hell of a crack shot
to hit a running man at ten meters with that snub-nosed
revolver she was pointing at him. But he couldn't leave
Inge. . . .

Likely, all four were armed, but the only one who had a
weapon out and ready for action was the woman, and Murdock
immediately tagged her as the most dangerous of the four. She
and her companion were five meters off now, the utility men a
bit further away in the other direction.

Always do the unexpected. Murdock charged.

"*Alt!*" the woman screamed. She was a hard-faced, short-

32

haired woman, with muscles that Murdock suspected had been honed with weight training. She brought the gun up to point at directly into Murdock's face, stiff-armed and one-handed.

Two mistakes—trying for a head shot against a moving target and trying for a one-handed stance like a gunfighter out of the mythical Wild West. Murdock sharply sidestepped, forcing her to pivot in an attempt to correct her aim, then lunged straight toward her, his left arm rolling up in a hard block, sweeping her gun hand aside as he stepped inside her reach. His right hand clenched, but when his right arm snapped forward, he carried the impact on the heel of his palm when it slammed squarely between the woman's small breasts, just at the bottom of her sternum. His follow-through was purely reflexive, his knee catching her between the legs so hard she was lifted from the pavement.

That particular blow was fully as incapacitating for a woman as for a man. The pistol was sent spinning through the air, and Murdock was past the woman before she could hit the ground, dropping his center of gravity, pivoting on his left foot, and bringing his right around in a savage roundhouse kick that caught the man in sports clothes squarely in his left kidney. The man *oofed* and went down, still fumbling at the pistol tucked into his waistband. Murdock snap-kicked him in the side of the head; there was an ugly snicking sound as the ball of his foot connected and the man's spine broke just below the base of his skull.

Spinning to face the remaining attackers, Murdock was just in time to see Inge, her shoes gone now, throw a hard forward kick into the groin of one of the utilities workers. The man gasped and doubled over, clutching himself; unfortunately, it was his partner who was carrying the tool kit and who was just pulling an Uzi submachine gun clear of the metal box's open lid.

The bad guys must have planned on muscle, numbers, and threat alone to force the two of them to come along, or they would have had their weapons out and ready instead of inaccessible. Murdock took three quick steps to the left and grabbed the man's gun hand, twisting him around and over into a wrist-breaker grip. Encumbered by the weapon in one hand

and the toolbox in the other, the man screamed and dropped to his knees, toolbox and Uzi both clattering noisily onto the pavement. Murdock held him down, swinging his knee up hard to connect with the man's face. The scream broke off in a gurgle of pain; Murdock kneed him again, then released him, scooping up the Uzi as the man's body slumped to the sidewalk.

The guy Inge had kicked was still on his feet, but doubled over. Murdock walked over, grabbed his hair with his free hand, then slammed his knee up into his face. The woman was on her hands and knees, one hand clutching her abdomen, but she was trying to crawl toward her companion, and the weapon protruding from behind his belt. Murdock walked up behind her and jackhammered his fist down hard against the base of her neck, and she collapsed facedown on the pavement without a word or a sound.

The roar of an engine exploded nearby. Spinning, Uzi at the ready, Murdock saw the panel truck jump a curb and careen into the street, its back doors still flapping open. In an instant it had cornered at the next intersection with a squeal of outraged tires, and was out of sight. So . . . there'd been a fifth attacker, and he'd gotten away. Not good.

"You okay?" he asked Inge.

The BKA woman was still standing over the man she'd kicked, fists clenched at her sides, her maroon dress was very much the worse—or perhaps from Murdock's point of view, much the better—for wear. Her kick had ripped the slit in the side of the dress clear to her waist, and he could see a torn stocking and a thin strip of something sheer, black, and lacy riding high across the tanned skin of her hip. She was excited too, breathing hard in tight, rapid, almost panting gasps, and the surge of adrenaline to her system had triggered a physiological reaction that made it quite clear that she was not wearing a bra beneath the thin material of her dress. "Yes," she said. She swallowed, then nodded her head. "I think so. God, Blake, you play rough."

He stooped next to the man at her feet, checking for a pulse. The guy's face was bloody and he was out cold, but he was still alive. Carefully, Murdock turned the man's head to the side so that he wouldn't strangle on his own blood. "When I have to."

Inge walked over to the woman. The man lying on the cement next to her was on his back, eyes open and very obviously dead. "You . . . you *kicked* her. . . ."

The sheer illogic of the statement, the dull edge to her voice, the glassy look in her blue eyes, all told Murdock that Inge was on the point of going into shock. He walked over to her and took her by both arms, turning her to face him. "Inge . . . remember what I was saying earlier in the car? There is no *fair* in combat. There can't be. You do what you have to do to survive. If that means you kill someone, if it means you use the dirtiest trick in the book, you do it, right? Because if you don't, it's a damned sure thing that the people you're fighting aren't going to show you a similar courtesy when they get the drop on *you*."

Jerkily, she nodded.

"They had guns, we didn't," he said. "But we're still here, right?"

She nodded again, then took a deep breath and gave him an awkward self-conscious smile. "I guess we are. Still think women can't handle themselves in combat?"

"Well, I know I'm not going to argue it with you. Not right now, at any rate." He nodded toward her torn dress. "I think you'd better go change, don't you? And maybe sit down for a bit, with a good, stiff drink."

She seemed unconcerned about her dress. "What . . . what should we do about them?"

Murdock considered the question. Stooping, he again checked each of the fallen ambushers. One dead, the other three incapacitated. The woman might begin showing some interest in her surroundings before too long, but he was pretty sure the two "utilities men" would be out of it for an hour or more, at the very least. The biggest problem was that the panel truck might come back for them . . . maybe with reinforcements.

"Get their guns."

"What?"

"I don't want the neighborhood kids wandering by and picking up their guns. The woman's pistol flew over there, somewhere, by those bushes. Then I want you to go inside and call the police. Or . . . maybe there's a department in the BKA?"

"I'll call Captain Halber," she said. "He's on duty at the watch desk tonight. He'll know who to send."

Inge began doing as she'd been told. Good. She needed something to keep her mind occupied, something to keep the emotional shock at bay. The woman's pistol was a Chief's Special, a snub-nosed .38 revolver, while the weapon in her dead companion's waistband was a German-made Walther PPK. The man with the tool kit had been carrying the Uzi, of course, and both "utilities men" were packing heavy artillery in the form of .357 Magnum revolvers, hidden inside their bulky coveralls.

"You have any enemies?" he asked Inge as she showed him the arsenal. "Someone who might want to even an old score?"

"No, Blake," she said. "This was an RAF hit."

"Red Army? How do you know?" In fact, he'd begun to suspect as much himself. The ambush had not been a robbery attempt. The idea had been to swiftly overpower Murdock and the BKA woman and bundle them into that van . . . a kidnapping, in other words. Since neither of them would raise much in the way of ransom, Murdock could only assume that the kidnapping had been for either political or intelligence-gathering purposes, and that pointed to a revolutionary or terrorist organization like the German RAF.

Inge knelt beside the woman, picking up her left arm and turning it so that Murdock could see the back of her hand. A small tattoo had been neatly incised into the skin, a small red circle with the unmistakable black silhouette of an H&K submachine gun.

"Rather stupid of them to advertise themselves that way," Murdock said. The H&K, he remembered from various SEAL briefings on terrorist cells and personnel, had been adopted by the Red Army Faction as a kind of logo back in the seventies. He studied the unconscious woman's face for a moment. It was hard, with knife-edged creases . . . an angry, bitter face, he decided. She might be in her early forties. Possibly the tattoo dated from the so-called People's Revolutions of the seventies, though he wondered how she could have gone for twenty years without someone noticing and reporting her to the authorities.

On the other hand, Germans were as likely to mind their own business and stay uninvolved as any other group of people.

Using strips torn from the dead man's shirt, Murdock tied the wrists and ankles of the three surviving attackers, just in case they recovered enough to wander off. As he worked, a small crowd began gathering. By the time Inge, dressed now in slacks and a white blouse, had returned from making her telephone call, a police car was on the scene as well. Weapons, prisoners, and body were all removed with a minimum of fuss, while uniformed officers dispersed the crowd. For over an hour, then, back in Inge's apartment, Murdock and Inge went over what had happened with the police again and again, with Inge serving as translator, until Lieutenant Hopke and Mac MacKenzie arrived.

When the police had departed at last, MacKenzie grinned at Murdock. "Can't you even have a nice night out on the town without getting into trouble, L-T?"

"Busman's holiday, Mac. Lieutenant Hopke?"

"Yes, Lieutenant?"

"I need some firepower. Think your department could arrange it?"

"I think so. I think it might be a good idea if both of you were armed while you are in the country. You seem to have attracted some unwanted attention."

"From my neighbors?" Inge said, shaking her head. "I still can't believe that."

"Did you know them well?"

"Not really." She'd already been over this several times with the police. "They moved in a few months ago. I saw them now and then, in the hallway or in the laundry. The man's name was Friedrick. The woman . . . I think her name was Erna, but I'm not sure. The name on their letterbox in the lobby was Dortman."

"Some of Komissar's people are in their apartment now," Hopke said. "The police will be there with a search warrant before long, but Captain Steiner authorized a black-bag operation, before the uniform people muddy up the scene." He glanced at Murdock. "This is not strictly legal, you see."

"Understood. SEALs have to operate outside the strict limits of the law too, from time to time."

"The trouble is," Inge said, "why do you think it was Blake who attracted their attention? It seems to be too much of a coincidence that two RAF terrorists just happened to be living on my floor."

"Quite correct, Inge," Hopke said. "My guess, and it is only a guess at this point, is that they took that apartment to keep an eye on you. When Lieutenant Murdock here put in an appearance, however, they decided—or were ordered—to move."

"Ordered?" Inge shuddered and closed her eyes. "By who?"

"Good question."

"Do you have anything on that panel truck we saw?" Murdock asked.

"Nothing. Police helicopters are up, watching for a vehicle of that description, but I doubt that they'll spot anything. The owners, if they are smart, will abandon it or get it quickly out of sight, and there are *many* white panel trucks on the Autobahn."

"Sorry I didn't get a license," Murdock said.

"I doubt that it would have helped if you had." Hopke shrugged. "These people are smart. They would have had fake plates."

"I'm not so sure they were that smart. If that was a kidnapping attempt, it was pretty badly planned."

Hopke smiled. "Perhaps, Lieutenant, they don't know you are a SEAL. Or that SEALs are such formidable opponents. They must have thought that the threat of four people, displaying guns, would be enough to make you submit."

"Maybe. If they didn't know I was a SEAL, though, the question remains why they tried to pick us up at all."

"If they have a mole with customs," MacKenzie pointed out, "they would know we came in on a military flight. We're in civilian clothes and we go straight to the BKA. One of us takes a lovely BKA agent back to her apartment. That's got to make them curious."

"Quite right," Hopke agreed. "We will know more when we have interrogated the prisoners." He looked back and forth between Inge and Murdock. "In any case, perhaps you two would like to resume your evening together?"

"I think Inge might like to get some rest," Murdock said.

"Nonsense!" All evidence of the shock that had threatened her earlier was gone. She seemed animated and very much *alive*. "After what we've just been through? I'm hungrier than ever now. That steak we were talking about sounds wonderful!"

"I'm not sure that's a good idea, L-T," MacKenzie warned. "Suppose they try again."

"About that gun," Murdock said, turning to Hopke.

"What kind do you prefer?"

"I don't suppose the Federal Republic would go along with me packing a shotgun. Or an M-16."

"How about something concealable?"

"First choice would be a .45 Colt. After that, just about anything in semi-auto and .45 caliber."

"I will see what can be done." Hopke removed his suit jacket, revealing a shoulder holster rig which he began unbuckling as he spoke. "In the meantime, why don't you take this. Just don't get caught with it until I can put the proper paperwork through."

"This," was an H&K P9S, a 9mm double-action semiautomatic with a nine-round magazine. Tucked into its holster with a Velcro strap and positioned under Murdock's left arm, it hardly showed at all when he put his jacket back on.

"Great," he said, shrugging, then moving his arms back and forth to settle the harness comfortably into place. "Of course, some official backup might be nice too."

"I'll see what we can do." He grinned suddenly. "Why do I have the feeling, Herr Murdock, that you are making of yourself a target?"

"I'm not really. And I wouldn't deliberately use Inge here for bait either. But my feeling at the moment is that no place we go is going to be all that safe." He shrugged. "Who knows? The guy in the panel truck may organize another try with some of his buddies. If we're ready for them when they do, so much the better."

• • •

The Cattle Baron was a pseudo-American restaurant located on the Büdingenstrasse in Wiesbaden. As Inge had promised, the steak was excellent, and both of them were hungry.

Their conversation, however, remained centered on things professional. At first, Inge was interested in the aspects of SEAL training. "Drown-proofing" fascinated her, though she thought the sink-or-swim mentality seemed a bit barbaric. The idea of tying a man hand and foot and throwing him into the deep end of the pool, literally to sink or swim . . .

Later, their conversation had grown more technical, with Inge probing Murdock's thoughts on nuclear proliferation . . . especially now, with the old Soviet empire gone.

"We've been especially concerned about the possibility of radicals in the former Soviet states getting hold of nuclear warheads before they can be disassembled or shipped back to Russia," she told him. "Even a so-called battlefield weapon, a tactical nuclear artillery shell, for instance, could kill tens of thousands of people, ruin a fair-sized city, and be extremely hard to track."

It was, Murdock reflected, not exactly light dinner conversation, but it was a topic he was keenly interested in. "Everybody said the world would be a safer place with the collapse of Soviet Communism, that we could enjoy a 'peace dividend' with all the money we'd save cutting back on our military expenditures. Stupid idea that, fit only for liberal, anti-military politicians and other assorted half-wits. I certainly don't want the Soviets back—never did—but at least they kept pretty good track of their nukes."

"You believe the current owners of the warheads do not?"

Murdock shrugged and kept cutting the steak on the plate in front of him. "There are just too damned many nukes, and too many people with reasons to sell them or steal them."

Inge nodded thoughtfully. "It sounds as though the—what is the expression? The nuclear genie has escaped its bottle."

"That's putting it mildly."

"So," Inge said. "What is the answer? How can we stop the proliferation? What will happen if we don't?"

Murdock didn't reply right away. Looking past Inge's

shoulder, he spotted MacKenzie, seated at a table across the restaurant with Lieutenant Hopke, and caught his eye. Mac nodded slightly but gave no other sign of having noticed Murdock. There was at least one other BKA team in the room too, Murdock knew, but they were good, and he hadn't been able to spot them.

Good backup, just in case. Chances were, though, now that they were ready for them, the RAF wouldn't try again, not in the same way, at least. The other patrons of the restaurant were going on with their meals, talking about weather or opera, the latest scandal in parliament or love, unaware of the topic being discussed at at least one of the tables.

"I really don't know, Inge," Murdock said. "Used to be, I thought the old nuclear balance of power would be enough. You know, they won't nuke us because then we'll nuke them. How do you nuke a terrorist group, though? You can't. You can't even nuke the country that sponsored the terrorists, because it's their *government* that's bad, not the people. Hell, most of the population of North Korea is one step removed from outright slavery.

"Later I thought SDI was the answer. You know, what the press called 'Star Wars'? But then the Russians folded and it was peace-dividend time, and everyone in Congress was scrambling for the easy kills, looking for money for welfare and free health insurance. Hell, even if we had a perfect ballistic missile defense, chances are those terrorist nukes would come by way of freighter or submarine or even a moving van coming across the border from Mexico, not in the warhead of an SS-19.

"I'm very, very much afraid that things have simply gone too far. One of these days pretty soon now, we're going to lose a city."

"I never took you for the fatalistic sort, Blake."

"I'm hardly that. I'll fight as long as I can, I'll fight whoever I'm told to fight to stop the holocaust. But I'm also a realist. In my line of work, you have to be."

"I know what you mean. Working with Komissar, you can often begin assembling a larger picture in your own mind while you are still feeding the machine with the snippets and fragments. For a long time now, there have been, well, hints of something very large, some operation involving many of the old terror groups, and it has left me with a dreadful foreboding. Like knowing that something terrible is about to happen, and being unable to do a thing about it."

Even with much of their conversation centering on what was for both of them shop talk, their relationship, their mutual feelings of camaraderie and comfortable closeness had deepened considerably by the time they reached Inge's apartment again, at just past twelve-thirty in the morning. She asked him in to have a drink and he accepted, with Mac waiting for him in a rented car outside. After two drinks more, she asked him to spend the night. Murdock signaled MacKenzie from her apartment's balcony with a flashlight, a quick-beamed long-short-short—not Morse for the letter "D," but an old Navy whistle or horn signal meaning, "Cast off and stand clear." MacKenzie replied with an affirmative flash from his headlights and drove off a few moments later.

When Murdock turned away from the window, Inge was waiting for him, beautifully, gloriously naked.

5

Saturday, April 28

0136 hours
Waterfront Rise
Middlebrough, England

The door banged open and Pak strode to the room, his anger tightly marshaled behind the impassive round mask of his face. The bedroom was cluttered with torn posters on the walls, empty beer and soda cans on the floor, and piles of laundry, cast-off clothing, and dirty sheets.

O'Malley lay naked in the bed with two naked women, the dark-haired one astride his hips, the other one at his side. As Pak stormed in, closely followed by Chun Hyon Hee and Gunther Weiss, both women screamed and rolled off the Provo man, clutching at the scattered sheets.

"What the bloody hell?" O'Malley shouted, heaving himself up from the pillow on his elbows.

Pak drew his weapon, a North-Korean-manufactured Type 68 automatic pistol equipped with a long, blunt sound suppressor.

"Kim!" O'Malley shouted, trying to scramble over the legs of one of the screaming women and onto the floor. None of the people here knew Pak's real name, of course. "Kim, you son of a bitch, have you gone completely nuts?"

"Take them aside," Pak told Chun, gesturing at the two women with the pistol. "By the wall. Keep them quiet. You!"

43

He swung the pistol to aim it squarely at O'Malley's head. "Out of the bed. Over there. Face to that wall and hands up!"

O'Malley complied, but his face was flushed dark red with a barely contained fury. "Kim, what the hell is this?"

"Who are they?" Pak demanded. The women's screams had died down to broken sobs and whimpers now. Chun had them on their knees, hands behind their heads, and was standing before them with her own pistol out. Weiss stood guard impassively in the doorway with an unsilenced 9mm Browning Hi-Power.

"Huh?" O'Malley blinked. "Who?"

"The women, you fool! Who are they? Where did they come from?"

"Aw, fer the love of—"

Pak jammed the muzzle of his pistol hard into O'Malley's left kidney. The man gasped and flinched. "Christ! Y'can't just come in here and—"

"You would be surprised at what I can do," Pak said coldly. "Now, for the last time. Who are these women and where did they come from?"

"Th' brunette's, uh, Sharon, and the blonde's . . . what is it, honey? Patty?"

"P-Patricia Summers," the woman said from the other side of the room.

Chun rapped her sharply in the side of her head with her pistol, and both women screamed again. "Silence!" Chun said. "He was not talking to you!"

"Where did you find them, O'Malley?"

"At a fuckin' pub! God damn it, Kim, I jus' brought 'em home fer a little—"

"You knew the rules. No contact with anyone outside the group until the operation was well under way!"

"But the operation *is* under way! C'mon, Kim! Lighten up, man!"

"Turn around. Keep your hands above your head."

Slowly, O'Malley did as he was told. The man was scared, but Pak could easily read the anger still in his face. He needed to be broken, and quickly. "Weiss!"

"Yes, sir," the German said.

"Come here."

The man walked across from the open door. "Sir?"

"Place your gun to O'Malley's head. If he makes any move, any move at all which I do not first tell him to make, shoot him."

"My pleasure."

"Spread your legs," Pak said, addressing O'Malley again.

"Huh?"

"Spread your legs apart! Do not make me repeat myself!"

The anger was nearly all gone now, drained away with the color in the Provo terrorist's face. His eyes were very wide now, and sweat was beading on his forehead and along his upper lip. Slowly, bit by bit, he inched his legs to either side, his spine pressed against the wall at his back, until his bare feet were about three feet apart.

Slowly, Pak lowered his pistol down the centerline of the man's torso. The man's eyes squeezed shut and his breath came in short, hard gasps. With great deliberation, Pak pressed the muzzle of the sound suppressor sharply against O'Malley's penis, which was still ludicrously encased within the glistening wet sheath of a condom.

"O, Christ, oh, God, please, no, no, no . . ."

"I should simply shoot you," Pak said quietly. "You appear unable to accept simple discipline, and your actions have endangered our entire operation."

"It was a mistake, oh, God-Jesus-Mary please, don't, it was a mistake—"

"On the other hand, I could simply hurt you in such a way that you would not break our rules in this manner again. Which punishment would you prefer?"

"Please, Jesus God, you don't have to do this, please. . . ." The man was crying openly now, and his knees were threatening to give way.

"Stop babbling. Now, tell me what I want to know, or I will castrate you here and now. Who are these women? Where did you meet them?"

"I swear to God, Kim, they're just a couple of whores! They don't mean nothin'! I picked them up at the King's Bull in town! I swear! I swear!"

"Prostitutes? How much did you pay them?"

"I ain't paid 'em yet! But, but they said we could have a great party if I gave 'em a twenty each."

"Forty pounds?"

"Yeah! Yeah, that's right!"

Pak sighed. "No wonder you people can't win your war with the English. You are so easily distracted. Did you approach them? Or did they approach you?"

"Huh? Hell, I don't know. They were at the bar and I come up to 'em and started talkin' 'em up, y'know? So yeah, I guess I approached them."

"Did they suggest you bring them back here?"

"Uh, I, uh—"

He jabbed the muzzle of the gun forward, hard. "Tell me!"

"They wanted to go to a fuckin' hotel, okay? But I said I had a place here! I thought it would be okay! That's God's truth, Kim! I swear it! I didn't think it would be any harm, I swear to God I didn't!"

Pak lifted the gun away from O'Malley's genitals and took a step back. As he did so, the condom fell away with a wet plop, followed by a dribble of urine. Then the terrorist lost control of his bowels, and Pak wrinkled his nose in disgust. These filthy *oegugin* had no self-discipline at all.

"I believe you," he said, and he squeezed the trigger. Pak's gun jerked with a loud but muffled thud, as a neat red hole appeared just above O'Malley's left eye, and a splatter of blood and brains exploded across the wall behind his head.

Behind him, the two women kneeling in front of Chun screamed again. Weiss gave Pak a leering grin. "So what are we going to do about these two lovelies, eh?"

Pak ignored him. *"Kot hasipsiyo,"* he told Chun. "Do it now."

Chun shot the brown-haired one, the sound-suppressed shot hitting her in the face, knocking her sprawling back against the wall with a scarlet splash of blood. With a flash of scissoring bare legs, the yellow-haired woman leaped up from the floor and bowled Chun aside, racing for the bedroom door.

"Stop her!" Pak screamed. Spinning, he raised his pistol and fired twice, both shots missing the woman and punching neat

side-by-side holes through the open wooden door. Beside him Weiss raised the Browning and snapped off another shot, this one explosively loud in the confines of the room. Chun was already racing after the fleeing prisoner. *"Ai ch'am!"* Damn it! Everything was coming apart, the situation completely out of control. *"Don't let her get away!"*

Patty Summers sprinted for her life. Out the door as gunfire crashed behind her, down the stairs and to the right . . . down the stairs again. As she rounded the bottom of the flight, she heard again that horrible, chirping thud of a silenced gunshot, and the banister a few inches to her right shattered in whirling chips of varnished wood.

If she remembered the layout of this place right, she was still on the first floor up . . . but now she could hear the pounding of feet coming up the stairs from below, and she knew they were going to catch her before she could get anywhere near the front door.

Directly in front of her was a door, a big set of French double doors, in fact, with tall, curtained windows.

"You!" a voice bellowed behind her. "Stop right there!"

She leaped forward, propelled by all the terror that had driven her from that bloody room. Bringing her arm up to protect her face, she hit the flimsy door full-on, smashing through the windows in an explosion of shattering glass and splintering wood.

Through the disintegrating door, she slammed into the iron railing of the balcony beyond and very nearly went over. She caught herself, though, just as a gunshot rang out from inside the house. The street twelve feet below was quiet, midnight dark save for the pools of illumination beneath the street lamps and the distant movement of traffic headlights on the main highway. The early April night air was bitterly cold on her bare skin, and for the briefest of moments, she hesitated.

Then she glimpsed movement on the pavement up the street, a shadow beneath a street lamp with an oddly shaped head. Was it? . . . yes! A bobby! Never, in her line of work, had Patricia Summers been so happy to see a policeman.

"Help me!" she shrieked. "Please! . . ."

Glass crunched underfoot behind her. Someone was coming through the shattered door to the balcony. Then another gunshot exploded close behind her, and she felt something like a red-hot wire sear through her flesh high on her right side. Without waiting for another shot, without even looking, she vaulted the railing. There was a dizzying rush of air past her body as she fell . . . and then she slammed into grass and soft earth with a thud that drove the breath from her lungs. She'd fallen about twelve feet, she guessed, and with a clumsy landing at the end of it, but at least she'd missed the wrought-iron fence topped by sharp spikes that lined the plot of earth where she'd landed. Quickly she scrambled to her feet, intending to run toward the policeman, only to have her ankle turn beneath her weight and pitch her to the ground once more.

"There she is!"

Rolling onto her back, she looked up at the balcony. The Oriental woman was there, looking as cold and as hard as ice. Beside her was a man with some kind of automatic weapon— she didn't know what kind, only that it looked dangerous. He started to aim at her, but the Oriental woman held up a hand. Had they seen the bobby up the street?

The woman was aiming her silenced pistol.

Patricia screamed as loud and as hard as she could and rolled away from the fence, banging up hard against the building's wall. She thought she heard the thump of the pistol, but she couldn't be sure; this close to the building, though, she didn't think the people inside could see her, and if they couldn't see her, they couldn't shoot her.

Her ankle burned like fire; she must have twisted it in her fall. Her side was burning where a bullet had scratched her, and she was bleeding from a dozen minor cuts she must have picked up coming through the window. Rising again, still screaming as loud as she could to attract attention, *any* attention, she began hobbling toward the street, leaning heavily against the wall. There was a gate in the iron fence ahead, a gate with a latch just opposite the building's front door, but to reach it, she would have to leave the relative shelter of the wall and run for the street.

At twenty-eight, Patricia Summers was a survivor. Her dad

had walked out on a family of six kids when she was just five, her mother thrown out of work during the big recession in the seventies; Mum had struggled along on the dole for a while but eventually lost herself in a bottle. With no education beyond the fifth grade, Patricia had supported herself and the other kids doing what work she could find. The promise of a career as a model—as if you had a chance at modeling without going to school!—had turned out to be the come-on for a London "escort service." It wasn't long after that before she'd been exchanging sex for money.

She didn't like it, but life was a bitch whether you liked it or not . . . and no matter what happened, she was *not* going to follow Mum into that bottle. Patricia knew how to do what had to be done, and she knew how to make quick decisions without second thoughts. The name of the game was *survival*.

Steeling herself, she took a deep breath, then lunged for the gate. The latch was stiff and her hand slippery with her own blood. She fumbled it twice . . . damn! Damn! Come *on*! . . .

With a grinding crack the gate swung open and Patricia dashed through. She could hear the lock on the front door of the house being turned. If only her ankle . . .

Shit! She was down again, on her hands and knees, but she kept crawling. Could they see her from the balcony? Were they shooting at her? She didn't stop to look, but kept crawling.

"'Ere now, miss!" an authoritarian voice said from the darkness just ahead. "What's the idea?"

It was the bobby, jogging toward her across the pavement.

Damn it, did all bobbies carry guns nowadays? She couldn't remember. Once, back in gentler, more innocent days, the British police has never been armed, but in recent years that had changed, especially in the rougher parts of England's cities.

But was *this* one armed? She desperately prayed that he was.

"Watch out!" she screamed. "They've got guns! They're trying—"

She was interrupted by a long, staccato burst of fire off the balcony from which she'd just fallen. Ricochets whined off the street a few feet away, and a fleck of broken stone stung her cheek. With a smooth, powerful movement, the police officer swept her up in his arms, spun about, and dashed down the pavement. Automatic gunfire followed them, stabbing at them through the dark . . . then abruptly ceased.

Moments later, in a sheltered doorway down the street, the bobby hung his overcoat over her shoulders and proceeded to question her. She told him everything, not even lying when he asked her what she and Sharon had been doing in the pub when O'Malley had picked them up, and minutes after that she could hear the wailing of approaching sirens.

Poor Sharon . . .

"Well, miss," the bobby said. She was shivering violently now, despite the heavy coat, and he guided her to the stoop within the doorway and made her sit down. "I guess that's one trick you'll always remember, eh?"

"Not if I can help it," she said, and then she started crying.

God, how she wanted to forget the sight of Sharon's ruined face.

0425 hours
Barracks, 23 SAS Training Center
Dorset, England

Someone was shaking Roselli by the shoulder. When he opened his eyes, a flashlight was glaring in his eyes. "What the fuck?"

"Sorry, mate," a Britisher's voice said from the blackness behind the light. "Rise and shine. We got a hot flash in a few minutes ago. Briefing in thirty, and you Yanks are invited."

Roselli groped in the darkness for his watch on the tiny nightstand next to his rack and peeled back the Velcro cover. When he squinted at them hard, the luminous digits told him what he already knew . . . that it was zero-dark-thirty in military parlance and entirely too early for civilized people to be up and about.

SEALs, however, never thought of themselves as civilized, and neither, evidently, did their SAS hosts. As he swung his legs over the side of the rack and set them on the cold linoleum deck, his tormenter straightened to shake Magic Brown, occupying the upper rack above Roselli's head.

"What's up, Razor?" Jaybird asked from across the aisle that divided the barracks into two long lines of double-decker bunks. He was already half dressed, pulling his fatigues from the seabag hanging at the head of his rack.

"Haven't the foggiest," Roselli replied, mimicking the Brits. "I suppose that's why God invented briefings."

"If this is another exercise," "Professor" Higgins said from his bunk, "I'm going to vote that we declare war on England without delay."

The briefing room was tucked away in one corner of the Dorset HQ complex, not far from the barracks, a wood-floored room half filled with folding metal chairs. Roselli, Higgins, Brown, and Sterling had arrived to find several SAS officers and noncoms already present, including Major Roger Dowling-Smythe and Sergeant Major Dunn, both of whom had supervised the CQB exercise, now impeccable in neatly pressed and creased fatigues. SAS Colonel Howard Wentworth was there as well, as was a rather plain man in civilian clothes, who had the look that Roselli had come to associate with intelligence people worldwide.

On a tripod at Wentworth's back was a corkboard to which several photographs had been attached. Roselli recognized them as photos he'd seen a few days ago . . . security shots from Heathrow Airport of a couple of possible North Korean agents. The L-T had flown over to Wiesbaden to talk to the Germans about those two.

"Gentlemen," Wentworth said, standing, a few moments after the Americans had found places for themselves and sat down. "This morning, about three hours ago, the Middlebrough police picked up a girl fleeing from a row house on the west end of the city. Shots were fired from the building.

"Normally, this would be a matter for the local police to handle, but it happens that the young woman in question was able to identify both O'Malley, late of the Provisional Irish Republican Army, and these two Koreans, Major Pak and Captain Chun . . . though according to their passports, they seem to be calling themselves Mr. and Mrs. Kim these days.

"This is something of a major break for our side. You see, it seems that Pak, his girlfriend, and O'Malley, who was his primary contact in this country, all gave our security people the slip two days ago." He glanced at the intelligence man, who looked away, clearly discomfited. "We still don't know what happened, but I gather that some highly placed ministers were quietly contemplating hara-kiri with the knowledge that two potentially dangerous enemy agents were wandering loose around the countryside, presumably in the company of some equally dangerous people from across the Irish Sea."

A murmur of low-voiced conversation rose in the room as the SAS troopers passed comments back and forth. Roselli heard one young man mutter darkly about a "bloody cock-up."

"In any case, we have them now. We suspect that this flat in Middlebrough is a safe house run by the Provos. From the woman's description, there were at least five people living there, probably more. It's a big house, four stories, and it could hold quite a mob. Most of the people she saw there were armed, and of course the bobby was able to confirm the presence of automatic weapons, though he wasn't able to tell what kind.

"Also, according to the woman, O'Malley is now dead. Apparently, well, it was O'Malley who brought the young lady in question and a girlfriend of hers home, and it seems that was a breach of the house rules. O'Malley was shot by Pak. Pak's girlfriend shot our informant's friend, but the informant was able to make a break for it and escape out onto the street, where she, ah, attracted the notice of the police.

"Naturally, the police were called in. The officer who picked up the girl reported being taken under fire, and there were reports of gunfire called in from other houses in the neighborhood. The police have cordoned off the area and are trying to open up communications with the people inside. They still don't have a good idea about how many people we have inside, or how well armed they might be.

"As of zero four hundred hours this morning, the Minister of Defense has put this unit on full alert, and I am calling a Class One stand-to. We have the helos loading now at the field. We will deploy A Troop, full takedown kit and harness, to a staging area two miles from the scene. Any questions?"

Roselli raised his hand. "Sir. Any chance us SEALs could tag along?"

Wentworth grinned at him. "Absolutely. I can't promise you a combat slot, but at least this will give you Yanks a chance to see how the SAS does things in the real world. Any other questions? Okay, let's move out!"

6

Saturday, April 28

0710 hours
Rüsselsheim, Federal Republic of Germany

Murdock awoke suddenly, momentarily wondering where he was. Then he sensed the sleek, warm, naked form of Inge Schmidt sprawled in the tangle of sheets at his side, and remembered. Carefully, so that he wouldn't wake her, he pulled away and stretched. His watch read 0710 hours . . . late for a SEAL who rarely slept past 0530.

But then, they'd been awake for a long time last night. He wasn't at all sure exactly when he and Inge had finally gotten to sleep.

Despite his careful movements, her eyes opened. "Good morning, my wonderful lover."

"Morning, beautiful. Sleep well?"

"Mmm. Delightfully." She reached over, running her fingers softly down the plank-hard slabs of muscle on his stomach. "You know, that steak was marvelous, but since last night, I've acquired a prodigious appetite for seafood. Especially SEAL. Delicious."

Gently caressing her left breast, he grinned at her from across the pillow. "Plenty more where that came from. Want another helping?"

"You know, I don't mind if I do. I understand the British eat fish for breakfast. What are they called?"

"Kippers?"

"Yes, kippers. Me, I much prefer raw SEAL for my breakfast." Raising herself up on one elbow, she leaned over, lightly kissing his chest, then slowly running her tongue down his torso, pausing here and there to lick or kiss, her golden, shoulder-length hair brushing lightly enough across his skin to tickle.

This shouldn't be happening, Murdock thought. It *couldn't* be happening. Not so suddenly . . . so unexpectedly . . .

Except for a low moan escaping from Murdock as he closed his eyes and slumped back against his pillow, nothing more was said for several minutes.

The telephone rang on Inge's bedside table, a harsh, intrusive explosion of sound.

"Oh . . . *damn*," Murdock said, with considerable feeling.

Inge reached across his body to pick up the receiver. "*Ja?*" She listened for a moment to a voice that Murdock could just barely hear as a murmuring buzz. Her eyes met his. "*Ja . . .* yes, Chief. He is here." She handed the phone to Murdock. "Your Master Chief MacKenzie."

"Good morning, Chief."

"Sorry for the interruption, L-T," MacKenzie's voice said. "Hope I'm not calling too early."

Damn the man. For a bleary moment, Murdock wondered how MacKenzie had known he was here. Then he remembered signaling the man out the window. Hell, Mac and Hopke had probably posted a security watch outside last night. So much for privacy.

"What is it?"

"Something's happening. You'd better get squared away and get on in here."

"Where is 'here'?"

"BKA headquarters, of course. I just had a call from Dorset. Seems there's an incident over in England, and it might affect our boys."

Inge had returned her full attention to Murdock's erection, and her ministrations were making it difficult for him to concentrate on MacKenzie's words. Reaching down, he gently stroked her cheek, then guided her away from his lap. Nodding her comprehension, she shifted her position to simply cuddle close against his side, her hand on his chest.

"What's up?"

"You know those tangos we were supposed to check on with Komissar?"

Tangos—military slang for "terrorists."

"Yeah."

"Seems the Koreans gave British intel the slip, then turned up in a row house in Middlebrough. There's been an incident, one civilian hurt or killed, another escaped. Police have been fired at. The SAS is being assembled for a possible assault."

"Okay." He sat up, swinging his legs out of bed. "I'll be in quick as I can get there. You start the ball rolling on getting us a first-available military flight out of here."

"Already taken care of, Skipper. A C-130 with 3rd Support, leaving Wiesbaden Air Base at zero-nine-twenty. You'd better hustle."

"You're talking to an echo." He hung up. Inge was sitting up behind him, her arms around his neck.

"Leaving so soon?"

"Sorry. Some of my boys might be about to get themselves into a firefight. I have to be there."

"I understand." She felt warm and very soft against his back. "I'll drive you to the BKA. Just let me get washed up and dressed."

**1230 hours
Waterfront Rise
Middlebrough, England**

Chun Hyon Hee gently eased aside the curtain on the third-floor window, keeping well back from the opening as she peered out into the bright daylight beyond. From here, she could see the police barricades, and beyond that the waiting, watching crowds of curious onlookers, the news media, the gawkers.

It was a pity, really. The location of this safe house, which originally had been a place for Provos on the run from the British to lie low, had been ideal. The brownstone building housing the Waterfront Rise flats fronted on Northport Street, just across from the main entrance to the BGA Consortium's Middlebrough port facility. From the third-floor front balcony, Chun had a splendid view of the entire expanse of the shipyard, from the storehouses and rail yards behind the fence, to the wharfs, piers, and shiploading machinery on the waterfront, to the harbor itself and the dozens of ships moored there, from lighters and small craft to mammoth oil tankers. To the right, beyond the Port Authority buildings at the south end of town, an enormous tank farm rose behind the skyline clutter of cranes and cargo gantries.

Middlebrough had long been an industrial center in this part of England, but in recent years the influx of oil from the North Sea fields had transformed parts of the port into an important petroleum distribution center. Pipelines from the important Ekofisk and Bouddica oil and gas complexes midway between England and the southern tip of Norway snaked across 150 miles of sea bottom to rise onto the oil-scummed beach and enter the Middlebrough refinery complex. The facility was known as Teeside, even though the town properly of that name lay some distance inland, up the Tees River.

Oil. Even now, twenty years and more after the embargoes and price hikes that had sent convulsions throughout the West, oil was the key to economic power in the industrialized world. And where one held economic power, one held political power as well. That was what Operation Saebyok was all about— power . . . political power enough to bring the West to its knees.

That idiot O'Malley had jeopardized everything, *everything*. If he hadn't brought those *maech'unbu* back to the safe house . . .

Carefully, Chun released the curtain and stepped away from the window. Sooner or later the enemy was certain to assault the safe house, though she thought it likely that they would wait until night, when the defenders were tired and their reactions were slowed. In a way, Chun was looking forward to the showdown, even though it would mean that she, personally, could no longer take part in Saebyok. The operation would continue, of course, even after she was dead. She took comfort—and great pride—in that simple fact.

Pak Chong Yong had escaped out the back of the safe house, moments after the prostitute had fled screaming out the front. Pak was the real key to Saebyok. The two of them both had the same training, the same knowledge, so that one could act as backup for the other should anything go wrong, but from the beginning, this had been Pak's operation, Pak's concept. Besides, Pak had been part of the original development team, and he knew the theory and the operation of the Device far better than did Chun.

It was good that he had been able to escape.

Of course, Pak had ordered her to escape with him, but she, with her usual practicality and sensibility, had pointed out that one of them had to stay behind and ensure that all of the records hidden at the site were destroyed, and that the German and Irish members of the unit would fight. Neither she nor Pak trusted their Western accomplices. The level of discipline, dedication, and obedience to orders among the Provos was appalling; they tended to be lazy, cowardly, and slow. The Germans among them were only slightly better. They were totally dedicated to the mission—especially the women, surprisingly enough to Chun—but always when given an order, it seemed they wanted to know *why*.

Reaching out, she drew the curtain back once more, staring hard past the buildings across the street at the waterfront and dockyard facilities beyond. Pak was out there somewhere. He should have been able to make it clear to the docks before the police barricades had been erected. The unit kept a small boat there, just for such emergencies as this. With luck, Pak was out to sea and halfway back to the primary base by now.

"*Haeng'un ul pimnida,*" she murmured, wishing him luck. She'd slept with him a number of times, at first out of socialist duty since the two of them were expected to look and act like husband and wife . . . but lately she'd developed a genuine fondness for him. Pak Chong Yong had the dedication necessary to see this operation through to its glorious end. She thought she was probably in love with him. "*Haeng'un ul pimnida, na e aein.*"

1245 hours
SAS Command Center
Outside Middlebrough, England

"We're not going to wait until tonight to take the bastards out," Colonel Wentworth said. An architect's blueprints were unrolled on the top of the folding card table before him. "We're going to hit them now."

"What?" Sergeant Major Andrew Dunn said in mock surprise. "In broad daylight?"

"Maybe we should go put our makeup on," Trooper Frank McIntyre put in. "Just for the telly cameras, you know."

"Hey, Roselli," Trooper George A. Cartwright said, laughing. "How do you SEALs like being on TV?"

"It's happened," Roselli said. He was thinking about the highly publicized Navy-Marine landing in Somalia several years back, when a joint SEAL/Marine Recon team had hit the beach smack dab in the middle of a waiting pack of journalists and cameramen, who'd been tipped off by someone in the high command. The result had been a cluster fuck if ever there'd been one, with the team taking up fighting positions squarely under the white glare of the film crew's lights. "We don't like it, but it's happened."

Roselli and the other three SEALs of the SAS exchange training group were standing inside the large tent that had been set up as Colonel Wentworth's operational field HQ, along with twelve SAS men in full battle garb—black Nomex coveralls, bulletproof vests, and combat harness. In one corner in the back, half-hidden in the shadows, a young, yellow-haired woman wearing camouflage Army BDUs several sizes too big for her and white bandages on her face and hands was talking quietly with a female British Army sergeant, who was questioning her and making notations on a large clipboard.

"What's the rush, anyway, Colonel?" Sergeant Vince Randolph wanted to know.

"Major Dowling-Smythe is at the scene now with a couple of observers," Wentworth said. He pulled a large and highly detailed street map out from under the blueprints and smoothed it out on the tabletop. "They have an infrared scope set up in this Port Authority office building on the top floor . . . right here. The major says there's a great deal of heat coming from the target's fourth floor." He stopped and glanced at Roselli. "That's the *fifth* floor to you boys from the colonies."

"Leave it to the Yanks t' get it wrong," Randolph said, and the others chuckled, including the four SEALs.

"What kind of heat?" Dunn wanted to know. "A stove?"

"Probably an open flame," Wentworth said. "Major Dowling-Smythe reports smoke coming from the windows as well. It's our guess that the terrs are busily burning the evidence.

"And that's why the minister wants us to go in quickly. If we can catch them now, before they've had a chance to dispose of the evidence of their dirty work, the goodies might give us a handle on the whole terrorist gang."

"So," Major Fred Billingsly, the colonel's chief aide, said as he looked up from the map. "No hostages this time?"

"Not that we know of . . . unless you want to count those records. I can't stress that part of the op enough, gentlemen. We suspect that this safe house was a storage facility—a library, if you will—for a very great deal of the gang's paperwork. There will be lists of contacts and informants, pay records, expense sheets, sources of money from overseas, lists of provisioners and gunsmiths and sources of weapons and explosives, rosters of active members, maybe even lists of sleepers they have hidden away in sensitive positions in the government or elsewhere."

"Hell," Roselli said. "Sounds like even the tangos can't escape the terror of bureaucracy anymore." The others laughed.

"Just so," Wentworth said. "If we're very lucky, there will be notes kept during their planning meetings, maybe write-ups or reports or schedules that will describe their current operations. We know this group has been damned active, both in uniting the RAF and the active remnants of the Provos into something new, something called the People's Revolutionary Front, and in planning for something new and very big either here or on the

Continent. We haven't been very successful in penetrating their new organization. This is our chance to see just exactly what they're up to."

"Are we sure they're all still in there, Colonel?" Higgins wanted to know.

"For that matter," Dunn added, "how many people are we facing in there? Any ideas?"

"Both good questions," Wentworth said. He nodded toward the woman in BDUs in the corner. "That young lady over there started this whole show, so to speak. Her name is Summers, and she was invited into the house by one of the terrorists. She, ah, didn't know he was a terrorist at the time, of course."

"Probably she didn't get to see his calling card," one of the SAS men joked.

"She claims to have seen five people inside," Wentworth continued. "The two Korean suspects, one male, one female. The man who took her and a girlfriend to the house . . . and he, according to Miss Summers, is dead. Plus two other gunmen, one of them with a foreign accent that Miss Summers thinks was German. Of course, it was unlikely that she would see everybody in there. Our observers have sighted in on two terrs on the roof armed with M-16 rifles, plus at least three more armed men visible inside the front windows on the fourth floor."

"Fifth floor," Roselli murmured. Higgins nudged him in the side with an elbow.

Wentworth ignored them both. "The IR scope may have as many as seven people spotted in that fourth-floor front room, though with the fire in there we may not be getting accurate readings. We've also gotten fuzzy readings from as many as four or five targets at a time on other floors. Based on this, our Intel chaps are guestimating the total hostile force at between twelve and sixteen shooters. I think we should extend that number to twenty, just to be on the safe side."

"Twenty, Colonel?" Cartwright said. "And you want to send in four whole sticks? One would do."

A "stick" was two four-man SAS teams, eight men in all.

Wentworth smiled, a cold expression. "Don't worry, gentlemen. I have a feeling that there's going to be more than enough fun to go around this time up."

Roselli had been in more than his share of house assaults, both in training and in real life. Looking at the small fortress represented on the colonel's blueprints, he was sure that Wentworth was right.

7

Saturday, April 28

1250 hours
SAS Command Center
Outside Middlebrough, England

"Okay, right," Wentworth said. "This is the way we'll do it. Hoskins . . . you'll have the first crack at them. Take your stick in on the helos. We've spotted two hostiles on the roof . . . about here. We'll hit them with snipers from across the road as you approach. Your boys should be able to abseil to the roof without opposition."

"Right."

"Jenkins."

"Sir."

"Your troop will take up position ahead of H-hour here, in the flat adjacent to the target. We've already quietly evacuated this whole section of the street, of course, and boys from S-section have been in there all morning, very, very quietly taking bricks out of the wall."

"They have a boroscope in place yet?"

"Not yet. There's always a chance your prey is going to notice that little black straw poking through his wall. Our lads have it down to the plaster, though, and you'll be able to take a quick look around before you go in."

"Right, sir."

"Dunn."

"Sir."

"Your boys will knock at the front door, then take the ground floor. We expect the heaviest concentration of enemy firepower to be there." Pulling several of the architectural blueprints to the top of the stack, he unrolled one to show the ground-floor plans. "You'll want to have a close look at these before jump-off," Wentworth continued. "Just inside the front door, here, you'll be facing a stairway up and down, with a landing overlooking the front lobby. Make enough noise there, and it might distract them, keep them from investigating upstairs."

"You can count on us, Colonel."

"Potter, you've got the fourth stick. You'll be in reserve across the street. I'll either throw you in where you're needed, or use you for the mop-up afterward. I'll also expect you to manage the sniper team."

"Yes, sir." Sergeant Major Christopher Potter sounded a bit disappointed at being left out of the initial assault.

"What about us, Colonel?" Roselli said.

"What about you? If you're thinking of coming along, forget it. Your bosses would flame my arse if anything happened to you boys."

"Shit, Colonel," Brown said. "We lose SEALs in training accidents all the time. This don't look no different to me."

"Yeah," Jaybird said, echoing the sentiment. "It's a piece of cake."

"Look, Colonel," Roselli said. "Tell you what. Brown here is one of the best snipers in the whole SEAL program. We call him 'Magic.' Give him a Barrett .50 or an M21 and he can reach out and touch someone from a thousand meters. You could put him with your snipers, as an extra set of eyes, couldn't you?"

"Well, I suppose. . . ."

"Of course you could! And as for the rest of us, I suggest you let us tag along with Sergeant Major Dunn. I agree that we might get in the way with the other groups. We haven't trained with you as a unit, and we might turn left when you're expecting us to turn right. That sort of thing is especially tricky working out of choppers or crowding through a narrow opening, like the one you're going to put in the wall.

"But that team going in the front door. You want them

making noise, and you need some extra muscle, if they're going in against the enemy's strong point, right?"

"Well . . ."

"And look here." He dragged his finger across the blueprint of the flat's ground floor. "You don't have anyone on these front windows at street level. Sure, your snipers could cover those windows, but you have a hell of a lot of windows to watch all over the building . . . and when the attack goes down, they'll be keeping their eye on the bad guys up on the roof anyway. Me and the Professor and Jaybird could cover those windows, maybe even break through and take the main defenses from the flank. Furthermore—"

"Enough."

"But—"

"Enough, Roselli! Let me think a moment."

Roselli knew when to shut up. Wentworth considered his arguments for several long seconds, studying the ground-floor blueprints.

"Very well," he said at last. "I was worried about being stretched as thin as we were on this op, and you make some good points. Your sniper will report to Color Sergeant Barnes here. I think he'll be able to provide you with an extra L96 out of stores. Is that satisfactory, Mr. Brown?"

Magic's teeth flashed white against his dark face. "Very. Sir."

"The rest of you can go with Sergeant Major Dunn. However, I want it perfectly clear that he is in command of this assault. If he tells you to stay back or get down or get the hell out, I expect you to obey. Clear?"

"Clear," Roselli said, and Higgins and Sterling echoed him.

"Mr. Billingsly, break out some weapons for our SEAL friends. H&Ks okay by you gentlemen?"

"Weapon of choice," Higgins said.

"They'll be just fine," Roselli added.

"Very well," Wentworth said. "Remember, now, we're going to play this one by the book. Advantage goes to the defender, and we have to assume the opposition will be well dug in and ready for us. Let's go over the layout of the place now. . . ."

1328 hours
Waterfront Rise
Middlebrough, England

Chun upended a cardboard box on the now-empty desk, spilling out a stack of manila folders. Each held neatly stapled stacks of closely typewritten papers, photographs, and newspaper clippings, a scrapbook record of terrorist coups stretching from Spain to Sweden, from Northern Ireland to the Gaza Strip. "Is this the last of them?" she asked Katarina Holst.

"I think so. The basement is empty now, except for the extra vests and military gear, and there's not much we can do about that."

"These things are so heavy." Chun patted the bulletproof vest she was wearing, wishing that she could take it off, knowing that if she did so it would be a bad example for the men. It seemed to be dragging her slight frame into the floor. "But you're sure everyone has been issued one?"

Holst took a double handful of folders off the spilled pile on the desk and dumped them into the flames. Steiner poked at them with a meter-long length of steel pipe. "Everyone," she said. "Not that it will help us that much when the time comes."

Chun heard something close to despair in the German woman's voice. She wanted to tell her to be strong, that death should be welcomed if it brought the opportunity to kill the fascist enemies of the People's Revolution, but once again, it wasn't wise to show softness to the men.

She longed for the siege to be over. . . .

A thunderous boom sounded outside, loud enough to make the walls of the flat tremble and the windows to rattle in their frames.

"What the hell was that?" Steiner cried. Turning from the burn barrel, he rushed toward the front windows.

"Karl!" Holst screamed. "*Nein,* get down! Get away from the window!"

"It's okay," one of the men already at the window called back. "Something just went up like fireworks in the dockyard across the street!"

Chun stayed well back from the window, but she moved to

one side so that she could see what the man was pointing at. A jet-black pillar of smoke was rising in an angry pall above the waterfront, uncoiling like a vast snake as it was caught by the gentle offshore breeze.

"My God," Holst said, staring.

"What do you think" Steiner asked. "Helicopter crash?"

"Ammo explosion, more likely." Holst laughed. "The bastards must have ignored their own no-smoking signs!"

"Don't be too certain of that," Chun warned. In the distance, a fire siren went off. Beyond the waterfront, well over the water, a military-looking helicopter was edging closer to the shore, apparently checking out the explosion. "It could also be a diversion."

Part of her specific training for this mission had been a careful study of the tactics and methods of the units who might be among the opposition. In 1977, four PFLP terrorists—two men and two women—had hijacked a Lufthansa with seventy-nine passengers after their takeoff from Majorca and flown them to the airport at Mogadishu, Somalia. Twenty-eight German GSG9 commandos, with two British SAS along as advisors, had stormed the aircraft with stun grenades, killing three hijackers and wounding and capturing the fourth. The attack had been launched in the middle of the night after an explosion and fire had been set off on the runway some hundreds of meters off the nose of the aircraft. Most of the hijackers had been clumped together in the plane's cockpit watching the fire when the commandos had blasted their way on board.

It was good to know the enemy and his methods.

"Everybody watch your sectors," Steiner snapped. Reaching into his hip pocket, he pulled out a small two-way radio and extended the antenna. "Ricky! O'Brien! What is your situation?"

"Ay, an' it looks to be a whopping big explosion over 'cross the road," a voice with a rich Irish brogue replied, crackling over the radio. "Lots o' people runnin' around there, as bright as the Belfast marketplace after a nice an' juicy bombing! There's an eggbeater up, Brit military job, but I think it's just lookin' over the situation, y'know?"

Chun glanced toward the ceiling. The two men Steiner had posted up on the roof with assault rifles that morning were supposed to be two of his best, one German RAF and one ex-Provo. But she had been up there once and knew just how little cover the rooftop provided. Those men would be the first to die if the enemy tried an assault, but they were invaluable where they were as early warning against anything the opposition might try.

"Keep your eyes open, O'Brien," Steiner told him. "It could be a diversion. I want to know the second you see a black uniform, a helicopter approaching the flat, anything."

"You got it, Karl. But it looks to us like they've got all they can handle across the way tryin' to put that fire out!"

1332 hours
Port Authority Building
Middlebrough, England

Magic Brown peered through the bulky sniperscope of the L96 PM rifle, which rested on its bipod on the concrete ledge of the Port Authority building's roof area and snugged up comfortably against his shoulder and cheek. From six hundred meters away, the two targets stood out as clear and as sharp as they might have at thirty feet. Both appeared to be wearing combat vests, probably with heavy Kevlar panels slipped into the inside pockets. Both were carrying American-made M-16 assault rifles with extended banana-clip magazines. Through the scope, Brown could see them looking intently off to the right, watching the carefully orchestrated consternation in the dockyard northeast of the sniper's position. The target on the right was standing up, carelessly leaning with his shoulder against a brick chimney and holding a pair of binoculars to his eyes; the other was lying flat on his stomach, holding a two-way radio and peering across the ridge of the peak of the roof.

"Chicks, this is Nest," a voice said in Brown's radio headset.

"Nest," the observer lying to Brown's left replied. He was the coordinator for the entire sniper team, which consisted of Brown and five British SAS shooters. "Go."

"Target traffic ended," the anonymous voice said. "Stand by."

The terrorist with the radio had been speaking into it, but according to the British army people monitoring the terrs' radio traffic, his report had just been concluded.

"Target," the voice said.

"Chick One, on the right," another voice said.

"Chick Two, on the right."

"Chick Three, on the right."

"And Four, I've got the left."

"Chick Five, left."

"Chick Six," Brown said, carefully drawing down on the terrorist with the radio, on the left. From this angle, with the target lying behind the pitch of the apartment building's roof, he could see the man's head, shoulders, and part of his back. It would have to be a head shot—rarely the preferred shot for a good sniper. A good hit meant an instant kill . . . but getting that hit was far more difficult than a shot against center-of-mass. "On the left."

"Chicks, you are clear for maximum force on my mark," the controller's emotionless voice said. Fire sirens wailed in the distance, rapidly growing closer. "And four, and three, and two, and one, and *fire*!"

Six Accuracy International PM sniper rifles, all equipped with long, sound-suppressor extensions on their muzzles, hiss-thumped in near-perfect unison. The standing man lurched suddenly, two puffs of smoke shredding the front of a vest bulletproof against small-arms ammo, but not against high-power explosive rounds. A third explosion, silent at this range, gouged a fist-sized crater out of the bricks just beyond his face. *That* was why head shots were risky . . . and why sniper kills were backed up by multiple shooters. The body jerked back against the chimney, bounced off, then tumbled forward in a lifeless sprawl across the peak of the roof.

At the same instant, three explosive rounds slammed into the terrorist lying to the left. One was low, nicking the peak of the roof in a cloud of splintering shingle and ridge beam; the other two detonated inside the man's skull, erupting in a bright red spray as his head exploded. The body jerked once, then slumped where it lay, motionless.

"Nest, Chicks," the SAS observer reported. "Two terrs down on the roof. Roof clear."

"Roger that. Shift to target area two."

Brown had already worked the bolt on his rifle, chambering another round from the box magazine, then dragged his sight picture away from the two bodies on the roof to the line of open windows on the building's upper floor. He could only see one tango there, lurking in the shadows behind the corner of the nearest window, but he didn't have a very good angle on the opening. It did look like the fire inside was out, for the haze of smoke that had been emerging from the upstairs room all morning was thinning out.

He wondered if that meant that all of the terrorist documents the SAS hoped to seize had been destroyed already, and the assault was to be for nothing.

Well . . . nothing but the offing or the capture of some major bad dudes. In Magic Brown's opinion, that was reason enough to go in.

"Chicks, Nest. What do you have?"

"One target, Area Two," the observer reported.

"Any reaction?"

"Negative reaction at this time."

"Hold one, Chicks."

The fire sirens were growing in volume second by second. Somewhere behind the Port Authority building, a bright red fire truck wheeled up to the blaze that was still pouring clouds of dense, black, oily smoke into the sky above the Middle-brough waterfront. Brown saw some movement at a curtain behind one of the windows, too sharp to be the wind.

"Nest, Chicks," the voice of the observer reported in Brown's headset. "Two targets, Area Two. Scratch that . . . three targets."

"Steady, Chicks," the command center warned. "Wait for the birds. . . ."

Brown could hear them now, the far-off *thumpeta-thumpeta* of helicopter rotors, just barely audible above the much louder screech of the fire sirens. Almost as if to add emphasis, another explosion went off with a dull *whoomp* in the open area north of the Port Authority. The wind was changing now, shifting over out of the north, and bringing with it an acrid bite of the oily smoke that brought tears to Brown's eyes. The curtains moved again . . .

"Chicks, Nest" sounded over Brown's headset. "You are now clear for Target Two." The thumping sound of the helicopter rotors was growing louder as the fire sirens dwindled, the one emerging almost seamlessly from the other. The terrorists would hear the helicopters' approach any second now, but the fire control officer had to delay the snipers' fire until the last possible instant. "And five, and four . . ."

1333 hours
Waterfront Rise
Middlebrough, England

Chun turned away from the window suddenly, stepping back into the room. She was certain now that she could hear something else, a dull and familiar thumping like a drumbeat behind the sirens.

Steiner was using a meter-long length of pipe to stir the fire in the barrel in the center of the room.

"I suggest you stay in radio contact with—"

There was a loud, rippling plop, and one of the Irishmen standing by the southernmost window spun back into the room, a pair of smoking holes gaping in his black bulletproof vest, and the right side of his head a violent scarlet smear. Next to him, another Irishman fell back as glass and wood splintered above his head, the raised window sash shattering in multiple explosions, another blast punching through his left shoulder. Curtains and windowsills all down the line of windows popped and fluttered as though blasted by a hot and deadly wind. Chun felt something sting her, high on her left arm.

"It's the attack!" she yelled . . . but needlessly, for in the moment of gunfire, the far-off thump had swelled to an avalanche of sound, drowning out the sirens, drowning out the exploding rounds smashing through the windows, drowning out the whole world as helicopters thundered in low across the rooftops of Middlebrough from the east, from inland, opposite the direction of the fires and explosions.

So . . . that blast and all of the smoke had been a diversion after all.

A third gunman yelled something mindless and swung into an open window, his G3 assault rifle to his shoulder. Before he could trigger the weapon, however, his head and chest exploded in bloody fragments, the rifle's plastic stock shattered against his shoulder, and his scream of rage turned to sheer agony, abruptly cut short as he tumbled in a bloody heap onto the bare wooden floor.

Steiner leaped clear of the barrel, grabbing the Uzi submachine gun he'd left on the desk. Katarina Holst, standing at the back of the room with another RAF gunman, shrugged her H&K subgun's sling off her shoulder and dragged back the charging lever with a loud snick. The thump and scuff of boots on the roof sounded through the ongoing thunder of the helicopters above the building.

The door to the room burst open and another Provo burst in, his eyes wild. "Christ! We got a team on the roof an' another comin' in at the front door!"

Then a distant explosion sounded from somewhere downstairs, and all of the building's lights went out.

8

Saturday, April 28

1333 hours
Waterfront Rise, front door
Middlebrough, England

Roselli leaned back as the lead SAS breaker aimed his shotgun against the front door's upper hinges and squeezed the trigger. The gun went off with a hollow boom . . . a boom repeated an instant later as he slammed a second one-ounce slug into the door's second hinge. The door breaker rolled back out of the way, chambering another round into his pump-action Mossburg, as the three SAS troopers waiting to either side plunged ahead, the first man up smashing the door aside and tossing in a stun grenade. Even outside on the street, the chain-reaction explosion was deafening; before the final echo had faded, the first man in the stick had lunged into the door, cutting loose with a burst of full-auto fire from his H&K subgun but never pausing for an instant as he cleared the opening, closely followed by his mates in a meticulously choreographed *pas de trois* that gave all three men clear fields of fire in mutually supported directions.

"Go!" Roselli snapped, and Higgins, unrecognizable in his hooded combat dress, mask, and goggles, swung his sledgehammer in a wide sweep that shattered one of the street-level windows. Sterling tossed a cardboard-bodied flashbang through the opening, and the three men pressed back against the bricks of the apartment as the explosions thundered inside.

Then Roselli was through the window, blinking into the smoky near-darkness of a small parlor just off the apartment's entrance hallway. His mask was hot and close and narrowed his field of view almost as sharply as night vision gear would have, and he wished he could pull it off; but he concentrated on sweeping every corner of the room. Enough light spilled in through the windows at his back for him to see, but he pulled a flashlight off his vest and held it ready, just in case.

There was one man already in the room, a scruffy-looking tango in jeans and combat vest, writhing about on the floor next to the door leading to the hallway, hands pressed to his ears and blood streaming from his nose. Roselli took three quick steps across the parlor floor, keeping the man beneath the muzzle of his H&K as he kicked the FN FAL assault rifle lying next to the man across the room. He kept the man covered as Sterling slipped in close, knelt by the tango, and frisked him for weapons. Normally, in a quick-moving assault, Roselli would have shot the man dead and moved on, but this operation wasn't hampered by the need to protect hostages . . . and the intelligence provided by live prisoners would be as useful as any documents they could hope to find.

"He's clean," Sterling said, reaching into a vest side pocket and extracting a clear plastic tie with one hand, as he used the other to grab the tango's right wrist and slam it into the small of his back.

"Eagle Four-one," Roselli said into his lip mike as Sterling efficiently cuffed the stunned terrorist. "South parlor on the ground floor secure. One prisoner."

Over his radio, he heard a second report close on the heels of his. "Eagle Two-two. Entrance achieved, second-floor bedroom. One terr dead, one prisoner."

"Eagle Three-one," Sergeant Major Dunn's voice added. "Entry at the front door. Front passage secure. Two down here."

"Two-two, Three-one," Roselli warned. "Coming in from the parlor."

"Come ahead."

Roselli moved through the parlor door and into the front hallway. The SAS men were already inside, deploying in different directions, each with a flashlight held next to his weapon, the beams probing through the haze and semi-darkness. One terrorist lay sprawled head-down on his back halfway up the stairs, while another was draped over the banister on the landing above. Both had been shot through the head. The entry teams, armed with submachine guns, weren't packing the explosive 7.62mm bullets used by the snipers' PM rifles to defeat the terrorists' body armor.

Burst-fire head shots at close range guaranteed an instant kill.

Gunfire sounded upstairs, harsh, sharp, and insistent. Seconds later, a tango in black jeans and a bulky sweater appeared running along the landing, running blindly, looking back over his shoulder, an M-16 in his hands as he fled some unseen threat at his back. Roselli brought his H&K up to his shoulder and triggered a three-round burst in the same instant that Dunn and another SAS man did the same; the terrorist was caught in a three-way crossfire of bullets that twisted him around, sending him slamming hard against the landing's banister. Wood splintered and the man catapulted into empty air in a shower of fragments, crashing heavily on the polished wood floor beside the stairway.

Two more SAS men, ominous in solid black, anonymous in their goggles and gas masks, appeared at the top of the landing. "Second floor, clear," said a voice over Roselli's headset. "Another down."

"Back of the flat," Dunn ordered, gesturing. "Down the passage. Watch for ambush."

Roselli moved deeper into the flat.

1334 hours
Waterfront Rise, top floor

"I'm going downstairs," Chun said, shouting to make herself heard above the clatter of the helicopters hovering low above the building's roof. She hefted her weapon, an Uzi. From the cacophony of explosions and muffled bursts of gunfire, mingled with the shouts and screams of the defenders, it sounded as though the attackers were storming up from the ground floor. She started toward the door.

Katarina Holst screamed a warning, and Chun whirled, seeking a target. Black shapes, like immense spiders, had slid down next to the exterior of each window. Karl Steiner raised his assault rifle, and gunfire stabbed in the dim light of the room, thunderously full-auto, as he wildly sprayed the windows in a shower of splintering wood and flying chips of plaster, but then return fire was slashing in through all four windows, pinning Steiner in a twisting, writhing dance before he pitched backward, finger still clenched on the trigger as his weapon chewed a ragged line of holes across the ceiling.

Something like a cardboard tube flew through an open window, bounced once on the floor . . .

By reflexes honed through long training, Chun squeezed her eyes shut, threw up her arms, and dropped to the floor. The explosion of the flashbang was like nothing she'd ever experienced before in her life, a chain of ear-shattering concussions accompanied by a pulsing, strobing flash so bright it burned bright red through her tightly closed eyelids. After the first cracking explosion, she wasn't even certain that she was hearing anything anymore, but she could feel the continuing detonations hammering at her body, slapping and clawing at her clothing like a high-pressure blast from a fire hose.

When the concussions ceased, she opened her eyes. Dimly, through a smoky red haze, she could see tall and bulky men swinging through the windows, landing on the floor, unfastening their rappelling ropes from the harnesses they wore over their torsos. The ice-cold sweep of those emotionless goggles was like the gaze of some huge and alien insect. The H&K MP5s strapped to their bodies swept the room, seeking targets, seeking prey. One of the commandos began unfolding a large, heavy blanket as soon as he was free of his line. With practiced speed, he advanced on the drum of burning records and threw the blanket over the top, smothering the flames. In seconds, the smoke in the room grew thicker, harsh white and choking, spilling from beneath the blanket.

Chin stirred, battling the paralysis that seemed to be pressing her down into the floor. They were trying to save the records still burning in the fifty-five-gallon drum! Someone was groaning on the floor close by, and Chun thought it must be Steiner.

She fumbled for her Uzi. Damn . . . where was it? She couldn't find it, she'd dropped it, and the men in black were bearing down on her like nightmares made flesh and blood. There was a short, harsh, three-round burst of gunfire into one of her compatriots—she couldn't tell who. Another burst . . . and Steiner's groans were silenced. Katarina Holst struggled to rise, an H&K in one hand, and one of the invaders triggered a burst that tore into her throat and face like a scythe. Without a word or even a sound, the German woman sagged back against a plaster wall stained by her blood, her subgun slipping from limp fingers.

"This 'un's dead," one of the figures said, his voice muffled by his mask.

"Here too."

"Live one here," another trooper said, bending over Chun. Carefully, he kicked her Uzi well away from her outstretched hand. "I don't think so, lady," he said. "Not today, anyway."

She felt his gloved hands moving to her face, her throat, checking for signs of life. She tried to back away and found she had no strength at all. He seemed to be studying her face closely.

With almost contemptuous ease, the man flipped her over onto her stomach, grabbed her right hand, and pulled it into the small of her back. She felt something thin and plastic snick tight over her wrist . . . and then the process was repeated for her left hand. Cuffed now, she was helpless. No . . . no, *no*! It wasn't supposed to end this way! Not with her a prisoner of the capitalist bastards! Briefly she considered trying to get to her feet and running; maybe they would shoot her, letting her escape the ignominy of capture.

But someone was securing her ankles as well, taking no chances with a potentially valuable prisoner. One of the men stood over her with his ugly black H&K, speaking into the microphone that must be hidden in that hideous mask. "Eagle One-one. Main room, fourth floor secure. Four terrorists dead, one captured. It's the Korean bitch."

She couldn't hear the response, and at this point she didn't

really care. One of her captors knelt beside her, and after
frisking her thoroughly and professionally for weapons, turned
her head to the side, and roughly probed the inside of her
mouth . . . searching, she supposed, for the inevitable hollow, poison-filled tooth of spy fiction. It would have been
funny if the situation had not been so desperate. She tried to
bite his finger, but he was wearing heavy gloves. In the center
of the room, two men were removing the blanket from the fire,
checking to make sure that the flames had been smothered,
while another carefully gathered up the records on the desk that
had not yet made it to the burn barrel.

Gunfire sounded elsewhere in the building, and then there
was silence. Chun forced herself to relax, closing her eyes to
shut out the sight of the enemy soldiers guarding their prizes.

This battle, the enemy had won . . . but the war was not
over yet.

She thought about Pak Chong Yong.

1345 hours
Outside the police perimeter
Waterfront Rise, Middlebrough

Murdock stood beside Colonel Wentworth and a number of
British army officers and security personnel. He was still
wearing his civilian clothing and felt out of place among all the
uniforms. The only other people in the immediate area in
civvies were obviously government types, "suits" in the
parlance of those like Murdock who claimed to work for a
living.

Wentworth was holding a radio headset to his ear. He looked
up at Murdock and cracked a grin. "Right, that's it," he said.
"Building secure."

"Excellent," Murdock said. "Any casualties?"

"One of my boys was winged going into that upstairs front
room. Nothing serious."

"Impressive. How long?"

The SAS colonel consulted his watch. "I make it three
minutes, forty seconds, give or take a few . . . ah, that's
counting from the time I gave the order to the snipers to take
down the people on the roof."

Speed was always the primary consideration in operations like this. If the entry team was fast, the bad guys didn't have time to kill their hostages, if they were holding any. Nor did they have time to coordinate their defense with one another, or to prepare a stubborn defense against an attack that could come from any or all directions at once.

Across the street, the British Army helicopters, which had been holding their positions above the roofs of the line of Middlebrough brownstones throughout the assault, were beginning to move off. Murdock could see black-clad soldiers filing across the roof and toward one of the machines, which dipped and swayed each time another heavily laden man clambered aboard.

Other SAS men were leaving by a more traditional route, exiting the flat's front door and walking across the street. Policemen and government agents were crowding in past them as they left, hurrying to begin their investigations, and to get the prisoners who were still under guard inside.

As they reached the police line and ducked beneath the barricades erected along the street, three of the SAS troopers veered away from the rest and approached Murdock. Roselli, Higgins, and Sterling; Murdock recognized them even before they'd revealed their faces.

"Well, gentlemen," Murdock said as they began divesting themselves of face masks and goggles and handing their unexpended ordnance over to a pair of SAS arms experts. "Having fun?"

"Hey, L-T!" Roselli said, his eyes lighting up. "Too bad you missed all the fun!"

"When'd you get in, Skipper?" Sterling asked.

"Just a few minutes ago," Murdock told them. "We heloed in from Lakenheath. Came in over the harbor just in time to see all the fireworks, and for a minute I thought one of you clowns had touched off some stores. I didn't find out it was a ruse until I was on the ground."

"Worked pretty neat, huh?" Higgins said, grinning. His face was streaked with soot . . . or possibly it was blacking off the rubber mask and goggles he'd been wearing. "Just like clockwork."

"Where's Magic?"

"Up that way, someplace," Sterling said. "He was with the sniper team. Probably be along shortly."

"So what was the take?"

"Eight prisoners, last I heard," Roselli told him. "Couple of them are wounded, though, and might not make it. One of them is what's-her-name. Kim. Or Chun."

"Chun Hyon Hee," Murdock said, nodding. "What about the guy?"

"Pak? No sign of him. Of course, the Brits are still going through the building. You should see some of the high-tech gimmicks they're using, looking for secret hidey-holes and such."

"Yeah, but they made us memorize the faces of a bunch of terrs before we went in," Sterling said. "They've got bodies laid out in there like keys on piano, and they're checking all of 'em real, real close. I didn't see any other Orientals in the lot. Just the Chun woman."

"That's not so good," Murdock said. "The people in Germany are pretty sure he's here on some kind of an op. A big one."

"Shit, L-T. No idea what?"

"Not a clue. Maybe Ms. Chun can help us on that."

Roselli laughed. "That's one mean-looking woman, Skipper. I don't think she's going to tell us a damned thing."

"Maybe. We'll let the MI5 boys worry about that. Now . . . maybe you'd like to tell me what the hell you three were doing getting yourselves involved in a firefight. I don't recall that being on the list of our assignments over here."

"Aw, L-T," Roselli said. He nodded toward Wentworth, who was deep in conversation with a couple of suits nearby. "We've been over all that with the colonel there. We were just observing SAS tactics and deployments in the field."

"Observing, huh? How many tangos did you observe to death in there, Razor?"

"Only one, Skipper." He raised his thumb and forefinger, holding them half an inch apart. "And he was just a little one."

"Maybe I should've told you guys that tangos were out of season over here, at least for SEALs."

"Shit, L-T," Higgins said with a grin. "You know as well as we do that tangos are vermin. Open season, anywhere, anytime, no limit."

Murdock thought about his own take in Germany and decided not to press the point.

"Besides," Sterling said. "This was part of our good neighbor policy. Hands across the sea, and all that."

"And when hands don't do the job," Roselli added, slapping the H&K MP5 still strapped against his combat vest, "a few rounds of nine mike-mike work wonders. . . ."

1925 hours
Cranston Moors
North York, England

It was very nearly dark when Pak pulled up to the airfield's gate and gave the password to the young PRF sentry in camouflage fatigues and lugging a British Army-issue rifle who challenged him. The sentry, one of the Provos, couldn't have been more than eighteen years old, and he certainly didn't look alert enough, or trained enough, to provide much of an obstacle should the SAS decide to hit this place as well. Pak said nothing, however, and merely nodded as the kid gave him a passable imitation of a military salute.

That was another thing, Pak reflected as he drove through the open gate. This make-believe that had infused the PRF fighters, this notion that they were a *real* army with uniforms and salutes and roll calls, might be good for morale, but it also tended to breed overconfidence. Pak had gone along with the idea hoping that the military forms and protocols might bring with them some military discipline. While the PRF army, so called, was somewhat better organized than a peasant mob, it still lacked the steel and the precision of a decent fighting force.

No matter. Children such as the play-soldier at the gate were expendable.

As expendable as the people he'd left behind in Middle-brough.

He felt as bleak as the moor country he'd been driving through for the past several hours. He'd left Hyon Hee,

knowing that she would have to face an assault by the enemy's
military, knowing that she would sacrifice herself for the cause.
Love was not an emotion discussed or encouraged among
members of the North Korean Special Forces. The first several
times he and Hyon Hee had enjoyed sex together had been
almost comical, with a couple of army officers present in the
room to make certain that the properly detached and clinical
nature of the exercise was maintained.

The times after that had been better . . . enough better that
Pak knew he'd grown genuinely fond of her.

He wished he could have convinced her to come along with
him.

Pak Chong Yong had been on the run all day, uncertain
whether or not he'd been seen or followed. Slipping out of the
back of the Waterfront Rise apartment minutes after gunfire
had erupted at the front, he'd made his way to the ancient but
well-serviced speedboat moored at a jetty just outside the BGA
Consortium's port facility fence. From there, it was a two-hour
run at a gentle and unsuspicious cruising pace to the landing at
Redcar, where a car had been left for just such emergencies as
this one. Four hours more, following a twisting and circuitous
route in case he was being followed, had brought him to
Cranston Moor, where the PRF maintained its field combat
training center.

Once, Cranston Moor had been a military base, an airfield
for the *other* RAF, the one that had won the Battle of Britain
against the Nazi blitz. During the '50s it had been converted to
a helicopter base for NATO antisubmarine missions over the
North Sea, and eventually had been sold to a developer, who'd
wanted to open a private flying club.

Several owners later, Cranston Moor had been abandoned, a
decaying symbol of the economic recession that continued to
dog England. Pak didn't know who the current owner was, or
why he'd made the facilities available to the People's Revolution, and he didn't really care. The ex-air base with its single
runway and its shabby, crumbling hangars and storage buildings was perfect for the PRF's needs. The nearest village was
Robin Hood's Bay, ten miles off, and the nearest neighbors on
this wild and lonely stretch of North Country moor were

perhaps half that distance away. That meant no one would complain about the frequent target practice that went on in one of the empty hangars, as recruits learned how to handle automatic weapons. There was even a grenade and explosives range on the moor out back.

The place was quiet today; Heinrich Adler had ordered all activities that might attract unwanted attention from the authorities suspended once the operation was under way. Even the troops, normally training outdoors on the obstacle course or standing to parade formation on the runway tarmac outside the control tower, had been dispersed.

Pak had agreed that the order was an excellent idea.

Pulling up to a parking area alongside one of the hangars, Pak stopped the car and got out. The base looked, *felt* deserted, despite the muffled roar of some machinery in use somewhere close by. The empty feel to the place was as it should be, of course. Only a few PRF troops stayed here all the time, maintaining security and keeping casual visitors, hikers and such, away. Adler had a healthy fear of American spy satellites, and while the paramilitary activities at Cranston Moor were officially explained as maneuvers and outings by one of Britain's numerous survivalist clubs, the PRF's leadership didn't want to attract undue attention to what, after all, was *supposed* to be an abandoned airfield.

"Pak!" a voice said behind him as he walked past the hangar's maintenance shack door. "You made it! Thank God."

"I made it," Pak replied, while thinking that *God* had nothing to do with it. A thoroughgoing and completely pragmatic atheist, as would be expected of someone raised since the age of six in one of Pyongyang's strictest military school-academies, he was frequently amused by Westerners' pretended reliance on divine intervention.

Heinrich Frank Adler walked out of the maintenance shack door, glancing back and forth as if to verify that Pak was alone. He was a tall, rugged, Nordic man with sandy hair and an engaging smile. Once he'd been a bronze medal winner on the East German Army's Olympic biathlon team, and it was rumored that he'd also been a high-ranking member of that country's notorious Stasi, the secret police. In 1989, he'd been forced to go underground—even further underground, that is, than he'd been already—to escape the purges that had followed the collapse of the East German government.

Adler had begun assembling the organization now known as the People's Revolutionary Front even before the formal unification of the two Germanies. He still styled himself "Colonel," after the rank he claimed he'd held in the army. Pak knew from intelligence sources in Pyongyang that Adler had never actually been more than an *unterfeldwebel,* a sergeant.

"Come on inside."

The door opened into a small area filled with ancient tools, engine parts, and rubbish. Beyond was the aircraft hangar proper, an enormous, open space that currently housed only a single craft, an aging Westland Lynx Model 81 helicopter. Acquired through the services of the same faceless man or men who owned Cranston Moor, the helo was government surplus and showed the signs of some years of rugged service with the Royal Navy.

Three men were at work on the machine now, wearing masks and goggles as they applied spray painters to the aircraft's body, methodically changing the color scheme from the blue-gray of the Royal Navy to a deep, glossy blue-black.

As always, Pak felt a rippling thrill when he saw the helicopter, the centerpiece to this entire operation.

Very soon now, he thought, *and my Hyon Hee will be avenged.*

9

Saturday, April 28

1930 hours
Cranston Moors
North York, England

The rumble of the generators and spray painter air compressors was deafeningly loud within the enclosed space of the hangar, and as the two of them walked across the hangar floor toward a small office in the back, Adler had to pitch his voice louder to make himself heard.

"I was afraid you'd all been taken," he told Pak. "Have you been listening to the news these past few hours?"

"No. The car had no radio. In any case, I would have expected a news blackout as soon as any assault was begun. Have you heard anything?"

Adler nodded. "Came over the television on the BBC evening news an hour ago. The government claims the Army assaulted a flat in Middlebrough, but the details are still sketchy. Was it the SAS?"

Pak shrugged. "I wasn't there to see. But I would be surprised if it was not. Did they identify who they were attacking?"

"Just 'presumed IRA terrorists,' though the announcer also mentioned the Red Army Faction once. Typical news botch-up."

"They won't know yet. About the People's Revolution."

"If by 'they' you mean the government, I doubt that they

would tell the press anything anyway. The BBC was taking a lot of wild guesses on this one, none of them particularly accurate."

"It would be helpful to know just how much the government does know," Pak said thoughtfully.

"Know your enemy," Adler said. "Say, where's your girlfriend? Did she get out of Waterfront Rise with you?"

"She . . . we thought it best that she stay behind, to ensure that incriminating documents were destroyed. Some of the papers you people insisted on keeping include sensitive information that could have led the authorities here."

Adler nodded, admiring the calm, the analytical detachment in Pak's voice. The man was cold as ice. "I know. Maybe that was a mistake, keeping those records . . . but what we're trying to do here, it's so big. We needed to keep track of the details, or else something small would have tripped us up."

Past the helicopter and the painting crew, the noise wasn't so bad. Adler opened the door to the office and ushered Pak through.

Inside was a desk piled with papers that would, if inspected, demonstrate that Cranston Moor was indeed a small private airfield that tended to struggle along in the red, with far more bills than income. A bulletin board on the wall by the door included cards advertising flying and skydiving clubs. On the adjacent wall was a detailed topological map of the area, a calendar hanging beneath a photograph of a World War II Spitfire in flight, and several pinups of provocatively posed naked women torn from various pornographic magazines.

"Do you know if anyone was captured at Middlebrough?" Pak asked.

"The BBC wasn't real explicit," Adler replied. "Deliberately so, I imagine. They don't want to tip us off."

"I was wondering if we should evacuate this site anyway, just in case."

Adler sighed. "I don't think that will be necessary. Even if they were able to capture the documents that point back here, it will take them days, at least, to sort through them all. And by that time, of course, it will be too late."

"I see the work on the helicopter is still only half complete. You are behind schedule."

"Don't worry, Major. It will be done by late tonight or early tomorrow," Adler told him. "We could fly it to our alternate location tomorrow afternoon if necessary, but I don't think that will be necessary. And after tomorrow, of course . . ." He let the thought trail off.

"Perhaps, then, our sacrifice of the safe house will have a good effect," Pak said. "It should provide something for the British government and security forces to worry about, while we complete our plans here."

"*Ja,*" Adler said. "My thought exactly. There is, however, one other disturbing piece of news."

"What is that?"

"This afternoon I received a cipher from Wiesbaden. The usual source."

"Yes?"

"There's been an . . . incident. Berg and two others have been captured by the German police And Waldemar is dead."

"That . . . is not good."

"Damn right it's not. The two were freelancers hired for the occasion and knew nothing, but Berg and Waldemar were members of the inner cells."

"And you say that Erna Berg was captured?"

"And is being interrogated by the BKA right at this moment, as we speak. At least, that's what Ulrich tells me."

"How much does she know? Can we get to her?"

"She doesn't know everything about the plan, of course, but she knows enough to link parts of our organization on the Continent with the operation here. She knows about me, and that I am running something here called Operation Firestorm. And . . . though she doesn't know the specific reason for your being brought over to England, she does know about you."

Pak's normally bland and impassive face twisted with something that might have been anger, then became expressionless once again. "How did she allow herself to be captured?"

Adler looked away. "Our nemesis over there is not an

organization so much as it is a machine," he explained. "The BKA computer at Wiesbaden. You're familiar with it?"

Pak nodded. "The one they call 'Komissar.'"

"Berg was head of a team keeping a particular BKA employee under observation, a woman named Schmidt who has some fairly high-level access to the Wiesbaden computer. We thought this person's activities might give us a clue to the nature of their investigations. Anyway, two days ago, Schmidt met with two unknown men. Our intelligence sources were unable to turn up any hard information on them, but a check of their passport records indicated that both were American, and both were active-duty members of the U.S. Navy. One was a lieutenant, the other a senior petty officer."

"American Navy. SEALs, perhaps?"

"It is a possibility. We are checking into that, though it is extremely difficult to learn anything about that organization. It is also possible that they were members of the American intelligence community, DIA or CIA or even FBI, working under the cover of Navy passports."

Pak grunted. "The American SEALs are very much a part of the American intelligence community," he said. "More so, perhaps, than your GSG9 is a part of the German intelligence apparatus. This news is . . . disquieting."

"I thought so too."

"What were the Americans doing in Wiesbaden, then?"

"Consulting with the Wiesbaden computer's records, obviously. With Schmidt's help."

"About what? Us?"

"There was no way to tell. Possibly the visit was simply coincidental with the onset of our operation in England. However, if the Americans are seeking information on Operation Firestorm—and it *will* strike at their interests in Europe, so we can expect them to become involved once they know what is happening—it is certain that the Wiesbaden computer would have data pertinent to their research. There is a way we could learn more. . . ."

"Yes?"

"One of the Americans, the officer, appears to have, ah, formed an attachment with the BKA employee while he was there. Spent the night with her. Understandable, of course. I gather she is quite attractive, not to mention something of a free spirit."

"What is your point?"

"It was Ulrich's idea to try to abduct both the BKA woman and the American officer . . . and that led to the incident."

"How was the attempt thwarted? The German police?"

"According to Ulrich's report, by the two targets themselves. The woman used karate, while the man . . . well, he appears to have been exceptionally well trained in martial arts. According to Ulrich, the fight was over in seconds."

"Which confirms, I think, that the American officer is a SEAL, and not a CIA bureaucrat." Pak considered the problem. "Trying to abduct an American was dangerous. And foolhardy. *Especially* if the man is a Navy SEAL! But even if the attempt had succeeded, it was not wise to focus the attention of the American intelligence apparatus on your European assets."

Adler shrugged. "Another incident of random terrorism. I doubt that the Americans would attach any unusual significance to it. I happen to believe that the reasoning behind Ulrich's decision was sound, even if the execution was flawed."

Pak nodded, almost reluctantly. "Perhaps. I dislike introducing random elements into a plan this complex, but the reward, if we could learn just what the enemy knows, what they are planning, would be invaluable, I agree. Can your people in Germany make another attempt against the Americans? Possibly against the other one, the petty officer."

Adler shook his head. "Not now. Both left the country early this morning." He shrugged. "According to my sources, they returned to London. It is possible they returned when news of the incident at Middlebrough reached them."

"Then they may already know something about Firestorm. What about the woman?"

"The one with the BKA? So far as I know, she is still in Wiesbaden. She has had a bodyguard assigned to her since the abduction attempt, but she is maintaining her old schedule. Are you suggesting that we try again to abduct her?"

"If she can tell us about the Americans, about why they are

here, yes. And if she was giving the Americans information from the Wiesbaden computer about us and our operation, then it might be worthwhile to interrogate her. We could learn exactly what they know about us."

"It would be risky. We mustn't alert them to our interest in their activities too soon."

Pak shrugged. "Having already gambled with one attempt, it will be worth the additional risk to try again. We have only another forty-eight hours, yes?"

"Less than that, now."

"Then I suggest that you talk to your people in Germany. They could arrange it with a minimum of risk."

"Very well. Where do you want her? Not here. And it wouldn't be safe back at our Hamburg site."

"No," Pak agreed. "You will have to arrange to have her flown to the operation, once it begins. She could be kept aboard the *Rosa*. Or on one of the targets, once we have them secured."

"Consider it done."

2040 hours
Lakenheath
England

Murdock and Chief MacKenzie stood side by side in the close and darkened room, staring through the two-way mirror. Alone in the brightly lit room next door, the North Korean woman sat on a straight-backed chair, looking frail and alone in the institutional gray slacks and shirt she'd been given. The only other furniture in the room was an empty table and one other chair.

"She must know we have her under observation, Skipper," MacKenzie said, watching her. He whispered, though the observation room was heavily soundproofed. "A mighty cool customer."

"So," Murdock said, turning to the other two men in the darkened spy chamber. "What have you learned so far?"

"That this lady is very well trained," Major Dowling-Smythe said. "She's not going to tell us a damned thing."

"She's already told us one thing unawares," Wentworth told

Murdock. "When they brought her in here, she was under some rather close scrutiny by some of your NEST chaps. They went over her and her clothing meticulously, with some fairly impressive equipment flown in from Washington just for the occasion."

"And?" Murdock prompted. Knowing something about Chun's background, he was the one who'd originally suggested summoning a NEST—a Nuclear Emergency Security Team—in the first place. The ultra-secret NESTs had been organized under the aegis of the U.S. Atomic Energy commission back in the 1970s, when it had first become apparent that the threat of nuclear terrorism might soon become a reality. They were trained to respond to any type of nuclear-related emergency, but their more secret tasks included monitoring for smuggled or hidden radioactive materials—such as the homemade nukes that might be employed by terrorists or by foreign nuclear powers.

"Your guess was right, Lieutenant," Wentworth said. "Definite traces of radioactivity, more than could be explained by the background count. There wasn't much, but their estimation was that she could well have been exposed to a secondary radiation source within the past few days . . . a week at the outside."

"Secondary radiation?"

"She wasn't in direct contact with plutonium or U235 or anything like that," Dowling-Smythe explained. "But I gather the radiation from something like that can trigger secondary radiation in other materials if they're dense enough."

"Cascade radiation," Wentworth added.

"That's the stuff," Dowling-Smythe said, nodding. "If they had a bomb that didn't have real good shielding, for instance, she could've picked up a dose from the lead or whatever they had protecting it."

"God help us," Murdock said quietly. "Then they *do* have a bomb."

"Not necessarily," Wentworth said, shaking his head. "They could have plutonium, which they're planning on dispersing with conventional high explosive . . . or by dumping it in someone's water supply. Or she could simply have come in contact with something else that had been exposed to radiation. For all we know the woman's just come back from having her chest X-rayed. . . ."

"Different kind of radiation here, Colonel," Dowling-Smythe said. "And a lot stronger too."

"Enough to pose a danger?" Murdock asked. "I mean, to people who've come in contact with her."

"Your men weren't at risk, Lieutenant," Wentworth said. "We're talking about very, very small doses."

"Good."

"This woman had a substantial and recent contact with a radioactive source," Dowling-Smythe said. "The doctor who supervised her physical said she hadn't received a lethal dose, but there was a definite possibility of complications down the line. Leukemia, that sort of thing." He shuddered, his shoulders drawing up and forward as he shook his head back and forth. "If the North Koreans were involved in some sort of home-grown basement nuclear program, they must not be taking adequate precautions when they're handling sensitive material. That's scary."

"These are scary people we're dealing with, Major," Mac-Kenzie said.

"I take it you've tried the usual tricks on her," Murdock said. "Tell her we got her boyfriend, that sort of thing."

Wentworth nodded. "Oh, yes. Told her we knew all about the bomb too, but that's such an old trick I'm surprised she didn't just laugh at us. She's just been sitting there and not saying a word."

"What will you do?" Murdock asked.

"Oh, we'll get her," Wentworth promised. "Sooner or later, we'll wear her down."

"What, torture?" MacKenzie asked.

Wentworth looked pained. "Oh, please. What do you colonials take us for anyway?"

"Outright torture tends to be counterproductive," Dowling-Smythe said, "especially when the person being interrogated is as well trained and mentally prepared as this one is. The victim tends to hang on for the sake of whatever he's already suffered. No, we'll wear her down bit by bit. Good cop, bad cop, that sort of thing, going on for hours on end. Disorientation, repeated questionings. Getting her to make small admissions, and building those into something more substantial."

"The problem is," Wentworth said, "is that all of that will take time. And standing back here watching her with the interrogators, I get the distinct impression that, well, time doesn't matter for her."

"What do you mean?" Murdock asked.

"Hard to put a name to it, Lieutenant. But I have the feeling that she figures she can stand anything because she won't have to last through it for long. Do you know what I mean? Like she's expecting a rescue."

"Or," Dowling-Smythe added, "because she knows that whatever it is she's protecting, some operation, some mission, will be too far along for us to do anything about it before we could possibly break her. Since she knows she can hold out that long, she's at peace with the world."

"Maybe she thinks her friends will try to set up an exchange."

"Could be," Dowling-Smythe said. "Though your people back in Washington have shown a keen interest in this bird, Lieutenant. Fairly champing at the bit to have a go at her. Doubt that they'll be too keen at letting her slip through their fingers."

"I don't think I want to know," Murdock said. He was a warrior, a profession that frequently demanded brutality. Two days earlier he'd killed a man with precision and efficiency, and very nearly killed a woman the same way, *would* have killed her had he needed to.

But he didn't at all like this tinkering with a person's soul.

"We also had something faxed through from Wiesbaden, Lieutenant," Dowling-Smythe said. "About those four people you pegged the other day."

"Yes?" He'd been expecting a distillation on the dossiers of the people who'd attacked him and Inge. "Anything useful?"

He shrugged. "Not much. They say that there were fairly complete dossiers in the Komissar computer. The two men who were captured were small-time thugs. Members of a criminal gang based in Hamburg. Bank robbery, extortion, but never any connection with terrorism."

"Freelancers," Wentworth suggested. "Hired muscle."

"A distinct possibility. Our source over there says they've questioned them, of course, but they claim not to know who they were working for. Their contact they knew simply as Ulrich."

"Chances are they wouldn't know," MacKenzie put in.

"True. But there was a difference with the other two." Dowling-Smythe pulled a folded sheet of paper from the inside of his uniform jacket and handed it to Murdock. "This came through for you, Lieutenant. From someone named . . . Inge?"

Murdock smiled, accepting the sheet. "A friend."

Swiftly, he scanned the faxed copy of a typewritten, single-spaced sheet. Inge's letter was curt and to the point, promising full dossiers to follow later.

"The man you killed, Lieutenant," Dowling-Smythe continued as Murdock read, "was Rudie Waldemar. The woman you captured was Erna Berg. According to Komissar, those two were members of the old Red Army Faction beginning in the middle 1970s."

"I thought as much," Murdock said, continuing to scan the information. He'd already described the woman's H&K tattoo to both men.

"Lately, of course, the German RAF is pretty much dead. Has been for ten years or more. But this strongly suggests that there's something new afoot. We've been hearing rumors for some time that the RAF and some of the other old terrorist groups on the Continent were banding together into something called variously the People's Party or the People's Revolution."

"This says that all four may have been working for something called the People's Revolutionary Front," Murdock said. He looked up, handing the paper to MacKenzie. "Is there a connection between that and our North Korean friend in the next room?"

"Hard to say," Wentworth said. He walked over to the two-way transparency and stared into the next window for a time. "We know that a large number of the terrs we put down

in Middlebrough this afternoon were either known Provos—
mostly hotheads who wouldn't accept the latest truce—or Red
Army Faction. And both Waldemar and Berg were RAF once.
I'd say it's a fair guess that the old RAF is changing its stripes,
turning into the People's Revolution . . . that or it's backing
the PRF, bankrolling it and providing personnel and shooters."

"And importing two North Koreans with experience handling nuclear materials," Murdock continued. "One of whom
has been handling nuclear materials within the past few days."

MacKenzie whistled. "*Fuck*, Skipper. I don't much like the
sound of that!"

"I think," Murdock said quietly, "that we'd better make a
full and complete report to Washington."

10
Monday, April 30

0825 hours
Rüsselsheim, Federal Republic of Germany
Inge Schmidt left her apartment, walking down the long hallway, turning into the foyer, and stepping out into the early morning sunshine. It was a glorious day, with a clear blue sky and the promise of an early spring.

She wondered if . . . no, *when* she would see Blake again.

The truth of the matter was that the American SEAL had really gotten to her, despite all of her promises to herself never to become emotionally involved again . . . not the way she'd been with Josef. Thinking about Blake, she couldn't help but remember the attack that evening, when she'd seen him take down three of their four attackers in the space of a couple of heartbeats.

"Guten tag, Fräulein."

She started. Glancing to her left, she saw Klaus Dengler's ironic smile as he leaned against the side of a trash dumpster, crisply dressed in a suit that betrayed the bulge of an automatic pistol beneath his jacket. "Hello, Klaus. All quiet?"

"So far."

Dengler was a Section Three man, one of those assigned to provide security for Inge since the incident here on this very street three days before. It was nothing so obvious as a constant guard; someone was simply . . . always about, walking around

96

the block, sitting in a car in the parking lot with a newspaper, or perhaps sitting on the front step, talking with a friend.

"Well, you can come on in to work now," she told him. "I don't think anyone will steal the building while I'm gone."

"Actually, Fräulein, I'll be following you in this morning." He shrugged. "The boss wants it that way, until we know more about why those RAF thugs tried to get you the other night."

"Well, I'll see you at work, then." She walked toward her Renault, parked in her numbered space in the lot.

She heard a shoe scrape on the pavement behind her. She assumed it was Klaus . . . but something tickled at the back of her mind, a warning, a tremor of fear, and she turned. A stranger was there, a big man in a heavy overcoat, coming straight toward her and only a few feet away now. He was reaching beneath his unbuttoned coat, pulling something out. . . .

Turning sharply, she started to run, but two more men had appeared, one emerging from behind her car in the lot, the other moving rapidly toward her from across the street. That stopped her . . . and an instant later a hand closed on her upper arm. "Be perfectly silent, Miss Schmidt," the man said in German.

She twisted hard, trying to gain the leverage she needed to break the hold, but something ice-cold and metallic pressed against the base of her neck. "Don't," the man said.

"What is it? What do you want?"

"Some information. You will come with us."

"Go to hell!" She opened her mouth and screamed as loud as she could.

The blow on the back of her head stunned her, an explosion of pain that made her gasp and turned her knees to jelly. Slumping forward, she felt the man in the raincoat grab her from behind, keeping her on her feet. She wanted to fight back, wanted to lash out, but the blow had stunned her to the point where she was having trouble coordinating any movement, or even managing to stand. "Help me," he barked in German to one of the others.

She heard running footsteps. As they dragged her off the sidewalk, she was just able to turn her head. Expecting to see still more assailants, she was momentarily relieved, then horrified, to see Klaus Dengler running toward her, an H&K pistol already drawn from his shoulder holster.

Gunfire erupted from at least two different directions—the muffled, hissing chirps of sound-suppressed shots—and Dengler stumbled, took another three steps, then collapsed facedown onto the pavement.

"Klaus! *No!*" Even stunned, Inge could still twist and struggle in her captor's grasp. God, they'd shot down Klaus!

Shock warred with shock. Somehow, she found the strength to scream again, louder, and someone clamped a leather-gloved hand over her mouth. "None of that, Miss Schmidt," he said in her ear. "Be a good girl and come with us and you will not be harmed. I am sorry about your friend, but . . . fortunes of war, yes?"

With a squeal of tires, a van careened around the corner, pulling up on the street opposite the parking lot, and her captors half dragged, half walked her across the road. Her eyes widened in terror. It was the same panel truck Blake had noticed the other night, the same vehicle that had carried the two "utilities men" to the attack in the parking lot. Desperate now, more desperate than she'd ever been in her life. She lashed out in a karate sidekick against one of the men holding her.

Her target yelped, then cursed; one of the others hit her again from behind, then propelled her forward, facedown onto a rug on the floor of the van. Someone else, a woman, she thought, was ready with handcuffs, securely locking her wrists together behind her back.

"You bastards—"

"Quiet, bitch." A hand roughly yanked her hair, hard, forcing her head up and back. A wad of something—a roll of gauze, she thought—was jammed into her mouth. She tried to spit it out, but they were wrapping tape around her head and over the gauze, effectively gagging her. One of the men tossed her handbag in after her. Doors slammed. The van's engine gunned, and she felt the lurch of acceleration, followed by a right turn at the next intersection down the street.

A man kneeled beside her, rummaging through her handbag,

then extracting the pistol she carried there. "Ah!" he said, smiling. "You were planning perhaps on using this on us?" Several of the others laughed.

The one who'd yanked her hair settled his weight across her buttocks, straddling her hips. Still tugging her hair back as he reached down over her shoulder, he fumbled with the front of her blouse, tearing buttons free, then reached his hand in and slipped it under her bra. Her skin crawled as he squeezed her breast, and she screamed into the gag, twisting back and forth, trying to throw her tormentor off.

"Johann!" The woman's voice snapped. "None of that!"

The hand lingered, then pinched her painfully before sliding out from under her clothing. "Shit, Felda," the man said. "I wasn't hurting her. . . ."

"Ulrich said no rough stuff," the man with her handbag said. "Leave her alone!"

Abruptly, the weight on her buttocks lifted and was gone. A blanket was dropped on top of her, smothering her in darkness.

In blackness, then, Inge sensed the van racing down the street. She tried to roll over, but someone dropped his legs heavily across her back, pinning her to the floor.

She was pretty sure from the turns she was sensing that they were headed toward the Autobahn, probably heading north.

Not that the knowledge helped her even the tiniest bit.

1140 hours
CQB house, 23 SAS Training Center
Dorset, England

Murdock stood with Colonel Wentworth next to an HMMWV, the ubiquitous "hum-vee" of the NATO forces. They appeared to be standing on the main drag of a small town, with narrow streets and neat two- and three-story buildings. Wentworth held a stopwatch in one hand. Sergeant Major Dunn was with them, pressing the earphone of a headset speaker to his ear as he monitored the radio net.

The mock battle was already very nearly over. Murdock heard another muffled three-round burst . . . then one more . . . and then Dunn, still listening to the radio net, announced, "Exercise complete."

Wentworth's thumb snicked the button on his stopwatch, and he peered at the final time with a skeptical stare. "Two-twenty-one," he said. "Slow . . . damned slow!"

Dunn, meanwhile, changed channels on his radio and spoke into his pencil mike. "All right, Freddy. Send 'em on through!"

Two more hummers drove up a few minutes later, both crowded with men. As the vehicles creaked to a stop and the doors banged open, Murdock immediately recognized the passengers spilling from them and onto the street.

A young U.S. Navy lieutenant j.g. with a SEAL's Budweiser on dress whites totally at odds with Murdock's green fatigues snapped to attention and saluted crisply. "Good morning, Lieutenant! Gold Platoon reporting for duty!"

"Two Eyes," Murdock said slowly, watching as seven enlisted sailors spilled into a rough line along the street. "What the hell is this?"

The j.g. was Ed DeWitt, known as "Two Eyes" for his position as "2IC," the platoon's second-in-command. "I guess Washington decided you couldn't handle the SAS all by yourself, Skipper," he said, grinning. He handed a bulky manila envelope to Murdock. "They sent us over to help you out."

Dubiously, Murdock accepted the envelope, unwound the length of twine sealing the flap, and glanced briefly at the thick sheaf of orders inside. The cover sheet on top told him what he needed to know. Stripped of its Navyese jargon and bureaucratic circumlocutions, it informed him that NAVSPEC-WARGRU-2—that was the Navy's Special Warfare Group stationed at Norfolk—had been placed on alert pending the possible unfolding of a terrorist scenario somewhere in northern Europe. First Platoon, SEAL Seven, was directed to continue with its current mission—meaning the exchange training program with the SAS at Dorset—but to maintain an alert readiness state in anticipation of further orders. To this end, First Platoon's Gold Squad was being transferred from Norfolk to Dorset. Operational equipment and expendables would be arriving on a MACV flight at Lakenheath by late tomorrow.

There was no word as to what the terrorist scenario might be, but Murdock was certain that the intelligence reports filtering back both from the interrogation of the Korean woman at Lakenheath and from the BKA in Wiesbaden must have gotten someone back in CONUS pretty damned well stirred up.

And about time too. Too often, especially lately, the White House had been totally adrift when it came to reacting to developments overseas. Maybe this time someone back there had finally read an intel brief on smuggled nukes and been scared enough to forget about apple-polishing, ass-kissing, and sound bites on the evening news.

Maybe.

Murdock tucked the packet of orders under his arm and let his gaze run down the line of men. Gunner's Mate First Class Miguel "Rattler" Fernandez, Gold Squad's big-muscled 60-gunner. Radioman First Class Ron "Bearcat" Holt. Chief Boatswain's Mate Ben "Kos" Kosciuszko. Torpedoman's Mate Second Class Eric Nicholson, variously called Red for his hair color, or "Nickel" for his last name. Mineman Second Class "Scotty" Frazier.

The seventh member of Gold Squad technically was Jaybird Sterling, but Murdock had shifted him at least temporarily to Blue Squad the week before. On paper, Third Platoon consisted of two officers and twelve enlisted men, but they'd suffered some casualties in recent missions; "Doc" Ellsworth was still recovering from a sprained ankle he'd gotten during a HAHO drop into Yugoslav Macedonia the month before, while "Boomer" Garcia had been taken off the active list after being shot through the lung. A new man sent out to replace Boomer, "Nick the Greek" Papagos, was now on TAD to Athens in the wake of the Macedonian op, all of which had left Third Platoon's Blue Squad two men short. Murdock had transferred Sterling to even out the two squads at six men apiece.

Only now, apparently, there was another newbie, a face in the line of SEALs that Murdock didn't recognize. "What's your name, sailor?"

"Mineman Second Class Greg Johnson, sir," the man snapped back. He had a powerful, muscular build, as did most SEALs, but he looked so young and had his hair shaved so close that Murdock was put in mind more of a high school linebacker than a Navy SPECWAR expert. "The guys all call me Skeeter."

"You're Ellsworth's replacement?"

"I guess so, sir. They, uh, they didn't really tell me anything. They just told me to pack my gear and go. Sir."

Murdock looked him up and down. Johnson seemed to be an unlikely replacement for the wild and often unpredictable HM2 Ellsworth . . . stiff and formal, the yes-sir polish of a raw FNG still as sharply evident as a fresh coat of paint. Murdock noticed that Johnson alone of all the men there was not wearing a Budweiser pinned to his shirt. "How long since Coronado?" he asked.

"Three months, sir. They sent me to Fort Benning to learn parachuting out of BUD/S, then back to California for SDV school. After that, it was straight to Virginia Beach."

Murdock nodded. Graduates of the Basic Underwater Demolition/SEAL school at Coronado, California, were put on a six-month probationary period, followed by a session with a review board before they could pin on their SEAL insignia. Training alone—even the rigors of Hell Week—did not make a SEAL. He wondered how the kid would fit in with the rest of the team.

"Bus driver, huh?" Murdock said, referring to the SEALs' swimmer delivery vehicles, or SDVs.

"Yes, sir."

"You'll be filling some pretty big shoes, son," Murdock told him.

"I'll do my best, sir."

"Good. You can start by dropping at least every other 'sir.' It makes me feel old." He looked up at the rest of the squad. "Well, gentlemen, all I can say is, welcome to England."

"Great to be here, L-T," Kos said pleasantly. "When do we get to kill something?"

"Yeah," Holt added. "We're ready to prowl and growl!"

"Loot and shoot!" Rattler exclaimed.

"Yeah, well let's just belay the 'loot and shoot' stuff," Murdock told them. "The British are our allies. At least so far. Colonel Wentworth, do you think your people can find barracks space for eight more shooters?"

"I think we should be able to accommodate you, Lieutenant," Wentworth said. "I'm beginning to wonder about you chaps, though. Haven't had this many Yanks running around underfoot since D-Day."

"If I were you, Colonel," Murdock told him, "I'd place every bar, pub, and brothel in a fifty-kilometer radius of this base on full alert. I'm not entirely sure whether to compare this bunch to D-Day . . . or the Blitz."

Three hours later, Murdock was sitting on a folding metal chair in First Troop's ready room, going over the stack of paperwork from Norfolk sheet by mind-numbing sheet. So far, his orders were typically vague, and as nearly as he could distill them, required only that he keep himself and his men in a state of readiness and take no direct action unless said action was specifically directed by CO-NAVSPECWARGRU-2, which was to say Admiral Bainbridge.

A British Army orderly stuck his head into the room. "Lieutenant Murdock, sir?"

"That's me."

"Telephone for you, sir. Main desk. Overseas call."

"I'm coming."

He wondered who the caller might be. Washington? He doubted that they would be moving quite that fast. The platoon's combat gear and other equipment hadn't even arrived yet.

He picked up the phone and punched the blinking, white-lit button. "Lieutenant Murdock."

"Blake?" a familiar, accented voice said. "This is Lieutenant Hopke."

"Yes, Werner! What can I do for you?"

"I . . . I fear I have some bad news, Blake. There has been another incident. Inge has been kidnapped."

"Shit! When? How did it happen?"

"This morning. In front of her apartment."

"Didn't you guys have security on her?"

The voice on the other end of the line sounded tired. "*Ja*, Blake. We did. He was shot down in the street."

"Who did it?" As if he didn't know. Anger flared white and hot deep within Murdock's mind. Somehow, he kept his voice calm. "Have they made any kind of contact with the authorities."

"We have heard nothing, but we must assume it was the same group that made the attempt on Friday. I probably should say nothing more. This is supposed to be a secure line, but . . ."

"Understood." The fact that the Red Army Faction, or the People's Revolution or whatever else they were calling themselves these days, had been keeping a close watch on Inge Schmidt suggested that the BKA's security might have been compromised in other ways as well. Informants within the organization, taps on the telephones . . . modern terrorist organizations were often as well provided for in the intelligence department as were the military units tasked with hunting them down.

Sometimes, Murdock thought, the opposition's intel was a hell of a lot better than what the SEALs had available.

Inge . . . kidnapped by terrorists? After thanking Hopke and telling him to keep him informed on every development, Murdock hung up the phone, his mind racing. The only possible motive the RAF had for such an act was their need for intelligence. With a terrible, burning clarity, Murdock could see the step-by-step reasoning that must have led the terrorist leadership to issue the orders to grab her. Unidentified Americans—members of the U.S. military, no less—were consulting with the BKA and their Komissar computer. That suggested an interest in possible terrorist activities.

Item: Murdock and MacKenzie had gone to Wiesbaden in the first place to check up on what Komissar had in its files about the two North Koreans Chun and Pak.

Item: Chun had been captured in the company of RAF and Irish Provo terrorists, involved in something called the "People's Revolution." She'd had traces of radioactivity on her clothing and skin that suggested that she'd recently been close to something nasty . . . like the plutonium in a poorly shielded nuclear warhead.

Item: While there was nothing definite, there were hints and rumors about that a major terrorist group was planning something big . . . and soon. A nuclear warhead would certainly qualify as "something big" in anybody's book.

Item: Inge had been kidnapped, probably by the same organization, probably to find out what she knew about American interest or involvement in European terrorist ops. The fact that they'd kidnapped her now suggested that the "something big" on his list must be going down damned soon, or they wouldn't have risked tipping their hand to the BKA or the SAS.

He thought about what Inge must be going through right now, and his neatly ordered chain of logic dissolved. Colonel Wentworth and British intelligence might disdain torture as a means for getting information out of a captive, but Murdock knew that the opposition held no such compunctions.

God, Inge . . . it was my fault. If you hadn't been seen spending time with me . . .

That kind of circular and self-destructive thinking would get him exactly nowhere. As he walked back to the SAS ready room, he concentrated on replacing the guilt and the fear with a cold, diamond-hard lust for the PRF bastards who'd orchestrated this.

One thing he was certain of. Whether the final orders ever came through from Washington or not . . . Murdock was going to find the people responsible for kidnapping Inge Schmidt.

And then he was going to kill them . . . if he had to force-feed them their own basement nuke one gram of plutonium at a time.

11

Tuesday, May 1

0115 hours
U.S. oil tanker *Noramo Pride*
The North Sea

"Captain? They're asking to talk to you."

Captain Dennis M. Scott swiveled in his vinyl-backed chair, his face stage-lit by the eerie green glow of the radar screen on the bridge console a few feet away. Greg Pelso, his radio officer, had emerged from the dim-lit recesses of the aft bridge space. He sounded both excited and worried.

Scott grunted. "Kathy? How far out now?"

"About ten miles, Captain," Kathy Moskowiec, the ship's third mate, announced from the bridge radar console. "Bearing one-nine-five. Closing at one-twenty."

"Anything else close by?"

"Nothing new. That fishing boat's still in our wake, about three miles back. *Rico Gallant* and *Perth Amboy* are to the north and north-northwest, eight miles, and I've got returns from the Viking and Ann production centers to the southwest. The rest is sea clutter."

"Very well." Behind them, just ninety miles astern, lay the eastern entrance to the English Channel, and one of the busiest waterways in the world, but if it wasn't for the ship's radar, it would be easy to look out those enormous, slanted wheelhouse windows and imagine that the tanker was completely alone in all that vast, black ocean.

It was pitch black out, a raw, moonless night with an overcast sky and five-foot seas that managed to make themselves felt even aboard so large and massive a vessel as the *Noramo Pride*. Earlier, it had been raining, with gusts of wind approaching thirty knots. Now, however, it was simply raw, wet, and blustery . . . in short, a typical mid-spring night on the North Sea.

Though not a supertanker, the *Pride* was a true monster, 883 feet long, 138 feet abeam, and massing some 120,000 deadweight tons. From keel to main deck she measured sixty-eight feet, and when fully loaded, her thirteen cargo tanks could carry some 35.5 million gallons of crude oil. Her crew numbered twenty-four. Moments before, they'd received a radioed message for assistance from a military helicopter a few miles to the south, a Royal Dutch Marine Luchtvaardienst flight out of de Kooij. Now it was up to Scott to make the decision about what they would—or could—do about it.

Scott slid out of the captain's chair and followed Pelso back to the *Noramo Pride*'s radio shack, a small area across from the chart room made cramped by the consoles and electronic gear arrayed across three of the bulkheads. Reaching up to his face, he eased his glasses off his nose and rubbed his eyes. He still felt groggy and not entirely awake. Until twenty minutes ago he'd been asleep—his bridge watch had ended at 2200 hours—but they'd called him when the distress message had come through.

Pelso picked up a microphone and held it close to his mouth. "Royal Netherlands Flight Three-one, this is the *Noramo Pride*," he said, holding down the transmit key. "Do you read me, over?"

"Noramo Pride, this is Flight Three-one!" came from the speakers mounted high on the bulkhead. The voice, speaking English with a thick, north European accent, was tight and carried a note of urgency; behind it, Scott could hear the hiss of static and the dull, rapidly throbbing boom that meant the speaker was aboard a helicopter. "We copy. Go ahead."

"Three-one, I have the captain here." Pelso handed the mike to Scott.

"Royal Netherlands Flight Three-one, this is Captain Scott. What is the exact nature of your emergency?"

"Ah, Captain. We're getting some very severe high-frequency vibration here. Probably means some trouble associated with the engine, a defective clutch, perhaps, or a bad bearing. We need to set down someplace, and quickly! I formally request permission to land on your deck. Over."

"Flight Three-one, the *Noramo Pride* is an oil tanker, not an aircraft carrier. Trying to land a helicopter aboard, a *malfunctioning* helicopter—"

"Captain," the voice interrupted. "This is an emergency or I would not have made the request. We have no warning lights showing. The engine is not overheating and there is no indication of fire on board. But I cannot possibly make it back to shore. I need a place to touch down, and your ship is the only choice available. I have fifteen passengers on board this aircraft. Do you have any idea how long they'll survive if I have to set down in the sea? Over!"

"I read you, Three-one. Wait one."

Scott thought hard for several seconds, trying to banish the grogginess and see the situation straight. For obvious reason, oil tanker skippers were hesitant about letting any potential fire hazard approach their mammoth charges . . . and hazard in that context didn't just mean a fire, but *any* possible source of a spark. That most certainly included turning rotors or possibly faulty engines. Still, tankers often received supplies, mail, or changes of personnel at sea via helicopter, and if the pilot was any good there shouldn't be a major problem having them touch down. Besides, there was a moral obligation. All vessels were required to go to the aid of any other party in distress at sea.

That helo pilot was very right about one thing. The water temperature in this part of the North Sea right now was something like forty degrees . . . frigid enough to kill an unprotected man in scant minutes, and in the middle of the night, it would be impossible to find everyone in time. Men were going to *die* if that helicopter ditched at sea.

At the same time, Scott was responsible for the safety of his immense charge and her crew.

Fortunately, the *Noramo Pride* was riding empty at the moment, her only cargo some ten and a half million gallons of ballast sea water, pumped aboard to hold the tanker deep and steady in the rough seas. There was always the danger of explosive gases trapped in her below-deck spaces, of course, but the ship possessed a state-of-the-art inert gas system, which pumped exhaust gases from the ship's engine into the empty tankage spaces below her forward deck, replacing the oxygen there so that explosive or inflammable gases couldn't ignite. It ought to be safe enough. If the pilot seemed to be having difficulties during the approach, Scott could always request that he ditch in the sea nearby while the tanker's crew stood by in lifeboats, ready to haul them out of the water.

In this heavy a sea, the rescue operation alone would put Scott's own people at serious risk. It would be a lot simpler and safer all the way around to let that Dutch helicopter set down on his forward deck.

He held the mike to his mouth, pressing the transmit key.

"Flight Three-one, *Noramo Pride*. What type of aircraft are you? And you'd better give me the dimensions of your rotor. Over."

"*Noramo Pride*, this is Three-one. We are a Westland Naval Lynx, Mark 81. Our rotor diameter is twelve point eight meters."

Twelve point eight meters . . . that was about forty, no, forty-two feet. There would be plenty of room, so long as the pilot had a good, clear approach to the deck.

"Will you be able to jettison most of your fuel before you land?"

"That is affirmative, *Noramo Pride*."

"Very well, Three-one. You are clear to land on my forward deck. We'll have a spot cleared and lit up for you. Over."

"That is very, very good news, *Noramo Pride*. Thank you!"

"I will have boat crews standing by in case you run into trouble." Not that boats would help much at night, in these cold waters, if the helicopter had to ditch.

"Roger, *Noramo Pride*. I'd still rather save the aircraft if I can. It feels like a simple mechanical problem. I may be able to fix it myself . . . but I can't do that until I'm down, and right now you have the only real estate within reach. Over."

"Copy that." Scott had a sudden thought. Fifteen passengers . . . might they be VIPs of some sort? Helos were always shuttling important people back and forth across this stretch of the North Sea, either between Great Britain and the Continent or between the beach and one or another of the oil- or gas-production platforms located in this mineral-rich region. "Three-one, who are your passengers, over?"

"*Noramo Pride,* my passengers are fifteen men of a company of Royal Dutch Marines. We were on maneuvers on one of the Dutch production platforms earlier this evening. We were on our way back to de Kooij when this happened."

"Understood, Three-one. My radio operator will be standing by on this channel. Captain Scott, out."

Handing the microphone back to Pelso, Scott turned and left the radio shack, making his way back to his bridge. He'd been sailing these waters and others around the world for nearly twenty years, and he knew of the Royal Dutch Marines. While the Dutch military was not especially highly regarded among the NATO nations of Europe, their marines, at least, had a justifiable reputation as an elite unit, with decent training similar to that of the British SAS or Germany's GSG9 in many respects. They'd seen plenty of action in various terrorist situations back in the seventies, Scott knew. Nowadays, they were charged with the safety of such diverse Royal Netherlands assets as Schipol International Airport, various seaports, and any Dutch-owned oil platforms in the North Sea.

No doubt the maneuvers the helicopter pilot had mentioned were part of the marines' counterterrorist training. De Kooij was the naval base ashore where the Royal Navy aviation units were stationed. Understandable, that training. Everybody with a piece of the carved-up North Sea was nervous about the terrorist threat, and justifiably so. A swath down the center of the North Sea, from north of the Shetland Islands to the Broad Fourteen just off the Dutch coast, was pocked by hundreds of oil rigs, production platforms, and tanker-loading buoys gathered together in sprawling clusters of various sizes that marked the oil and natural gas fields discovered so far. This area was

among the richest oil- and natural gas–producing regions in
the world; the surrounding nations—especially Great Britain,
Norway, and Germany, but including other nations as well—
had invested hundreds of billions of dollars in these fields,
investments that substantially reduced or even eliminated their
dependence on the politically uncertain influx of oil from the
Middle East. Those drilling and production rigs were attractive,
lucrative targets for terrorists . . . especially Middle East
terrorists who knew very well just how closely tied were the
world's economies to oil.

Hence the considerable interest by elite military units such
as the British SAS and SBS, or the Royal Dutch Marines, in
defending those investments.

Several minutes passed, in which time Scott gave the orders
to several of his crew to make certain that the area on the
forward deck chosen for the landing was clear of anything that
might get caught up in the rotor wash, and that all potential
obstacles such as overhead lines, railings, or the ship's big hose
derricks were secure or well back out of the way. A six-man
boat crew was told off as well and was waiting on *Noramo
Pride*'s second deck fully rigged out in foul-weather gear and
life jackets, with two lifeboats already swayed out on their
davits and ready to put into the sea. Searchlights mounted high
up on the tanker's bridge wings and along the main deck's
railings were switched on and swung about to paint a brilliant
oval of illumination forward, giving the ship the cheery look of
a football stadium lit up at night. The helicopter would be
directed to touch down on the forward half of the hull, between
the foremast rising from the forecastle and the two tall king
posts with their hose-handling derricks mounted amidships just
aft of the ship's loading station. Though the *Pride*'s forward
deck encompassed a full two acres, finding a clear spot to land
was still a challenge, for much of the deck surface was taken up
by a maze of piping, deck machinery, winches, fire hoses and
foam dispensers, and the tangle of fittings for the ship's inert
gas system. Still, a suitable area had been marked out by the
lights, and crew members detailed to secure the helicopter once
it was down.

"Captain," a voice called over the bridge intercom speaker.

"Starboard wing lookout here. We've got an aircraft of some kind approaching from the south."

"That's him, Captain," Moskowiec confirmed from the radarscope. "Bearing now one-eight-nine, range one mile."

"Very well."

Scott walked across the bridge to the starboard windows in time to see the helicopter's lights passing abeam. Off the starboard bow, the lights slowed, pivoted, then brightened as the helo nosed in toward the *Noramo Pride,* quartering in from downwind. The thutter of the rotors could be clearly heard above the wind now. If there was a problem with the engine, Scott couldn't hear it. Whatever the trouble was, then, might not be too bad after all. From the tension in the pilot's voice, he'd half expected to see the chopper limping in, smoke spilling from its manifold, its rotors barely turning fast enough to keep it aloft.

He was happy to be proved mistaken. Despite empty cargo tanks, despite inert gas systems, despite damage control crewmen waiting with foam dispensers in the bows, the *Noramo Pride* could be turned into an inferno in an instant if something went wrong enough to send that helicopter and its load of aviation gasoline crashing into the tanker's deck.

As the helo entered the crisscross of the tanker's search-lights, seemingly balanced atop the white shaft of its own spotlight shining beneath its nose, Scott could make out its blue-black paint scheme, the tripartite red, white, and blue roundel on the fuselage, the words "KON. MARINE" picked out on the tail boom in large, white letters. Dutch Navy, sure enough. The nose came up as the aircraft flared out for touchdown, gentling down precisely between forecastle and king posts despite the wind. The pilot, whoever he was, was *good.* Almost as soon as the helicopter's wheels touched down, the rotor blades began slowing. Several of the *Noramo Pride*'s deck crew raced toward the aircraft, heads bent to avoid the dipping blade tips, carrying chains and chocks to make the helicopter secure. The wind might be down now, but if it came up again tonight, that helicopter could be overturned, smashed in an instant into crumpled and possibly burning wreckage.

Scott raised a pair of 7x50 binoculars to his eyes. The

helicopter's side door had been slid back, and soldiers were spilling out one after another, lining up and moving aft across the deck. They were big men, made bulky by the cold weather gear, combat vests, satchels, and weapons they carried. They were wearing watchcaps instead of helmets, and their faces were blacked with camouflage paint. It looked like they were carrying a mix of exotic-looking weapons, including both submachine guns and military assault rifles, but Scott had heard that elite units like this one often carried different kinds of guns, and lots of them. One of the men, a tall, heavily built man with a shock of very pale, almost silver-blond hair poking out between painted skin and black watchcap, appeared to be the leader. He paused to talk briefly to the crew securing the helicopter, talked a moment more with the aircraft's pilot, then started walking aft with the rest of the men.

"Kathy?"

"Yes, Captain?"

Scott stopped himself. He'd been about to send the third mate down to the galley on an errand, and that sort of thing had been a source of friction more than once already on this voyage. Kathy Moskowiec was a bright, attractive woman five years out of Kings Point Maritime Academy. Sensitive about being the only woman aboard ship—women had been serving with tanker crews only for the past ten years or so, and never in great numbers—she took her professional image very seriously.

"Take the wheel, please," he said, changing his order. "David?"

"Yes, Cap?"

The A/B—the able-bodied seaman—standing at the ship's wheel was David Ramos, a stocky Filipino who'd been in the merchant marine, then in tankers, for almost as long as Moskowiec had been alive.

"Haul yourself down to the galley," he told the man. "Tell the cook to make sure there's plenty of tea and coffee laid on. I imagine that bunch is going to want to get warmed up."

"Right you are, Cap." Kathy took David's place at the wheel, and the A/B hurried off the bridge. For several minutes, there was no sound save the warm hum of the bridge ventilators and electrical systems. The searchlights outside were switched off, and the *Noramo Pride* again plowed ahead through the sea in a blackness relieved only by her red, white, and green running lights.

Then one of the aft bridge doors opened, and five of the visitors entered, led by Mike Beatty, the ship's chief mate. The silver-haired man was with them, looking particularly ominous in his black combat garb, and with a wicked-looking submachine gun strapped across his chest.

Scott frowned. He'd been in the U.S. Navy for four years before he'd gone into tankers, and he knew something about the military. While he'd never worked with SEALs or similar commando units, he'd had the impression that they didn't haul loaded weapons around, especially aboard ship or on a helicopter, in order to reduce the risk of accidents. These men all had magazines plugged into the receivers of their weapons.

Well, maybe the Dutch did things differently. Or maybe those magazines were empty. Perhaps he could speak to the unit's commander about it after the amenities were over. "Welcome aboard, sir," Scott told them. "Do you speak English?"

"Ja," the leader replied, smiling. "A little, anyway. Some of my men, maybe not so good."

"Well, we've laid on coffee and tea for you all down in the mess, and I imagine Cookie can rustle up some midrats, if you're interested."

"Midrats?"

"Midnight rations. Something for your boys to eat."

"Ah! Thank you very much for your hospitality, Captain," the man replied slowly. "It was . . . how you English say? A bit dicey out there."

"Actually, sir, we're Americans." He extended a hand. "The *Noramo Pride* is an American vessel. Captain Scott, at your service. And you are? . . ."

"Delighted to meet you, Captain Scott. I have one rather urgent request, before we do anything else. Might you show me, please, your radio room? I need to report to base that we are okay."

"Of course. This way, if you please."

Scott had led the man—followed by two of his black-garbed soldiers—up to the door of the radio shack before a question occurred to him. "Uh . . . excuse me, sir," Scott said as he opened the radio-room door and held it for the man, "but why do you need to use our radio? You could have used the one aboard the helicopter to call—"

The gunfire was shockingly loud contained within the narrow, steel-walled confines of the ship's passageways, as the black-garbed commando opened up with his submachine gun from the open doorway, spraying the radio shack from bulkhead to bulkhead, from overhead to deck. Greg Pelso was just rising from his seat, his mouth gaping open in astonishment as half-a-dozen bullets slammed into his torso in a bloody, splattering tattoo that sent him crashing backward, arms flailing, into an electronics cabinet.

What the hell?—"

For a nightmare moment, Pelso seemed pinned upright by the bullets slashing into his body, as radio equipment around him exploded in a shower of sparks and the thunder of gunfire and the crash and ping of bullets smashing delicate equipment drowned out his gurgled shriek. When he collapsed onto the deck, the front of his shirt was sodden and stained bright red, his face was an unrecognizable pulp of blood and skin tatters and shockingly naked bone, and a very great deal of blood was pooling on the linoleum beneath his body.

Scott was still lunging for the gunman, a scream of protest in his throat, when the butt of an assault rifle slammed into the back of his head, tumbling him forward onto the deck across a clattering spill of brass casings from the commando leader's submachine gun. In the distance, he could hear other sounds of nightmare chaos—shouts and wailing curses from the bridge and, farther off still, the rattle of automatic gunfire.

A heavy boot nudged him in the side, rolling him onto his back. Stunned, his head throbbing from the blow, he blinked up at the black, pain-blurred form of his captor, silhouetted against the lights in the passageway's overhead.

"Captain Scott," the man said, and his voice, while still accented, no longer carried the bumbling and somehow disarming clumsiness of someone who knew only a little English.

"I am Heinrich Adler of the Army of the People's Revolutionary Front. Your ship is mine, and you and your crew, what is left of them, are my prisoners." He shifted position, so that the ugly black muzzle of his weapon was pointed directly at Scott's face. "Most of your people are expendable, and I will not hesitate for an instant to shoot some of them in order to force the compliance of the rest. Do you understand me?"

Scott blinked, not sure whether a response was called for.

The man's boot swung back, then shot forward, hard, cracking into Scott's ribs and sending a blinding pain shooting through his body. *I said do you understand me?*

"Y-yes!" Scott gasped, trying to capture the breath driven from his lungs. "God . . . what . . . what is it you want?"

"For the moment, Captain, we have what we want, but I assure you that when I require more of you, you will be the first to know." He looked up at the other two soldiers, snapped something that sounded German to Scott, and jerked his head. Rough hands reached down and grabbed Scott's arms and shoulders, and started dragging him across the deck back onto the bridge.

"Captain!"

Kathy was standing at the wheel between two of the invaders, but she pushed past them as Scott was dropped onto the deck.

"Easy, Moskowiec," Scott said, rising. His head hurt like hell, but he didn't think there was any serious damage. "Just do what they say, okay?"

"But who *are* they?"

"I'm not sure," he said, eyeing the commando leader, who was now talking rapidly and unintelligibly to someone on a small radio attached to the shoulder of his load-bearing vest. "But somehow I don't think they're really members of the Royal Dutch Marines."

12

Tuesday, May 1

0940 hours
Fishing trawler *Rosa*
The North Sea

The *Rosa* was typical of the small independent trawlers that made their living off the shoals and fishing banks that ringed the North Sea, from the Frisian Banks off the Netherlands to the Viking Banks between Norway and the Shetland Islands. Originally part of the Norwegian trawler fleet, she'd been appropriated by the Germans early in World War II, ended up in Poland as part of the reshuffling of the German border at the end of the war, and finally been sold to a fishing cooperative back in East Germany. Thirty years later, aging, so rusty in spots that her owners insisted that only the rust was holding her together, the *Rosa* was ready for the breakers' yard.

Before she could be transformed into 210 tons of scrap, however, money quietly changed hands, a certificate was forged, and the *Rosa* was quietly moved from her port at Warnemünde through the Kiel Canal to an out-of-the-way pier on the Hamburg waterfront.

There, she was repainted and her engines refurbished. There was still some question about her seaworthiness, but after all, it was only necessary that she make one final voyage. One week after departing Hamburg, she could sink forever beneath the waves of the North Sea, and it would no longer matter.

She'd already been at sea for three days, having departed the

German port early on Sunday. That was a day earlier than originally planned, but a certain amount of flexibility had been built into the operation, just in case there were last-moment complications. On Tuesday morning the *Rosa* was loitering at an otherwise undefined spot in the North Sea fifty miles east of Flamborough Head when a thirty-foot cabin cruiser out of the English port of Great Yarmouth approached. Signs and countersigns were exchanged, first by carefully worded radio exchanges until they were within visual range, then by flashing lights. After some preliminary maneuvers to bring the cabin cruiser in under the lee of the larger vessel, three men—Major Pak and two RAF gunmen—clambered up a cargo net and onto the ancient trawler.

Pak's first question as soon as he stepped onto the *Rosa*'s main deck and faced the vessel's captain was sharp and to the point. "Where is it?"

"Main hold forward," the captain replied. "Under our nets, for camouflage."

"Take me there."

The forward hold stank of fish, but Pak ignored the stench as a couple of *Rosa*'s crewmen pulled the nets off the massive wooden crate, which rested on wooden supports and was still fitted with the straps and snap-swivels used to hoist it aboard. "Compressor, Air" and the name of a well-known industrial manufacturer were stenciled on the crate's side, along with the usual shipping information and serial numbers.

Actually, there were two large crates in the *Rosa*'s hold, the second much larger than the one Pak was examining now, but that other piece of cargo had been Hyon Hee's special charge, and Pak doubted that it would serve any purpose now. He ignored it, concentrating instead on the "air compressor." Using a pry bar, he popped open the top and looked inside at the dull, lead-gray cylinder a meter and a half long and nearly a meter thick resting inside. Then, with the crewmen and *Rosa*'s captain standing nearby, Pak unlocked a hinged access plate on one end of the cylinder and swung it open, revealing a clotted tangle of wires, cables, and electrical connections inside. The rough handling the device had endured so far didn't seem to have harmed it. A thorough manual check of its power supply, arming circuits, and antitamper mechanisms suggested that everything was in working order.

There was, in fact, little that could go wrong with the thing, for its design was almost idiot-proof. Pak couldn't even see the real guts of the bomb, for those were sealed away in the front half of the device, behind massive lead shielding. Inside that shielding, however, a hollow sphere shaped from roughly two kilograms of plutonium was surrounded by nearly fifty kilos of plastic explosives, in which were embedded scores of electrically fired detonators. Most of the rest of the bomb consisted of the battery, a complex arming device that Pak himself had had a hand in designing, and the outer casing, which was little more than a shell two meters long. Dozens of wires penetrated the inner shielding, passing through rubber-plugged openings. The entire device weighed just under a ton, most of that from the lead shielding.

Those openings in that shielding for the detonator wires were a serious weak point in the bomb's design, Pak knew, and one that had been responsible for unfortunate levels of radioactive contamination already both in North Korea and in Germany. If the *Rosa*'s captain knew just how hot the exterior of the device and the crate carrying it were, he would never have volunteered himself and his crew for this operation; certainly, he never would have come this close to the thing while Pak had it open!

Pak knew the risks since he'd worked with the assembly team back in Yongbyon in the first place. He suspected that he was dead already, though it might take a few more years for that death to manifest itself. He'd been exposed to the low levels of radioactivity trickling through the rubber-sealed holes drilled in the shielding for hundreds of hours. Exposure was insidiously cumulative.

But that, of course, was of no importance, since Pak didn't expect to survive long enough to develop cancer or radiation sickness. Even if the mission succeeded perfectly in every detail, even if he was able to make good his escape afterward, he knew well that an unknown but large number of the world's governments would never permit him to live, not when the degree of his participation in this operation became clear. It was distinctly possible that even Pyongyang would join in the hunt, if only to convince the rest of a very angry world that North Korea's government had not actively participated in Operation Saebyok, that Pak and a number of others had done what they'd done independently.

Pak was more than willing to accept that. He preferred a quick and sudden death at the hands of comrades to the lingering agonies of leukemia. Besides, the prize to be won in this game was so much vaster than any one man's life.

"Is it safe to be this close?" the captain asked, peering a little nervously over Pak's shoulder.

"Of course," Pak lied. He patted the dull surface of the shielding. "This is lead, five centimeters thick. It is perfectly safe."

"That thing's not armed, is it?" one of the crewmen said.

"Of course not. That will be taken care of tomorrow, once we're at the objective."

Following a carefully memorized routine, Pak began an electronic check of the device, examining each of twenty-four electrical circuits and the battery itself using a small voltmeter with silver probes that he touched to various connections, one after the other. The *Rosa*'s crewmen watched him with a morbid fascination, and so intently that Pak could practically hear the sweat dripping from their faces.

The materials used in the construction of the device had come from widely different sources. Most important, of course, had been the plutonium, part of a much larger cache purchased from an ex-Soviet Strategic Rocket Forces colonel who'd needed enough gold to set up himself and his harem in comfort somewhere in Argentina. The story of how the plutonium had been smuggled from Chelyabinsk to Vladivostok to Yongbyon, despite the efforts of the Russian government, the Chinese, and the Russian mafia, was a small epic in itself.

The electronics had come from Japan—specifically from one of Japan's larger industrial corporations, one that had been in trouble more than once selling restricted materials to the Soviets. The plastic explosives, on the other hand, were of American manufacture; there was a company that did a lot of ordnance work for the U.S. government but was more than willing to deal with anyone who offered their CEO enough money. It was incredible, Pak thought, just how eagerly individuals from the various Western nations would participate in their own cultures' destruction. *The West will hang itself*, Lenin had once prophesied, *and we will sell them the rope to do it.*

Just as it was incredible how easy it was to manufacture such power as this. A surge of electric current, and the detonators would set off the plastic explosives. The resulting explosion, expanding in all directions but tamped by the lead shielding, would crush the plutonium sphere, initiating critical mass. The nuclear scientists who'd worked on the device estimated a potential yield of somewhere between fifty and one hundred kilotons.

More than enough for what had to be done.

Pak checked the final set of connections, watching the swing of the needle on his voltmeter. Everything was working, ready for him to throw the switches in the proper order. Another series of checks proved the pressure sensor and timer were operating as well. Carefully then, he closed up the trunk and locked it, then replaced the lid on the transport crate.

"It is ready," he said.

And this time he told the truth.

1630 hours
RAF Lakenheath
East Anglia, England

The Royal Air Force base at Lakenheath is located in East Anglia, the thumb-shaped extrusion of low hills and quaint villages, of farms and cattle-raising country extending into the North Sea between the Thames River and the gulf known locally as the Wash. The first thing a visitor sees as he enters the base's main gate is a replica of the Statue of Liberty, dedicated in 1981 to commemorate the fortieth anniversary of the base and of the 48th Tactical Fighter Wing, known—after its insignia—as the "Statue of Liberty Wing." The replica is impressive, though not so big as the one overlooking Upper New York Bay; it was cast in bronze from one of F. A. Bartholdi's first-step models for the original Statue of Liberty.

When Mineman Second Class Greg Johnson had first seen the statue it had made him homesick, and he hadn't even been out of the United States for twenty-four hours yet. Well . . . perhaps *homesick* was the wrong word. But he did wonder what he was doing here . . . wondered if he'd made a mistake in becoming a Navy SEAL.

The C-130 had rumbled in to Lakenheath's Number One runway half an hour earlier and was standing now in an out-of-the-way corner of the base while an Air Force working party emptied the transport's capacious hold. The SEALs were on hand to take charge of their gear as soon as it had been off-loaded, but for the moment they were standing at ease in formation, watching the airedales unload their gear.

Johnson stood a little apart from the other SEALs of the First Platoon, still uncertain of his standing with them. Twenty-six weeks of grueling BUD/S training had failed to completely erase the awe he'd felt for the Navy SEALs ever since he'd first heard about the unit. But in fact he'd never given more than a passing thought to actually *becoming* one, not until he'd already signed up and reported for duty with BUD/S Class 23.

By then, of course, it was too late to back out without looking like a wimp—*pussy* was the vulgarity used by the other men—and that was something Johnson refused to accept from anyone.

"So what do you think, Skeeter?" Jaybird Sterling asked him, jolting his thoughts.

"Huh? About what?"

Fernandez, standing next to Jaybird, nodded toward the C-130. "About the bus, man. We were just wondering if she was gonna be of any use over here."

"You said you just got out of bus driver's school," Sterling added. "We were just wondering if you'd logged any hours on that thing."

"Not many," Johnson admitted.

"Hell, I still don't know why they shipped the thing over here," Brown said. "Without a mother sub, we can't go very far in that thing." SDVs were generally carried on the deck of specially modified Navy subs. Without a big sub to piggyback a ride with, the SDV would be sharply limited in range and usefulness.

"You know the Navy." Fernandez laughed. "Always prepared."

"That's the Boy Scouts."

"A bunch of amateurs. I bet *they* don't pack Mark VIII SDVs with them when they go on a hike."

"I wish it was one of the new babies," Johnson said. "One of the real hot deep-divers."

Gregory Lawrence Johnson had long been fascinated by the sea and by the various means that man had employed to explore it. He'd first heard about Navy frogmen as a boy of ten or eleven when he'd read an account of the Navy Underwater Demolition Teams of World War II . . . and of how they'd pioneered SCUBA and cold-water dry-suit research in the late forties and into the fifties.

Born and raised in southern California, not far from Malibu, he'd already been an experienced swimmer and an expert with SCUBA gear when he'd joined the Navy at the age of eighteen. More than anything else, Johnson had seen the SEALs as a chance to continue his love affair with diving. It had sounded like a real adventure, for the Navy was doing things with deep-diving submersibles and underwater breathing gear still totally unknown in the civilian world.

Skeeter Johnson possessed a determined singlemindedness of purpose that his buddies often laughed about. He'd enlisted in the Navy wanting to be a diver, and his recruiter had suggested that he choose one of two possible routes . . . through EOD school—that was Explosive Ordnance Disposal—or as a SEAL. In fact, he'd originally put down EOD school as his first choice, and SEALs second. EOD divers, he'd been told, spent a lot of time practicing their trade in and under the water, and they had to learn to use some pretty exotic gear while they were about it. His interest in the SEALs stemmed mostly from the fact that his recruiter had told him that the men who drove the Navy's small submersibles were SEALs first. After Navy boot camp, he'd gone to Mineman School simply because that rating would open a direct route to advanced EOD training.

Unfortunately, the continuing military cutbacks that had begun with the collapse of the Soviet Union and the end of the Cold War had cut sharply into the Explosive Ordnance Disposal program. Not even the problems the Navy had faced from enemy mines in both the Tanker War in the eighties and the brief but spectacular Gulf War with Iraq in 1991 had convinced a shortsighted budget oversight committee that EOD needed more ships, equipment, and personnel. Minesweeping and disposal, after all, had always been the tediously boring part of modern warfare; Harpoons and Tomahawks, Sea Wolf submarines and Stealth aircraft were all a lot more sexy, and even some of those programs were all in serious trouble. There'd been no openings at all for new EOD personnel when Johnson completed his basic mineman training.

SEAL recruits, however, were still much in demand . . . not so much because the Navy felt it needed them for war, but because there was such a high attrition rate among the SEAL candidates. The dropout rate for would-be SEALs averaged something like sixty percent; only five percent of all recruits actually finished with the class they started with, and the SEAL program aggressively sought volunteers for BUD/S training . . . fresh meat for the grinder. Though the demand rose and fell according to the vagaries of politics and the world situation, it had happened that SEAL recruits were needed when Johnson was in Mineman School, and his application had been granted.

Johnson had been disappointed but game. He knew enough about the SEALs to know they didn't like quitters, and there was always the possibility of learning those new SCUBA techniques, maybe even of becoming an SDV driver.

But he wasn't a SEAL yet, wouldn't be until he'd completed his probationary training and received the coveted Budweiser. To tell the truth, Johnson wasn't sure he wanted that gaudy, heavy gold pin since his request for additional, more advanced training with the SDVs had been turned down and he'd been assigned instead to SEAL Seven.

BUD/S training had been everything that Johnson had ever heard it was, and far, far more. It had been a grueling, muddy, exhausting nightmare that had challenged him physically and mentally like he'd never been challenged before. He'd learned just how far he could push his endurance in the water, in repeated two-mile swims across open ocean, in fifty-foot-deep tanks with hands and feet bound, in buddy exercises with a shared SCUBA tank. Hell Week had been just that, a solid week of hell when he'd been allowed just three hours of sleep total, spread out in fitful catnaps and dozes while lying neck-deep in cold ooze or stretched out on the sand or even while standing in formation.

Somehow, somewhy, he'd stuck it out.

He still wasn't sure why. SEAL trainees were no longer followed about on their evolutions by a brass bell that could be rung three times to announce a DOR—a Drop On Request—from the program, but they could still give up after a couple of counseling sessions and be transferred back to the Fleet. He'd come *that* close to bagging it all and giving up.

It had been during the fourth day of Hell Week. He'd staggered out of the mud pit where he and twenty-eight other men had been wallowing for the past several hours, declared through chattering teeth that he'd had enough, and stumbled off toward the trailer where an officer waited to hear his request.

But he'd gone back to the mud and the cold. Why? He still wasn't entirely certain. During his first counseling session, he'd been asked if he really wanted to quit, told to consider what he'd already invested in becoming a SEAL . . . but his final decision had more to do with the fear that the others would think that he was a quitter than anything else. The shame that attended that failure of nerve and strength and soul had seemed a worse fate than dying in the program, worse even than the humiliation of being assigned to a Navy minesweeper as just another ordnance man, screwing fuses in and out of mines.

He'd stuck . . . *somehow* he'd stuck out of sheer, stubborn pride, and now he was seriously wondering if he'd made a very bad mistake. More interested by far in the technical end of Navy diving, Johnson had never actually thought much about one decidedly non-technical aspect of his new career specialty, the fact that the Navy SEALs were looking for *warriors,* for men who could kill instantly, without hesitation, without remorse.

And that was what he thought separated him from the others.

It wasn't that he couldn't kill. He wouldn't have completed the program had he not satisfied his instructors that he could, if necessary, take an enemy's life. The issue had more to do with his inward focus as a SEAL; he didn't *think* of himself as a warrior, didn't feel that warrior's bond shared by his comrades, had trouble imagining himself ever fitting in. His greatest love was still diving, exploring the ocean depths, losing himself in the weightless joy, so like skydiving, of a free-dive descent into an alien, emerald world.

"C'mon, Skeeter!" Brown's voice snapped. "Wake up!"

The other SEALs were filing toward the C-130 Hercules— "Herky Bird" in military parlance—leaving Johnson behind. He jogged to catch up.

The airedales were just unloading the last piece of SEAL special equipment off the Herky Bird. It was big, a very special package, vaguely torpedo-shaped despite the bulky wrappings and tarps that enfolded it like a blanket swaddling a baby. Twenty-one feet long and four wide, it was gentled out of the C-130's cargo bay on a tractor-towed cart and wheeled off toward the hangar used to stow the SEAL Team's equipment.

The bus had arrived.

13

Wednesday, May 2

0419 hours
Oil Production Facility Bouddica
The North Sea

"*Noramo Pride, Noramo Pride,* this is OPF Bouddica. Please respond, over."

The platform's radio officer listened for a moment to the burst of static, mimicking the hiss of wind and rain outside the monster oil platform. Her brow furrowed in concentration as she tried to pick out a reply from all the noise. Nothing . . . nothing but static, punctuated by the sharper, harsher crackle of lightning somewhere close by.

The storm had come up hours ago, howling in out of the northwest just after midnight, and while the front's first burst of wild violence had swiftly passed, the black night was still being lashed by hissing rain and hail, blasting along on a thirty-five-knot wind.

Sally Kirk was worried. Earlier on her watch, just before the storm had struck, in fact, one of the hundreds of green-yellow blips smeared across the facility's radarscopes had gone off course. It was a big one too . . . one rapidly identified as an American oil tanker, the *Noramo Pride*.

The straying of one of those blips was hardly unusual. The North Sea carried an enormous amount of surface traffic, from oil tankers to freighters and container ships, from oil-field workboats and tugs to fishing boats and pleasure craft, a mob drawing its members from as many different nations as there were seafaring countries. Imposing order on that mass of shipping was, frankly, next to impossible, though neatly aligned shipping lanes that kept traffic well clear of the forest of oil-recovery platforms in the area had been drawn up and well marked by radar buoys.

"*Noramo Pride, Noramo Pride,* this is OPF Bouddica. Respond, please. Over."

Still no response, and the *Noramo Pride* was ten nautical miles off. If they didn't turn soon, there was going to be a collision. A very large, very nasty collision.

The BGA Consortium's Bouddica oil production facility consisted of two separate platforms connected by a partly enclosed bridge suspended fifty feet above the churning black waters of the North Sea. To the north was the command center, Bouddica Alpha, also called "Big B." South was the drilling platform, Bouddica Bravo, or B-2. Each structure was enormous; together, viewed as a single complex, they were titanic, a small city rising on stilts from the depths of the North Sea. At night, illuminated by twin galaxies of white and yellow and green lights gleaming like Christmas tree lights from the dark and thickly tangled branches of both structures, and by the bright orange flare atop the burn-off stack above Alpha's processing center, the center took on the aspect of some fantastic, far-future city from some science-fiction movie, an eerie and not quite believable sight.

The facility was brand-new, five years in the making and only brought into full production last September. The British-German-American Consortium—BGA for short—had invested hundreds of millions of pounds, marks, and dollars in this facility, which rested in just under 250 feet of water squarely atop one of the most recently discovered of the dozens of large oil deposits of the central stretches of the North Sea.

Oil. It had first been discovered in the late 1960s, just after the various countries ringing the coasts of the North Sea had arrived at an agreement neatly carving up the sea and its resources for exploitation. Bouddica had been constructed just west of the dividing line sundering the British claim from the Norwegian.

Bouddica was not entirely British, however, even though most of the personnel serving aboard were British nationals and the platform itself was technically British soil. These were the 1990s, and the oil that had been so astonishingly plentiful and easy to reach in the early seventies, transforming the economies of those countries able to draw upon it, was long gone. Rigs like Bouddica had been constructed in much deeper water—the depth increasing with each advance in the technology that shaped the raising of these structures—and were correspondingly far more expensive. The BGA Consortium had been formed as a means of pooling the resources— technical, personnel, and economic—of three important oil prospecting nations: the British, who owned the claim to the area of the North Sea where Bouddica had been built; the Germans, who'd made astonishing advances in the technology of oil drilling and production; and the Americans, who were bankrolling the lion's share of the project . . . just as they would take the lion's share of the oil once it was pumped to the surface and refined.

Though most of the structure was invisible to Kirk in the darkness and the rain, she knew precisely what it looked like, having approached it by helicopter or by service ship dozens of times, in all weathers, in all lights. The eastern side of Alpha looked like a displaced apartment building, with smooth walls and neatly spaced rows of windows. Built on the leeward side of the structure where it was sheltered from the worst of the wind in a North Sea blow, it housed the living quarters for the 312 men and women who lived and worked on Bouddica for two-week stretches at a time. The structure's large heliport was perched atop the apartment complex like a graduate's mortarboard cap. To the west were the gas and oil processing facilities, a vast, roughly cubical tangle of girders and struts, towers and pipes, conduits and storage tanks, all nestled together beneath the three-hundred-foot thrust of the burn-off tower and its flaring tip of orange flame. The whole enormous, brilliantly illuminated structure was perched atop four pillars that rose like sequoias from the sea, growing thicker toward their tops to support Alpha's 615-million-ton mass.

South, across the bridges, Bravo appeared much smaller, a

box-shaped affair of girders and steel much like her larger sister's production facility, but less than a third as massive and far less imposing. The single largest structure aboard was the drilling tower, most of which was enclosed to protect the machinery from storms and salt spray. Unlike Alpha, the platform was supported by a spidery forest of pylons that held its deck forty to fifty feet above the waves, depending on the winds and tides.

Stretched taut between the two structures was a steel-girdered causeway that sang and danced ominously during any blow of more than about thirty knots. Most of the bridge was taken up by a massive cluster of meter-thick pipes that channeled oil from Bravo to Alpha, and gas recovered from the processing plant back the other way. Bouddica used an expensive and modern gas-injection system that forced natural gas back into the oil deposits below, increasing the oil recovery to better than fifty-five percent of what was in the field. The wire-mesh enclosed walkway running along the top of the pipeline cluster looked like something designed for insects rather than men.

As massive as a small city, which, in fact, was as good a definition for the twin structures as any, they were nevertheless vulnerable. Though they were built to withstand the worst winds and winter storms the notoriously savage North Sea could fling at them, the threat posed by the off-course *Noramo Pride* was greater by many orders of magnitude than any storm.

"*Noramo Pride, Noramo Pride,* this is Bouddica. Respond, please. Over."

She'd already sent for the facility's senior manager, but it might be some minutes before he reached the control center. One distinct disadvantage to working aboard Bouddica so far as its inhabitants were concerned was the structure's sheer size and complexity. At four in the morning, Brayson *ought* to be in his quarters just across from the center and down one level in the apartment complex . . . but the man had something of a reputation among the female employees aboard Bouddica. He might well be in someone else's quarters tonight instead of his own.

"James?" she asked the officer of the desk. "Shouldn't we call Brayson up here over the Tannoy?"

James Dulaney was one of Bouddica's assistant plant managers. The son or the nephew or some such of some BGA poobah, he was young for his position aboard the facility . . . and he was obviously having some trouble with the responsibility that attended it. He looked up from the radar, his face creased with worry and indecision. "You mean . . . *wake* everybody aboard!"

"Damned straight I mean wake everybody. Send someone down to Brayson's cabin to make sure he heard my call buzzer." With a facility this new, there were endless teething problems. Possibly the buzzer simply wasn't working. "And if he's somewhere else, maybe he'll hear the loudspeaker."

Dulaney considered this. "But we don't know if this is really an emergency. I mean, the ship is still—"

"Take my word for it, Dulaney!" Kirk shouted. "It's a fucking emergency! Now send someone to find the boss . . . or go down there yourself!"

Dulaney vanished, leaving Kirk alone on the command center deck. She peered out through the curtains of black rain, straining for a glimpse of running lights, of anything. She decided she would give Dulaney a few minutes to check Brayson's cabin. If he wasn't there, she would put out a call over the facility's loudspeakers herself.

"Bouddica, this is *Noramo Pride,*" a voice rasped in her headset.

Thank God! "*Noramo Pride,* this is Bouddica! You are off course!" Kirk cried. "You are entering a restricted area and may be on a collision course with this platform!"

"Bouddica Facility, *Noramo Pride,*" the voice on her headset said. The accent to the English words didn't sound American . . . or British either, for that matter. The man sounded German. "I wish to speak with your senior manager."

Yeah, so would I.

Cutting the circuit on her microphone, she reached for the microphone that served the facility's loudspeakers. "Mr. Brayson, Mr. Brayson," she said, and her voice boomed from the overhead speakers with a shrill squeal of feedback. "Please report to the control center immediately!"

That would bring everyone not working on the early shift spilling out of their bunks. She opened the ship-to-ship channel once more. "*Noramo Pride,* our radar has you on a collision course with this facility," she said. "You must change your course at once."

"We seem to be having a bit of difficulty, Bouddica. Please let us speak with your manager."

Kirk was certain now that something was seriously wrong. An oil tanker as massive as the *Noramo Pride* was not a speedboat that could be stopped or turned in moments. Even if she reversed her engines immediately, at her current speed of ten knots it would take her something like five miles before she could be brought to a stop, and turning presented much the same difficulty. The tanker was now just eight miles from Bouddica, moving on a straight-ahead course that would bring her nearly nine-hundred-foot bulk blundering into the complex in about forty minutes. If there was something wrong with the tanker's steering—her rudder jammed, for instance—then they only had about ten minutes more to do something about it before the Bouddica complex was doomed.

"Our manager is on his way," Kirk told the unseen speaker somewhere out there in the rain and darkness. "Please, please change your course immediately! Over!"

"We will discuss that with your manager, Bouddica."

"*Noramo Pride,* do you need assistance? Over!" It would be murder getting a helicopter aloft in these winds, she knew, but if the tanker required some special help . . .

"*Noramo Pride, Noramo Pride,* do you require assistance? Over!"

Her only answer were the mingled hissings of static and the wind.

0421 hours
U.S. oil tanker *Noramo Pride*
The North Sea

"We have to start slowing the ship now, damn it," Captain Scott told the blond-haired German with the submachine gun. A whole minute had passed since Adler had stopped talking with the Bouddica complex. "You can't stop these monsters on a dime, you know. And in these seas, any close maneuvering around that platform's going to be dangerous as hell."

"I am perfectly aware of the capabilities of this vessel, Captain," Adler replied. "And I have supreme confidence in your abilities as a seaman."

"Fuck you," Scott muttered, half under his breath.

If Adler had heard the obscenity, he didn't respond. Instead, he took another long look into the bridge console's radarscope, as the half-dozen other armed men on the bridge stood by silently, impassively. He still wore a radio headset, however, as though he was expecting to hear again from Bouddica at any moment.

At last, Adler nodded as if satisfied with what he'd divined from the glow of the radar's sweep. "You may make all preparations for bringing this ship to a halt. We will be docking at one of Bouddica's mooring buoys."

Even in ports, oil tankers rarely tied up alongside a pier to take on fuel or cargo. Instead, they used mooring buoys offshore, huge, cylindrical drums firmly anchored to the bottom. This was especially true in deeper waters, alongside oil rigs or production facilities far out on the continental shelf, where the water was too deep to anchor. Tankers coming alongside an oil rig to take on crude directly would tie up to a fueling buoy, where hoses could be passed aboard and the oil channeled straight into the tanker's holds without risking an unexpected swing by a 12,000-ton ship into the facility's vulnerable supports with a sudden change in the weather.

Scott peered ahead through the rain-swept forward window, where the windshield wipers were making their fitful *scrape-scrape-scrape* in an almost useless attempt to keep up with the rain. Eight miles. Usually you could see one of these big production platforms ten miles off; at night, with all of the lights and the flare stack going strong, you could see them from fifteen miles out. In shitty weather like this, though, just seeing the running lights up on the ship's bow was next to impossible. It reminded him again of just how enormous his charge was.

God in heaven. Did these maniacs plan on *ramming* Bouddica? It was possible. The *Noramo Pride* would make one hell of a battering ram, though Scott couldn't imagine what the terrorists' motives for such an act could possibly be. Glancing back over his shoulder, he took in the grim expressions of the men under Adler's command and the weaponry they carried. Earlier, before it had gotten dark, he'd watched from the bridge as several of the invaders unloaded several crates from the helicopter forward. He had no idea of what the crates contained, though his guess was explosives of some kind. Perhaps the PRF terrorists had other weapons in their arsenal besides the *Noramo Pride* herself.

He wondered what was going on aboard the platform right now. Knowing only that a tanker was bearing down on them, they must be running scared.

Scott knew that *he* for one was damned scared, and he didn't like it one bit.

0421 hours
Oil Production Facility Bouddica
The North Sea

John Brayson hurried onto the command center deck, puffing from the long jog from the cabin—not his own—where the loudspeaker announcement had caught him sound asleep. He was a short, soft-voiced, dumpy-looking man who was often underestimated by those who'd never worked with him. His mild, gray eyes and thick glasses gave him the look of an accountant rather than a production rig manager; certainly he didn't look the part of a man expected to boss a crew of derrick workers and oil hands.

Still, the economics of a productive drilling project were as hard and as balky and as demanding as any drunken work hand, and Brayson could be just as hard when the occasion demanded it. One look at Sally Kirk's ghost-pale face when he entered the control center was enough to tell him there was trouble.

"Okay, Sal. Let's have it."

"*Noramo Pride* is a tanker, one hundred twenty thousand deadweight tons," Kirk told him, her words crisp and precise despite her obvious fear. "American registry, no cargo. We noticed she was off course four hours ago. During the past thirty minutes, it became clear that she was on a direct heading toward us, speed ten knots."

"How far?"

"About eight miles. A little less."

"You've raised them on radio?"

She furrowed her brow, an expression of exasperation and puzzlement. "*Finally.* But . . . he doesn't make sense. He just wants to talk to the facility manager and won't discuss what his problem might be."

"It's okay, Sal," he told the woman. "Let me have it."

He took the headset and microphone from the radio officer and slipped them on. "*Noramo Pride, Noramo Pride,*" he said. "This is John Brayson, the manager of the Bouddica facility. What can I do for you?"

"Attention, Bouddica," the voice said. "This is Heinrich Adler of the People's Revolutionary Front. We have taken control of the American oil tanker *Noramo Pride* and are holding her crew hostage."

Brayson's heart caught in his throat. *Terrorists . . .*

"As you are no doubt already aware," the voice continued, as cold and as implacable as the sea outside, "this vessel is on a collision course with your facility. If you do not accede to our demands, we will do what we can to give Bouddica a small nudge. I ask you, Mr. Brayson, to imagine, if you will, a tanker like the *Noramo Pride* attempting to wedge itself beneath the bridge connecting Bouddica Alpha and Bouddica Bravo. The pipelines carrying natural gas from your refinery to the gas-injection modules would be ruptured. If a spark, or a burst of gunfire, or a rocket from one of the man-portable launchers I have on board the tanker should happen to ignite it—"

"We get the picture," Brayson said, his voice dry. "Just what is it you want, Mr. Adler?"

"Very little, for now," the voice replied. "First, you will accept a boarding party of my men, who will come over by helicopter. You will conduct them to the command center of your facility, where they will tell you what we require of your crew. Your people are to be instructed to follow their orders precisely, to the letter. Any disobedience, however slight, any attempt to escape or to communicate with the outside by any member of your crew will result in the immediate execution of *five* of your people, selected at random. Do you understand that, Mr. Brayson?"

Brayson licked his lips. God, it was a nightmare . . . the worst nightmare he ever could have possibly imagined. "Yes. Yes, I do."

"Second, you will have your safety tug alerted and standing by, ready to secure us to one of your mooring stations."

Whoever Adler was, he knew the layout of Bouddica, and he knew how the facility operated. What the hell kind of game where they playing? "Very well."

"My remaining demands will wait until I am aboard your facility. I warn you, however, Mr. Brayson, not to attempt to communicate with your headquarters in England. We are monitoring the airwaves and will know if you radio for help. If you try it, I will ram Bouddica Alpha, and that will cause a great deal of damage and could result in a number of deaths. I also warn you not to attempt any unfortunate heroics, such as hiding armed men in the hope of overpowering my forces after they come aboard. Any attempt at armed resistance will result in the immediate execution of *ten* of your people, selected at random, in addition to the people who resisted. Your one hope for survival, Mr. Brayson, is to assemble all of your people and assure them that complete cooperation is in their best interest. You are, all of you, salaried employees and have nothing whatsoever to gain by risking the death of yourselves or your coworkers in vain heroics. Do you understand?"

Brayson could hardly speak. He exchanged glances with Sally Kirk, then realized that she'd not heard anything of this conversation save his responses. She looked afraid, though. Almost as afraid as he felt. She must have guessed at least partly what was going on, simply from the tightness of his voice, and his expression.

"I understand."

"*Sehr gut.* Do what you are told, and all of you will come through this safely." He sounded almost considerate. Business-like. It added to the surreal horror of the moment. "We will talk further when I come aboard. Until then, Mr. Brayson, this is the *Noramo Pride,* signing off."

"God," Brayson said softly as he set the microphone down. "Dear God in heaven . . ."

"What is it, sir?" Kirk asked.

"We're . . . being hijacked," Brayson said quietly. He was wondering if anybody had ever been held up by oil tanker before. The *Noramo Pride* was not exactly your typical deadly weapon, but it was deadly. It would have been funny . . . if the situation had not been so dangerous. "Better sound the alarm, Sal, and get everybody up. We've got a lot to do."

He was already wondering just how he was going to explain this to his bosses ashore.

14

Wednesday, May 2

0540 hours
Home of Sir Thomas Ruthersby
London

The shrilling of the phone brought Sir Thomas groggily awake.
It took a few moments to focus eyes and mind; the clock on his
bedside table read twenty of six, fifty minutes before his usual
hour of rising. He groped for the telephone, already angry.
Whoever was calling at this ungodly hour had better . . .

"Yes?"

"Sir Thomas? This is Harlow."

Anger evaporated. Donald Harlow was Sir Thomas's personal secretary, an able and competent man who most certainly
would not awaken Her Majesty's Minister of Defense without
damned good cause.

"Yes, Donald. What is it?"

"Sir Thomas, I'm sorry to wake you. There is . . . a
situation."

Sir Thomas was fully awake now. He sat up, swinging his
legs off the bed. Behind him, his wife stirred sleepily. "Go on."

"A few moments ago, the headquarters of the BGA Consortium in Middlebrough received a telephone call. It was from
the manager of their Bouddica facility in the North Sea.
Apparently, terrorists are in the process of taking the place
over."

"Good God! Who?"

138

"No word on that yet, Sir Thomas. The manager—his name's Brayson, by the way—did say the terrorist he'd spoken to by radio was named 'Adler.' We've contacted MI5, of course, and they're looking into the name now."

"Good. How did this Brayson make contact? Are the terrorists using him to make their demands?"

"Actually, the word I have is that the terrorists have forbidden anyone at Bouddica to contact anyone on the outside. Apparently they assumed all communications are by radio, however, and were unaware of the land lines. Brayson talked to his people in Middlebrough before the terrorists reached the platform and told them what he knew."

Sir Thomas blinked. Had he missed something? "I don't understand. The terrorists communicated with Bouddica before they arrived? Doesn't the facility have its own security force?"

"A small one, Sir Thomas. According to Brayson, this Adler had already hijacked an oil tanker—the *Noramo Pride,* American registry. We're looking into that, of course. The terrorists were threatening to ram Bouddica if they were not allowed to come aboard."

"I see." A tanker would be a formidable, if somewhat clumsy weapon. Who were these madmen? "And no word about who the terrorists are, who they represent?"

"Not so far, sir."

"What is being done?"

"The Prime Minister, the Ministers of Energy and the Interior, and Her Majesty are all being alerted now, of course. A cabinet meeting is being set for nine this morning, and the Prime Minister's office recommends that you have options available regarding a military response."

"Of course." That meant either the SAS or the SBS. Or both. They shared responsibility for the security of Great Britain's North Sea oil assets.

"Other than that, of course, there's little we can do in the way of a response until these people make direct contact with us and make their demands," Harlow said.

"Something outrageous, I shouldn't wonder. Hijacking a billion-pound oil platform seems a desperate act."

"Foolhardy, Sir Thomas, given the reputation of the Special Air and Boat people. Unless . . ."

"Unless what?"

"Well, unless they have something pretty powerful in reserve."

"From the sounds of things, Donald, we're dealing with terrorists, probably politically motivated, who from the nature of their objective must be afflicted by delusions of grandeur. They will scarcely be able to muster the resources of a national government."

"Of course not, sir."

"I'm on my way. You're at the office now?"

"Yes, Sir Thomas."

"I'll see you in thirty minutes. Have the staff briefed, and have Charlene pull the folders on the 23rd Regiment. I want to know who's available for immediate deployment."

"Very good, sir."

Sir Thomas hung up and reached for his robe. His wife sat up in bed. "A little early for telephone calls from the office, isn't it, dear?"

"It's probably nothing, pet. Go back to sleep. I'll get something to eat at the Ministry."

But she was already up, pulling on her robe. "At least let me fix us some tea."

"Damn."

"I beg your pardon?"

"Eh? Oh, sorry. Yes, some tea would be nice." His brain was only just getting into gear. He'd forgotten to ask Harlow whether the Americans had been notified. They would have to be, of course, if they hadn't learned already. And the Germans as well. The Americans and Germans owned part interest in the Bouddica facility, and Harlow had mentioned that the hijacked oil tanker was American as well.

That was all they needed . . . a bunch of clubfooted Americans muddying up the scene. Chances were, this confrontation could be handled diplomatically, and if not, by a quick, silent strike by Britain's finest covert warriors. The

Americans were far too much the Wild West cowboys to suit Sir Thomas's taste.

He hoped they could be kept out of this.

0725 hours
Oil Production Facility Bouddica
The North Sea

The tanker had arrived less than an hour later, sliding gently through the rough, dark water and coming more or less to rest close by Fuel Mooring Station 3. There were a number of fuel mooring stations scattered across the surface of the sea within sight of the Bouddica complex. They were places where an oil tanker, even a super-tanker far larger than the *Noramo Pride,* could tie up and take on a full load of crude, without coming so close as to pose a hazard to the platform. Tankers rarely tied up at them anymore. Two years before, the main seafloor pipeline threading northwest toward the Ekofisk Center had been completed, linking Bouddica with the largest of Great Britain's North Sea oil facilities and with the eighty-mile pipeline running from Ekofisk all the way back to Middlebrough.

Brayson had watched from Bouddica's control center as the rig's safety boat ferried out the massive hawsers used to secure the 120,000-ton behemoth. It was still dark, but he could follow the operation well enough by the lights; searchlights from the *Noramo Pride*'s superstructure bathed the *Celtic Maiden,* the anchor tug used as the facility's safety boat, in a glare reminiscent of a football stadium lit up for a night game.

A second radio call had arrived from the tanker at 5:30. Adler had warned Brayson once again that he was not to communicate with his superiors ashore—well, it was too late for *that* warning to have meaning—and informed him that the men aboard the *Noramo Pride* possessed portable rocket launchers, trained now on Bouddica Alpha's gas-processing plant and separators.

That announcement had crushed any thought Brayson might have been entertaining about resisting the terrorists, now that their tanker was at rest and no longer a threat to the platform. In retrospect, Brayson had to admit that this operation had been carefully planned, each step designed to force only the next level of compliance from the BGA people on Bouddica. He dared not resist in the face of threatened rocket fire, not when an explosion in the separators could loose a fireball that would engulf the entire platform.

The terrorists, obviously, were counting on his reluctance to risk the one disaster most dreaded by all oil-platform workers.

The helicopter landed on Alpha shortly after dawn, touching down on the helipad atop the crews' quarters and disgorging a small army of black-clad men carrying automatic weapons. Adler had radioed further instructions. As directed, Bouddica's full complement, save for the *Celtic Maiden*'s crew, was waiting in the platform's main recreation hall when Adler finally made his appearance. It had been a rude awakening for the off-duty crew members. Many were still in their underwear or were wearing bathrobes. Brayson watched with slowly mounting anger as three of Adler's men made a careful count of everyone present.

"*Drei hundert zwei,*" one of the terrorists reported when the last person was counted.

"Which with the ten on the tug makes three hundred twelve," Adler said, nodding with apparent satisfaction. He was standing with Brayson near the center of the enormous room, with the crowd ringed around them in near-silent, watchful dread. "Good. I am pleased to see that your crew is well behaved, Mr. Brayson. That will make things considerably easier."

He was a tall, powerful, blond-haired man with the evident self-confidence born of training and experience. Unlike the others, he wasn't carrying a submachine gun, but he did have an automatic pistol tucked into the waistband of his trousers. He did not require the gun, however, to convince Brayson that he was a dangerous man.

"That was not my intent," Brayson said through clenched teeth. "Listen. I don't know what your political philosophy is, what you hope to gain here, but—"

"My *philosophy*," Adler said quietly, "is to accept no interference from anyone." He paused and looked about the room. As big as a fair-sized school auditorium, it was luxuriously furnished, with thick carpeting, modern furniture, and an enormous central open fireplace. The room was located near the center of Bouddica's living quarters module, and there were no windows. At the moment, with over three hundred BGA employees crowded inside, with black-garbed men holding submachine guns standing around the crowd's perimeter, it felt claustrophobic.

Adler raised one hand and ran it along the edge of the gleaming copper-colored hood above the central fireplace pit. He smiled. "A fireplace? I'd heard you people were extraordinarily careful about sparks and flames in a place such as this."

Brayson said nothing but wondered what Adler might be driving at. It was true that care was taken aboard the platform to avoid igniting the odorless and invisible natural gas fumes that could spread from an unsuspected leak. Visitors to Bouddica's work areas were asked to remove everything that might cause a spark, even the tiny batteries for the light meters and flashes in their cameras. The main rec room, however, was carefully sealed and was in fact one of the safest areas on the platform, reinforced against blast and equipped with elaborate automated-sprinkler and foam devices. Large amounts of money had been spent in Bouddica's construction to attract and keep skilled workers on this lonely North Sea outpost, on tours of duty that balanced two weeks of isolated and demanding work here with four weeks off ashore.

"Your people will stay here," Adler said after another moment's inspection of the area. "I see sanitary facilities down there at the end, and we can have food brought in from your commissary as needed. My men will organize small working parties from your group to go to the sleeping quarters and bring mattresses here. It should be quite cozy."

"You sound as though you plan to stay for a while."

Adler regarded him coldly. "As long as is necessary, Mr. Brayson. If all goes well, I and my men will leave in a few days, taking a few of you with us to ensure our safe passage to our destination. Those whom we select will be released once our own safety is guaranteed. I assure you that we are not murderers. If you do as you are told, all of you should come through this safely. Understand?"

Jerkily, Brayson nodded.

"Good. Your people will be searched to ensure that none are hiding weapons. Your employees aboard the safety craft will be brought here shortly. After that a count will be made at intervals to make certain that all are present. If anyone is missing, five of your people will be shot for each missing person. Do I make myself clear?"

The captain nodded again.

"You will impress upon your people the necessity of obeying our orders. First among these." Adler glanced about the crowded room. "There are four doors out. A guard will be posted at each. A line will be marked in tape on the floor ten feet from each door. Your people are forbidden to cross those lines. If they do, they will be shot. After the sanitary facilities have been thoroughly searched, your people can come and go there as they please."

Almost irrationally, Brayson felt a small surge of appreciation for this one concession to dignity, and fought it down. He was furiously angry at this, this interruption of routine, this intrusion into his life and career. He wanted to fight back, yet felt pathetically inadequate before this hard and competent man.

There was another factor involved as well that Brayson was keenly aware of. Alicia Roberts, one of the facility's office managers, was sitting on the floor close by, her large eyes riveted on him as she followed his every move. Five hours ago, he'd been in bed with her. More than once during his two years as head of this facility, Brayson had enjoyed the charms of one or another of the women in his employ, something he'd always thought of as a perquisite of the job. Alicia, however, black-haired, pretty, bright, had become much more than mere recreation. He'd been sleeping with her every time she was working on Bouddica for the past several months, and it had reached the point where he was seriously considering getting a divorce from Jane so that he could marry Alicia.

He knew she was watching him. He wanted to protect her from all of this, to shield her from these monsters . . . and he didn't want her to see the fear that was hammering away inside his chest and throat right now.

Adler was looking at his watch. "It is now seven-thirty. At precisely eleven o'clock this morning, I will make a radio broadcast from your control center. I will require you and one of your radio operators to open the correct channel and to initiate the appropriate protocols."

So these terrorists weren't omniscient, Brayson thought. Their knowledge of the facility's layout had half-convinced him that there were traitors within his crew or, possibly, in the BGA headquarters staff ashore. If they didn't know the radio procedures, they might well be unaware of the seafloor land line that serviced the station's telephone system.

He wasn't sure yet what kind of advantage this gave him, but it was an advantage, to be sure. He felt new hope . . . and a flash of bravery.

"Before we make that radio broadcast, however," Adler continued, "there is an important unloading operation that must be completed. Mr. Brayson, who is the best crane operator you have aboard?"

"You can go to hell!" Brayson said. He felt Alicia's gaze on him, and it hurried his words along. "You can hold us all hostage, but you aren't going to make us work for you. You're not *paying* us enough for that!"

"Your *lives* are your payment, *Mister* Brayson! You are the man charged with the safety of the lives of three hundred twelve men and women aboard this facility! If you wish to preserve those lives, you will do what I say!" Adler's hard gaze sweep across the crowded room. Then, with a swift, smooth motion, he slid the automatic pistol out from under his belt, and half a dozen of the platform workers shrieked as Adler brought the weapon up and aimed it directly into the crowd.

He's going to kill someone, Brayson thought with an inward cry of despair and horror. *He's going to kill someone just to show his power over us!* And for a horrible, irrational moment, Brayson thought the man was going to shoot Alicia.

Then Adler shifted his aim suddenly to the left and held it, arm extended straight out from his body, the pistol's barrel aimed directly at James Dulaney's head.

"I told you, Mr. Brayson," he said with a voice as cold as the North Sea's bottom currents. "*Any* act of disobedience will result in the immediate execution of five of your people. I will start with that one."

"No!" Brayson shouted. He started forward, but one of Adler's men grabbed his arms and held him back. "No," he said again, more softly, all trace of rebellion or defiance gone in that one brief flash of horror. "I'll . . . I'll tell you anything you want to know. *Please!*"

Adler continued to stand with his arm and the pistol extended. Though the others sitting near Dulaney had pulled back, the young plant manager had remained where he was. His eyes were closed, his face ghost-white, and he seemed to be muttering something under his breath. Adler remained motionless . . . then finally seemed to make up his mind. He relaxed, raising the muzzle of the weapon and snicking the safety up with his thumb.

"Your best crane operator?"

"That's me," another voice said from the crowd. Jeff Nolby stood slowly, an immense giant of a man, with powerful hands and arms, and with a bushy red moustache that somehow complemented his completely bald head.

Adler looked to Brayson for confirmation, and he nodded. "That's him."

"Name?"

"Nolby," the giant growled.

"Well, Mr. Nolby. Within a few more hours, another vessel is going to arrive, a German fishing trawler named *Rosa*. She is carrying some very special cargo aboard. I will expect you to use all of your no-doubt-considerable skill to hoist that cargo out of the *Rosa*'s hold."

"What is it?" Brayson said softly, his voice close to shaking. "A bomb?"

"Insurance, Mr. Brayson. Insurance to guarantee the success of my mission."

15

Wednesday, May 2

"The announcement was put out over the BBC on their noon news," Phillip Buchalter said. He looked down at his Rolex, tugging back the cuff of his Saville Row jacket to reveal its face. "That was just over two hours ago. There have been no further communications from this Adler person since."

"He can't be serious," Frank Clayton said, shaking his head. "God, he can't be fucking serious!"

Gloom and worry permeated the room, as heavy as the ornate, nineteenth-century decor so carefully restored over the past decade. Nine men sat at one end of a long, polished oak table large enough for sixty. Together, they were facing a nightmare long expected.

Each had hoped it would be a nightmare deferred. With the BBC broadcast of two hours before, that hope had just been dashed. After years of being the stuff of fiction, spy thrillers and the like, nuclear blackmail by terrorists had just become reality.

Buchalter was the current President's advisor on national security, and as such was responsible for the day-to-day operation of the National Security Council. Most of the men present were members of the NSC Principals Committee, one

147

of the three subgroups of the Council formed during President Bush's reorganization of the group in 1989. Among them were Frank Clayton, the new White House Chief of Staff; Secretary of State James A. Schellenberg; General Amos C. Caldwell, the Chairman of the Joint Chiefs of Staff; Secretary of Defense Ronald Hemminger; and, rumpled as always in his tweed jacket, Victor Marlowe, Director of the Central Intelligence Agency.

Normally, each of these singularly powerful men was attended by a small army of aides and staff members, but this afternoon the foot soldiers were restricted to a half-dozen or so men and women who waited, standing, at the far end of the room until they might be needed. This meeting of the Principals Committee was both secret and urgent. A special brief was being prepared for the President, a man not known either for his expert grasp of foreign affairs or for his patience, and there was no time to be lost on preliminary meetings or group discussions.

Three of the men at the table were not members of the NSC but had been brought in to assist with the brief's preparation. The white-haired, professorial-looking man at Marlowe's side was a second spook, Brian Hadley, the head of the CIA's Office of Global Issues. Next to him, dapper and trim as always, was Sir George Mallory, the British ambassador to the United States.

The ninth man at the table wore one of the two military uniforms in the room, but his was the blue and gold of a Navy rear admiral, as opposed to the khaki of General Caldwell's Army uniform. Admiral Bainbridge was the commanding officer of Navy Special Warfare Group Two, a simple enough name that was generally reduced in true Navy acronymic fashion to the jawbreaking mouthful NAVSPECWARGRU-2. The unit included the East-Coast based SEAL teams: Two, Four, Seven, and Eight, plus Helicopter Attack Squadron Light Four. He'd been in Washington attending a series of meetings at the Pentagon when an NSC driver had appeared, with orders for him to report to the Situation Room Support Facility at once.

Bainbridge was no stranger to this room. He'd been here

many times before during his career, as advisor during other crises, though it certainly didn't look like the popular view of such a place—all computers and consoles and wall-sized monitors and screens. The room, once known as the Crisis Management Center, had been carefully restored so that there was no hint that the nineteenth-century decor hid twenty-first-century electronics and telecommunications equipment. For eighty years, in fact, Room 208 of the Executive Office Building had been the office of the Secretary of State, starting with Hamilton Fish during the Administration of President Ulysses S. Grant, and ending with George Marshall in 1948. Cordell Hull had ejected Ambassador Kichisaburo Nomura and Special Envoy Saburo Kurusu from this very room early on a certain Sunday afternoon in December 1941. Forty years later, the Reagan White House, seeking to expand the hopelessly cramped and inadequate facilities of the Carter Crisis Management Center in the White House basement, had taken over this room for the purpose. Sometimes the President himself met here, though more often, as today, it was used by members of the National Security Council to make their decisions and prepare their recommendations, which one or several of them would submit to the Oval Office later.

Bainbridge couldn't help thinking that this was one time when the President really ought to be in the meeting. Action was needed, and cold, hard decisions . . . not meetings.

"Let's hear the damned thing again," Clayton, the President's Chief of Staff, said. He was a small, pinched lawyer of a man who looked as though he was always expecting the worst.

This time, Bainbridge thought, Clayton's notorious pessimism could well be justified.

A crackle of static sounded from a hidden set of speakers in the room. "Nations of the world," a voice said a moment later. Bainbridge thought it sounded German . . . or possibly Dutch. Northern European, certainly. "This is Heinrich Adler, and I am speaking to you from the operations center of the BGA petroleum consortium's Bouddica oil production platform in the North Sea. My name is not important, but my message most assuredly is. I and the people with me represent the People's

Revolutionary Front, an organization dedicated to redressing the wrongs and imbalances of a world political system designed to take advantage of the poor, the oppressed, the technologically backward peoples of this earth. You, the rich and powerful, have long been able to ignore the plight of the billions of human beings who have needed your help; you have raped this planet, upset the balance of nature, impoverished whole nations by your callousness and greed.

"For too long, the majority of the world's population has had no say whatsoever in affairs that concern them . . . the distribution of food and consumer products, the benefits of the technology so esteemed by you richer nations, or the use of the mineral wealth torn from their own soils.

"For too long, the majority of the people of this world have had no voice because they have been powerless in the face of the capitalist nations, disenfranchised simply by accident of birth. We, the People's Revolution, will redress this wrong. We will be their voice. We will be their power.

"In short, the People's Revolution is declaring itself to be another state among states, a nation as legitimate and as real as any other nation on the face of the earth. The single difference is that we are a state without boundaries. We exist everywhere, for the benefit of the disenfranchised everywhere, for the redressing of social wrongs everywhere.

"It would be easy enough, of course, to dismiss my words as the ramblings of a madman. I assure you all that I and the people behind me are saner than any of those who now occupy the halls of power in the world's capitals. However, since we have been forced to play the game according to their rules rather than according to the rules of moral right and of justice, I am taking this opportunity to announce that the People's Revolutionary Republic is, as of this moment, a *nuclear* power and worthy of the respect due any of the world's nation-states that hold similar power."

There was a pause in the broadcast, as though the unseen Adler were waiting for the real meaning of his words to sink in. The vault-ceilinged emptiness of Room 208 was silent, save for the hiss of recorded static.

"A nuclear device has been transferred to the Bouddica oil

production facility," Adler's voice continued after a moment. "It will be detonated if our demands are not met. These are our demands.

"First. The United Nations, meeting in special session, shall vote to recognize the People's Revolutionary Republic as a legitimate state and to admit that state to the UN, with all rights and powers accorded any other member state of that organization.

"Second. Since the People's Revolutionary Republic is not limited to any one geographical area, it requires a place where it can do business as a state among equals, a place to receive ambassadors, conduct trade negotiations, and the like. An office suite within the United Nations Building in New York City will be made available for this purpose. Our representatives will consult with the appropriate agencies at a later date in order to guarantee such matters as security, privacy, and our specific requirements for space and personnel.

"Third. The governments of the United States of America, Great Britain, Germany, France, Italy, and Russia will all immediately and formally recognize the People's Revolutionary Republic, and agree to an exchange of ambassadors and other representatives, which will take place at our United Nations office as soon as such a meeting can be arranged.

"Fourth. Arrangements will be arranged for the transfer of six thousand million American dollars to an account in the name of the People's Revolutionary Republic to be opened in the British Bank of Commerce at its London office. This sum is to be raised as follows: one thousand million American dollars *each* from the United States of America, Great Britain, and Germany, the three governments whose combined investments are represented by the BFA petroleum consortium. In addition, five hundred million American dollars apiece will come from the governments of Norway, France, Belgium, the Netherlands, and Denmark, all of which have a serious stake in this matter. Finally, to make up the total sum, another five hundred million American dollars will come from Lloyd's of London, which, of course, insures the Bouddica complex. This money will become the initial operating capital for the PRR. Even states without boundaries require a national treasury.

"Fifth. Citizenship in our nation will be free to any who ask it and who can demonstrate that their legitimate needs have not been met by their former governments. Any attempt against the lives or liberty of members of the People's Revolution, against our representatives anywhere in the world, or against citizens wishing to join us in any country, will be considered an act of war against the PRR.

"Sixth. We have a list of our people already apprehended by various governments. Among them are two PRR people now being held by the government of Germany, and eight more who were taken prisoner in Middlebrough, England, last Saturday. These people are to be released without delay. Failure to do so will be considered an act of war against the PRR. Furthermore, one of the PRR personnel now being held by the British government is a Korean woman, a Ms. Chun Hyon Hee. Arrangements are to be made to fly her at once to the Bouddica facility.

"If you fail to satisfy us that our conditions are being met in good faith in every particular, we will have no alternative but to detonate our *first* nuclear device. We estimate a yield of approximately one hundred kilotons, or roughly five times the power of the explosion that destroyed Hiroshima in 1945, and the blast will have three immediate consequences.

"First, the three hundred twelve civilians on Bouddica and the twenty-four crewmen of the *Noramo Pride* will die. Next, the blast will do considerable damage, both from shock and from heat effects, to the infrastructure of the North Sea oil fields and the attendant drilling and pumping apparatus. It is impossible to guess how extensive this damage will be, but at the very least, a great many of the seafloor pipelines that now supply Germany, Great Britain, and Norway with crude oil will be ruptured, as will dozens of well heads, sea-bottom pumps, and surface derricks. I'm sure the representatives at Lloyd's will be able to give you a succinct estimate of the damage purely in terms of dollars, pounds, and marks. The Bouddica complex alone is worth several thousand million pounds, and that is only one of many such production platforms that could be destroyed or heavily damaged by blast or rendered unin-habitable by fallout. In particular, the oil platform and other facilities at Ekofisk, as well as the seafloor pipeline to Middlebrough, will all sustain considerable and possibly ir-reparable damage.

"Further, we suspect that the oil leaking from hundreds of ruptured well heads will be rather difficult to stop. The well heads are located on the seafloor at depths ranging from one hundred to five hundred feet and are not easily accessible. Shutting them down will not be so simple a matter as putting out the oil well fires in Kuwait, or as easy a cleanup as the effort to repair the damage caused a few years ago by the *Exxon Valdez*. Those tasks were completed in a number of months. How long will it be before the radioactivity reaches levels at which it will be safe to send divers or submarines into the area? I leave that to the experts to decide. Frankly, we believe that the majority of the North Sea oil deposits, what is left of them anyway, will be forever unusable simply because it will be too expensive to reopen them. In the meantime, hundreds of millions of barrels of oil will be released over a period of time, much of it contaminated by radiation. The smoke from the oil fires left burning on the surface could blacken Europe's skies for months. The soot and the resultant rains will be radioactive. Beaches and seaside towns and cities from Oslo to Calais, from Aberdeen to Hamburg, could be threatened, depending on the wind and weather patterns and on the prevailing sea currents.

"Finally, the blast will hurl a tremendous amount of radio-active water into the sky. Again, depending on the weather patterns, the 'footprint' of radioactive fallout will almost certainly threaten densely populated areas in England, in Scandinavia, or on the Continent, and quite possibly all three. The cost in human life and suffering would be appalling.

"Believe me when I say that we have no wish to unleash this horror. No sane people would. But in the interests of national sovereignty, we will do what we must do to preserve our cause and our sacred mission to the disenfranchised peoples of the world.

"It is now five past eleven, GMT. By the time this message is broadcast, it will be early afternoon of Wednesday, May 2nd. While I realize that it will take time to discuss my, ah, demands, you must understand that I have neither unlimited time nor unlimited patience. We will expect to see Ms. Chun here by 2400 hours on Friday. All other demands, including the transfer of funds to our accounts, must be carried out and confirmed by noon, GMT, Saturday. If all of these conditions have been met, the nuclear device will not be detonated. Armageddon, for the North Sea, will have been averted.

"I will not negotiate and I will not tolerate attempts to wear me down or play psychological games. Your next communication with me will signal your agreement to my terms, or you will suffer the consequences."

The static hissed on for a moment, punctuating the echo of Adler's words.

"Extortion, plain and simple," Schellenberg said, shaking his head. "Never mind the crocodile tears for the disenfranchised. That character's just hitting us for the money."

"Interesting point," Hemminger observed. "How interested is he, really, in the people he claims to represent? Is he serious about this stuff?"

"If he is, he's a complete lunatic," Clayton said, shrugging. "This 'country without borders' idea *sounds* okay, but it would never work in practice. Do its citizens still pay taxes to the government of the country where they live? Do they obey two sets of laws? Is the country where they live going to have to treat them as aliens, complete with green cards and visas and all of that? Do citizens of the United States lose all the entitlements, food stamps, welfare, Social Security, whatever, that they had before they join the PRR?" He shook his head. "None of it makes sense. It seems to me it's not very well thought out."

Caldwell laughed. "Doesn't need to be, Mr. Clayton. It just has to *sound* good . . . one of the great evils of our age. You think people are going to wait for all the loose ends to be tidied up first?" He jerked a thumb over his shoulder at the wall behind him. "Soon as word of this gets around, there's going to be lines a mile long looking for where they can sign up. We could be facing a complete breakdown of the social order."

"I don't see how you can equate a bit of social disorder with the catastrophe that this nuclear explosion would bring on

Europe," Sir George said softly. "Tens of thousands could die. Great Britain's economy will be plunged into chaos . . . and not simply from the loss of North Sea oil, though that loss would be staggering. An ecological disaster of the scale this man is proposing, my God. We could lose half of our fishing industry, or more. Whole cities would have to be evacuated, their citizens moved and resettled into camps of some kind, I suppose. Industry would be brought to a standstill. Presumably, the Arab countries would raise oil prices as well. Gentlemen, this catastrophe could ruin the economy of the entire world!"

"Which, of course, is what Adler is threatening us with," Buchalter said. "Compared to all of what Sir George has just said, six billion dollars is chicken feed."

"Six billion dollars?" Schellenberg asked with a sniff. "That's hardly enough for a national treasury. Is it possible we're dealing with simple thieves here? Con artists?"

"It's a possibility," Caldwell said. "I don't believe for a moment that their demands will stop with six billion dollars. They'll be back to hit us again once we show that all they need to do is rattle a nuke at us to get us to give them whatever they want."

"Yeah," Clayton said. "That could be. But maybe they're bluffing too. Maybe they don't have an atomic bomb after all."

"You really want to take that chance?" Hemminger said. Clayton glared back at him.

"They have a bomb," Marlowe said, speaking for the first time. "At least, we have to assume that they do." Briefly, he outlined for the others the events of the past few days in England, particularly the SAS raid in Middlebrough. Most of the men present had heard about the assault, of course, but the information about the North Korean woman captured in the raid and the traces of radiation picked up on her clothing was new.

And shocking. "Good God," Clayton shouted at the CIA man. "Why weren't we told?"

"We were . . . we *are* still assessing the situation. We're still trying to acquire independent corroboration."

"Corroboration be hanged," Hemminger put in. "We've got

a crazy out there who claims to have an atomic bomb! This requires action!"

"And just what, Mr. Secretary," Marlowe said coldly, "would you have us do?"

"Easy!" Hemminger declared. "This fucking PRR wants to be treated like a real country? Declare war on 'em!"

"And what targets do we attack?" General Caldwell said quietly. "Their, ah, national capital in the UN building? Their treasury in London? Or do we simply attack their population, which happens to be the poor or the homeless or the underdogs or the radical militants in any of a hundred countries?"

"Including our own," Clayton put in. "This Adler guy's message is going to play great with black extremists right here in the U.S.A."

"And Hispanics," Buchalter added. "Native Americans. Hell, radical environmentalists. Even militant feminists, maybe. Anybody in the damned country who claims to have a beef with the government or with society as a whole could sign on to this guy's PRR movement. General Caldwell is right. If this gets going, it means social chaos, a complete breakdown in order."

"Did you hear his comment about this being their first device?" Hemminger said. "What about that, Victor? How many bombs do these guys have?"

"Unknown," Marlowe said.

"Actually," Hadley said, leaning forward on the table, "since we suspect that North Korea is the agency responsible for supplying these people with a nuclear device in the first place, we have to assume that they could have provided the PRR with more than one, but that they probably did not do so."

The Defense Secretary frowned. "Why not?"

"Our best estimates are that North Korea doesn't have more than five to seven nuclear devices in all. That's not much of an arsenal. Simple math. Seven bombs take away one leaves six. Seven take away two leaves five. The leadership in Pyongyang will want to see how it goes before giving away almost thirty percent of their entire nuclear capability."

"They may not be giving them away, you know," Clayton

said. "North Korea is desperate for money. For all we know, they just sold their whole arsenal."

"Maybe," Marlowe conceded. "But a conservative involvement seems more likely, given North Korea's dealings with foreigners in the past. Remember, we're dealing with an insular, isolationist regime, one that doesn't trust any outsiders, no matter what their politics might be."

"I thought this had all been ironed out with North Korea." Schellenberg put in. "After the confrontation with them a couple of years ago over their nuclear program, we promised to give them a new, safer nuclear reactor in exchange for certain guarantees—"

"And why is it, Mr. Secretary," Caldwell said softly, "that you people in State always assume that other nations in the world are going to play the game by *our* rules?"

"In any case," Marlowe added, "we don't have enough information yet. This could be the work of a small clique in their military, rather than a policy decision by Pyongyang."

"None of this gets us anywhere, does it?" Hemminger pointed out. "It all comes down to a question of whether or not we're going to pay the price this guy demands."

"The United States does not accede to blackmail," Caldwell said flatly.

"Come off it, Amos," Buchalter said. "We're not talking about a few hostages here. We're talking about a single bomb that, at the very least, will do unimaginable damage to the economies of half a dozen of our allies, and could, possibly, through radioactive contamination kill tens of thousands of people. You know as well as I do that we'll negotiate if we have to, if the alternative is—"

"Pay the blackmailer and you'll never be rid of him," Marlowe stated softly. "Worse, you'll have a dozen more like him knocking at your door the next day."

"What alternative do we have?" the British ambassador asked. "As with you, Her Majesty's Government has a standing policy of never negotiating with terrorists. This time, however, we may have no choice. The risks, to our economy, to our people, are simply too great."

Buchalter turned to face Bainbridge. "Admiral. Your thoughts on the matter?"

Bainbridge shifted uncomfortably in his chair. He knew why he'd been called here, and he knew what he was expected to say. Still, he was not entirely comfortable with his role.

"As per orders," he said slowly, "we have positioned a SEAL platoon—that's two officers and twelve men—in England, with orders to stand by. It, ah, happened that some of these men were already training with your SAS, Sir George. We merely had to send a second detachment with their equipment."

"I've heard about your SEALs," the ambassador said. "Impressive."

"SEALs," Clayton said thoughtfully. "Could they pull off some sort of mission? Maybe go in and disarm that bomb?"

"We are looking into alternatives," Bainbridge said, a bit stiffly. "My staff in Norfolk is working on several options, including an assault." He spread his hands. "I should caution you not to put too much hope into that possibility, however. Fourteen men, however well trained, are not much of an army in a situation like this. Our intelligence is woefully inadequate. We have no idea where the bomb is being kept, or how many terrorists are there, how they are armed, how they are positioned. Assaulting them blindly would be insane."

"An open invitation to Adler to push the button," Schellenberg agreed.

"Then why did you pre-position the SEAL platoon?" Buchalter asked.

"To give us some leverage," Bainbridge replied. "And in case NAVSPECWAR can provide the necessary intelligence. I had in mind the possibility of using a minisub, one of our SEAL delivery vehicles, to carry out a covert reconnaissance of the situation."

"That makes sense," Buchalter said. "I want you to write me up a plan. Tell me what you need. You'll get it."

"Thank you, sir."

In fact, Bainbridge was more uncomfortable than ever with the idea. Though he commanded the Navy's East Coast Special Warfare Group, he'd never entirely believed in the concept of special warfare . . . and that meant the SEALs. Oh, they had performed splendidly in the past, certainly. SEAL Seven's recent rescue of hostages, including an American congress-woman, from a terrorist stronghold in what had once been Yugoslavia had been a classic.

But the Navy SEALs, he knew, were unpredictable, and damned near uncontrollable. Like many in the senior levels of the U.S. military, Bainbridge did not trust Special Warfare forces. This situation in the North Sea was one place where gun-toting cowboys could *not* be allowed to interfere.

Not even if the only alternative was surrender.

16

Wednesday, May 2

1825 hours
The Golden Cock
Dorset, England

"The boys seem to be hitting it off pretty well," Colonel Wentworth said.

Murdock tossed off the last of his gin and nodded. Another roar of approval sounded in unison from the two groups of men—SEALs and SAS troopers—who'd taken over the pub a few hours before by the simple expedient of being louder and more obnoxious than anyone else in the establishment.

"They make noise together all right, Colonel," Murdock said.

Chucking everybody else in the place out was a strange way to preserve operational security, he thought, but it was just as well that most of the civilians had long since taken their business elsewhere. None of the men were in uniform, but even in civvies, the British and American elite troops stood out alike in their hard-muscled fitness and swaggering banter. They *looked* military, and Murdock was more aware than ever that that could mean trouble.

When he'd first taken command of SEAL Team Seven, Murdock had made a point of making the men adhere to the Navy dress codes . . . and more. No mustaches that could break the seal on a face mask. Short hair. *Discipline,* and the uniformity of appearance that helped build good unit morale.

Over the past few months he'd changed his mind, though. As a vital part of the U.S. military's intelligence gathering network, Navy SEALs had to be able to blend in with the population at large. There'd been a particularly nasty terrorist incident in the early eighties, when three Navy divers on a hijacked passenger plane had been singled out by their terrorist captors despite their civilian clothes, beaten, and finally murdered. The word was they'd been picked out from the other passengers by their athletic builds, clean-cut looks, and white-walls—the close-shorn hair that left them nearly bald on the sides of their heads.

That, Murdock had declared, was not going to happen to *his* boys, and as the men liked to say among themselves, the Old Man had loosened up considerably since taking command of SEAL Seven's Third Platoon. Roselli and Fernandez both sported black mustaches now, and all of the men had hair a bit longer than Navy regs normally allowed.

Besides, as he watched the men, it was clear they didn't lack for unit morale.

Someone stumbled against a table and there was a sharp report of shattering glass.

"Go easy on the crockery, eh?" The bartender growled at Murdock's back.

Murdock sighed. Reaching into his hip pocket, he pulled out his wallet, then unfolded a five-pound note, which he slipped across the counter. "Sorry."

"No problem, mate," the bartender said, making the money disappear. "Long as we settle up when I call time, right?"

"Right."

The bartender, Murdock reflected, didn't seem too upset at the fact that so many of his customers had been driven away tonight. With all the heavy-drinking SEALs and their new SASmen buddies, he was probably doing three times his normal business.

While Murdock retained enough of his officer's training formality to keep him from joining in the fun—even a SEAL officer was expected to maintain a certain amount of decorum in front of his men, after all—he'd come along to unwind with his men . . . and maybe to look after them as well.

Though details of any upcoming mission were still vague, everyone knew, with that undeniable and insistent sixth sense that the shooters in any elite team always possess, that something was going down. By way of preparation and possibly of initiation, the SASmen had invited their SEAL compatriots to a pub in Dorset's strip district as soon as they'd stood down from the last of their training exercises that afternoon, and the party promised to get even more raucous as the evening wore on.

With the pub named The Golden Cock, the SEALs could hardly have refused, even if they hadn't felt the need to uphold their international reputations as hard drinkers. There'd already been a great deal of ribald bantering between the Brits and the Americans over that noun, which, though not exactly common in refined company in England, was still a perfectly legitimate term either for a rooster or for nonsense. Somewhere in the shared linguistic past of the two countries, the term "cock and bull story" had been broken in two, with the English taking the cock while the Americans got the bull. Polite Americans, it was noted, didn't like using the word "cock" under any circumstances, and the SASmen delighted in ribbing the SEALs about getting drunk on "rooster-tails" before dinner, or about going off half-roostered.

MacKenzie and DeWitt had stayed back at the Dorset base, continuing to go over the platoon's gear and filling out the paperwork for the munchkins back in CONUS, but the rest of the men had joined up with First Troop and descended on the objective with the enthusiasm of Sherman's visit to Georgia.

"Good to let the boys have one over the eight," Wentworth said. He signaled the bartender for two more.

Murdock looked at him and blinked. "Beg pardon?"

"Get sloshed."

"Pissed?"

"Don't think they've quite reached *that* point yet, Leftenant."

"Let's have another round, gents!" an SAS trooper called out.

The crowd began clamoring at the bar. Murdock and Wentworth grabbed their drinks and a half-empty bottle and moved off to a table, safely out of the way. The men jostled one another happily and noisily, and it was impossible—unless you knew their faces—to separate the British SAS from the SEALs.

"So what do you think, then?" Wentworth asked him as they took their seats.

"About what. The men?"

"The situation, actually. About being on alert and not knowing when the curtain's going up. Or even *if* it's going up." He toasted the men at the bar with an upraised glass. "*Them* I know about!"

"Not a lot to go on, is there?"

The standby orders had been routed through to the SEALs late that afternoon, but with precious little explanation. According to the background faxed through to SAS headquarters from Norfolk, terrorists had taken over both an oil-production platform and an American tanker and were threatening to touch off a nuke if anyone so much as came close. The British had a bit more information available, thanks largely to the BBC broadcast at noon that day. The group responsible was the PRF . . . the same group that had been involved in the Middlebrough takedown.

That strongly suggested that *this* was the big operation hinted at by the German BKA.

The Third Platoon's orders directed them to be "made ready for possible immediate operations against hostiles in connection with the current situation on the Bouddica oil production facility."

Yeah, right. The bad guys had a fucking nuke in there, and the SEALs were to be "made ready."

The orders passed down to the First Troop of the 23rd SAS were a bit more explicit. A reconnaissance operation was being contemplated for the following afternoon—sometime after noon on Thursday. Wentworth had been in on some of the early planning missions, and was scheduled for another at 0800 hours the next morning. Initial planning had concentrated on the use of a BGA service boat out of Middlebrough to deploy an SAS assault force, possibly backed up by SBS commandos.

"No, not a lot to go on," Murdock finally said. "SOP, really. Not enough intelligence and we're operating in the dark."

"I've been wondering about why you SEALs were put on alert," Wentworth said. "Not really your bailiwick, is it?"

"Well, the way I see it, Colonel, the brass'll probably make it a political decision. You Brits will take on the oil rig, since that's British property, while we hit the tanker."

"If the brass ever gets off its collective arse," Wentworth said, "and decides to do anything. If you ask me, I think they're afraid to move."

"Well I suppose a one-hundred-kiloton nuke could have that effect on someone," Murdock said. "But damn it, we have to do *something*."

"Of course." Wentworth downed a slug from his glass. "We will await further orders. Or do you Yanks do things differently?"

Murdock turned his gaze on the men gathered at the bar. "I wonder."

Wentworth's eyebrows arched up. "You're worrying me, Yank. I can hear the gears clicking away from here."

"Yeah. I was just wondering about a quiet little exercise."

"Exercise?" Wentworth took a deep breath, then poured himself another couple of fingers from the bottle. "I suppose you mean a reconnaissance exercise."

"Full gear. Full simulation. Open ocean."

"Possibly with a 'simulated' target?"

"I had in mind one of those North Sea oil rigs. A big one."

"I was afraid of that." Wentworth took a deep breath. "You know, Yank. I should say no right now. What you're suggesting, going in without orders? They could bloody hang you from the yardarm."

"Actually, I think I have the orders end of things pretty well covered. UNODIR."

"What's that?"

" 'Unless otherwise directed.' The Special Warfare warrior's friend. They just want me to stay where they can reach me . . . and that means keeping them informed at all times of where I am." He patted the beeper in his jacket pocket. "Like this. So, I write out a set of orders. 'Unless otherwise directed,

SEAL Seven Third Platoon shall under the command of Lieutenant Murdock, et cetera, et cetera, conduct an independent reconnaissance in preparation for possible operations against hostiles in connection with the current situation on the Bouddica oil-production facility.' I transmit that to Norfolk a few hours before we get wet. By the time someone back in Norfolk reads it and starts getting nervous, we've gone in, done it, and gotten out again."

"You're mad. There's a procedure to these things. They'd never accept that."

"I don't know about you Brits," Murdock said, considering his glass. "In my neck of the woods, the main consideration is always, *always* CYA."

"CYA?"

"Cover your ass. Or arse, as you Brits might say. As long as the people reading the document as it makes its way up the ladder can truthfully say, 'This looked as though it was done according to proper procedure, and I handled it according to proper procedure,' they never have to actually *think* about the damned thing. Somewhere up the line, someone will have enough weight to really read the thing and say, 'Huh?' By then, though, they'll have to go along with it. What are they going to do, call up the bad guys and say, 'Uh, excuse me but have you seen our SEAL Team?' "

Wentworth laughed." 'Won't you please send them home?' "

" 'They've been very bad boys. I'm sorry if they bothered you.' "

"Assuming your own people don't shoot you," Wentworth said after a moment, "we do still have a problem. Have you thought through the implications of what might happen if we fail?"

Murdock looked up sharply. " 'We'? I don't remember inviting you."

"Be reasonable, Leftenant. You're going to need help to deploy, right? A boat. Or a helicopter. And you'll need backup. Extraction cover and transport. Maybe special weapons and ammo. Reinforcements. Radio net coverage. Am I right?"

"Well . . ."

"Besides, we need that intel too, and if the Defense Ministry makes up its mind to launch an assault, it would be nice to have our team already in place. So First Troop is in too. Now, answer my question. What if we fail? Can we *risk* failure?"

"You're asking whether we can afford the possibility of the bad guys setting off their bomb." Wentworth nodded, and Murdock pressed ahead. He began ticking off points on his fingers. "Okay. First, we don't *know* they have a bomb. That has got to be the number-one question Washington and London are both asking right now, and we can answer it for them."

"Maybe. If we get close enough."

"Two. Assume they do have a bomb."

"We *have* to, damn it. If nothing else, there's the radioactivity on that Korean woman's clothing."

"Agreed. And they're not going to touch the thing off at the first sight of combat swimmers."

"You seem awfully sure of yourself about that."

"Stands to reason. Push the button and . . ." Murdock shaped a mushroom cloud with his hands. "Boom. And that leads to some very serious consequences."

Wentworth laughed, a dry, forced bark. "No! Now pull my other one."

"No, I mean it. Serious consequences for *them,* for their cause. Remember how Saddam's eco-terrorism backfired on him?"

"Yes." Wentworth hesitated, then his eyes widened. "*Yes!* You think this PRR is going to be concerned about world opinion."

"Hell, they have to. Saddam threatened to blow up all the oil wells in Kuwait if the forces leaning on him didn't back off. He also threatened to set loose an enormous oil slick in the Persian Gulf. When Desert Storm kept storming, he did both. All he managed to do was convince the rest of the world that he was as crazy, as *vicious* crazy, as we'd been saying all along."

"That was war, of course."

"And terrorism isn't? In fact, my impression always was that the terrorism of the seventies and eighties was designed to convince nice, soft, comfortable people in the West that they were now in a war zone, potential targets. Americans . . . hey. Wars between Arabs and Israelis, that didn't bother them, right? Didn't strike home. But when an airliner blows up and some of the passengers are from your home state, when suddenly it takes a couple of hours longer to check aboard your flight because of the security precautions, when laws are being passed that take away some of the freedoms you'd taken for granted up until then . . . when suddenly you're fucking *inconvenienced,* you've become part of the war. And that's exactly what those groups were after.

"Well, after a while, most of the terror groups learned that they were sending the wrong message. Westerners started thinking of *all* Arabs as barbarians or worse, as crazed fanatics. Elite units that fought terrorists—the SAS, the SEALs, Delta Force—well, they were the heroes. It hurt the tangos' cause, drove a damned stake through it. After a while, terror groups like the PLO that needed legitimacy started talking about diplomacy and peace instead of car bombs. The only ones left tossing bombs around are the ones who really do think they're at war with the West, or who do it for revenge."

"Or for the thrill of seeing the write-up in the *London Times.*"

"Maybe. Better example . . . when the Provos started getting bloody in the seventies, the IRA's funding in the States started drying up. A lot of their money originally came from Irish-Americans, especially in Boston and New York, but Americans wouldn't bankroll terrorists."

"Most Americans, anyway. But I take your point. Setting off a nuclear device in the North Sea, ruining the economics of the five or six countries that depend on North Sea oil and fishing productivity, causing massive unemployment, spreading radioactive fallout across a quarter of the continent and blackening the beaches with radioactive sludge . . . bad show, really. And a *very* bad press."

"I think it was Mao who said a guerrilla has to swim with all the other fish in the sea. He can't alienate the people he's trying to liberate. And that nuke, believe me, would alienate a lot of people."

"You don't think the general population will respond to this idea of a nation without boundaries? If it means membership in the nuclear club?"

"Look at the hits in world opinion that the U.S. has taken for being the only nation in history to use atomic bombs in war. These people know that if they touch off a nuke, they're going to be remembered the same way."

"Some of those people out there," Wentworth said. He stopped, then shook his head. "They might like the publicity."

"Not *these* people. They're looking for political power. And they won't rock the boat, won't want to rock the boat, I mean, with the North Koreans bankrolling them and providing them with noisy toys. My guess is that they'll be damned careful about setting off their device, if only because they need Pyongyang to supply them with more bombs, and the North Koreans don't need to find themselves at the receiving end of an antinuke crusade any more than the tangos do."

"So, what's your point? That the terrorists won't set off the bomb? Assuming they have one, of course."

"No. That they're not going to be so itchy-twitchy to set it off that they'll push the button the moment they catch sight of one of us. My guess is they won't push the button until they have absolutely no other choice. As long as the bomb hasn't gone off yet, they still have a hold on us, a way to manipulate us. If they set it off, they've got to know that the whole world is going to brand them as monsters, as outcasts, and at least a dozen governments aren't going to rest until every last one of them is hunted down. Where's their political power then?"

"You know," Wentworth said with a faraway look in his eyes. "That actually makes a crazy kind of sense."

"There's one more reason nothing will happen," Murdock said.

"And what is that, then?"

"The crazy sons of bitches aren't going to see us, that's why. In and out, sneak and peek. SEALs are *good*."

"Not to mention modest."

"And truthful. At least while operating UNODIR."

"Okay. Let's say I buy into all this. What's your idea?"

Murdock had been thinking about such an operation for some time now, ever since the communication had arrived from Washington. He began sketching the outline for Wentworth, and the SAS colonel, listening carefully, began to smile.

"I have access to the blueprints for Bouddica," the SAS colonel said after several minutes of listening. "I can download them through my fax back at headquarters. We'll have to talk with someone higher up about the notion of a prisoner release . . . or an exchange, and that will give us the excuse we need to get a boat in close. The powers that be might go for that in any case, just to be able to talk with the opposition."

"That's what I thought. Sounds like the people on Bouddica are especially eager to get that Korean woman, Chun, back."

"Yes. Yes, they are. Getting MI5 and the people at HQ to go along with the idea, though . . ."

"We can try. What have we got to lose?"

"Our commissions, for one thing. But I think you've got a decent plan there. I'll get on it with my staff people right away."

"Thank you, sir."

"Just one thing, Leftenant."

"Colonel?"

"Why do you insist that *you* be along as one of the scouts? Wouldn't things be better served if you coordinated from the rear?"

"That's not the way SEALs do it, Colonel."

He didn't look convinced. "Maybe. But I was wondering if you had . . . personal considerations in this."

Murdock didn't answer immediately. Of *course* he had personal considerations . . . and Wentworth damn well knew it. He'd been worrying about Inge Schmidt ever since Monday, when he'd heard the People's Revolution had kidnapped her.

Where was she? There were, essentially, two possibilities as he saw things. They might be holding her in a safe house ashore, probably somewhere in Germany. If that was the case, there was almost nothing he could do about it . . . nothing, that is, except carry out the raid against the tangos on the Bouddica platform. It was just possible that a prisoner taken there, or a document, or some other piece of intelligence picked up in either the preliminary reconnaissance or in a full-blown takedown later would yield some clue as to where they were holding her. The moment such a clue surfaced, Murdock would see to it personally that Lieutenant Hopke of GSG9 had it too . . . and then God help the terrorists who were holding Inge captive!

The second possibility was more intriguing. The bad guys must have kidnapped Inge to find out more about the Americans who'd been seen with her. If they knew Murdock and MacKenzie were SEALs, they'd be questioning Inge about how much the American SEALs knew, about why they were in Europe, about how they might react to the Bouddica takeover. Depending on how the tango command structure worked, it was distinctly possible that they would take Inge out to Bouddica and hold her there. It would be more secure than any safe house ashore; the terrorists must be afraid that intelligence picked up by the SAS in Middlebrough would compromise their operation all over the continent. They might see Bouddica as the safest place to hold their hostages.

Either way, Murdock was determined to be on that recon team.

"I'm going, Colonel," he said quietly. "Let's leave it at that, shall we?" He shoved his glass back across the table and stood up. "Perhaps it's time I got my boys out of the pub, off the streets, and away to someplace where they'll do no harm."

"That lot?" Wentworth asked. He laughed. "No chance there. Your lads, like mine, were *born* to do harm, and heaven help the poor soul who gets in their way."

17

Thursday, May 3

1710 hours
Anchor-handling tug *Horizon*
The North Sea
Five miles southwest of the Bouddica facility

Captain Ronald Quentin Croft stood on the afterdeck of the wallowing tug, wondering how anybody could do this for a living. The North Sea, predictable only in its rough and unruly character, seemed determined to swamp the vessel from astern, and each passing wave pitched the work-boat aft-high and forward, then surged beneath the keel with a queasy, rolling motion. Croft knew the SAS prided itself in fighting anywhere, in any conditions, but this particular venue he would gladly have left to the SAS's sister unit, the SBS.

While the Special Boat Squadron was on alert as well, however, it had happened that the 23rd Regiment was already set to go with full kit . . . and the Old Man, Colonel Wentworth, had seemed particularly eager to push this one through. Croft wondered if it had anything to do with that tin full of Yanks aft. . . .

The *Horizon* was properly classified as an anchor-handling tug and had originally been designed to haul oil-drilling platforms from one North Sea site to another. She was 250 feet long, with a high prow, with all of her superstructure crowded as far forward as it would go, and with a long, low afterdeck that gave her a decidedly unbalanced look. For the past twelve years she'd served as one of the supply boats that kept the North Sea oil platforms linked with the shore. On her voyages out from her home port in Middlebrough, she carried food, drilling mud, bits, shafts, piping, and all of the other myriad supplies and spare parts necessary to keep a small community of oil-field workers going. On her voyages back, she carried garbage.

This time, however, *Horizon* was carrying a piece of equipment unlike any she'd ever hauled before.

Forward, just aft of *Horizon*'s white-painted superstructure, a massive winch as thick as a man was tall rested on its supports, a six-inch steel cable paying out astern and vanishing into the churning white foam of the tug's wake. A second cable, no thicker than Croft's little finger, paralleled the first. It was attached to a com unit near the winch, where half-a-dozen SAS men were huddled together, keeping down and out of sight. The twin towers of Bouddica had slowly risen above the horizon over an hour ago, and it had to be assumed that men with binoculars were there, observing all that they could of the approaching supply boat. In Croft's case, it didn't matter; he was wearing civilian clothes—jeans, a heavy leather jacket over a wool sweater, and a balaclava—but most of the SAS men aboard were in their combat blacks.

Ready to go.

Briskly, Croft walked toward the crouching men. Sergeant Major Dunn acknowledged him with a nod but did not stand. He was listening to a headset pressed against his ear.

"How are they?" Croft asked.

"All's right so far," Dunn replied. The *Horizon* gave a heavy lurch as she slid into another trough, and Dunn grinned. "I'd say they're getting an easier ride than we are."

Croft nodded, then walked around to the side of the superstructure, peering forward. He could have gone up to the bridge for a precise figure, but he estimated—a guess close enough for government work, he decided—that the Bouddica complex was about five miles off.

"Pass the word to Tagalong," he told Dunn. "Release in another minute."

"Yes, sir." Dunn held the headset's mike close to his mouth. "Tagalong, Tagalong, this is Big Brother. Do you copy?"

It was time.

1715 hours
"The Bus"
The North Sea
Five miles southwest of the Bouddica facility

It was cold. Even in the British-designed dry suit, the bitter chill of the North Sea seeped through the stubborn material and permeated Skeeter Johnson's bones.

Crammed into the cockpit of the bus, he scarcely had room to breathe, much less stretch or move to unkink muscles too long cramped into a space smaller than any coffin. Worse, visibility was zip. Even though it was broad daylight above the surface, the light filtering down through the silt-filled water at a depth of forty feet was just enough to turn the world around him to a soft, gray murk. Before joining the Navy, Johnson had dived in plenty of different conditions, including at night, but he'd never gone diving in really deep water. Always before there'd been a bottom to give some sense of scale, perspective, and movement, even if only glimpsed in the moving beam of a hand-held diver's light.

SDV evolutions, however, rarely had the luxury of light save for the faint green luminescence coming off the console instrumentation, and there was nothing beneath him now but the blackness of a night unchanging across a span of time measured in tens of millions of years. The bottom along this part of the central North Sea averaged forty fathoms—240 feet. The sensation was less like being aboard a small submarine than like what Johnson imagined it would be flying through the depths of space.

Certainly, this wasn't what he'd dreamed about before joining the Navy, exploring the ocean depths and the wonders of the sea. There was almost nothing whatsoever to see here; his vision through the sub's tiny forward window was sharply limited. His breathing sounded harsh in his ears. The submarine's cockpit, like its passenger compartment aft, was flooded. Johnson was wearing a full-face mask, one equipped with a radio. His backpack rebreather had been switched off, and his mask hooked to the SDV's life support.

"Tagalong, Tagalong" sounded in his earphones. "This is Big Brother. Do you copy?"

Peering ahead and up, he could just make out the vast shadow of the *Horizon*—Big Brother—churning through the water forty yards ahead. The sound of her screws was a pounding, hollow thunder.

"Big Brother, this is Tagalong," Johnson said. His own voice sounded strangely muffled inside his mask. "I copy."

Normally, the SEALs would have avoided communications this close to a target . . . but the link this time was by cable, not radio.

"Okay, Tagalong," the voice said. "We're five miles out now. We can see the complex fine. Any closer, and they might spot the tow. The boss says it's time for your guys to let go."

"Roger that," Johnson said. "Any word on what the reception's going to be like?"

"They've given us permission to come to one hundred meters" was the reply. "Don't imagine they'll sink us right off, not if they want to negotiate for their friends back on shore. But they don't sound friendly."

"Copy that. I'll pass it on."

"Right. Here's the skinny. Your target is at a bearing of three-five-five true, range five miles. Any questions?"

Johnson took a last look at his instrumentation—not that he had that much to look at. The Mark VIII SDV didn't pack that much in the way of fancy electronics. "Ready when you are, folks," Johnson said. "Let 'er rip!"

"Hold on t'your hats, then, mates. Cast off!"

For the past four and a half hours, ever since leaving Middlebrough, Johnson had been riding the SDV's diving and control planes to keep the vessel at a depth of between thirty and forty feet, but nothing else had been required of him in the way of steering. The *Horizon* had four times the SDV's maximum speed and far, far more endurance.

It was for that reason that Murdock had suggested the idea of having an anchor tug tow the SEAL recon team most of the way to the objective.

Johnson hit the shackle release. There was a rattling clank from somewhere above his head, then a sudden lurch and a loss of forward velocity as *Horizon*'s cable slid free. His communications headset went dead too as the simple jack popped free of its receptacle on the SDV's hull. The control yoke assumed a life of of its own as the vessel's nose tried to come up, and Johnson forced it down.

The SEALs were all alone now.

Reaching to the channel select, he switched on the SDV's intercom system. "Yo," he called. "How's the ride back there?"

"I've seen coffins with roomier amenities" came back the reply. A few feet behind Johnson's back, in a separate compartment, four SEALs were crammed into a space only slightly larger than a typical phone booth. "I just hope those other guys can drive."

Johnson chuckled. "Roger that. They said the target was in sight. Range five miles."

"Yeah," Roselli's voice added. "Assuming, of course, they found the right rig. Don't know about *them*, but all those derricks look the same to me!"

Johnson leaned forward, peering upward through murky water. The wake was thinning overhead in a churning wash of gray light. The *Horizon* was pulling away. Gently, gently, he eased the SDV's yoke forward, taking the vessel deeper.

By craning forward and looking up, he could see the surface, a vast, shifting ceiling of liquid silver stretched overhead, with occasional shafts of pale light slanting through the water, illuminating myriad specks of drifting gunk. Below, the light faded rapidly into pitch blackness. The thunder of the *Horizon*'s screws were fading into the distance, and in another few moments, near-silence descended on the tiny undersea craft. The only sounds were Johnson's breathing and the high-pitched whine of the Mark VIII's electric motor. Like a World War II glider cast off from its tow plane, the bus was now on its own.

The bus was a Swimmer Delivery Vehicle, an SDV in military-speak. Standard equipment for the Navy SEAL teams, it was nonetheless an awkward compromise between politics and practicality—a compromise that more often than not was practicality ignored for political considerations.

The submarine navy had lobbied long and hard—and with complete success—to keep the Navy SEALs from appropriating money for submarines of any kind. Yet the SEAL Teams needed a vehicle that could travel underwater and undetected to its target, carrying the commandos and all their gear. They needed a vehicle that could travel hundreds of miles, so that the process of getting the thing launched wasn't under observation by the enemy, and they needed one small enough that it could be transported by air anywhere in the world at virtually a moment's notice. SEALs were trained to insert into an enemy area in many ways—by HAHO and HALO parachute drops, by helicopter, by the ubiquitous SEAL IBS. But SDV insertions theoretically gave the SEALs a covert insertion shared by none of the other services, one that they should have been able to use to supreme advantage.

And would have, had it not been for the infighting over the proper definition of a submarine, and over who got to use them.

As a result of the infighting, the SEALs were not allowed to acquire any *dry* submarines at all, meaning enclosed boats sealed against the sea that would allow their passengers to travel in relative safety and comfort for the hundreds of miles usually necessary in this sort of a deployment.

SEALs had to ride in boats that, while enclosed for streamlining purposes, were filled with seawater, their passengers and drivers breathing off life-support tanks stowed behind the bulkheads. Every minute in the water—especially in cold water—sapped a man's strength and endurance, even when he was wearing a supposedly cold-proof dry suit, which meant that the time spent traveling to the objective had to be counted against his overall dive endurance time.

It was, Johnson reflected, a perfect example of the ancient adage learned by every recruit in boot camp: There were just three ways of doing anything in the Navy—the right way, the wrong way, and the *Navy* way.

As Johnson steered the SDV left, angling out of the

Horizon's wake, the little vessel lurched hard, rolling momentarily to starboard.

"Good afternoon, ladies and gentlemen," Johnson said into his face mask mike, "and thank you for flying with SDV airways. We will be traveling today at an altitude of *minus* forty feet, so please make sure your cigarettes are extinguished, your seat belts are fastened, and your seat backs are in their full upright position. . . ."

"Just watch those barrel rolls over the runway," Murdock's voice came back. "Listen, Skeeter. How's it look up at your end? You think you can find the thing without going active?"

"Hey, just sit back and relax," Johnson quipped, shifting metaphors by mimicking an old bus commercial, "and leave the driving to us."

His heart was hammering, his hands inside the gloves covering them were sweating. He'd never been this keyed up in his life, and he wasn't sure whether the emotion was from excitement or stark terror.

Navigation—navi*guessing*, as Murdock had called it before they'd embarked—was an almost mystical blend of sixth-sense awareness and pure luck. Since it was assumed that terrorists sophisticated enough to own an atomic bomb would also be sophisticated enough to rig some sort of simple hydrophone arrangement so that they could listen for the ping of an approaching sonar, the SEALs would be restricted to passive sonar for their approach.

Active sonar, using bursts of sound, "pinging," like underwater radar to pinpoint objects such as ships or oil-rig platforms, was far better for undersea navigation, but it carried the risk of being detected by the target and alerting the enemy that a submarine was in the area. Passive sonar was strictly listening and therefore safely covert; hydrophones aboard the SDV could pick up the sounds other vessels in the water made. The problem was there was a lot of traffic in the North Sea, and the surrounding water was filled with eerie clanks, thumps, whirrs, and the churning throb of engines and screws.

In particular, the nearby screw sounds made by the *Horizon* just ahead drowned out nearly every other sound in the area, and Johnson had to listen hard over his headset to try to pick out the more distant noises. A small screen on the console in front of Johnson's face gave a graphic representation of those sounds, what submariners referred to as the "waterfall" because of its appearance, like falling sheets of colored water. Most of the display was the jagged pulse of the *Horizon*'s powerful twin screws . . . but there was another element beyond the screw noise, a rhythmic clanking, that probably was coming either from the Bouddica complex or from the tanker moored nearby.

The current flowed southwest to northeast, coming up out of the English Channel at about three knots, and Johnson welcomed the added boost it gave him from astern, just like a tail wind for an aircraft.

At five knots, however, even adding in the assist from the following current, it would take the SEAL SDV well over half an hour to traverse five miles—longer when you added in the extra time required for maneuvering.

It gave Johnson a lot of time to think about what could go wrong.

All things considered, he thought, it was miraculous how fast things had come together when the plan depended on the cooperation of the men on the front lines instead of the REMFs who normally made the decisions. The way Johnson had heard it, the British SAS colonel had cleared the whole thing with his superiors, right down to arranging for the tow from the oil-field supply tug. The plan called for him to take the SDV up close to the pilings supporting Bouddica Bravo and park it there. While *Horizon*—with a hidden contingent of SAS commandos—moved in close and opened negotiations with the terrorists, the SEALs would climb the pilings, taking advantage of the distraction offered by the *Horizon* to make their move without being seen. Normally, such an operation would have been carried out under the cover of darkness, but Murdock had made the decision to go in during the daytime for two important reasons.

First and foremost was the time . . . or the lack of it. According to their intelligence briefing, the bad guys had set a deadline of 1200 hours Saturday for the last of their demands to be met. The sooner the SEALs could get aboard and find a convenient perch for an OP, the better. *Horizon*'s presence was important too, if for no other reason than that the tug was needed to tow the SDV close enough to the objective to make this operation possible. Having the tug approach at night, however, would definitely make the opposition twitchy, and more alert to the possibility of approaching combat swimmers.

And finally there was the simple and quite practical matter of *finding* the place. Right now, at a depth of forty feet, there was just barely enough light to see out to a range of perhaps ten or twenty meters. The Bouddica complex was enormous, almost a thousand feet long from one end to the other, counting both platforms and the bridge between them . . . but the sea transformed even the largest oil platform into a speck lost in emptiness. At night, the speck became harder still to find, especially if the SDV couldn't use lights for fear of being spotted from the surface. Since they didn't dare go active with their sonar to spot the thing, while passive sonar was notoriously imprecise, it was possible that they could spend hours aimlessly circling about, passing within a few yards of the objective and unable to see it in the darkness.

Not that it was a piece of cake pulling this stunt off in daylight. The murk ahead played tricks on the eyes, with the wavering shafts of sunlight from the surface creating the illusion of large and solid structures. As Johnson increased the angle of separation between the SDV and the *Horizon,* he began trying to pick up that rhythmic clanking he'd heard earlier. He was also keeping his eye glued to the compass bubble on his console. The *Horizon* had been lined up perfectly with Bouddica before the sub's release. By watching his compass heading, his clock, and his speed, he could hold a mental image of the platform's direction as the SDV changed course. Bouddica was—should be—*that* way.

He hoped. He glanced at his console clock. Though the exact timing was the subject of considerable guesswork—their speed through the water couldn't take into account the speed of the water itself, and that could vary quite a bit with depth or position—it had been almost fifty minutes since their release from the *Horizon* . . . enough time, perhaps, to have missed the objective entirely.

He continued to listen for that intermittent clanking sound

that had been, if not a certain guide, then at least a reassuring
confirmation. It still seemed to be coming from more or less
dead ahead. There were other sounds to contend with as well:
the whirr and chug of some sort of equipment, probably a
generator; the sharp, sudden, and unrepeated bursts of sound
known to sonar operators as *transients* . . . caused by such
unpredictable events as someone jumping off a ladder onto a
steel deck, or dropping a heavy tool; and finally, the welcome
throb of *Horizon*'s engines, backed down now to a gentle purr
and interspersed with occasional blasts that sounded like steam
hissing from a vent. That meant that the tug had come as close
to Bouddica as the tangos allowed; her engines were running,
and the sharp hisses were bursts from her fore- and aft-
maneuvering thrusters. She was station-keeping and, in the
process, providing a rough beacon for the SDV while SAS
Captain Croft negotiated with the tangos.

Horizon's engine sounds were well off to the right now and
starting to pass astern. That suggested that he might not have
passed the oil platform yet, but it must be getting damned
close.

The operation was like a colossal, high-tech game of
blind-man's buff. And the stakes of this game . . .

Johnson didn't want to even think about that.

And just when he'd begun assuming that the SDV must have
missed the objective, that he would have to circle around and
try another pass, the gray-lit backdrop of the water ahead
seemed to take on a faintly more solid feel, a tenuous
something that gradually formed a spiderweb of wavering
shadows against shadows that was nonetheless more substantial than the light-shaft phantoms he'd been watching earlier.
Banking slightly to the left, Johnson slowed the SDV's forward
motion to a crawl and steered for the apparition, which slowly
solidified into a dark framework of struts and pilings, descending out of the silvery light of the surface and plunging into the
black emptiness below. The bus was scant yards from the
nearest of the pilings before any detail at all was visible, a dark
and muddy-looking encrustation of algae, barnacles, and muck
adhering to the surface of a vertical post four feet thick.

"End of the line back there," Johnson said into his face mask mike. "We're coming up on Bravo."

"Good naviguessing, Skeeter," Murdock's voice said in his earphones. "Bang on the money."

The skipper's praise warmed him.

For the first time since he'd been transferred to SEAL Seven, Johnson felt like he belonged.

18

Thursday, May 3

Carefully, moving slowly and with great precision in almost total darkness, Murdock switched on his rebreather rig, checked the gas flow, then unhooked his umbilical from the SDV's life support. MacKenzie had the side door open. Murdock waited as Roselli squeezed through the opening and into the water outside. Sterling followed, and then it was Murdock's turn.

After the claustrophobia of the SDV's interior over the past five hours, the freedom of movement outside was sheer heaven. Swimming was not quite as easy out here as it might have been otherwise, for the SEALs had abandoned their usual swim fins for rubber-soled, dry-suit boots, the better to scramble about on the oil rig topside without having to worry about carrying extra footgear. They were further burdened by the waterproof gear bags, which were secured by nylon straps to their load-bearing vests.

At a depth of forty feet, the ocean's swell was mostly well over their heads, but they could still feel the mighty surge of water moving above them. Together, the four swimmers used lines to secure the delivery vehicle to a cross beam on the submerged platform alongside, working carefully in the murky light to avoid mistakes. Once the SDV was secure, Murdock moved close to the cockpit and signaled Johnson with an upraised thumb. Johnson responded the same way, then cracked his hatch. Normally, the bus driver would wait with the bus, but there was no telling how long the SEAL team would be here. The SDV had a strictly limited battery life; in fact, the only alternative was for Johnson to turn around after dropping the other SEALs off and head back out to sea for a rendezvous with the *Horizon* or another tug like her somewhere out of sight of the objective.

And if the SEALs needed to extract in a hurry, he wouldn't be there to pick them up.

Not that extraction was a particularly important aspect of this recon, Murdock thought with an uncharacteristic stab of pessimism. This one was for all the marbles, and if the SEALs or the SAS or anybody else along the way screwed up, well, it wouldn't be a particularly bad way to go, not from ground—or rather from water—zero. A sudden, heaven-searing flash, and you'd be incinerated before your nerve endings could transmit the sensation of pain to your brain.

The nightmare would be reserved for all of those thousands of people on the fringe of the effects, the ones having to deal with radioactive rain or soot from the North Sea oil fires, for the fishermen and roughnecks and workboat crews swamped by the radioactive base surge, for the kids made sick by contaminated milk and grain and livestock ashore.

Murdock was ready to risk that blinding, instant flash for himself—if it gave him a fighting chance of avoiding that slower, more agonizing death for all of those thousands of civilians.

He just hoped to hell that his assessment of the tangos' mentality, tossed off in a casual conversation last night in the Golden Cock, was accurate. If these people were psychopathic nut-cases instead of dedicated political terrorists, then all bets were off. Hell, even if his guess about the bastards was right, the sight of SEALs clambering around on Bouddica Bravo would make whoever was holding the firing button damned nervous.

And nervous men made mistakes.

Johnson pulled himself free of the SDV's cockpit, and

Murdock clapped him on the shoulder, giving him an OK sign of approval. The newbie had performed well, in a dangerous and difficult assignment. The entire operation could have been doomed had he missed the bearing of the oil complex by even a single degree. Murdock waited as Johnson retrieved his own waterproof bundle of weapons and gear. Then, together, the five men pushed away from the moored SDV and began swimming into the forest of struts and supports beneath Bouddica Bravo.

They'd decided to approach the complex from the smaller Bravo platform for several reasons. Perhaps most important, Alpha was supported above the waves by four massive steel-and-concrete pylons, each many meters thick and all narrower at the water than they were at their tops. Climbing those structures at all would be next to impossible; climbing them unseen would be more difficult still.

Bravo, on the other hand, was a more conventional oil-rig platform, built on a structure like the gantry crane surrounding a rocket about to be launched. The rocket, in this case, was the drilling rig itself, which extended down through the center of the platform and was completely surrounded by the supports. The underwater portions of the structure had to be serviced periodically by BGA divers; there were handholds and an access hatch to the rig's main deck, the pylons themselves offered lots of handholds—assuming you could climb like a monkey—and a man could almost certainly make his way all the way from the water's surface to the well deck proper without being seen from any other part of the complex.

The terrorists, most of them anyway, those who hadn't remained on board the *Noramo Pride,* would be on Alpha, up in the operations center and in the east-side living quarters complex. They might be terrorists, but they weren't fools. It was *cold* outside, and except for a few routine guards taking turns out in the brisk, North Sea wind, most would be inside where it was warm.

Up . . . up . . . up. Murdock could feel the water growing rougher, in powerful, mountain-sized surges. With his equipment load and no fins, the uphill swim swiftly became a small torture. His weight belt had been set for neutral buoyancy at twenty feet; halfway to the surface, it became harder to keep moving up, harder to support the drag of all of the weight he was carrying. He moved himself along up the cross struts, hand over gloved hand. All the way up, he watched for other movements within the pylon forest. Though unlikely, it was not impossible that the terrorists' first string of defense included a pair or two of frogmen of their own.

Murdock broke the surface first, clinging with one hand to a steel cross brace as he pushed his mask back with the other. The cold of the water was so raw it hurt, biting into the skin of his exposed face like a knife. The air temperature was in the high forties; the water itself must be a whisker or two above freezing. Back in Virginia Beach they were having a heat wave on the heels of an early spring. And here he was, worrying about major exposure. . . .

Carefully, Murdock took a long, hard look around. This, arguably, was the most dangerous moment. If the opposition was alert, if the guards were ignoring the potential threat posed by the *Horizon* and were watching the surface of the water close to the derrick pilings, then the SEAL recon was doomed before it had properly begun. Nothing . . . no sign of life anywhere. Bouddica Alpha's lowest work deck stretched like a raftered ceiling forty or more feet overhead, while the pilings rose about him like the trunks of fantastic, otherworldly trees. Sterling's head broke the surface with an oily ripple a few feet away . . . and beyond him, MacKenzie, Roselli, and Johnson.

The team's next set of steps had all been worked out and rehearsed again and again back at Dorset. Satellite photos provided to the British government by the American Defense Intelligence Agency had shown the general layout of the platform area, and Wentworth had shared those maps with the SEALs as soon as they'd reached his desk. As Murdock bobbed in the sea beneath the platform, he used each lift provided by a passing wave to check the actual layout with what he'd memorized off the satellite maps.

Nothing, apparently, had moved in the past few hours. The tanker *Noramo Pride* was still moored east of the platform, about a mile off. A red-and-white-painted anchor tug outwardly identical to the *Horizon* was moored close beside one of the four main supports beneath Bouddica Alpha. That would be the *Celtic Maiden,* assigned as Bouddica's safety boat. Not far from the *Maiden* was an aging fishing boat, dilapidated and rust-streaked, looking very much out of place alongside so much twenty-first-century hardware. Murdock had heard nothing about that craft's identity, but her presence here meant trouble. Either she'd been used by the terrorists in their takeover of the original tanker, or she was an honest fishing vessel, somehow swept up in the drama unfolding over the North Sea. Either way, there were probably tangos aboard, and they would have to be neutralized.

The sheer number of large and complex targets here was daunting. Bouddicas Alpha and Bravo alone represented a small city, with thousands of niches, corners, and hidey-holes for the bad guys. Same for the *Noramo Pride,* an enormous vessel that could have any number of people aboard. And both the *Celtic Maiden* and the old fishing trawler would have to be considered too.

Clearly, the assault was far beyond the capability of SEAL Seven's Third Platoon. Most of the op would have to be in the hands of the SAS and—Murdock had been pleased to learn just before their departure that morning—the GSG9. The Germans, evidently, had decided to pitch in to protect their North Sea interests by sending a squad of GSG9 troopers. Murdock hadn't seen them, but he'd heard that Lieutenant Hopke was with them.

Knowing Hopke's feelings for Inge Schmidt, feelings shared by Murdock himself, he somehow wasn't surprised.

They would all be welcome on this one. The single disadvantage in a multi-unit op, of course, was the fact that so many elite teams could end up getting in each others' way, literally tripping over one another, even opening fire on one another, once they'd broken into the confused tangle of a firefight inside the objective.

After verifying that the various ships were still where the satellite data had originally placed them, Murdock signaled to the others. Roselli, MacKenzie, and Johnson all began unbuckling their diving rigs and pulling their equipment off. While

Jaybird Sterling and Murdock stood—or rather swam—watch, the other three shucked themselves down to combat blacks and load-bearing harnesses, with their weapons and other combat gear still sealed in black, waterproof pouches fastened to their backs. Their rebreathers and other swim gear, along with Murdock's and Sterling's weapons bags, were attached to a floatation bladder that Sterling inflated with a small CO_2 bottle equipped with a pull ring. The bladder's buoyancy had been calculated to keep the bundled gear adrift just beneath the surface. Any curious eyes that glimpsed the tarp-covered bundle would assume that it was a piece of flotsam bumping against Bravo's structural supports

With the gear safely afloat and lashed to a piling, it was time to begin climbing the platform. Roselli was the best climber in the group. He looked at Murdock and Murdock nodded vigorously. God, it would be good to get out of this cold! Roselli groped upward for another cross support just within arm's reach, grabbed it in one gloved hand, and chinned himself up. A moment later, his rubber-suited legs slid clear of the water, and he began his nerve-wracking climb.

Murdock ran his gloved hand over the piling beside him. Damn . . . that was ice! Not a solid layer, but a slickness of frozen vapor. Roselli must be part mountain goat to be pulling this off.

A surge of icy water caught Murdock from behind, raising him several feet along the piling, slamming him forward, then dropping away beneath him as he clung precariously to his slippery handhold. A moment later, the water returned, the current whirling him about and breaking his grip.

MacKenzie reached out with one strong hand and grabbed Murdock's arm, hauling him back. "Easy, L-T," he said, just loud enough to be heard above the surge and hiss of the waves.

Murdock spat salt water, then gulped in a lungful of cold air. "Thanks, Mac. Let's link up."

Each of the four men held fast to the framework with one arm, and with the other snagged hold of the load-bearing harness of the man on his left. Together, they clung to one another and the piling, as wave after ice-cold wave of seawater cascaded about them.

Blinking though the salt, Murdock stared up at Roselli, now a tiny black shape half lost among the black, crisscrossing beams and support struts of the derrick platform. Murdock knew a sharp thrill of fear. If he slipped on that ice-slicked perch now, lost his grip, and fell, he could easily break his back or neck in the fall or hit the water so hard he'd lose consciousness and drown before the others could reach him. Murdock watched the twisting, upward-inching shape, willing him to go on. . . .

Roselli vanished forty feet overhead, a telephone pole's height above the surging, angry water. For a breathless moment, the four SEALs clung to each other, waiting, and then something came spilling toward them from the derrick platform above, something that unraveled as it fell, then jerked to a halt, dangling free, its end swinging about in the wind.

A caving ladder. MacKenzie, closest and with the longest reach of any of the men still in the water, reached up and out and snagged the end as it swung past just overhead. Carefully, he released his hold on Murdock and the piling, letting his full weight drag down on the ladder and pull it taut. Johnson gave a final check to his gear bag, making certain the snaps and fittings were all secure, then swung up onto the caving ladder's rungs and began swiftly climbing up out of the water.

With Roselli on the platform and Johnson on his way up, it was time for Murdock and Jaybird to pull a small reconnaissance of their own. Murdock locked eyes with the other SEAL, nodded twice, then pulled his face mask back down and settled it in place. A last look around to get his bearings, and then he ducked beneath the surface again, striking out toward the north.

Toward the moored anchor tug *Celtic Maiden*.

The distance was only about four hundred feet, but it was tough going nonetheless without flippers, even without the added weight of the weapon bags and ammo they'd been carrying. After hours of forced inactivity inside the bus, Murdock was already beginning to feel the effects of exhaustion and exposure.

But he particularly wanted to check out the *Celtic Maiden*'s strange cargo. The sat photos from Washington had not included any analysis, and Murdock doubted that the folks at

the National Photographic Interpretation Center in Washington—
NPIC, for short—had advanced any solid guesses yet. Murdock
had studied an enlargement of the stern of the *Celtic Maiden* for
quite a while early that morning, however, and was disturbed by
what he'd seen there. Something was resting on the *Maiden*'s
fantail, an elongated, vaguely torpedo-like shape swaddled in
canvas.

If there was even the tiniest chance that the object wrapped
in tarpaulins on the *Maiden*'s deck was the PRR A-bomb,
Murdock wanted to know it. Half of the battle would be won
if the SEALs could just confirm where the bomb was being
kept, and if the tangos had been stupid enough to leave the
thing so easily accessible to the sea, then Murdock might be
able to pull the appropriate wires and end this whole crisis,
right here and now.

Not that it would be that easy. Things never were, and on
tricky and dangerous ops like this one, the ubiquitous Murphy
of Murphy's Law was always likely to be tagging along.

At last, the *Celtic Maiden*'s hull loomed overhead, vast and
dark against the silver light of the surface. From beneath the
water, nothing seemed out of the ordinary. Taking his place at
the workboat's stern between the two massive propellers,
Murdock waited while Sterling got into position a few feet
away, then cautiously the two men surfaced together.

They'd been lucky in one aspect of the positioning of the
various players in the drama. The *Celtic Maiden* was moored
beneath the bridge that spanned the gap between Bouddica
Alpha and Bouddica Bravo, her bow facing east. That meant
she was facing the *Horizon* almost bow-on, and the SEALs had
been counting on the distraction offered by the *Horizon* in
order to get aboard the facility. Anyone on board the *Maiden*
was, Murdock fervently hoped, up on the bow or in the
wheelhouse up on the superstructure, keeping a wary eye on
the other tug.

No one was visible from the water astern. Reaching up onto
the *Maiden*'s transom, Murdock chinned himself smoothly out
of the water . . . then froze. Movement!

But it was someone's back, a man wearing what looked like
commando garb, walking away from the tarp-shrouded object

on the afterdeck and vanishing around the corner of the superstructure forward.

The aft end of the tug was deserted now, so far as Murdock could see. Leaning forward, he rolled out of the water and onto the waffle-ribbed steel deck. Sterling joined him a moment later.

Silently, exchanging hand signals, the two SEALs split up, circling the big package from either side, and checking beneath the cradle that supported it. If it *was* a bomb it was a damned big one, far larger than even the first U.S. bombs used half a century ago on Japan.

Keenly aware that someone might return at any moment or glance down on the afterdeck from the superstructure forward, Murdock and Sterling took cover behind the object. It was securely wrapped, but Sterling found a loose flap extending from beneath the steel strap that held the tarp in place, and worked open a large enough opening to see inside.

Murdock had not been expecting this. He found himself looking not at a homemade A-bomb, but at the aluminum and plastic-cowling enclosing a fair-sized propeller.

Silently, Sterling pointed to some characters impressed in part of the prop shroud. They looked Chinese, but both SEALs had learned to recognize the different types of Oriental characters that were descended from the original Chinese, even if they couldn't read them.

Korean.

Sterling already had his camera out, a small device manufactured by TRW that recorded images digitally. He got several shots of the lettering and of as much of the propeller and shroud as he could get at. Then, still in complete silence, the two men replaced the loose corner of the tarp, pulled down their masks, and rolled into the sea off the workboat's transom with scarcely a splash to mark their entry.

Washington, Murdock thought as the two SEALs swam the four hundred feet back to the pylons beneath Bouddica Bravo, would be interested in this one.

The other three SEALs were all gone when they returned. After finding the equipment bundle, they removed their swim gear, added it to the cache, and reset the inflation on the bladder to keep it suspended just beneath the surface. Then, Murdock in the lead, they ascended the caving ladder, which had been left in place for them.

It was a wild, dizzying climb, one made interesting by the buffeting wind and the biting cold. Murdock could feel the water freezing in his hair, where it stuck out from beneath his dry suit's hood. He climbed with an awkward-looking frog's posture, his knees splayed out to either side, to keep from pushing himself out too much from the ladder and losing control of the thing. Despite Sterling's weight on the bottom end, the wind kept threatening to spin him about, or worse, to bash him against the side of the piling.

Then he was at the top, and the platform stretched above him like a vast, gray, steel ceiling. The ladder threaded its way through a narrow manhole, and he squeezed his way up and through.

Roselli was on the platform on the other side, his equipment bag on the deck, his 9mm Smith & Wesson Mark 1 Mod 0 Hush Puppy clutched in both hands.

Murdock touched him lightly and flicked a sign with his fingers. *Anything?*

Negative, was Roselli's hand-sign response. *You?*

Later.

Mac and Johnson . . . that way.

Okay.

Together, the two men surveyed their surroundings, automatically positioning themselves back to back and rotating slowly to the left, covering one another and maintaining a 360-degree lookout.

From their vantage point on the oil platform's main deck, they had a clear view of the causeway stretched across open water to Bouddica Alpha, which rose like a fantastic, far-future city on its four massive pylons a hundred meters to the north. Murdock could see the windows of the operations center, but they were blank and empty. If there were people up there—and there must be—they weren't close to the windows and they weren't looking this way. They too must be watching the *Horizon*, which was still riding the heavy swell well clear of the facility, highly visible with its bright red hull and odd, far-forward white superstructure. Even further east, moored to one of the area's huge fueling buoys, was an oil tanker, a black and rust-red cliff topped aft by a white superstructure like the face of a four-story building.

Murdock shifted his full attention back to the twin platforms. Nowhere on all that vast and tangled structure was a human shape visible.

He grinned to himself. There were four more working decks on Bouddica Bravo above this one, and Alpha was bigger still, an incredibly complex forest of cranes and gantries, tanks and towers, in which an army of SEALs could hide out for days, if necessary, undiscovered. The SOBs would've needed an army of their own to adequately protect a facility this large and this complex. They'd bitten off more than they could possibly chew.

He sensed movement behind him. Sterling was there, dripping wet, clutching his Hush Puppy automatic. Swiftly, the two of them adjusted the radios attached to the insides of their hoods, pulling the pencil mikes out until they rested on their lower lips. They would be maintaining radio silence at first, for obvious reasons, but when they needed communications links, they would need them fast. Murdock had to concentrate, though, to keep his lip, which he imagined was pretty blue by now, from trembling. This shit was worse than Hell Week back in Coronado.

When all was ready, Roselli led them away from the deck opening, threading up several steel ladders and deeper into the platform, until they were climbing the weather shroud on the central drilling derrick itself. Halfway up, in a position identified from the plans of the facility back in Wentworth's office, was a spot where a walled-in section gave way to the more traditional open latticework of girders and braces. There was a platform there, giving the roughnecks access to the drill, with plenty of heavy machinery—winches, hoists, and the pumping gear for drilling mud—which would provide the SEALs with cover, the perfect site for an observation post.

They'd code-named the spot Eyrie. The other two SEALs were already in place and in the process of setting up the rest of their gear.

The most important set of hardware was the HST-4 satcom unit, its attendant decoder, and the small satellite uplink unit that went with it. MacKenzie had already carefully aligned the folding satellite dish with an invisible point in the sky. With that gear properly set up and aimed, they'd be able to converse directly with Washington through one of the MILSTAR communications satellites if they wanted to, though that particular call was probably a bit premature just now.

More important, it would let them talk directly with Wentworth, back in Dorset, or with Captain Croft aboard the *Horizon*. The SEALs had a great deal of help available, if and when they needed it.

Though they had personal communication with each other as well, they didn't use it, since the enemy might have scanner gear in operation, set to watch military channels.

The first information beamed out over the tiny satellite dish was the digital recordings stored in Sterling's TRW camera, followed by a brief report of what they'd seen so far.

Meanwhile, Murdock and Roselli set out to reconnoiter the rest of Bouddica Bravo . . . and this time they found some tangos.

There were two of them, rough-looking men armed with H&K MP5 submachine guns much like those carried by the SEALs, though they were not the SD3 suppressed version with the heavy silencer barrels. They'd found a place for themselves on the east side of the facility, tucked away out of the cold and the wind behind an immense stack of barrels and drilling-shaft segments. Indeed, the SEALs could easily have missed them entirely, except that Murdock's sharp sense of smell had first detected a whiff of cigarette smoke, fresh and sharp above the clinging stink of oil and machinery. Murdock and Roselli watched them for a time, dispassionately, until they were certain that there was no alarm, no sense of urgency or worry on the part of the enemy. Then, stealthily, moving with death-silent footfalls, the two SEALs backed away, rejoining the others.

Back in the Eyrie, MacKenzie had a pair of binoculars out and was studying the sheer white cliff-face of Bouddica Alpha. "Anything?" Murdock asked quietly.

"I've got two guards spotted on top of the command center," MacKenzie replied. "And I've been following some movement inside. Hard to get a good count, though."

"Two more back that way," Murdock added. "It's going to be a bear getting an accurate head count. Especially if they keep moving around."

"Roger that."

The SEALs settled down to wait.

19

Friday, May 4

"Who authorized this!" the Secretary of Defense demanded, his face flushed with rage. The transcript of the report from England was spread out before him on the table. "Who let these . . . these *cowboys* loose over there?"

"The terrorists?" Caldwell asked, momentarily confused.

"No, damn it! These SEALs! Who gave them orders to board that oil platform?"

"As near as we can gather, Mr. Secretary," Admiral Bainbridge said quietly, "the SEAL commander on the scene interpreted his orders rather, um, broadly. He wrote up what we call an UNODIR report, a report telling us precisely what he was going to do unless we told him otherwise. Unfortunately, his report did not reach levels cleared to know what was going on until too late."

"At this point," Marlowe, the CIA director pointed out, "we'd do a hell of a lot more damage pulling them out than we would leaving them there."

"That's easy for you to say," Hemminger snapped. "What if they're seen, damn it? What if that SEAL over there gets excited and launches a takedown? He could trigger the very disaster we're trying to avoid!"

"I must remind you, Mr. Hemminger, that the British government has already authorized a takedown," Caldwell pointed out. "They are proceeding with their plans as we speak."

The President's Chief of Staff looked shocked. "God! Why weren't we consulted?"

Caldwell gave a thin smile. "Great Britain is still a sovereign country, you know, Frank. We were informed because it is our oil tanker which is at risk, but they are taking the steps they feel are necessary and justified to protect their interests, which in this case is a very expensive oil-production facility, half the oil-production capabilities of the North Sea, and the North Sea itself, for that matter."

Marlowe stood up and walked to the far end of the table, where part of the rococo scrollwork and ornate wooden paneling of one wall had been slid back to reveal a large screen. "Can we have the first shot, please?" he said, raising his voice for the benefit of the unseen techs running the room's electronics.

The scene on the monitor appeared to be an aerial photograph of the two Bouddica platforms, shot from an altitude of several hundred feet. Long shadows on the water indicated a time close to dawn or sunset; lines of white alphanumerics in the upper right corner listed security codes, and a time of 0734:15 GMT, with Wednesday's date.

Marlowe pulled a pen-sized laser pointer from the inside pocket of his jacket and switched it on. The intense, ruby-red spot of light from the pointer danced wildly across the photo image. "This is a KH-12 series, with the first shot taken early Wednesday morning," he said. "We started moving satellites as soon as the word came through that something strange was going down at Bouddica. We shifted KH-12 Delta into a new orbit with its apogee above the North Sea. Gives it a line-of-sight on-station time of almost sixty minutes. You can see here Bouddica Alpha . . . Bravo . . . Over by the edge, this fat cigar is the *Noramo Pride*. This speck alongside Alpha is the *Celtic Maiden*. That's a workboat assigned to the oil platform." The laser-light pinpoint zipped across to Alpha's helipad and circled an insect centered in the pad's bull's-eye. "This is a helicopter that had apparently touched down in the early hours. Our analysts tell me it's painted with the markings and hull insignia of an aircraft with the Royal Dutch Navy."

"The Dutch!" Schellenberg exclaimed. "Has anyone consulted with them?"

"Their Defense Ministry assures us it's not one of theirs, Mr. Secretary," Marlowe said dryly. "It's counterfeit, probably to let the terrorists board the *Noramo Pride*. Next!"

The scene on the monitor flashed to another view, this one from a different angle. The shadows were shorter and differently aligned; the date was still Wednesday, but the time was 0913:35 GMT. The *Noramo Pride* was nosed up to a buoy, visible as a small, gray blotch next to her bow. Another ship, a third the length and bulk of the tanker, was moving toward the platform, her wake indicating a speed of no more than a few knots.

"Almost two hours later, another ship came on the scene. We've identified her as the *Rosa*, fishing trawler, German registry. Interesting thing is she's listed as scrapped. We're trying to track down her current owners, but that may take a while. At first we were concerned that another civilian ship had blundered into the scenario. Now we think the *Rosa* is part of it. Next."

On the screen, time leaped ahead once more. *Noramo Pride* was still riding at her mooring. The *Rosa*, however, was tied up close alongside Bouddica Alpha. A crane had been swung out over her cargo deck. The workboat *Celtic Maiden* was tucked in between the *Rosa* and the platform, partly hidden by the crane and by the bridge connecting the two platforms Alpha and Bravo.

"Enhance, please," Marlowe said. The scene on the monitor zoomed in tight, the complexity of the southeast corner of Bouddica Alpha and the bridge expanding swiftly to almost fill the screen. At this magnification, only a portion of the *Rosa*'s deck was visible. An open hatch in the deck gaped at the sky; the platform's crane was hoisting something clear of the opening, while a number of men clustered on the deck guided it along with upraised hands.

What the "something" was was not clear. It was large,

certainly, roughly cigar-shaped, and bundled up in tarpaulins and packing straps.

"When we first caught sight of this," Marlowe went on, "we assumed it might be the terrorists' bomb. The only problem was, it's way, way too big, lots bigger than any A-bomb would need to be. In fact, some of our analysts thought the PRR might have taken a shortcut and put together a whopping big conventional bomb instead. Next."

A second enhanced view showed that the package had been moved from the *Rosa*'s cargo hatch and onto the afterdeck of the *Celtic Maiden,* after which the *Rosa* had moved clear, tying up at another mooring nearby. The tarp-bundled package was resting on some sort of cradle on the *Celtic Maiden*'s after deck.

"Our satellites could tell us a lot about the thing. It's a bulky, oblong object about six meters long bundled in a tarp and resting on a wooden cradle. We could estimate that it weighs between eight and twelve tons." The laser-light pointer flicked past the images of two armed guards standing next to the object. "We could even tell that the bad guys had posted guards armed with H&K submarine guns, which suggests they want to protect it."

Marlowe flicked off the pointer and turned to address the room. "This, gentlemen, should be an object lesson to those of us who tend to put too much reliance in spy satellites and other long-range, high-tech spy equipment. We never would've had a prayer of learning what this thing was if it hadn't been for the report from our SEALs. In my trade, it's called HUMINT. That's human intelligence. You can only rely so far on machines."

"So what is that thing?" Clayton asked. "If it's too big to be a bomb . . ."

"Next."

The aerial view was replaced by a close-up of what seemed to be the rear end of a very large torpedo or small boat, with a propeller encased in a smooth, shiny shroud. Someone's black-gloved hand was visible to the left, pulling back a corner of the tarp.

"Enhance." Writing filled the screen, blocky Oriental characters and several numerals that might have been serial numbers.

"Korean characters," Marlowe said. "It reads 'People's Defense Ministry, Special Project' . . . and that number. This down here might be a part number. And this on the shroud is the Korean equivalent of 'no step.'

"We were able to trace the numbers. What we are looking at here is the stern of a small one- or two-man submarine, similar to the Shinkai-series research subs of the Japanese, or our own *Alvin*. It appears to be of North Korean manufacture but is basically Japanese technology . . . probably openly purchased, though the material's supposed to be restricted. I'm sure you're all well aware of the problems we've had with several major Japanese corporations on that count.

"We think this must be a special project of the North Korean Navy that they call 'Mul ojing o,' or 'Squid.' Designed for salvage work, sabotaging or tapping undersea cables and the like during war, probably mine clearing as well. Like the Japanese model, it's equipped with teleoperated arms. It would probably be particularly useful for undersea assault."

"What, with frogmen?" Hemminger said. He shook his head. "It doesn't look that big. What'd you say, six meters?"

"No, sir. With those remote-control arms, it could plant a bomb against an underwater objective. A *big* bomb."

"An underwater objective," Schellenberg said thoughtfully. Then realization dawned and his eyes opened wide. "You mean like Bouddica."

"Precisely. It's likely that the Squid is there to plant the A-bomb beneath the platform."

"Damn," Clayton said, his fist clenched on the tabletop before him. "Why didn't those SEALs take out that sub when they had a chance? What'd they do, just leave it there?"

"They did," Admiral Bainbridge said. "And I have to believe they did the right thing. According to the report from the officer in charge, they didn't have time for more than a quick look. Worse, they haven't found the A-bomb yet. Blowing up that minisub would've been a great way to tip our hand and set off the fireworks, don't you think?"

"What are the SEALs doing now?"

Marlowe looked toward the ceiling and raised his voice slightly. "Can we see the telephoto shots, please? Run through the series."

On the monitor, a new photo appeared, grainy but distinct. It showed a rough-looking man in watchcap and combat harness, lighting a cigarette. An H&K subgun was slung over his shoulder, muzzle-down. That image was replaced a moment later by another, showing a different man, similarly armed and equipped. He was leaning on a railing, looking out across the sea with an almost pensive expression on his face. Next there were two armed men, obviously engaged in conversation. A long, flat, open wooden box rested on a fifty-five-gallon drum at one man's elbow. One of the men was pulling something from the box, something like a black spindle on the end of a stick that Bainbridge instantly recognized: rocket-propelled grenades for an RPG.

"To answer your question, the SEALs have been running an OP—an observation post—right under the terrrorists' noses. They've got a digital camera with them, with a telephoto lens, that records images electronically instead of on film. They've been shooting pictures of everyone they can see and all of the equipment they can find, then uploading the camera's catch onto the satellite net for us to decipher here.

"So far, they've recorded fifteen different men, though there are certainly more than that present. We've been able to identify six of the faces—two are die-hard members of the Provo IRA, the other four were spotted by the German BKA as former members of the Red Army Faction. The SEALs have also catalogued an array of weapons that includes rocket-propelled grenades, submachine guns, and at least one U.S.-made M-60 machine gun."

"And how many SEALs are aboard?" Hemminger wanted to know.

"Five. And there are twenty-eight SAS men in the anchor tug, which left the immediate area after concluding the first round of negotiations but is maintaining station just over the horizon."

"Thirty-three? Against what amounts to an army?"

"Seems to me we've got a more serious problem that that,"

Clayton pointed out. "All those weapons, all of those explosives aboard an oil-production rig, for God's sake. They start shooting, and the PRR isn't going to need an A-bomb. Remember Piper Alpha?"

Everyone there had received briefings on the history of North Sea oil platforms, including some of the notable disasters. In 1988, the British platform dubbed Piper Alpha had exploded when an undetected gas leak had been touched off by a spark. Of the 231 workers aboard, only 64 had survived.

"Maybe that would be for the best," Hemminger said, his long face growing longer. "If someone touches off a gas explosion in there, maybe we won't have to worry about the bomb."

"That's for damned sure." Clayton brightened. "Yeah! That's right!" He turned to Caldwell, on his right. "How about it, General? If we launched an attack, I mean, a really massive, all-out air strike. Laser-guided bombs, missiles, the works. Could we just blow that baby right out of the water? Before anyone in there had time to push the button?"

Caldwell looked pained, then shook his head. "I don't think—"

"No, really!" Clayton said, enthusiastic now. "I know it's kind of drastic. There could be lots of—what do you military guys say? 'Collateral damage'? But fuck it! This gives us a fighting chance!"

"Ignoring for the moment the more than three hundred hostages being held at the objective—"

"Damn it, General, we're balancing three hundred hostages against how many thousands of people who die if that bomb goes off? I find those losses to be acceptable!"

"Ignoring the hostages," Caldwell repeated, pushing ahead, "and ignoring for the moment our own military forces at the objective, there are some serious basic problems with that approach. We don't know how the nuclear device is shielded, armed, or triggered. Any atomic bomb, however, depends on a conventional explosive charge to compress the fissionable material of the warhead to critical mass. Set off as big an explosion as we're talking about here, and there's a good chance, a *very* good chance in fact, that the bomb's conventional explosive would be triggered through something called sympathetic detonation. And that, of course, would create critical mass and a nuclear explosion.

"Second, we still don't know where the bomb is being kept. We haven't seen them unloading it and don't even know what it might look like. Maybe it's already on the platform. Maybe it's aboard the tanker. Maybe it's on the fishing boat where the minisub was stored, but it hasn't been unloaded yet. While we could easily trigger a natural-gas explosion on the platform, there's no way in hell we could get all of the possible targets. In the case of the various ships and boats on the site, even a large number of direct hits wouldn't make the target explode or sink immediately. Someone, either on Bouddica or on the ship, would have plenty of time to evaluate the situation, decide all was lost, and push the button."

"I would have to agree with that assessment," Hemminger said. "But with the proviso that it does give us some hope. I think my recommendation would have to be to leave the situation to our people there, but have the air strike ready, just in case. If things get bad, if the assault is beaten off, we can hit them with the F-15s and hope for the best."

"Hope for the best?" Bainbridge laughed. "We're talking about a nuclear weapon here, gentlemen!"

"I'm well aware of that, Admiral," the Secretary of Defense said coldly. "Which is why this must be a *political* decision, not a military one. The detonation of that device could ruin the economy of a vital ally and would seriously threaten U.S. strategic interests in the area. If we have any chance, any chance at *all* of stopping that detonation, we must take it. *Must* take it. Do you understand that?"

"Yes, Mr. Secretary," Bainbridge said coldly. "I understand you very well. I just wonder, though, if you'll give the order."

"Eh? What order?"

"The order to those airmen who'll have to fly in and fire the missiles that will kill over three hundred civilians and a number of comrades-at-arms."

Hemminger shot Bainbridge a black look but said nothing.

"So what are we saying?" Schellenberg asked.

Clayton shrugged. "I suggest we let them go. Go! We've got

men on the platform already. The Brits have their SAS people
on the tug. I say we deploy the rest of the SEALs to the
Voramo Pride, back up the Brits with every scrap of air and
supply at our disposal, and run with it!"

"But Christ," Schellenberg muttered, his eyes wide. "I
mean . . . *Christ!* We don't have any control over those
people, those SEALs! We can't leave leave something this
important to trained killers like them! We have no control!"

"Maybe," Marlowe said with a faint, tight smile, "that's the
way it should be."

1325 hours GMT
The North Sea
Bouddica Bravo

Murdock watched as Sterling listened intently to the head-
phones plugged into the HST-4 receiver. Was he receiving
orders from Washington? Had to be, since he'd been listening
without comment or acknowledgment for five minutes now.
The question was . . . would the orders require the SEAL OP
to support the expected assault? Or order them out . . . and
home to a court-martial?

It had to be an assault. It *had* to be. If these tangos got away
with their nuclear blackmail . . .

The past twenty hours had been fairly typical for a long-term
SEAL OP watch. They'd prowled both platforms during the
night, looking for intel, identifying tango security elements and
positions, familiarizing themselves with the facility's maze-
like layout. During the day, they'd kept to their perch save for
brief forays to keep tabs on the terrorists who were also on
Bravo, down on the first level. The rest of the time, they took
telescopic photos of terrorists and equipment, watched the
movements of men aboard the *Rosa* and the *Celtic Maiden,* ate
cold packaged rations, and endured the numbing chill of wind
and weather. Much longer, Murdock knew, and the men would
begin suffering from the effects of exposure, despite the
protection afforded by their dry suits.

Still, BUD/S had shaped all of their minds as much as it had
shaped their bodies. They might grumble about the cold quietly
among themselves, but they endured it.

They had to. *You may not like it,* ran the old SEAL adage *you just have to do it.*

They did it. In Vietnam, SEALs had trained themselves to deliberately assume uncomfortable positions in order to stay awake, while waiting at an ambush for hour after aching hour. This, Murdock thought, was much like that . . . though he did make his men take turns catching a few hours of sleep at a time.

He checked his watch impatiently. Waiting. Not knowing. That was the hardest. Always.

Let's get it on!

"Watchdog, Eyrie, Sierra three-five," Sterling whispered into his mike after an interminable wait. "Acknowledged, Eyrie, out."

"Well?" Murdock asked.

"Orders, L-T," Jaybird Sterling said, replacing the headset from the satcom unit in its case. "Looks like we stay. . . ." He paused, then grinned wickedly. "And kick some tango ass!"

Murdock felt a surge of relief. He'd risked everything with his decision to bend the rules this far, both for himself and for his men, by coming here instead of adhering to a strict interpretation of his orders and staying on alert ashore.

"Yes!" Roselli said, clenching his fist and jerking his arm back. "All right!"

"Are we gonna hit them?" Johnson wanted to know.

"Let's keep a sock on it, people," MacKenzie said, lowering his binoculars and turning to face the others. But he was grinning. "What's the story, Jaybird?"

"Okay. They're gonna want to talk to the L-T to finalize shit." He looked at his watch, peeling back the Velcro cover. "Thirty-five minutes. Fourteen-hundred hours, our time. But an assault is go. They're bringing in the rest of Third Platoon to hit the tanker out there, and more SAS to take down Bouddica Alpha. We're to stay put, but act in support from the Eyrie. And . . ."

"What?" Murdock asked as Sterling hesitated.

"The station's radar. They want both of them taken out, just before the show goes down."

"We don't have much with us in the way of bang-clay," MacKenzie said. "What . . . three kilos?"

"That would be enough to take both radars down," Murdock decided. Bouddica had two radar towers, visible above the main platform as a pair of slender towers capped by what looked like large, white golf balls—the weather shrouds housing the radar dishes.

"There's more," Sterling added.

"What?"

"Any preliminary data we can acquire about the location and nature of the, quote, possible nuclear device, unquote, as well as any information on the location of the hostages and the disposition of tango security elements on any of the targets, including the fishing trawler *Rosa* . . ." Sterling stopped, and drew a deep breath, before proceeding. "Would all be greatly appreciated!"

"Tall order," Murdock said. He was already considering possible approaches to the main personnel habitat over on Alpha. If they could just slip across the bridge unobserved, at night . . . "We'll have to see what we can do about that. When it's going down?"

"Tonight. Time's not set yet, but tonight. The British government has been in radio communication with the terrorists. I gather they've agreed, at least in principle, to all of the tangos' demands, though they're claiming some problems."

"Delaying tactics," MacKenzie suggested.

"Sounds like it," Sterling agreed. "Things like, the UN can't make an official vote on admitting the PRR until a full session of the General Assembly can be arranged Monday."

"They bought that?" Roselli asked. "The tangos, I mean?"

"They're probably more interested in the money transfer," Murdock suggested. An earlier burst-transmission picked up from MILSTAR had brought the SEALs up to speed on the terrorist demands.

"Probably."

"What about the prisoner release?" MacKenzie wanted to know.

"The British have promised to release the prisoners," Sterling said. "One of them, the Korean woman, will be sent out to

Bouddica tonight. The terrorists were demanding that she be flown out to the platform by helicopter, but the Brits are pleading that bad weather in the area might pose a danger. So they're sending her out on the *Horizon*."

"Which lets Wentworth get his boys in close when they come in to hand her over," Murdock said, nodding. "Slick."

"If they can manage it, the tug will move in close and provide a diversion while SEALs and SBS take down the tanker and the trawler. We'll hit the facility's radar so that the main assault force can come in by helo."

"What about the minisub?" Johnson asked.

"The SAS'll hit that off the *Horizon*."

"Sounds like it's all covered then," Roselli said.

"Yeah," Murdock said. "Except for one little thing."

"What's that?"

"Where the hell's the A-bomb? Sounds like Washington is expecting us to find that out for them."

Sterling nodded. "I guess they're working out a set of code words now, Skipper. They'll discuss that with you when you talk to them later. So we can tell them where the thing is, or even call the whole thing off."

Roselli laughed, a short, bitter sound. "Which makes it our fault if the thing goes down bad."

"Shit, Razor," Murdock said, grinning. "Isn't that the way it always is?"

"Scars and stars, L-T," Roselli said, shrugging. An old SEAL saying held that others got the stars—meaning promotion to admiral—while the SEALs faced the actual combat. "It's always scars and stars. . . ."

20

Friday, May 4

1920 hours GMT
The North Sea
Eight miles south of the Bouddica Complex
DeWitt released his equipment pack, which fell to the end of its tether with a sharp jerk, then dangled there five meters beneath his feet. Looking up, he checked the canopy of his ram-air chute, making certain that it was fully deployed and hadn't twisted into a deadly Mae West. Doc Ellsworth, he remembered, had been the victim of a faulty chute deployment over the Balkans; he'd been able to work with his reserve okay, but he'd ended up coming in off course and slammed into a tree.

Incidents like that always tended to make everyone a little more careful afterward.

The wind was blowing from the east at a fairly gentle five knots, which meant that DeWitt and the other jumpers had to quarter slightly into the wind to compensate for drift to the east. This op had been pretty restrictive in what was available for insertion. There weren't enough minisubs available for eight men, and if they were to reach their objective by IBS, they would have to come from the south or the west to keep from fighting the current . . . and an approach from the west would take them right under the noses of the tangos on Bouddica.

The current mission plan then, as were so many of them, was a series of compromises forced by available equipment and the lay of the land. The objective was at least in sight now . . . the long, low, black and white smudge of the tanker *Noramo Pride,* lying on the horizon just to the right of the tangled gray tower that marked Bouddica.

To DeWitt's right, just visible as a blue-on-blue patch against the sky, was another chute, he couldn't tell whose. Seven other SEALs were in the sky all around him, but DeWitt couldn't see any of them, a fact that was oddly reassuring. If he couldn't see them at a range of a mile or so, the terrorists on Bouddica and aboard the tanker wouldn't see them either.

The plan was simple—the best kind when it came to combat. There were fewer things to go wrong, or to screw up, that way. The SEALs had leaped from an Air Force C-130 moments before at an altitude of thirty thousand feet, which put the aircraft easily beyond the range at which it could be seen or heard from the platform. The SEALs, wearing heavy coveralls and jackets against the cold, with oxygen bottles strapped to their sides and connected to the full-helmet masks they wore, had fallen to ten thousand feet before opening their chutes.

It was, in fact, a mix of HAHO and HALO techniques. High Altitude, High Opening approach would have had them pulling the ripcord above 25,000 feet, then literally flying to their target for as much as fifty miles across the open sea. They could damn near have jumped over the east coast of England and flown all the way to Bouddica on the power of the wind alone.

High Altitude, Low Opening gave the jumpers no distance but let them fall almost on top of the target, literally yanking their rip cords at the last possible moment, scant hundreds of feet above the surface.

The compromise, however, had them fall a long way in order to stay off the enemy's radar. Bouddica had a decent radar setup, both to monitor the ever-changing weather and to watch the steady flow of surface traffic moving through this part of the North Sea. A skilled operator might detect the blips that were approaching parachutists, and while it seemed unlikely that terrorists would have radar experts within their ranks, SEALs only reached old age when they planned for all

possibilities and were very, very careful in how they dealt with
them.

They would splash into the sea five miles south of Bouddica,
where they would home in on a Chemlite stick held by Brown,
who'd jumped a few moments before the rest of them in order
to serve as pathfinder. Once everyone was down, they would
inflate two SEAL IBSs—one of them was part of the heavy
bundle dangling beneath DeWitt's feet—climb aboard, and
begin motoring toward the *Norumo Pride*.

They would deliberately hang back out of sight, however,
until 2200 hours, almost half an hour past sunset, when it
would be dark enough to approach on the surface of the sea
without being easily spotted.

Once they reached the tanker, of course, everything was
easy. Just climb the damn thing, neutralize every terrorist
aboard, and wait for further orders. Meanwhile, all hell would
be breaking loose around them. The anchor tug *Horizon* would
be returning to the area at just about 2200 hours, with the North
Korean woman on board. There would be some final negotiations, and then Chun would be handed over to the tangos, just
as they'd demanded.

Washington and London had agreed on that one, at least,
though DeWitt imagined there'd been some pretty acrimonious
infighting over the question at first. But they needed to bring
Chun in close, even let her go across to Bouddica, so the
terrorists could see her and perhaps believe that the government forces had capitulated; while the exchange was taking
place, at precisely 2230 hours, DeWitt's SEALs would take
down the tanker, Murdock and the four men with him would
knock out the facility's radar, and the SAS men aboard *Horizon*
would storm the main platform. A small SBS team, DeWitt had
been told, would deal with the trawler *Rosa,* just in case the
A-bomb was hidden in her hold. The final blow would be
delivered minutes later, when a flight of British helicopters,
ferrying in SAS and GSG9 commandos, would come skim-
ming in out of the west at wave-top height. If Lieutenant
Murdock and his people were able to take down Bouddica
Alpha's radar, the helos ought to make it all the way in without
being sighted until literally the last moment. More helos would

be coming in behind the first wave, these carrying American
NEST agents and Navy EOD experts, with the tools and the
know-how to disarm a live nuclear warhead.

Simple.

Except that there'd been no time to rehearse this thing, no
time even to be sure of the preliminary intelligence. DeWitt
had at least been told that most of the intel they'd received had
come courtesy of Lieutenant Murdock and the other SEALs in
the recon force, which meant it could be trusted as gospel, but
there were so many unknowns still. How many tangos were
there aboard Bouddica, aboard the *Rosa*, aboard the *Noramo
Pride*? How alert were they? Could the separate assault teams
of SEALs, of British SAS and SBS, of German GSG9 troopers
all work smoothly together and coordinate their separate
attacks without either giving away the show by jumping the
gun or confusing an already confused situation by blundering
into each other's fire zones?

And most vitally important of all, where was the PRR's
atomic bomb?

So vital was that last bit of intelligence that the entire
operation had a built-in hold. Lieutenant Murdock and the
others were supposed to be looking for the thing, starting at
2200 hours when the tangos would be busy watching the
handover of Miss North Korea. Murdock had a satellite uplink;
what he put out over the tactical net would be heard by
everyone in the assault team. If Murdock could learn the
whereabouts of the bomb, all of the teams involved had several
alternate and fallback plans to cover various possibilities. The
code phrase "snapping turtle" meant to concentrate everything
on the freighter, that someone had picked up hard intel that the
A-bomb was there. "King cobra" meant the tanker, *Noramo
Pride*. "Copperhead" meant that the attack would go as
planned—but immediately, whether or not everyone was in
place and ready to go. "Copperhead" would be invoked if one
of the OICs on the site—meaning Murdock or Croft on
Bouddica, or DeWitt aboard the tanker—discovered the bomb
and thought that the assault's best chance would come from a
quick rush *now*, rather than waiting for the 2230-hour deadline.

The reptilian code word that no one wanted to think about,

however, was "crocodile," transmitted by Murdock or one of his SEALs. Crocodile meant that the SEALs had discovered something about the bomb that made assaulting the platform too damned risky, something like a tango with a dead-man switch, or the bomb placed where it couldn't be reached and disarmed.

Lieutenant Murdock literally had it in his power to call off this whole damned show, even after things had already started going down.

It was not the sort of responsibility that DeWitt envied in anyone.

1930 hours GMT
OP Eyrie
Bouddica Bravo

"Say . . . L-T?" MacKenzie had returned to his lookout and was peering once more through his binoculars. He had them focused on the freighter, riding on her mooring several hundred yards off the platform's east face. "Something happening here. I'm not sure, but this sure as hell could be it."

Sliding down alongside MacKenzie, Murdock accepted the binoculars from the big Texan.

Murdock too had been thinking hard about the responsibility that had been assigned to him that afternoon. It was, he thought, a typical dodge pulled by the spineless bureaucratic types who so often screwed up a slick, simple mission with impossible add-on requirements—this "crocodile" abort code he'd been given, or worse, the code word "copperhead" that literally meant *charge!*

Of all the pencil-necked fucking stupidities. Giving that kind of power to a junior officer in an advance OP was begging for trouble. An inexperienced man might panic or chicken out; an overeager one, or one just burned out by combat, could ignore the danger and blunder full ahead . . . right into a nuclear disaster. It would have made a hell of a lot more sense if the powers-that-were had simply worked up their plan, relied on the SEAL intel to find the bomb or not and *then* deploy, based on what they'd learned.

Possibly, the brass in both Washington and London had

decided there simply wasn't enough time, that gathering the intel and launching the raid both had to be carried out almost simultaneously. But Murdock didn't like it, not one small bit.

He tried to push the doubts aside as he concentrated on focusing the binoculars on what Mac was pointing out.

"They're bringing the *Rosa* in close again," he said.

"That's sure what it looks like to me, Skipper."

Murdock glanced back over his shoulder. Sterling and Roselli were both out cold, taking their turns at catching some sleep, stretched out on the steel deck with their rucksacks as pillows. He wouldn't wake them yet . . . but this could be what they'd been waiting for. He could see tangos on the trawler's deck, some of them holding coils of line as though they expected to tie up alongside Bouddica Alpha.

Even more significantly, someone was moving one of the cranes mounted on Alpha's superstructure, swinging it around until its arm was out over the water.

As though they were getting ready to unload something heavy from the ship's hold.

"What's your guess, Mac?" Murdock said softly. He handed the binoculars back to the other SEAL.

"About what, L-T?"

"Where's the damned bomb?"

"Well," MacKenzie said, drawling the word with an exaggerated Texas accent. "It would have to be in the trawler, in the tanker, or it's already on the platform somewhere, hauled in on that helicopter. I don't see any other option. But our satellites would have spotted an unloading operation out of the trawler, for instance, even if they did it at night or under the cloud cover. Right?"

Murdock nodded. "Right so far."

"But to get it onto the tanker, they'd have had to pull a transfer at sea. That's a tricky maneuver, even for experienced hands, and I doubt that these guys have that kind of experience. The sea's been rough the last couple of days, too. Seems risky, for something as heavy as an A-bomb.

"And I don't think they'd use the helo either. They'd need all the payload for troops for their first assault. And in dirty weather like we've been having, well, I just can't see them trusting an atomic bomb, maybe a one-of-a-kind and very expensive bomb, to the possibility of a crash at sea, or something going wrong when they land their troops. So if it was up to me, I'd have to guess the thing was still on the *Rosa*."

"Right. Just what I was thinking. Only now they're moving the trawler in close to the platform again, and it looks to me like they're readying the crane. What do you want to bet they're making the transfer now?"

"Why'd they wait so long? They've been here two days."

Murdock shook his head. "Hard to say." Then he reconsidered. "No . . . maybe it's not so hard to read after all. By now, they've gotten word that the *Horizon* is coming back with the Korean woman on board. These people aren't stupid. They have to assume at least the possibility that we're going to try something when the *Horizon* gets here."

MacKenzie grinned. "We are."

"Sure, but they don't know one way or the other. If they suspect the Special Boat Service people are out, hell, if they know the SEALs are in town, they're going to be worried about combat swimmers hitting the ships. Up until now, it was safer to keep us guessing about the bomb, maybe keep it squirreled away on the *Rosa*, out of sight belowdecks. Now they figure it'll be safer on the platform, easier to defend, at least from frogmen."

"Sounds logical. What can we do about it?"

"Depends on what they do with the bomb. I'm still wondering about that Korean submarine. If they mean to use it to plant the bomb, they might put it down right alongside, on the *Celtic Maiden*."

"That would be a little *too* easy, don't you think?" MacKenzie said.

Murdock smiled. "Hey, we can dream, can't we?"

"Only if we pull a reality check once in a while. Why would they move the thing out of the trawler, which they think is vulnerable to SEALie types, only to plant it on the afterdeck of a tug three feet from the water?"

"Okay, okay, so they've got something else in mind. What?"

"Damfino, L-T. But if we watch, maybe we'll find out."

During the course of the next half hour, the *Rosa* was moved in close beside Bouddica Alpha and the moored *Celtic Maiden* and was lashed in place, her bow almost thrust beneath the bridge between the platforms. That gave Murdock and MacKenzie—and Sterling and Roselli when they woke up a short time later—virtually a bird's-eye view of the whole operation. The crane was carefully positioned, the hook lowered into the *Rosa's* open forward hold. There was a long and breathless pause . . . and then the slack was taken up and something was hoisted slowly clear of the trawler.

"Do you think that's it?" Sterling asked, taking his turn at the binoculars.

"It's about the right size," MacKenzie pointed out. "And it looks heavy enough. I'd bet on it."

"I'll give it a sixty percent chance," Murdock said, taking the binoculars from Sterling and studying the object suspended on the end of the crane's hoist.

"Sixty? Why so low?"

"Hmm. If you were hiding an A-bomb and were expecting a boatload or two of commandos to show up, where would you hide the thing?"

"I don't follow you, sir."

"I didn't make it clear. You said earlier that it would be too easy if they put the bomb on the deck of the *Maiden,* where we could get at it."

"Sure."

"Suppose they put something there that we might *think* was the bomb, while the real one was still stashed away someplace else?"

MacKenzie looked stricken. "Oh . . . shit . . ." Murdock handed him the binoculars and he took his turn, studying the ungainly cylinder as it swayed gently in the stiff, westerly breeze. "Then that could be a dummy. Something to distract us, just in case of an attack. We go after it, and they've got the bomb safely down in the *Rosa's* hold."

"Something like that. We're going to have to check it out, if we can. The problem is, if the attack begins at 2230, we're not going to have much time to work with. Not much time after it gets dark, anyway."

"At least," Roselli pointed out, "we've got a target now."

"Skipper?" MacKenzie said, peering through the binoculars. "Maybe you should have a look at this."

A partly enclosed metal stairway had been swung out from the bridge between the platforms and one end lowered to the fishing boat's deck. A number of people were leaving the ship now, making their way one after the other up the ladder toward the catwalk encircling Bouddica Alpha's crew quarters module. From just over three hundred feet away, the powerful 7x75 binoculars clearly revealed the faces of the people as they lined up by the ladder.

Five rough-looking, armed men, all terrorists by the look of them. At his side, Murdock heard the tiny click of the digital camera, as Sterling started collecting another string of tango mug shots for Washington.

A sixth man whom Murdock had seen before: the Korean special forces agent and nuclear expert, Pak Chong Yong, looking cold and impassive.

And a female hostage. The front of her blouse was torn and she was barefoot. Her business-suit skirt seemed wildly inappropriate in this marine setting. They had to help her stand; she seemed to be having trouble standing upright on the trawler's slightly rolling deck.

Murdock recognized her instantly with an anguished pang that very nearly drew a moan from his lips.

Inge . . .

2004 hours GMT
Docking area
Bouddica Alpha

"Easy, Fräulein. Watch your step."

Inge blinked into unaccustomed bright light, trying to get her bearings. There'd been no porthole in the tiny cabin aboard the fishing boat where she'd been a prisoner for the past several days, and no light save that from a single small overhead fixture. Using the meals they'd brought to her as a rough measure of time, she was pretty sure this was the fourth day since her kidnapping, but suddenly being dragged out under so much open sky was disorienting.

The deck pitched heavily beneath her bare feet, nearly throwing her off balance. She'd never cared much for sea passages, especially rough ones, and in the terror of the moment, she'd not been able to eat much. She felt weak and sick.

Worse, though, was the *not knowing*. Not knowing what these people wanted with her. Not knowing where she was being taken. Not knowing what was going to happen to her the next time she heard the rattle of keys at her cabin door.

Now, though, she suspected that she was going to find out what it was all about, and she already knew that she was not going to like the answers to her questions.

When she'd seen the skeletal thrust of the oil platforms looming far overhead, she'd immediately recognized where she was: the names BOUDDICA ALPHA and BOUDDICA BRAVO were printed in one-meter type on signs affixed to the sides of the platforms, and she knew the BGA logo, a winged oil derrick on a globe, printed above each.

Why, *why* had they brought her here? It made no sense.

The only ones paying much attention to her at the moment, she realized, were the two men who'd come to drag her from the cabin a few moments ago. There were a number of heavily armed terrorists on the trawler's deck, but their full attention at the moment was riveted on the gray, metallic cylinder that was being swayed on a derrick up out of the trawler's forward hold. One man she recognized . . . an Oriental-looking man in civilian clothing and a heavy leather jacket, appeared to be in charge. The North Korean, Pak.

"Careful with that!" the man shouted in English. "Don't bump it against the side!"

A bomb? It hardly mattered. She was more interested in the fact that so much attention was being focused on the trawler's cargo. Possibly . . . possibly . . . there was a chance here for her to escape. Inge knew her chances of survival for more than a few minutes in the cold water of the North Sea weren't good, but the oil-production platform offered hope. The thing was enormous, the size of a small city. The terrorists couldn't have men enough to search the whole damned thing.

If she could find a hiding place . . . and a way to communicate with the outside world . . .

Desperate hopes, clutching at straws, at fantasies. But Inge was not the sort to simply allow herself to be herded from place to place, helpless. Her captors shoved her along, away from the unloading operations, guiding her toward a metal gangway hung over the trawler's side. One of them, the one they called "Johann," went first. The second urged her forward with the barrel of his gun.

Feigning submission, she stumbled down the ladder, then stumbled again on the smooth, hard steel of the temporary floating dock below. Johann reached out to steady her. . . .

Her snap kick caught him in the knee, dropping him to the deck and eliciting a yelp of pain. She dashed past him as he crumpled, sprinting for the long, narrow ladder leading up the side of the platform called Bouddica Alpha.

Two steps up, a powerful hand snagged her left ankle and yanked her leg out from under her. She fell heavily, bruisingly against the steps, and as she started to struggle up on trembling arms, the butt of an assault rifle cracked the back of her head.

She tumbled back to the deck, head throbbing, as Johann leaned close, his leer blotting out the sky. "You'll be sorry for that, *Fotze!*" The word he'd called her was sexually graphic, a foul vulgarity reducing her from a person to a *thing* to be used more completely than anything done to her in her captivity so far. She spat in Johann's face.

"Scheisse!" he howled. *"Dirne!"*

She tensed and squeezed her eyes shut as he raised his fist. . . .

2006 hours GMT
OP Eyrie
Bouddica Bravo

Murdock bit off a savage obscenity as he watched the drama come to a close on the floating temporary dock four hundred feet away. One of the gunmen, the one she'd kicked, struck Inge twice with his fist before the second man pulled him off of her. Together then, they lifted her between them and half walked, half dragged her up the steps.

God! Why had they brought her here? Presumably they'd been holding her aboard the trawler until they felt it was safe to move her across. Or maybe they were simply getting her beyond the reach of any possible naval commando attack. He followed her through the binoculars as two of the tangos forced her up that long, long, steel-rung stairway.

A few hours ago, he'd been willing to accept the judgment of some military planner in the Pentagon about whether or not to launch an assault in the middle of hostage negotiations. Now he was watching one of those hostages climb that ladder, a woman he knew.

A woman, he realized with a small, almost guilty start, whom he cared for very much. The guilt, he thought, arose from the fact that he shouldn't allow personal considerations to intrude at this point.

But intrude they did. There was no escaping them.

"We're going over there to get her, Mac," he said quietly. "Before the show goes down."

"Yeah, I thought you might want to do that," MacKenzie replied. "You sure it's a good idea?"

Mac's words were level, calm, and unhurried, not questioning Murdock's reasoning so much as . . . forcing him to examine it.

"I know what's percolating through that thick skull of yours, Mac," he said. "It's not what you think."

"No?"

"They've been holding her aboard that trawler. With that . . . thing that looks like it could be a bomb. If we can get her to tell us what she saw down there . . ."

"She *could* help nail it down for us, L-T," MacKenzie said, taking the binoculars back from Murdock and focusing them on the trawler's deck. The bomb—if that was what it was— was hanging out over the water now, as the crane operator slowly reeled it higher. "Well, we were going to have to talk to some people over there anyway. Wonder what they're having for dinner in the mess hall?"

Murdock rolled on his side, drawing his Hush Puppy and

checking the action. "How about nine-mike-mike parabellum?" he asked.

"*Cordon* blam," Roselli said, grinning.

"Yeah," Johnson added. "Shot cuisine. I like it."

They would have to move before it got fully dark.

21

Friday, May 4

It was still light. Sunset this day, in this part of the North Sea, had been at 2136 hours, and the sky was still suffused with a deep, royal blue light. The moon, which would be just past full tonight, had not yet risen.

Murdock, MacKenzie, and Roselli were making their way across the bridge between Bouddica Bravo and Bouddica Alpha, sticking to the shadows among the bundles of oil and gas pipelines, and avoiding the narrow, partly enclosed catwalk stretched along the top of the span. Ahead of them, the south side of Alpha's crew habitat module rose like a white cliff before and above them; a series of railed ladders and catwalks zigzagged up the otherwise blank, white-painted wall like a fire escape. At the highest level, a full one hundred feet above the water, a lone terrorist guard paced the fifth-level walkway, his submachine gun slung over his shoulder. Forty feet below the bridge, two more guards maintained watch on the stern of the *Celtic Maiden*. The unloading operations taking place aboard the *Rosa* had been completed, at least. The trawler had maneuvered clear of the platform, and the bomb—or whatever it was—hung suspended above the water now, twisting slowly back and forth with the wind about fifty feet above the water, and in plain view of all of the guards.

It was an interesting tactical problem. The SEALs would have no trouble reaching Alpha unobserved. The tangle of pipelines and railings offered plenty of cover for their stealthy crossing. But once they started climbing that fire escape, they would be in plain view of the guard at the top, of the two on the *Maiden,* and of the two terrorists positioned behind them, on the east side of Bouddica Bravo. There was no way to approach the object suspended beneath the crane at all, not without getting at the crane controls on the upper deck and physically bringing the thing aboard the platform.

There were two possible approaches, once the SEALs reached Alpha. The sneaky-Pete approach would be to move around to the left, vanishing into the forest of tanks, pipelines, and processing machinery that made up the western side of Bouddica Alpha. There were stairways and ladders back there that would get them up to the fifth level and the platforms operations center.

But Murdock was favoring a more open approach.

No matter how stealthy they were, there was always the possibility that by sheer bad luck and the malign intervention of the god Murphy, someone would see them sneaky-Peting their way through the refinery area. But what if they walked up that outside ladder in full view?

The SEALs had shed their dry suits and were wearing the ordinary combat blacks they'd had on beneath the bulky neoprene garments. Over that they wore combat harnesses very similar to the load-bearing vests worn by most of the terrorists. On their heads, they wore black wool watchcaps, again much like the headgear worn by a number of the tangos. Seen in poor light, glimpsed for a second or two, any one of the SEALs would simply be one more man in black among many. Weapons might present a problem; many of the terrorists carried H&K MP5 submachine guns, while the SEALs carried MP5SD3s, the sound-suppressed version of the same weapon, with heavy, cylindrical muzzles as thick as a man's arm.

Still, some of the tangos had been seen on the platform with other weapons, Uzis and even American-made M-16s, and in poor light, the SD3s weren't that dissimilar from the weapons carried by the bad guys. People tended to see what they thought they *ought* to see, so the silenced subguns probably wouldn't attract any attention. Anyone who caught sight of the SEALs as they walked around on the platform superstructure would assume that they were comrades. All they needed to do was walk in as though they owned the place, instead of sneaking around like commandos.

No problem. It was all part of the SEAL knack of blending into their environment.

And Murdock was about to put that knack to a brutal test.

Once they reached the upper levels of the platform, Mac-Kenzie would take out the radar, while Murdock and Roselli tried to find an isolated tango to question. A quick-and-dirty interrogation or two was the only way Murdock could think of to verify that the object suspended from the crane was, in fact, the terrorist bomb. With luck, and the appropriate threats, they could even find out how it was fused, and whether or not there were booby traps on the thing.

Whatever they learned would have to go out over the satellite net; Johnson and Sterling would handle that . . . as well as keep an eye on the terrorist sentry post on Bouddica Bravo.

Then, when all the rest was complete, Murdock was determined to find Inge Schmidt, somewhere within that imposing fortress towering above him.

And they had to pull it all down by 2230 hours—forty-five, no, make that forty-four minutes from now—when the joint British, American, and German assault went down.

Movement caught Murdock's attention, high overhead, on the fourth-floor level of the living quarters. He froze in place, raising one warning hand to stop Roselli and Mac behind him. His breath caught in his throat. Two men were walking around the corner from the west side of the building, and between them was a woman, blindfolded and handcuffed.

It was hard to tell at this distance and at this angle, but Murdock was certain from the skirt, the blouse, and the matted blond hair that it was Inge once again. The group was only in sight for a moment or two. Murdock watched in helpless fury as the men led the woman up the outside ladder from the fourth level to the fifth, then ushered her through a door off the top-level catwalk after exchanging an inaudible comment or two with the guard there.

Swiftly, Murdock plotted the movement against the mental map he carried of the complex. That brief glimpse of Inge had been a damned lucky break; three SEALs could have spent hours searching the labyrinth of rooms and passageways that was the living quarters for the platform personnel before finding her. Even now, all he knew was that she was still alive—for the moment, at least—and being held somewhere on the structure's top deck.

The rest of the mission—verifying the position of the bomb, taking out the radar, gathering other intel and getting it to the assault force—would have to come first.

But when all of that was done . . .

2148 hours GMT
Room 512, Deck 5
Bouddica Alpha

In all that time since they'd picked her up on the street outside her Rüsselsheim apartment, they'd not asked her a single question, told her they were demanding ransom, or even threatened her directly with death, and her capture was beginning to seem more and more senseless, a random, brutal, and arbitrary interruption of her normally orderly life.

After dragging her off the trawler, they'd taken her first to a large recreation area somewhere deep within the facility's third level, tossing her in with a large number of hungry, dirty, miserable, and thoroughly frightened BGA employees. Less than an hour later, however, her captors had returned for her, leading her away to a tiny cabin on the fourth level and locking her in. Two men had come to her new prison at dinnertime, but instead of bringing food, they'd handcuffed her as they had in the van, then blindfolded her and led her step by step with rough hands gripping her arms. They'd walked a long way . . . down an echoing, empty passageway, turning right, then left again. For a short time, they'd been outside. Despite the blindfold, Inge could sense the difference in the light, could taste and smell the salt in the air, could feel the cold bite of the wind on her bare skin. They'd gone up a steeply climbing ladder, with her captors tightly holding her arms to keep her from falling. Up one level, and then they'd gone inside again, down another corridor, and finally into what she'd sensed was a small room.

Roughly, they'd removed her handcuffs, forced her down into a straight-backed chair, then shackled her wrists once more behind her, pinning her in the seat.

She waited for what seemed like hours, though in fact it was probably only a minute or two. Then she heard the door open to her right, heard footsteps, felt the movement of air as someone leaned over her.

"Good evening, Fräulein," a man's voice said, speaking German with the precise fluency of a native. From the trace of an accent, she guessed that he was from eastern Germany somewhere. "How is your head?"

She didn't answer, but she listened with a fierce concentration to the voice, to his movements, to the sense of his presence, somewhere to her left.

"From what I've been told," the voice said, "you crippled one of my men back in Rüsselsheim. And this afternoon you just missed crippling Johann. He was upset about that."

"I wish I'd killed him," she said through clenched teeth.

"Yes, I'm sure that's true. That, incidentally, is the reason for the handcuffs. I would prefer that you keep those pretty hands to yourself for the time being. And if you attempt to kick me or one of my people now, we will have to tie your feet as well. I think it better if we can have a more dignified discussion, yes?"

Dignified, with her helpless and blindfolded? The irony nearly brought a wild laugh from her throat. She was, she realized with a new stab of fear, frighteningly close to the thin, ragged edge of hysteria.

"In any case, I wish to discuss with you your meetings with some Americans last week."

"Go to hell."

"Now, now. Dignified, Fräulein. Remember?

"You are Fräulein Inge Schmidt," the voice went on after a moment, speaking as though reading from a file. "A civilian employee, level ten, of the Bundeskriminant. You initially began training with the GSG9, but failed your preliminary physical evaluation. You are currently assigned to the BKA's data-processing division and work as liaison between the GSG9 and other law enforcement agencies and the computer network known as Komissar. You see, Fräulein, we know all about you. We want you to describe your contacts with the Americans."

"If you know so much about me, you can describe them yourself."

The man sighed. "I really would like some answers, Fräulein. You were seen in the company of American Navy SEALs. We want to know what they were doing in Wiesbaden, and we want to know precisely what you told them."

"Fuck yourself," Inge told him, turning her head toward the sound of that hateful voice.

"Hardly necessary, my dear," the voice said reasonably. She felt something—fingers?—brush her cheek and flinched. "Not when you are available, eh?"

"Rather cheap melodramatics, threatening me with rape," she said. She forced a bitter laugh but the threat shook her nonetheless. She already felt used, violated. She hoped her captors couldn't tell from her voice what she was feeling . . . or sense her dread of what might happen next. She thought, from the feel of it, that her blouse, torn by that bastard in the van, must be hanging open, and wished she could close it up now.

"Rape would be only the least of it, I assure you. Fräulein Schmidt, I have thirty-nine men here on board this facility and aboard the various ships in my little fleet, and after each of them has sated himself with you, loosened you up for me, so to speak, they will bring you back to me. And then the *real* interrogation will begin." And then in stark and utterly clinical detail, her interrogator began describing what he would do to her, what he had done to other women he'd had to question in the past, and what had happened to them along the way. Things involving electricity . . . or scalpels . . . or ropes slowly and relentlessly tightened with twist after twist to an iron bar. Things that would leave her helplessly broken, she knew that, knew with desperate, despairing certainty that she could never stand that kind of pain. Despite herself, she was trembling now, and beads of sweat were trickling down her face beneath the blindfold.

"And, in the end, my dear, you will *tell* me exactly what I want to know. You'll beg to tell me things I haven't even asked, just to make the hurting stop." She could hear him smiling, and she couldn't stop the trembling. "They always do."

"Who was your teacher," she snapped. "Mengele?"

But the small bravado left her feeling very small, and very empty.

"I think a demonstration," she heard him say. Hands fumbled with the front of her blouse, then with her bra, rolling it up above her breasts. "Ah. Lovely. Johann? The electrodes, please."

"No—" Then she clamped her mouth shut. *I won't beg,* she thought with a fierce and desperate defiance. *I won't beg.* She started to twist against the handcuffs, and hard hands from behind grabbed her shoulders, holding her motionless in her seat.

"Even a few volts of electricity applied to a tender part of the body can be excruciatingly painful," the voice said casually, as if discussing the weather. "I think we'll start . . . here." And something bit her left earlobe, the sharp tiny pain in a completely unexpected place startling her so badly she jumped despite the hands holding her and nearly upset the chair. "And here." Something clamped on her right ear. "We should remove the earrings too, I think, Johann. So we have better contact. There. That is better."

She was shaking so hard now she could scarcely sit upright in the chair. It felt like they'd attached alligator clips to both ear lobes; she could feel the wires lying across her shoulders.

"Now, Fräulein. Would you like to tell me about your American SEAL friends?"

"Bastard! Go to hell!"

The pain exploded in her head like a thunderbolt.

2157 hours GMT
The bridge
Bouddica Alpha

Murdock heard Inge scream, faint, far-off and muffled by walls and distance . . . but unmistakably a scream.

Damn those fucking bastards!

But he held himself in check, forcing a cold and calculating deadliness to replace that first hot surge of fury that threatened to drown rational thought in a combat frenzy. *No . . . take it easy. We're going to do this right. . . .*

The SEALs were more than halfway up the zigzagging ladder on the south wall of the crew's quarters. It had taken them nearly all of the past ten minutes to work their way invisibly across the rest of the bridge and clamber onto the catwalk running around the outside of the crews' quarters' first deck. The scream had been very faint, almost lost in the rush of the wind, but the sound had been enough to chill him far more than the cold bite of the North Sea.

"Easy, L-T," MacKenzie said from just behind Murdock on the ladder. "Don't let the bastards—"

"Don't worry, Mac," he said, his voice sharper and colder than the stiff breeze plucking at his combat vest. "Whatever they do to her, they're gonna pay for it in blood."

"Roger that."

They kept climbing, their weapons casually slung over their backs, with no evident response from the sentry overhead or from the other platform off to the south.

Those two men on Bravo worried Murdock more than the lone guard. Murdock couldn't see them, though he knew precisely where they were. Sterling and Johnson were keeping an eye on them while the other three SEALs penetrated Alpha, and would take them down if they seemed to notice anything amiss across the way on Alpha. The problem was that while Murdock trusted Jaybird's and Skeeter's judgment, the moment they took out the two sentries the clock would be running. It would be possible to explain the disappearance of one guard, if they had to take him down, as an isolated accident.

The disappearance of three, at two different locations, would tip off the enemy that they were under assault, just as soon as they realized the three were missing.

The risk—to the SEALs, the hostages, to the whole operation—was appalling, but all Murdock could do was play out the hand.

He kept climbing.

2157 hours GMT
Room 512, Deck 5
Bouddica Alpha

The telephone rang, a jarring, explosive sound, and Adler looked up from the shaking, whimpering girl, irritated. Now what? He'd told Karl he was not to be disturbed. Walking over to the small desk, he picked up the receiver and stabbed the internal call button with its blinking light. "What is it?"

"Sorry to interrupt you, Herr Adler," Karl Strauss's unpleasantly nasal voice said on the other end of the line. "But that workboat is coming back. They say, they say that the Korean woman is on board. We've won, Heinrich!"

"No, we haven't," Adler replied. "Not yet." But it was an important first step, and Adler felt a thrill of excitement. It was happening! Just as Pak had assured him it would! "Very well," he said. "I will be up immediately."

Hanging up the receiver, he turned, then walked back to the girl. She was slumped in the chair now, no longer struggling, no longer whimpering. Her earlobes were fiery red where they'd been burned, the skin already blistering. When he lifted her chin with one hand and pulled off the blindfold, her eyes stared past him, glazed and unfocused. "Are you ready to tell us what we need to know yet, my dear?"

There was no answer, not even a groan. It was possible, he thought, that he'd pushed her too hard, too fast. Carefully, he pried one eyelid open wider, checking the dilation of the pupil. Then he checked the other. Was she going into shock? Both pupils were the same size.

"I must go up to Ops," he told Johann, who was standing next to the table with the car battery and switch. He removed the alligator clips from her ears, then handed them across to the other man. "Take her back to her room and watch her. I don't want her to hurt herself."

Johann smiled. "What if I hurt her instead, Herr Adler? I could continue the interrogation, you know."

Adler reached down and pressed his fingers against the woman's throat, probing for a pulse. There it was . . . strong and pounding, not the weak and thready flutter of someone deep in shock. It was possible that she was faking it, trying to avoid more pain, but Adler couldn't be sure.

Adler was drawing on years of highly specialized training with the old East German Stasi. All of his earlier statements—the threat of gang rape, the threats of slow torture with knife or flame or rope—had been made as part of a deliberate campaign to elicit an emotional response. He was looking for a handle on this woman. He needed to break her, and quickly, because he was certain that the enemy wouldn't capitulate to the PRR's demands without at least the attempt to board the platform.

He suspected that she knew something about the American SEALs and their interest in the PRR, and he was determined to find out what it was. Unfortunately, they were running out of time. If the enemy was going to try something, their plan, their deployment must already be in motion, and though something so obvious was unlikely, it was still distinctly possible that an assault had been timed to correspond with the arrival of the workboat bearing Major Pak's comrade. It was for that reason that he'd given the order to go ahead and remove the bomb from the *Rosa*. It had been Pak's suggestion that they suspend it high in the air above the water where no one could reach it unobserved.

"Go ahead, Johann," he said, still probing. "Have fun. Just don't damage her too seriously, at least not until I have a chance to get my answers."

He was watching her eyes carefully as he said the words, watching for a reaction. Had her nostrils flared slightly? Hard to tell. Perhaps she really was in shock . . . or simply in a deep, psychological withdrawal. He snorted. Obviously, the girl was psychologically soft, with no tolerance for pain at all. Breaking her would not take long.

But first, he had to see to Chun's arrival . . . and to make certain his men were ready, just in case this was a diversion of some sort for an assault. "Do what you want with her," he said, reaching for the door.

Johann grinned unpleasantly. "It will be my very great pleasure, Herr Adler."

Adler had known Johann Schneider since the two of them

had worked together in the Stasi. He never had liked the man.

He enjoyed his work too much, and that could make a man get sloppy.

2159 hours GMT
External catwalk 1, level 5
Bouddica Alpha

Clomping noisily up the last few rungs of the ladder, Murdock mounted the top catwalk and turned to face the guard. The man was leaning against the walkway railing, casually lighting a cigarette . . . despite the prominent NO SMOKING sign posted on the wall nearby.

Idiot. The terrorists were as likely to destroy Bouddica through stupidity or carelessness as they were by triggering their bomb.

Murdock suspected—judging from the mix of Irish Provo and German RAF terrorists so far identified—that not all of them knew one another that well. In fact, he was counting on that. As he walked toward the guard, the man flicked the glowing tip from his cigarette, glanced incuriously over his shoulder directly at Murdock and the other SEALs, then looked away again.

Silently, Murdock and MacKenzie exchanged hand signals, and then Mac turned and vanished down the catwalk around the building's southwest corner. He would take out Bouddica's radar facilities while Roselli and Murdock looked for intel.

Murdock stopped at the door through which they'd taken Inge a few minutes ago. He glanced in through the small, square window; the door opened into a small foyer with another door beyond, with no one visible inside. He tried the knob; it opened. Keeping a cautious eye on the guard's back, he held the door open for Razor, who casually walked through and into the foyer beyond.

As Roselli pushed open the inner door, however, Inge—it was unmistakably Inge, and much closer now—screamed again, a raw-throated wail that could only have been wrenched from her by some terrible pain. The guard turned at the sound, and from three yards away, his hard, pale blue eyes locked with Murdock's.

A half-smile played at the man's lips, *"Laute Tussi,"* he said. Murdock's few words of German weren't up to translating, but it didn't sound pleasant.

But translation was the last thing Murdock had to worry about. Almost as he said the words, the German terrorist's eyes narrowed suddenly, and the half-smile vanished. Murdock could read the realization in those eyes that the man standing before him was a stranger. Widening, the eyes dropped to Murdock's load-bearing vest . . . the radio strapped to his left shoulder . . . the Kevlar pouch bulging with flash bangs on his right hip . . . the thousand other tiny details of equipment and manufacture that separated the SEAL from the terrorist . . .

. . . and the man was already pulling his submachine gun up to the firing position. . . .

22

Friday, May 4

The tango guard was still fumbling with his slung weapon, his mouth opening to give a shout of warning, when Murdock took a half-step forward, then slammed the stiffened knuckles of his right hand squarely into the man's Adam's apple. With a tiny crunch, the guard's trachea collapsed, and the shout turned into a fish-like gasping for air, the lit cigarette popping from the mouth and sailing away with the wind. Murdock's follow-through brought his elbow snapping back into his temple. The guard sagged and Murdock caught him; a step and a shift of balance, and the terrorist went backward over the railing, falling silently one hundred feet into the dark gray water below.

"No smoking!" Murdock called softly after him. The sound of the splash was lost in the wind, but an instant later, someone yelled from far below, on the after deck of the *Celtic Maiden*, "Man overboard! Man overboard!"

"Achtung!" another voice cried from four levels below. *"Mann über Bord!"*

Murdock glanced around. No one else in sight. He ducked through the door. With a bit of luck, the guard's fall could be attributed to an accident.

But the SEALs couldn't ride on luck alone for long.

2159 hours GMT
2nd deck, east side
Bouddica Bravo

The two guards stationed on Bouddica Bravo had not been paying any particular attention to the three black shapes making their way up the outside of the other platform to the north. In fact, for the past hour their chief concern seemed to be simply to stay warm, so they'd been hunkered down out of the wind, sharing cigarettes and what looked like a bottle of Jack Daniels.

Smoking . . . on an oil platform. Watching from his hiding place among the pipes and fittings twenty feet away, Johnson had been wondering if he should suggest shooting those guys simply to keep them from blowing the facility sky high with a lit match—never mind their nuke—but the gunfire posed as much risk or more. Better to let them go . . .

. . . until, at just exactly the wrong moment, one of them stood up, stretched prodigiously, and glanced across the open gulf toward Bouddica Alpha just in time to see one black-clad figure tip another over the railing on the fifth-level catwalk.

"Hey, Georgie," the man said with a thick, Irish lilt, reaching down and shaking his partner's shoulder. "We got us a problem!"

Georgie was already reaching for the walkie-talkie, which rested on a coiled length of cable nearby.

Johnson locked eyes with Sterling, who was in a second hiding place a few feet to the left, and exchanged nods. Together, as though run by the same computer program, they raised their S&W Hush Puppies, Johnson drawing down on the man on the right, while Sterling aimed at the one on the left. Sterling called the time, a whispered countdown so soft it was more felt than heard. "And *three* and *two* and *one* . . ."

Both Hush Puppies spoke simultaneously, their muzzle flashes and the crack of the shots alike swallowed by the heavy muzzles of the sound suppressors. The reports were two closely paired triplets of shots, the thump of each report louder than the hiss of silenced pistols in movies, but still too soft to be heard more than a few meters away, especially above the rush of wind and waves. Johnson's man was just picking up the radio when the first 9mm round slammed through the side of his head. He was probably dead before the second and third shots tore out his throat . . . or before the radio smashed loudly on the deck. Sterling's man was just turning toward the SEALs—he might have seen something moving in the shadows—and then his face puckered with a savage impact, followed swiftly by two more.

The bodies crumpled into black piles, as spent brass clinked and bounced on the steel deck. "Two up," Johnson said over his radio. "Two down." With hand signals, he directed Sterling to collect the tangos' weapons. No sense in leaving them for the enemy . . . or in wasting precious 9mm ammunition.

They were going to need a lot of it damned soon now.

2200 hours GMT
Operations center
Bouddica Alpha

Heinrich Adler had just stepped into the operations center, where five PRR gunmen stood watch over two of the platform's personnel, an administrator named Dulaney and a female radio operator named Sally Kirk. The terrorists had been bringing facility personnel up two at a time for two-hour shifts, in order to run the radar and radio equipment, under close supervision, of course.

Karl Strauss met him at the door. "We've warned them to keep off," he said. "Just like last time. They're holding position two kilometers off to the east."

Major Pak was in ops as well. "They have Chun," the man said impassively. "I demanded to be allowed to speak with her."

"And?"

"It's her. She's there, on board the *Horizon*."

"Then we'd better have them bring her on over, hadn't we?" Adler said easily. "Put out the word. Everybody keep alert. This could very easily be a trick." A telephone buzzed, and one of the other PRR men picked it up. "I don't want anybody to be alone, do you understand? Everybody in pairs at all times."

"Herr Adler?" the man with the telephone called.

"What is it?"

"Trouble, sir. That was Kemper, on guard down by the minisub. One of our boys just fell overboard."

"Who?"

"Don't know yet. They're still fishing him out. But they say he's dead. Probably broke his neck in the fall."

"I want armed parties out, checking the catwalks and exterior platforms."

"I will tell them."

Pak's eyes narrowed. "I do not like this. It seems conveniently timed for an 'accident.'"

Adler glanced at the Korean. "I agree. The question is, do we let that anchor tug come close? Or not? Your call. You're the one who wants to get your friend back from the Brits."

Pak seemed to consider the question. "We do need her. Not to arm the bomb. I can handle that. But I would feel better about the success of this operation if we had her to handle the Squid."

"Doesn't seem to make that much of a difference, does it?" Strauss said, his voice betraying his nervousness. "I mean, if that thing goes off, we're all dead anyway, right? Does it really matter whether the explosion is up here on the surface or two hundred feet underwater? We're not going to care, that's for sure!"

"It matters insofar as whether or not we can inflict maximum damage on the enemy's facilities," Pak said. "An underwater burst will guarantee that the British, Germans, and Americans will never again be able to draw oil from the North Sea. The effects on their economies will be incalculable. A surface burst would not be nearly so effective."

Adler considered this. Originally, the North Korean–inspired plan had called for using the borrowed minisub to plant and arm the bomb deep within the tangle of struts, supports, and drilling pipe somewhere beneath Bouddica Bravo, the idea being that it would be almost impossible to find and disarm down there.

But Strauss had an excellent point. "The idea," Adler said carefully, "is for us not to have to detonate the bomb in the first place. I would much rather live. To see the PRR established as

a state. And to spend some small part of six billion dollars. So
far as the Americans and British are concerned, the threat to
their facilities is the same, whether the bomb is above water or
below. I think, given the likelihood of a ruse, we will be safe
warning them to stay away."

Pak blinked. "Perhaps you're right. However, I would still
like to bring Chun over here. If we are successful in this . . .
enterprise, there is no telling what they might do to her."

"They'll release her unharmed, Major. That's part of the
agreement, part of our demands."

"We could send the helicopter for her. It could hover, in clear
view of here, while she and she alone climbed aboard. If
nothing else, she might provide us with intelligence about what
it is the enemy is planning. Perhaps she saw enemy troops
aboard that boat."

Adler thought about that a moment longer, then nodded
sharply. "Very well. But only if we can keep that boat at least
two kilometers away. See to it, Karl."

"Ja wohl, Herr Adler."

The best way to frustrate any planned enemy assault was to
be unpredictable, to throw changes in troop dispositions and
patrol patterns and unexpected obstacles up at every possible
juncture. If there were troops aboard that workboat, they'd
have a damned hard time reaching Bouddica unobserved.

The change in plan might even flush their people into the
open.

He would welcome that. Heinrich Adler was a patient man,
but he much preferred facing an enemy in the open, one to one,
without all of this sneaking and maneuvering.

And very soon now, the issue would be resolved, one way or
another.

2201 hours GMT
Room 512, Deck 5
Bouddica Alpha

"I think we should get those clothes off of you, Fräulein, and
make you more comfortable." The man's voice was oily with
black promise. "Let me help you."

Inge felt the man fumbling behind her back with the keys to her handcuffs, freeing her wrists. It was all she could do to keep from shaking, to keep her body as limp and as lifeless as a pile of rags. The bastard had sent that last jolt of electricity through her nipples, and the scream that it had elicited from her had destroyed any hope she'd had of convincing him that she was already unconscious or in shock. Still, she thought, if she stayed limp, if she faked a muscle spasm or twitch and seemed to have trouble standing—and at the moment she didn't think she'd have to work very hard to fake that—then she still might find the opening she was so desperately looking for.

The man had a pistol tucked into the back waistband of his trousers. She'd seen it there, as he'd moved back and forth between her chair and the table with the battery and the switch. If she could just get her hands on it . . .

The handcuffs came off. Her captor grabbed her by her right upper arm and hauled her to her feet. "On the desk, I think," he said as he steered her toward it. She took a step, stumbled in a headlong fall. . . .

"None of that, bitch!" He yanked her arm, hard, spinning her around to face him. She took that momentum and fed it, bringing her arm up, fingers clenched above her palm, hurling all of her weight and every ounce of strength she could muster in a blow that slammed the heel of her hand squarely into her captor's nose.

The strike jolted her clear to her shoulder; using her karate training, she'd instinctively focused the blow well behind the man's eyes, and her follow-through snapped his head back and brought an ugly splatter of blood from his ruined nose.

Perfectly timed and delivered, such a strike could kill, driving shards of cartilage into the brain. Inge had been rushed, however, and throwing the strike at an awkward angle. Johann wasn't killed; he didn't even let go of her arm, but he did go down, crumpling backward onto the floor with a strangled yelp, dragging Inge down on top of him.

For a horrible moment, the two of them thrashed about in an awkward tangle of limbs until Inge was able to connect a second time, hitting him in the nose again. Blood flecked the carpet, dark droplets sprayed as Johann twisted around. He was reaching for the gun, he had the gun and was pulling it out. Inge yelled, a wail of defiance and anger and hurt as she kept hammering at the man's battered face.

The gun clattered free, bouncing across the floor. Johann struck out, knocking Inge clear with a blow that set her head ringing, but she used the momentum, turning to fall into a roll, landing beside the gun and scooping it up.

Johann came to his knees at the same instant, rising, face bloodied, eyes staring, as Inge's fingers closed about the automatic pistol's butt, her thumb snapped off the safety, and her finger squeezed the trigger.

Had the terrorist not been carrying the weapon with a round already chambered—always a dangerous practice, Inge knew from her own weapons training with the BKA—she would have been dead, for her opponent was much stronger than she was and would have had no trouble at all taking the pistol away from her.

But instead there was a startling and ear-piercing bang and the pistol leaped in her clenched hands. Blood exploded from the terrorist's left shoulder, a bright flower that staggered him as he tried to get to his feet. Inge held tight and corrected her aim. The gun barked again, and the back of Johann's head exploded in a gory spray of pink and red. Adding injury to insult, the bullet had punched its way in through his mangled nose.

Inge rose to her feet, the pistol still trained on the sprawled corpse in front of her. She'd never killed a man before, and the shock, the sheer, numbing realization of what she'd just done was almost overwhelming.

But the gunshot would bring others, and she didn't want to be found here. Pausing only to tug her bra and blouse back into place—the fabric burned her where it dragged across the tenderness at the tips of her breasts, but she ignored that—she hurried to the door, opened it, and peered out.

An empty passageway. Which way to go? She'd been brought here from the left, so somewhere in that direction was the doorway going outside. A plan was forming, still maddeningly hazy in its details, of hiding herself in the refinery area behind the living quarters. It would take them a while to find her there. Adler had boasted of having thirty-nine men—thirty-*eight* now, she amended with grim joy—and he couldn't spare that many just to search for her. Perhaps she could find a way to signal the government forces that must have this platform surrounded by now.

But voices were sounding from the right. Men were coming this way, and at a dead run from the sound of it. Just a little way down the corridor to the right was the intersection with a cross passageway. Almost without thinking, she turned right, then stepped off to the side, out of the main corridor.

Almost immediately, two black-clad men raced by in the main corridor. "This way," one yelled in German as they passed her hiding place. "In here!" Neither saw her.

If they found Johann's body, however, there would be more men here almost at once, and they would search and search until they tracked her down. Coolly, she stepped back into the main passageway, glanced right to make sure no more were coming, then brought her pistol up, aiming at the backs of the two running men.

There is no fair *in combat,* Blake had told her a century or two ago. She opened fire just as they reached the door to the room where Johann's body was and started to turn the knob. Two shots . . . three . . . four . . . five . . . Again and again she squeezed the trigger, the gun thundering in the narrow corridor. One of the terrorists staggered back, slamming into the wall opposite the door. The other twisted around, staring into Inge's eyes with a horrible mix of surprise and pain, but he wasn't going down . . . he was still on his feet and he had his own weapon out now, a gleaming black submachine gun that was swinging up and around to aim at Inge's head.

Then his face was obliterated by a splash of blood, and he hit the floor on his back with a loud thump. A hand touched Inge's shoulder; still working on instinct, she let go of her pistol with the left hand, caught the wrist, threw her hip into her assailant and sent him spilling across her leg and onto the floor. He was wearing black military-looking garb like the others. She raised her pistol, centering it on his stunned expression. . . .

Another gloved hand reached past her from the right, dropping across the breech of her pistol just as she pulled the trigger. There was a dull snap as the gun's hammer closed on the glove, right where the webbing between thumb and forefinger would be. Another hand closed over her mouth. Struggling, she tried to bite it but couldn't penetrate the leather. She tried to fight, tried to throw him off, tried—

"Easy, Inge! Damn it! *Easy!* It's Blake!"

Blake! . . .

He released her mouth and she turned, looking up into his face. It was Blake! It was!

It took a blurred moment to sort out what had just happened, so fast had things taken place. She'd shot one of the terrorists, but the bullets hadn't penetrated the Kevlar armor the other was wearing; Blake had killed the man with a burst from his silenced submachine gun, while the other SEAL had grabbed her shoulder, probably to pull her out of the way. She'd thrown him and come *that* close to putting a bullet between the SEAL's eyes.

Except that Blake had been there, just in time.

"Oh Gott! How? . . ."

"Never mind. Are you all right?"

She felt like she was going to collapse right there on the floor if he let go of her arms, but jerkily she nodded. "I—I'm fine."

"We heard you scream."

"They . . . never mind. It's okay. I'm okay, really. My God, Blake . . . what are you doing here?" Then realization dawned. "It's a takedown?"

"The beginning of one. Our side needs intelligence. That's why we're here."

"One of them told me he had thirty-nine people here," Inge said. "On the platform and on what he called his fleet. With him, that's forty." She looked at the two bodies sprawled in the passageway. "I guess that makes thirty-seven."

"Well done, Inge! Heinrich Adler?"

"One of them called him Herr Adler, yes."

"Okay. Let's get the hell out of here." Murdock looked at the other SEAL. "Did she hurt you, Razor?"

"Lucky throw," the SEAL muttered, but he was grinning. "I like the lady's style, L-T."

"Me too."

"Razor? I nearly shot you. I'm sorry. . . ."

"Don't sweat it, ma'am. I'd only've gotten pissed off if you'd actually shot me. Y'know, L-T? I think we oughta make her an honorary SEAL."

"Maybe later. C'mon. Let's move out."

"Blake, wait!" she said. "What about the bodies? And there's another one in that room."

"Leave 'em," Murdock said. "By now, everybody on this platform has heard gunfire, and a check will show those men missing. If we leave the bodies, though, they might think that all they have to contend with is one very wild escaped prisoner . . . not a bunch of SEALs."

"SEALs always eat their kills," Razor explained quietly. "We're very neat and tidy that way."

Quickly, they led her down a side passageway, deeper into the platform's living quarters.

2205 hours GMT
Operations center
Bouddica Alpha

"Gunfire!" the frantic voice said over the telephone. "Gunfire on level five! Three men are down!"

"Where?" Adler snapped. But he knew what the answer would be.

"Room 512. Johann is dead—"

Shit! "The prisoner we brought over today from the *Rosa*. Is she still there?"

"*Nein*, Herr Adler. She is gone. There are just the bodies."

"Find her. Everyone on full alert!"

He slammed the receiver down. Was it possible that Schmidt had somehow gotten Johann's gun away from him, shot him, and then shot two more? He shook his head, rejecting the possibility. No, not her. He'd seen the weakness in her. It was much more likely that the enemy already had commandos aboard the facility.

And then his eyes widened. Perhaps even . . . American SEALs . . .

23

Friday, May 4

The quarters module roof
Bouddica Alpha

Major Pak burst through the doorway opening onto Bouddica Alpha's upper deck, just below the helipad. Ahead, the refinery's flare stack jutted out over the sea at a sharp angle, still capped by its wavering halo of orange flame; nearby were the twin towers, each capped by a spherical white shroud, that supported the facility's weather and surface traffic radars.

His destination, however, was off to the left on the far side of a maze of air-conditioning ducts and blowers. The cab to the platform's number one crane was standing empty, the arm still stretched out over the sea to the east, supporting the PRR's Korean-made nuclear device.

As soon as he'd heard that there'd been gunfire somewhere inside the Bouddica complex, he'd known the time had come to act.

He was a man with a mission.

That mission did not necessarily match the mission parameters of Adler and his PRR.

It never had.

Operation Saebyok—the word meant "Dawn"—had been conceived by the hard-liner military clique within the Pyongyang government as a means of beginning a new day in the exercise of international power, a way of striking back at the hated

243

Americans, a means of crippling, or at least slowing, the quickly expanding economies of the European community. Behind it all, Pak knew, was the determination of the militarists to confirm their own positions of power; when Bouddica was incinerated, their long-argued program of expanded covert warfare against the West would be proven viable, their own power base secured.

The next bomb to detonate beneath the World Trade Center towers in New York City might well not be conventional explosives.

And so, contact between the North Korean secret police and the scattered and demoralized remnants of the old RAF and other European terrorist groups had been strengthened. A seed had been planted within the RAF leadership, the idea of the state without borders, of a nation born in terrorism but rising to become the idealistic champion of the downtrodden peoples of the earth.

North Korea had provided the nuclear weapon for some much-needed hard currency and provided as well the experts to arm and place it and to advise the PRR in the seizure of the BGA oil platform. Adler and the other European fools thought the Americans and the British would capitulate to their demands, leaving the PRR with their nuclear device, a means of preserving their existence and of providing themselves with negotiating power in the future.

Pak and his superiors knew better. The world would never allow the PRR to keep its nuclear hardware, not if they had to hunt down every one of the People's Revolution members and assassinate them one by one. Besides, Pyongyang had other plans for the PRR's new weaponry. The threatened nuclear devastation of the North Sea, the collapse of Britain's economy, the tottering even of the titanic American economy as it tried to stop the collapse of its friends, all much better suited North Korea's future plans.

So the nuclear weapon was to be detonated whether the enemy capitulated to the PRR's demands or not. Ideally, it was to be detonated during the expected enemy assault, so that it would look to the world as though the Americans and British had brought the disaster down upon themselves.

He was grinning as he broke into a run, trotting past the air conditioning machinery toward the crane's waiting cab.

Before long, the world would know what *terror* really was.

2208 hours GMT
Radar Tower 1
Bouddica Alpha

MacKenzie had climbed the service ladder on the first of the two radar towers and used his diving knife to pry open the service access panel just below the spherical white weather shroud housing the unit's rotating dish. Disabling the radar would be a simple matter of reaching in, grabbing a handful of wires, and yanking hard . . . but the idea was for both radars to go down at once after the tangos realized something was going down.

He'd already manufactured two small bombs, each a fist-sized lump of C-6 from the team's small supply, a pencil-sized detonator, and a small unit that included a 9-volt battery and a digital timer. After pulling one of the devices from a pouch and checking his watch, he punched the buttons on the timer, setting the alarm, as it were, for 2230 hours. Then he reached into the access hatch and mashed the plastique in among the circuit boards and wiring.

As he pulled back to replace the access panel, movement on the roof of the platform crew's quarters caught his eye. A lone man was jogging from a doorway opening out onto the roof just below the helipad.

He was wearing civilian clothing—a light-colored shirt and trousers—and MacKenzie's first thought was that one of the hostages had managed to escape.

But he'd seen the same shirt earlier that day through binoculars and through the telephoto lens of the digital camera. "L-T!" he whispered into the lip mike suspended just below his mouth. "This is Mac!"

2209 hours GMT
Room 570
Bouddica Alpha

Murdock, Roselli, and Inge had taken shelter inside another room on Bouddica Alpha's fifth level. Unlike Room 512, which had been a small office of some kind, this one was one of the apartment-cabins provided for personnel working their two-week shift on the oil platform. It was small but comfortably furnished, with a tall, narrow window that admitted the cool blue eastern light of the dying evening, carpeted decks, and even a small television in the bulkhead above the desk.

The most important amenity it possessed, however, at least so far as the SEALs were concerned, was privacy. The five levels of the towering crew's quarters module were as complex and maze-like as a five-story hotel. Forty men could not possibly search it all in less than many hours—the main reason, Murdock thought, that the PRR tangos had waited so long to remove the bomb from the trawler. The terrorists had probably searched the structure at least cursorily after collecting all of the personnel in the main recreation area, but they didn't have enough men to guard it, or even to patrol it on a regular basis.

Inge had just begun describing for the SEALs what little she'd seen of the layout of the Bouddica platform when Mac's call sounded over the speakers clipped to their left ears. "L-T! This is Mac!"

If Mac was breaking radio silence, it had to be urgent. Murdock held up one finger to silence Inge, opened his transmitter, and said, "Go!"

"I've got Pak in sight. He's double-timing for the crane!"

Which told Murdock immediately what he most needed to know. If the object suspended from that crane was a dummy, the PRR's resident nuclear expert wouldn't be that interested in it.

If he was running toward the crane controls, however—

"Inge. When you were aboard that fishing boat, there was a Korean man there too."

She nodded. "Pak. One of the men you were investigating last week."

"Was he interested in that device they pulled out of the ship's hold with a crane?"

The woman thought for a moment. "I wasn't really watching, I'm afraid, but I'd have to say yes. He was there on the deck shouting at someone in English to be careful with—"

Confirmation! "Mac! Take him down!"

"Rog."

"Jaybird! Skeeter!"

"We're here, L-T." Sterling's voice replied.

"Put the word out over the satcom. *Copperhead!* I say again, *Copperhead!*"

There was a small, shocked silence. "Affirmative. Copperhead."

Murdock turned to Inge. "They wouldn't let you join GSG9, huh?"

"What about it?"

"You may have just saved this platform and everyone on it."

"Told you, L-T," Roselli said. "She's SEAL material."

2209 hours GMT
Radar Tower 1
Bouddica Alpha

Still standing on the rungs that led up the radar tower to the access hatch, MacKenzie unslung his MP5 and took aim at the running figure. He estimated the range to be fifty meters—half the length of a football field.

Submachine guns are brutal, close-range weapons and not designed for sniping, but SEALs were trained to use a wide variety of weapons under every possible set of conditions. Leading Pak slightly, he squeezed the trigger, loosing a three-round burst with a fluttering hiss, but the runner kept moving. MacKenzie adjusted his aim and fired two more bursts, and the runner stumbled, then went down, vanishing behind a tangle of air-conditioning ducts.

MacKenzie would have to get close to make sure the job was done. First, however, he opened up the access panel again and reset the timer, giving himself sixty seconds.

The code word "Copperhead" Murdock had just ordered Sterling and Johnson to transmit meant that the assault would be going down *now,* not twenty minutes from now.

The cavalry was already on the way in, and those radars had to be taken down first.

2209 hours GMT
Room 570
Bouddica Alpha

"An atomic bomb!" Inge's eyes were wide. *"Mein Gott!* That was an atomic bomb they had out there?"

Murdock reached into a pouch and extracted one of the long, curved magazines he carried for his H&K. Bullets gleamed, copper and gold, as he began thumbing them out of the mag and into his hand. Counting out ten rounds, he handed them to Inge, spilling them into her cupped hands. "You know how to reload your magazine?"

She looked up at him and nodded.

"Good. Load up . . . just in case. I don't think the bad guys will bother you here. If you hear anything outside that door, though, just get down on the floor behind the bed and stay there."

"But . . ."

"Razor and I have to go. You'll be safe here."

Damn it, she didn't *want* to be safe! But she knew from Blake's expression, from the tone of his voice, that he would accept no argument. "Very well . . ."

"Good girl. I'll be back for you as soon as I can."

And then the two SEALs were gone.

Inge stared at the door, the bullets still in her hands. "Like hell I'm going to sit here and wait for you, Herr SEAL!" she muttered after them.

Then she reached for the empty pistol.

2209 hours GMT
The quarters module roof
Bouddica Alpha

Pak lay flat on his belly, his pistol drawn, searching the direction from which the shots must have come.

He'd been hit. One moment he'd been running across the upper deck, and the next he'd felt twin hammer blows against his right leg, one halfway between his knee and his hip, the other just below his knee. The impact had knocked him down, and blood was pooling beneath his leg on the concrete deck.

There still wasn't any pain—not really—but he felt the dizziness and chill of impending shock. From the way his lower leg was twisted, he was sure that it was broken.

Lifting himself on his elbows and using his good leg, he pulled himself forward, the broken limb dragging behind until he could get a better view past the machinery he'd fallen behind. The radar towers. The shots must have come from the radar towers, but he couldn't see anyone there. No! There was someone, a dark shape climbing down the tower's side.

Fifty meters. Too far for him to have any hope at all of hitting a man with a handgun, not without an extraordinary stroke of luck.

Pak didn't believe in luck. The crane's cab was ten meters ahead.

He kept crawling.

2209 hours GMT
Helicopter Falcon 1/1
25 miles southwest of the Bouddica Complex

"Colonel!" the pilot called, twisting around in his seat and shouting to make himself heard above the thunder of the rotors. "We just got a flash over the satellite taccom! The word is 'Copperhead.'"

Wentworth's eyes narrowed, and he jerked his head in a curt, short nod. "Okay. Pass the word to all Falcons. We're going in!"

Copperhead. The SEALs had located the bomb, and it was aboard the Bouddica complex, vulnerable to a quick dash by the assault force.

Wentworth unholstered his Browning Hi-power and checked the action, before snapping home a loaded magazine. *This* time he would not be waiting out the op in a command post somewhere.

Outside, beyond the thin metal skin of the big Westland Sea King HC.Mk4, four other Sea Kings of 846 Squadron, an aerial armada configured for commando assault, stretched out in a huge V-formation nearly half a mile across, dipped their noses and accelerated as one toward the northeast. They were twenty-five miles from the objective. At a maximum low-level speed of better than two and a half miles per minute, they would be there in ten minutes.

2209 hours GMT
Tanker *Noramo Pride*

DeWitt and the other SEALs of SEAL Team Seven had heard the Copperhead call. Six were already aboard the *Noramo Pride,* with the last two coming up three caving ladders dangling off the stern passageway to port, just under the towering white loom of the ship's superstructure.

The rendezvous at sea had gone precisely as in training, though the size and strength of North Sea waves had been a lot nastier than they'd been during any training run. As the twilight had deepened, the two small rubber raiders had closed on the titanic ship riding at her moorings a few miles away, slipping along with electric motors that made scarcely more than a purr as they brought the SEALs in close.

Once under the hull, port side aft, Fernandez had tossed a grappling hook up and over a railing thirty-five feet above the water, then swarmed up the line after it, a maneuver practiced and practiced again by all of the SEALs. Moments later, three caving ladders had dropped over the side, and the SEALs of Third Platoon Gold Squad, plus Higgins and Brown from Blue, had been on their way up the side.

Copperhead! That meant the A-bomb wasn't here, and DeWitt felt a small, almost guilty sense of relief. If there was a screwup and they all died in a nuclear flash in the next few minutes, at least it wouldn't be his fault!

Bemused by the universal human tendency to place blame somewhere else, even in the face of disaster so absolute that who was at fault mattered not at all, DeWitt waited until the last two SEALs joined the party on the tanker's fantail. They were almost invisible, in black wet suits, with hoods and gloves, and with faces painted so black that the whites of their eyes were startlingly luminous by comparison.

The ship was quiet, and mostly darkened save for a blaze of lights from the bridge, topside on the superstructure, and forward. Breaking out their weapons and checking them carefully, the SEALs split into two teams. Higgins, Brown,

Fernandez, and Kosciuszko started down the portside gangway, moving forward. DeWitt led Holt, Nicholson, and Frazier
around the stern of the ship, then forward along the starboard
gangway.

They met their first tango coming aft, his M-16 slung over
his shoulder, his right hand in his trouser pocket. DeWitt shot
him with a sound-suppressed burst through the chest and
throat, then with Nicholson's help, tossed the body over the
side.

The outside ladder leading up to the pilothouse was there.
He signaled his men to hurry.

2209 hours GMT
The quarters module roof
Bouddica Alpha

MacKenzie dropped to the deck below the radar tower, then
glanced at his watch. It would have been nice to have been able
to take care of the other radar . . . but he had to make sure of
the man he'd put down first. H&K at the ready, he scanned the
labyrinth of machinery in front of him, selecting a route that
would put him between the target and the crane.

A shout sounded from the left, followed by the clatter of
boots on cement. Men were spilling onto the facility's roof
from the open doorway, and in one sudden twist of events,
MacKenzie had gone from being the hunter to the hunted.

Could he pass himself off as one of the tangos? Another
shout, followed an instant later by a burst of automatic fire,
answered that question with a decisive no. Either he had no
business being up here in the first place, or some sort of
security plan was in operation that identified him as an enemy.
Bullets shrieked off the cement nearby; others punched through
the thin metal of the air conditioning ducts with the sound of
hammers striking sheet tin.

MacKenzie dropped and rolled as the shots, wildly aimed,
snapped over his head. He came up with his MP5 pressed
stock-to-shoulder, squeezing off two three-round bursts in
rapid-fire succession. One tango threw out his arms, pitched
backward, and sprawled face up on the deck; a second clutched
his belly and crumpled into a ball, rolling heels over head as he

fell. MacKenzie found cover behind a massive blower head as four more tangos spread out to right and left, trying to flank him.

Suddenly, things weren't looking good at all.

2210 hours GMT
Corridor 1, Operations level
Bouddica Alpha

According to Inge, Adler, the PRR leader, had told Johann he was going up to Ops after getting a phone call. The enemy's defense of the installation would probably be directed from there in any case, and this was a splendid opportunity to catch a number of the PRR force's leaders in one place.

So Murdock wanted to hit Ops fast, before the SAS/GSG9 helos arrived. He knew that the installation rose like a futuristic afterthought above the rest of the quarters module and overlooked the helipad. He told Sterling what he planned to do, and then he and Roselli had raced off down the passageway toward a central, interior stairwell that led up one more level to Ops.

At the top of the stairs, a fire-door opened onto a long passageway that ran along the center's west wall. South were storage rooms and a door leading out onto the main upper deck; north were the entrances to the helipad and to Ops.

Murdock and Roselli came through the door one after the other, Murdock rolling to the left while Roselli took the right, weapons already at their shoulders. A tango was jogging toward the door as Murdock burst into the corridor, obligingly sliding across the tops of his sights just as he clamped down on the trigger.

The sound-suppressed MP5 made a noise like flags cracking in the wind and the terrorist twisted right, slammed into a wall, then collapsed at the same moment that Roselli's MP5 went into action at Murdock's back. "We're in Corridor One," Murdock announced over the tactical net. He glanced back over his shoulder to confirm Roselli's kill. "Two bad guys down. Moving to Ops."

His words, transmitted over the open satellite network, would keep listeners in Dorset and in the Pentagon informed of exactly what was happening. Gunfire sounded, unsuppressed but muffled, outside the walls of the building.

They ignored it. Together, the two SEALs dashed for the door leading to the Operations Center.

24

Friday, May 4

2210 hours GMT
The quarters module roof
Bouddica Alpha

MacKenzie's plastic explosive bomb detonated with a sharp bang that blasted the service access panel off and sent it fluttering off over the sea. The report took some of the heat off MacKenzie too, for the terrorists trying to flank him suddenly ducked for cover and opened fire, blazing away at the radar tower.

The distraction was enough for MacKenzie to rise from cover and open fire himself—not at the PRR terrorists who were scattered across half of the quarters module's roof—but at the large white shroud covering the second radar dish. Snapping his select-fire lever to full auto, he emptied the rest of his magazine at the target, watching bits and tatters of the plastic cover flying away under the caress of the steady stream of 9mm bullets.

His weapon clicked empty and he dropped to cover again, dropping the dry magazine and slapping home a fresh one. Rising again, he emptied another twenty rounds at the radar, until the tango gunmen started throwing shots his way once more; sometimes, the subtlety of carefully prepared and packaged explosive charges had to give way to the sheer, brute force of full-auto fire.

Sure that he'd shredded that radar dish enough to take it off the air as effectively as the first, MacKenzie dropped to his belly and started crawling. The tangos were closing on him fast now from two directions, and he wanted to reach the crane before they did.

2210 hours GMT
Operations Center
Bouddica Alpha

Heinrich Adler looked left and right, panic gibbering like a looming black beast somewhere in the back of his mind. Pak! Where was Pak? The Korean must have dashed out, but Adler hadn't seen him go.

He didn't trust Pak, never had trusted him completely. The man was unpredictable . . . even dangerous.

The operations center had huge, slanted windows fronting on three sides of the long, east-facing room. The north windows overlooked the helipad, where the Lynx in its Royal Dutch Navy livery still rested. East there was only water, and the dark shapes, almost invisible now in the rapidly deepening twilight, of the *Noramo Pride,* the *Rosa,* and the *Horizon.*

South was a view of Bouddica Bravo and the bridge connecting it with the main platform. The yellow-painted arm of the crane extended past the window, the atomic bomb suspended in space some eighty feet below the level of the windows.

He could hear the chatter of automatic weapons fire outside and knew the enemy commandos were storming the facility. An instant ago, both radars had gone down, first one, then, seconds later, the other, and he'd known that the end was in sight.

"Sir!" Strauss yelled, fear visible in his eyes and in his stance. "Sir, what do we do?"

Adler yanked back the slide on his Austrian-made Glock automatic pistol. What should they do? He stared for a moment at the two hostages, sitting together at the control center console, and his wild gaze and the way he was holding the weapon must have convinced them that he was about to shoot them both.

"No!" the man shouted, standing and putting himself between Adler and the young woman. "Don't do it!"

"Ruhe!" Adler snapped, his English forgotten for the moment. *"Halte die Klappe!"*

Turning, he raced down the long room to the south window, where he could peer back at the elevated cab of the crane. Despite the near-darkness, he could see enough by the light off the flare stack to make out a solitary figure in civilian clothing raising himself painfully to the ladder that led up toward the open cab.

Pak! And he was going for the bomb release.

In that nightmare moment, Heinrich Adler saw how the People's Revolutionary Republic, how *he* had been used by the North Korean agent. Pak wasn't interested in the national autonomy of the PRR. For Adler, the bomb represented power . . . but only if the bomb remained as a *threat,* not as a rising pillar of superheated vapor and radioactive fallout. Detonated, the bomb would no longer confer power or immunity on the PRR. Adler himself would be dead, incinerated along with most of the PRR's paramilitary strength, its bargaining power, and its credibility. The organization's survivors, those left ashore on this op, would be hunted down and exterminated one after the other by the more civilized members of the world community.

Pak, clearly, was determined to set the hellish thing off no matter what.

And maybe that had been the North Korean agent's plan from the very beginning.

Adler raised his gun, then lowered it. The windows of the Ops Center were reinforced with plastic and very tough; designed to deflect the winds of a North Sea storm, they'd have little trouble deflecting bullets. He would have to go outside to stop the Korean. Maybe he could find some of the SEALs and—

The door from Corridor 1 at the northwest corner of the room burst open, and a cardboard tube sailed through the opening. Adler had presence of mind enough to dive for the floor, throwing his arms over his eyes and ears as, an instant later, the flashbang erupted in a shattering chain of explosions.

The woman screamed and fell off her chair; two of the four PRR gunmen went all the way down, while Strauss and Kelly dropped to their knees.

Two men in black combat garb spun through the doorway, sweeping the room with their MP5SD3s. Kelly's head exploded and he toppled backward, arms flailing. Strauss fired his own H&K with an ear-splitting chatter, then pitched backward under a double fusillade of silenced fire, his finger still clamping down on the trigger as he stitched a ragged line of 9mm bullet holes along the soundproofing in the Ops Center's ceiling.

Acting almost instinctively, Adler sprang forward, grabbing the civilian woman by the waist and hoisting her in front of himself as a shield. "Stop!" he shouted, and the gunfire stopped and both commandos pivoted their weapons to aim directly at Adler's head. He scrunched down behind the struggling woman, pressing the muzzle of his Glock against the side of her skull. If he could just talk long enough to warn them of the danger. "We must talk about the—"

Someone landed on him from behind, grappling with his arm, clawing at his throat. *"Nein!"* Adler shrieked, and he let go of the woman, trying to fling his attacker clear. . . .

The male civilian was riding Adler's back, one arm around his throat, the other grabbing desperately at his right arm and the Glock pistol. The two commandos froze in place, both aiming their weapons but unable to fire with the civilian in such close and wildly spinning proximity to their target. With a powerful thrust, Adler hurled the BGA employee clear, smashing him back into the radar console. He pivoted left, bringing up his Glock to cover the commandos—

Twin bursts of 9mm rounds slammed into his chest, knocking him backward, knocking him down as both commandos continue to trigger three-round bursts that riddled him again and again.

"The bomb!" he tried to shout, but then his throat and mouth were filled with blood. He spat, trying to clear his throat, trying to speak. *"Die bombe—"*

It was growing dark at last, the night outside filling the control center, blotting out even the advancing feet of the enemy commandos. . . .

2213 hours GMT
Operations Center
Bouddica Alpha

"He's dead, L-T."

"You two okay?" Murdock asked the woman.

She glanced at the man who was standing next to her, an arm around her shoulder, and nodded. "Yes, sir."

"What'd the tango mean about the bomb?" Roselli wanted to know.

"Don't know, Razor. Maybe we'd better get out there."

"Roger that."

Murdock looked at the two civilians. "Quick. Was this the leader?"

"Yes, sir," the man said. "He was the one giving all the orders. And making the threats."

"Did he say anything about a bomb? Anything at all?"

"No," the woman said. "He threatened to shoot us, not blow us up."

Maybe Adler hadn't told his hostages that he had a nuclear device outside. There could be a good reason for that. Terror could be used to control hostages, but too much terror might make them even harder to handle.

Roselli was on his knees, searching the dead terrorist's jacket pockets. "Did he have any kind of controller on him? Maybe a push-button remote control device? Anything like that?"

"I never saw anything like that," the man said. "There was that Chinese guy, though—"

"What Chinese?"

"Little man, this high," the woman said, measuring five-seven or so with her hand. "He had something like a little box, with buttons on it. I thought it was a portable computer."

"Where is he?"

"He went out a few minutes ago." She pointed at the door. "That way."

"You two stay here. Lie down on the deck, stay away from the windows, and don't move. Understand?"

They moved to comply. "Yes, sir!"

Murdock hesitated, then checked his watch. The cavalry

would be here in another few minutes. "Eagles!" he called over the radio net using the code word agreed upon for all SEALs. "Eagles, this is Eagle Leader. Show your colors!"

Acknowledgments came in from the other SEALs. Murdock reached into one of his vest pockets, retrieving a Velcro-backed American flag which he pressed onto a Velcro patch affixed to his dry suit's left sleeve.

The act was not one of flag-showing patriotism, but of deadly practicality. When the SAS choppers arrived, their gunners would have one hell of a time telling friend from foe, and the flags would help. Even among the SEALs, with Mac alone out on the deck somewhere, and Roselli and Murdock moving to help him, misidentification was a terribly real possibility.

Friendly fire could kill as easily as hostile fire.

Nonetheless, Murdock felt a surge of pride as he settled the flag in place. Patriotism might be outdated in most sectors of the American public these days. But not here. Not among SEALs.

"Let's go, Razor."

2215 hours GMT
The quarters module roof
Bouddica Alpha

MacKenzie winced and ducked as a ricochet stung his cheek. This was turning into a goddamned cluster fuck. If the bad guys had rigged their A-bomb to blow with the push of a button, it would all be up now. He sensed movement among the shadows to the right and loosed a burst in that direction. Bullets shrieked and clanged among steel generators and air ducts, but he couldn't tell if he'd hit anything.

Probably not. The tangos were working toward him crabwise, cautious now that some of their buddies had been tagged.

He would have to try something different. He just needed to wait for them to get close enough. . . .

2216 hours GMT
Tanker *Noramo Pride*

As the flashbang's final crack rang off steel bulkheads, DeWitt rolled through the starboard side door into the tanker's pilothouse, dropping to his knees and rolling to clear the door as Frazier came in close behind him. At almost the same instant, Higgins and Brown smashed through the port-side entrance.

Several men were there, close by the ship's wheel. With a skill born of long practice in killing houses and practice mock-ups of tankers like this one, DeWitt picked out the ones with weapons and triggered his MP5.

The two tangos still standing went down hard before they'd even acquired a target. Two more, gasping on the deck and with blood streaming from their ears from the flashbang detonation, were put down an instant later. A fifth, crouched against the instrument console forward hurled both hands high above his head. From his face, DeWitt guessed that he was seventeen or eighteen years old.

"Nicht schiessen!" the kid screamed. *"Ach! Scheisse! Nicht schiessen!"*

The only other man left—dazed but unhurt—was one of the ship's officers, judging from his uniform jacket.

"Name!" DeWitt snapped, covering him with his weapon.

"S-Scott! Dennis Scott! I'm the *Pride*'s skipper."

"Lie down on the deck, please, Captain! Facedown, hands out from your body!"

The man complied. Higgins crossed the pilothouse and knocked the stunned terrorist facedown on the deck; Brown covered him as Higgins cuffed his wrists behind him with a plastic tie, then started frisking him. Nicholson appeared out of the door leading aft to the radio and chartrooms. "All clear back there, Two-eyes," he said.

"Engine room secured!" Kosciuszko's voice called in De-Witt's radio earpiece. *"One tango down!"*

"Roger that, Chief," DeWitt added. "Bridge secure! Four tangos dead, one prisoner. And we've got Captain Scott."

At the moment, they had Captain Scott flat on the deck, as Higgins tied his wrists. Since the SEALs hadn't seen photographs of any of the tanker's officers and crew, they would follow SOP and keep even the rescued hostages immobile until their identities could be confirmed—just in case.

DeWitt moved to the port wing of the bridge, stepping out into the open night air and peering into the gathering darkness, first at the immense and dazzlingly lit towers of the oil complex a mile ahead, then at the much nearer, darkened form of the trawler *Rosa*. It was hard to tell; was there movement on the *Rosa*'s deck? A flicker of light . . . or gunfire?

"Two-eyes!" sounded in his headset. "This is Rattler! We're secure forward!"

"Roger that. Kos! Make sure the plugs and fuses are pulled in the engine room. Then everybody get up here, on the double." If there were still tangos wandering around loose in the cavernous labyrinth of the *Noramo Pride,* the SEALs' best course of action was to make certain the tanker was immobilized, then turn the upper decks of the superstructure into an easily defended strong point. By daylight, someone would be along to relieve them.

Reaching into a pouch in his load-bearing vest, he extracted a pen-sized flare launcher, armed it, aimed it at the sky, and triggered it. A yellow flare arced through the night, trailing sparks.

An instant later, an answering yellow flare speared into the night from the *Rosa*'s bridge, and DeWitt felt a heady thrill of excitement . . . and of accomplishment. They'd done it! The SEALs had secured the tanker, while the SBS people — shadowy and rarely heard-of British counterparts to the American SEALs — had taken down the trawler.

For once, DeWitt thought with a burst of sheer joy, old Murphy had been left at home. For once, the operation was going down perfectly!

2217 hours GMT
Anchor tug *Horizon*
Fifty meters east of Bouddica Alpha

The *Horizon* had been fully powered up and ready to move all evening. The instant the word "Copperhead" had been flashed over the tactical net, Captain Croft had given the order to move. The twenty-eight SAS men aboard had been packed away out of sight aboard the miserable little workboat, until the spaces below decks were a fetid hell of stink and vomit.

By now, Croft thought, his boys were *mad*. Heaven help the sods who got in their way!

Standing on the tug's bridge, next to the SBS man in civilian clothes who'd been seconded to the *Horizon* as one of the stand-ins for her crew, Croft had to step forward and look up through the bridge skylight windows to see the full, tangled majesty of Bouddica Alpha towering above them. Dead ahead, the *Celtic Maiden* rode the North Sea swell, tied up alongside a temporary floating platform with a spidery metal stairway running up the forty feet to the platform's lower deck.

"There's the sub," the helmsman said. "Looks like they have 'er cleared for launch."

"I see." Bathed in spotlights on the main structure, the North Korean minisub was resting on its complex wood- and aluminum-frame cradle, still on the afterdeck of the other anchor tug. "Put us alongside," Croft ordered. "Our boys will cross over and secure the *Maiden* and the sub both, then hotfoot up the ladder."

"Aye, sir."

He heard a noise and glanced behind him. The Korean woman, Chun, was there, standing impassively beside the SAS man detailed to guard her. Damn! He'd forgotten all about the woman. He'd brought her onto the *Horizon*'s bridge half an hour ago in case he'd needed her to talk to her mates on Bouddica, but things had been a bit frantic since then. "Get her below!" he snapped at the woman's guard.

"Sir!" The trooper grabbed her arm and steered her away, off the bridge.

"Better 'ave the lads get ready," the helmsman said. "Another minute or two'll do it."

Croft passed the word for the assault teams to get ready.

2218 hours GMT
The quarters module roof
Bouddica Alpha

MacKenzie hurled the flashbang in the direction of his nearest opponents. When the first detonation cut loose, he broke from cover in an unexpected direction, zigzagging back toward the command center's west wall, leaping across a dark, wet trail on the cement, plunging behind a line of steel pipes and ducts, then twisting around and opening fire at the terrorists closing on him from that side.

Stunned and blinded by the grenade, they were helpless. Two went down . . . then the third. Mac tossed another burst at the farther group of terrorists, driving them to cover. Then he turned and sprinted south, racing toward the crane.

That black trail was blood! He must have hit Pak earlier, but the tough little bastard had kept on going.

Well, MacKenzie knew that he would have done the same thing, had the situation been reversed.

The crane was just ahead, the cab mounted twelve feet above the cement deck atop a steel pillar. Pak was there, dragging himself toward the opening. Mac raised his subgun and pulled the trigger. There was a single shot, and then the bolt snapped shut on an empty chamber.

"Fuck!"

He dropped the empty mag and reached for a reload. . . .

25

Friday, May 4

Pak's leg had started to hurt.

It was sheer agony to cling with both arms to one rung of the ladder leading up to the invitingly open door of the cab and, with his right leg dangling limp and useless, lift his left foot to the next rung and push himself up one more grueling step. The pain below his knee as the splintered ends of his tibia grated across one another with each short, jerky movement was excruciating, and it had slowed his progress to an inch-by-inch creep across the deck.

But he was almost there now.

Inge reached the roof of the quarters module by finding her way back to the fire-escape ladder running up the south side of the building and going up from there. She knew she wasn't combat-trained, for all the joking about her being an honorary SEAL, so she elected to avoid the sounds of the heavy firefight coming from directly overhead.

But she was damned if she was going to be left all alone in that cabin, waiting for the men to finish with their killing and get back to her. With a cool and professional detachment, she'd reloaded her magazine, snapped it home, and chambered the first round with a metallic snick of the slide release.

Then she'd headed for the roof.

She still wasn't entirely sure why she'd done so. That first shock she'd felt after realizing she'd killed a man had faded, replaced by a wild, almost enjoyably furious pounding of heart and quickening of her breathing. She wanted to be where the action was, not sitting in that cabin, wondering what was going on outside.

Besides, Blake had talked about these terrorists having an atomic bomb, and that fit with the information she'd found for him back in Wiesbaden, helped piece it all together. She'd been a part of this operation from the beginning. She didn't want to be left out now.

Inge Schmidt wasn't sure what she would be able to do, but she ought to be able to do *something*.

So she grabbed her pistol and went.

A pitched battle was still being fought on the module roof when she stepped off the ladder. She couldn't tell who was shooting at whom, especially with the darkness closing in fast, but stuttering, flaring muzzle flashes off to the left suggested that quite a few people were there, firing in her general direction. Ducking low to take advantage of the shelter offered by air ducts and machinery, she ran barefoot across the poured concrete roof in the direction of the big crane.

Thunder filled the night, louder, *vaster* than the crackle of small-arms fire, and Inge stopped, leaning back against a sheet metal duct. The thunder grew, wind stirred . . .

. . . and then the night sky exploded in light. Helicopters! She couldn't see them clearly, couldn't tell how many there were, but she could sense huge, insect shapes sweeping low over the platform, searchlights stabbing and sweeping out of the night. One helicopter passed right overhead, the rotor wash whipping her hair and skirt with a frigid blast of howling, shrieking wind. A machine gun mounted in the aircraft's open, right-side door spat flame, though the *thump-thump-thump* of the rotors was so loud she couldn't hear the gun's bark.

A stray round hit the duct two feet above her head with a

sound like a clashing garbage can. Inge ducked, then started running.

The crane was just ahead. . . .

2219 hours GMT
Helicopter Falcon 1/4
Above Bouddica Alpha

"One-three, this is One-four," the helicopter's pilot called over the air tactical net. He was Lieutenant Gerald Gerrard, "Jerry" to his mates, and he'd been flying Sea Kings for 846 Squadron for almost five years now. Rigged for commando assault, the 846 helos were deadly, their crews the best in the business. "Watch your tail, Manny. We're on it!"

The lights and forest-like tangle of towers rising from the Bouddica complex swept past the cockpit windows in a dizzying blur, as though trying to claw the Sea King from the sky. Gunfire stabbed. Something thumped loudly in the rear . . . a piece of gear gone adrift possibly, or a round punching through metal. The controls continued to respond, however, and the gauges all showed everything was champion.

"Roger that," One-three replied, the voice strained behind the static of the radio. "We're picking up fire from the helipad, fire from the helipad. Over!"

"All Falcons, this is One-one," Wentworth's voice announced. "We'll put down suppressive fire on the helipad. The rest of you drop your chicks."

"Ah, roger, One-one. We're on approach."

Falcon One-two was drifting toward the helipad, sweeping the area with fire from the machine gun in its cabin door. Flame leaped, then exploded skyward in a dazzling fireball and, for a horrifying instant, Gerrard though the whole rig was going up . . . but it was just the Royal Dutch navy helicopter resting on the helipad, the fuel in its tanks touched off. Falcon One-three banked left, came nose high, and drifted toward the center of the platform. Men in black combat garb spilled from the side, fast-roping to the complex's roof in a fast-moving pearls-on-a-string line.

"Falcons," Wentworth's voice warned. "One-one. Mind the Yanks now! Watch your fire until you're sure of your targets!"

"Yes, Mother," One-four's co-pilot said, and Gerrard laughed. The helos were operating under damned stringent restrictions for this assault. In the first place, indiscriminate fire could knock holes in natural gas lines down there, especially in the bridge or in the forest of pipes and storage tanks on Bouddica Alpha's west side. A stray round going into *that* lot could touch off the whole complex, which was why he'd winced when that helo had brewed up. Hell, a firestorm of flame and destruction like that would be overshadowed only by the flash of a nuclear detonation, something Gerrard didn't like thinking about.

To make things even more complicated, both the terrorists and the Yank SEALs down there were running around in basic black. Picking out one from another wasn't going to be easy . . . though it was safe to assume that anyone firing at the helicopters was not friendly.

So the five helicopters of 846 Squadron had been ordered to fire only at targets that were shooting at them . . . and then only when the field of fire would sweep the roof of the platform complex *away* from the refinery section next to it.

Still, everything was going perfectly, a smooth op, money for jam.

The pilot banked the helo out over the sea, angling for an approach that would place him and the twenty-eight commandos at his back down on an open area between the crane and the Operations Center.

2219 hours GMT
Bridge
Anchor tug *Horizon*
Alongside Bouddica Alpha

The anchor tug was nosing up beneath the bridge now, close alongside her sister tug, the *Celtic Maiden*. Croft watched from the starboard side of the bridge, peering up at the platform's superstructure. The tug's nose bumped into the *Maiden*'s port side aft, thumping heavily along the fenders hung over the rail.

"Go!" he shouted over the radio. "Go! *Go!*"

On *Horizon*'s bow and starboard side, thirty SAS troops, all in combat black with the blue, white, and red of St. George's

Cross Velcroed to their sleeves, leaped from one tug to the after deck of the other. Two terrorists stepped out from behind the submarine, subguns raised . . . but a fusillade of fire from the *Horizon*'s superstructure and from the men going over the side nailed the gunmen in a withering crossfire, tattering their bodies in a hail of bullets. Neither got off a shot; one crumpled beside the minisub, the other pitched sideways into the cold, black water off the *Maiden*'s stern.

SAS troops swarmed across the *Maiden*'s deck, moving forward. Gunshots sounded. "*Maiden's bridge secure! One terr down!*" someone called over the net.

A flash grabbed Croft's eye. He looked up, looked into the crisscross of beams and struts and piping that supported the whole of Bouddica's crews' quarters module like a fantastic, high-tech bird's nest. A dazzlingly bright star flashed out from a catwalk there, passed just to the right of the *Horizon*'s bridge, and slammed into the superstructure astern. The explosion sent a shudder through the anchor tug's hull. Rocket!

"RPG on Alpha's belly!" he called. "Hit the bastard! Hit him!"

A second star flashed, hissing down toward the tug and exploding amidships with a shattering wet roar.

2219 hours GMT
Gangway, starboard side
Anchor tug *Horizon*
Alongside Bouddica Alpha

The first explosion had thrown both Chun and her guard to their knees. It had struck low, close by the waterline, and the icy cascade of water from the geysering spout drenched both of them and sluiced across the deck.

Chun grabbed the gangway railing and pulled herself upright. Her guard was just rising when the second grenade detonated just meters away, and the air sang with thumb-sized chunks of shrapnel. The SAS soldier yelled and grabbed his shoulder, his H&K jolted from his grasp. Chun rose to a crouch, pivoting sharply, snapping her leg up and around and kicking the man in the side of his head, knocking him back against the side of the tug's superstructure.

Gunfire snapped and howled nearby. Ahead and high above the water, a dark shape screamed and dropped from a catwalk. Spotlights from the anchor tug pinned a second shape crouched on the walkway, a man frantically trying to reload his clumsy RPG launcher. SAS men already spilling onto the catwalk from the ladder up opened fire and cut him down.

Chun knew she didn't have a moment to lose. They would be coming any second to check the damage from the two grenades. Bending over, she picked up the unconscious guard's H&K and checked to make sure a round was chambered. Then, kicking off her shoes, she vaulted the gangway railing and leaped into the icy black sea.

A helicopter thundered slowly overhead, closing on Bouddica Alpha's roof in a blaze of lights.

2219 hours GMT
The quarters module roof
Bouddica Alpha

Gunfire burst and rattled behind him as Pak struggled up the ladder just below the crane's cab. One round slapped against steel six inches to the side of his good leg, but with a last, desperate heave, one that drained almost the last of his endurance, Major Pak of the PDRK Special Forces hauled himself up and over the lip of the door and sprawled across the leather-covered seat.

An array of controls confronted him, black-knobbed levers for controlling cab rotation, for raising or lowering the crane arm, for winding in the cable. While they'd gotten one of the hostages to do all the crane work so far, Pak was familiar enough with the general layout of this type of heavy equipment. A special forces commando had to know how the thing worked in order to most effectively destroy it . . . or to use it to destroy something else.

There. That would be the cable release.

He reached for it. . . .

2219 hours GMT
The quarters module roof
Bouddica Alpha

MacKenzie slapped the fresh mag into the receiver and closed the bolt, chambering a round. In the handful of seconds it had taken him to reload, Pak had vanished into the crane. Mac-Kenzie broke into a run. The night was filled with light and violence, and the thunder of helicopters circling overhead.

Out of the corner of his eye, off to the right, he saw three tangos sprinting toward him across the roof, but he had to stop Pak and stop him *now*.

2220 hours GMT
The quarters module roof
Bouddica Alpha

Murdock and Roselli had burst through a fire door and onto the roof of Bouddica Alpha just below the helipad several minutes before. Almost at once, they'd come under heavy fire and been forced to take cover.

Then the helicopters had arrived, a deafening arrival of the just-in-time cavalry.

"Eagle, Eagle, this is Falcon Leader!" Wentworth's voice called in Murdock's ear. "How about a rundown on your lads so we don't nick 'em by mistake? Over!"

"Falcon Leader, Eagle Leader," Murdock called back. "Don't worry about us. We're scattered all over the place, but we'll try to keep down until your boys are on the deck. Over!"

"We copy, Eagle Leader. Do you have any special targets in mind? Over!"

"That is affirmative, Eagle Leader. Hit the crane at Alpha's southeast corner. But be careful of the baby on the hook. Over!"

"We read you." The voice was grim. "We'll have it secured quick as thought. Good luck, Eagle."

"You too, Falcon. See you on the deck!"

2220 hours GMT
Bridge
Anchor tug *Horizon*
Alongside Bouddica Alpha

"All units!" Croft called, fiercely depressing the transmit key on his microphone. "All units! The Korean woman's escaped over the side. She's got a gun!"

In the excitement of the moment, he didn't realize he was

transmitting on the general tactical frequency to all of the combatants in the area.

2220 hours GMT
The quarters module roof
Bouddica Alpha

Inge reached the crane housing from the south side, ducking beneath the guy wires that helped counterbalance the long, yellow arm, and circling to the east side where the cab door was still open. Looking up, she could see Pak manipulating the levers.

"Pak!" she shouted, raising the pistol in the BKA-approved, two-handed grip. "Hands up!"

2220 hours GMT
The quarters module roof
Bouddica Alpha

Pak stared down at the woman, who stood below him in an aggressive, straddle-legged stance, barefoot, wearing a skirt and a torn white blouse. Would she actually shoot him? If it had been Chun standing there he would have had no doubt about that whatsoever, but this was a Westerner, coddled and soft, weakened by notions of fair play.

Still, indecision held him there, immobile. If she *did* shoot, if she managed to hit him, he could be dead before he could release the bomb.

Suddenly, a huge, black vision of insect-faced horror heaved itself up from beneath the railing encircling the upper deck, hanging from beneath its clattering rotors, blinding lights beneath its nose obliterating the night. A hurricane of wind caught the woman from behind, shoving her forward a step as her yellow hair whipped in frenzied disarray.

Pak grinned, reaching again for the cable release.

2220 hours GMT
Helicopter Falcon 1/4
Above Bouddica Alpha

"What was that?" SAS Lieutenant Kevin Donovan yelled. He was standing on the Sea King's cargo deck, trying to hear as the pilot shouted something over the intercom channel.

"I said we just got a flash from the *Horizon*," the pilot repeated. "Something about an escaped woman with a gun!"

"Sir!" one of the men tugged on his sleeve and pointed out the open door.

Speak of the devil! A woman was there, pinned in the helicopter's lights, trying to get up off her hands and knees as the helo's rotor wash struck her. She was holding a pistol, about to shoot someone inside the crane's cab. . . .

"Put her down!" Donovan yelled, slapping the machine gunner on the shoulder.

2220 hours GMT
The quarters module roof
Bouddica Alpha

Something struck her from behind just as she got to her feet. There was no pain . . . just a savage blow that slammed her forward, knocking her down and leaving her stunned, almost paralyzed. Blinking back tears of shock and rage and adrenaline-charged fury, she rolled over and saw the helicopter edging closer.

No . . . *no! It wasn't goddamned fair!* She wasn't supposed to be shot by the guys on her *own side*! . . .

Men were running toward her . . . terrorists. She tried to rise, but her left arm refused to support her. They were firing, though whether at her or the helicopter behind her she couldn't tell. She did know they would be on her in seconds. . . .

Then fire stabbed again from the helicopter's open side door, cutting into the running PRR terrorists and scattering them like tenpins.

And then the big SEAL from Texas, Blake's friend Mac-Kenzie, was there, sliding to a halt next to her, helping her up. "No!" she shouted above the helicopter's thunder. "In the crane! In the crane!"

In a heartbeat, she'd pushed free of MacKenzie and raised her pistol again, one-handed, aiming once more at Pak, who was illuminated now by the light inside the crane's control cabin, struggling with one of the levers.

Gasping against the crushing paralysis that was clamping down on the entire left side of her chest, Inge squeezed the trigger. The gun bucked in her hand and she kept firing, slamming round after round into the cab. *Damn!* She couldn't hold the target! Miss! Another miss!

She kept firing. . . .

2220 hours GMT
The quarters module roof
Bouddica Alpha

Bullets slammed into the cab, smashing the windshield, pocking the metal roof. Turning in his seat, Pak saw the woman sprawled awkwardly on the deck outside, firing round after round directly at him. One of the SEALs was there too, aiming his H&K,

One bullet slammed into Pak's side, nearly knocking him out of the seat, but the woman was too late, the SEAL and the noisily hovering helicopter were too late, they were *all* too late. . . . Laughing, the sound a bit hysterical even to his own ears, Pak grasped the release knob and pulled, just as a string of rounds struck him in the side, higher up, just beneath his left arm.

There was an agonizing delay . . . and then the atomic bomb suspended at the end of the cable dropped away; the cable leaped into the air, dancing at the release of so much weight. The bomb plummeted through darkness toward the surface of the water fifty feet below.

Pak didn't hear the splash when it hit two seconds later.

26

Friday, May 4

Murdock had seen the bomb's release as he raced across the rooftop toward the crane, seen it drop from the hoist and arrow fifty feet straight down, vanishing into the gray water with a splash. He reached the railing above Alpha's southwest corner and stood there looking over the edge, hands gripping the railing so tightly his knuckles ached, holding his breath, waiting for that searing, final instant that could come any second now.

No one knew how the thing might be armed and triggered. The assumption all along had been either a remote-control device of some sort that would detonate the thing at the press of a button, or a timer, set either manually or through a remote control. The former was a nightmare possibility; the latter was deemed more likely. The PRR terrorists who set the thing would almost certainly allow some leeway for their own escape. There were terrorists who seemed suicide-minded enough to go to certain death, but that didn't fit the usual profile of terrorist shooters drawn from the old RAF or the Provos. Politically motivated, they seemed to go for the main chance, seeking to create havoc but rarely allowing themselves to get drawn into suicide situations. They shot it out to the last bullet only when there was no other way out.

274

If these terrorists had been members of the Japanese Red Army now, it would have been a lot more worrisome from the start. Some of *those* guys deliberately sought martyrdom, like the Hezbollah crazies who'd driven an explosives-laden truck into an American compound in Lebanon.

As the minutes passed and there was no blinding flash, Murdock started to relax. Maybe the bomb hadn't been armed after all. Perhaps it had dropped by accident.

Or . . . Pak was supposed to have a remote control of some sort. Turning from the rail, Murdock raced back toward the crane . . . then came to a dead stop. Mac was there . . . and, oh, God, *no*. . . .

"*Inge!*"

Mac was there, cradling Inge's head. There was a lot of blood on her blouse, and some on her face as well, next to her mouth. SAS and GSG9 commandos had circled off the area, creating a perimeter around the crane. A young officer looked up as Murdock approached.

"I'm sorry, Yank," he said. "We thought—"

"Inge!" She was unconscious. He looked up at Mac. "How is she?"

"Don't know, L-T. She took a fifty through her back."

He probed her shoulder, front and back. Entrance and exit wound were clean and no wider than his gloved finger, punching through her left shoulder blade from behind and emerging beneath her collarbone; a fifty-caliber round was so powerful it must have punched clear through her and scarcely slowed. Still, there was a hell of a lot of blood. Mac or someone had plugged the wound with a cloth that was already sodden through with blood.

"We've got a medic coming down now," the SAS officer said.

"Where's Pak?" Murdock demanded.

MacKenzie nodded toward the crane. "Up there. She got him, L-T. You would've been proud. But he pulled the damned lever anyway."

"We're still here," he said. "Take care of her."

"Right, L-T."

He left them and started up the ladder to the crane cab.

Crackling radio calls over Murdock's earphone followed the progress of the assault inside the quarters.

"*Charlie-five, Charlie-three. I'm on Level One, Corridor Two. Two prisoners here. Moving!*"

"*Delta-one, this is seven. We are in the rec hall. Repeat, in the rec hall. Two terrs down. The hostages are okay.*"

"*Seven, one. Keep 'em there. Medics and handlers are on the way.*"

"*Echo two, Echo one. Watch yourselves. We're coming down Corridor Seven.*"

"*Roger that.*"

Elsewhere, the battle was rapidly dying out. British helicopters remained hovering off each corner of Alpha, as dozens of SAS and GSG9 troops scoured the roof, penetrated the doors, filtered down into the depths of the labyrinthine installation. Occasional scattered bursts of gunfire sounded from below, but by and large, all resistance had ceased. Several tangos had been rounded up by SAS troopers and were lying flat on the deck, hands in the smalls of their backs, as commandos cuffed and searched them.

Pak was crumpled in the corner of the cab, bleeding from a dozen wounds but still alive. Murdock thought the man was unconscious, but as he started searching him, as he found and retrieved the remote-control unit in an inside jacket pocket, the North Korean's eyes opened.

"Too . . . late."

"What do you mean, 'too late'? What'd you do?"

Pak started coughing, vomiting blood. "Too late," he managed to say again as his eyes drifted shut. He was dying.

Murdock glanced down at the twisted, broken leg. His hand snapped down, slamming against the broken ends. "Wake up, you bastard! What did you do?"

Pak's eyes opened again. The pain seemed to brace him, to give him strength. "Pressure switch," he said. "I set it for eighty . . . for eighty . . ."

The eyes glazed over. Pak was dead.

A pressure switch! That was why the bomb had been suspended over the water. It could be jettisoned easily, possibly with the non-suicidal PRR gunmen being told it would be detonated by a simple timer after they'd had a chance to escape. Probably the idea had been to use the minisub to plant the thing if there was time. Then arming the pressure switch would be like a direct trigger, detonating the bomb as soon as the button was pushed. In either case, having the bomb detonate deep underwater would be certain to cause maximum damage to all of the bottom installations in this part of the North Sea.

He'd set it to detonate at eighty something. Eighty what? The water in this part of the North Sea averaged forty fathoms . . . about 240 feet. Murdock frowned. Pak was North Korean . . . and the Koreans measured everything in meters.

Eighty meters?

That would be 248, almost 250 feet.

Oh, God! Could it actually be that simple? Had Pak miscalculated . . . and armed the bomb to explode eight feet *deeper* than the water around the Bouddica Complex? Murdock sagged back against the crane's support, suddenly weary. That bastard Murphy had been up to his old tricks on *both* sides of the battle this time.

He dropped from the cab and started walking back toward Mac and Inge. Other helicopters were approaching now, with more troops, with NEST personnel, with medics and doctors.

Roselli met him. "I just heard about Inge."

"She'll be all right," he said. *She's got to be.*

"Yeah, she's tough. They'll have her on a medevac chopper in another few minutes. What's the word on Pak's bomb?"

"He said there was a pressure switch, set for eighty meters." Murdock managed a weak smile. "I think he miscalculated. The water's not that deep here!"

Roselli laughed. "Ha! That's a good one! All that high-tech, and the son of a bitch forgot to check his depth charts!"

The moon, just past full, was rising over the southeastern horizon, enormous and silver, its light casting cool illumination across the sea.

The moon . . .

And with a terrible, icy certainty, Murdock knew that he was wrong, that Pak had made no mistake, that the bomb deposited moments ago at the base of Bouddica Alpha was still very much alive and very, very dangerous.

"This is Eagle Leader!" he shouted over his mike. "I need to talk with a senior man with the complex! One of the civilians!"

There was a confused rustle of sound over the net. Then an unfamiliar voice came on. "Uh, this is John Brayson. I'm the senior facility manager. What can—"

"Mr. Brayson! How deep, exactly, is the water underneath Bouddica Alpha? Do you know?"

"Of course," Brayson's reply came back, sounding a trifle hurt. "Two hundred forty-seven feet. That's the average depth, of course—"

"And what's the variance from tides?"

"Tides? Oh, well, that depends of course—"

"Damn it! How high are the fucking tides out here?"

"Between low tide and high, they average five meters," Brayson said. "About fifteen, sixteen feet. Of course, with a storm surge, they can be—"

Murdock cut him off, switching to the main tactical channel. If the moon was just rising, it ought to be close to low tide here. Murdock cursed himself for not checking the local tide tables before leaving on this op, but there'd been so much else to think about. If it was low tide now, the water must be somewhere in the neighborhood of 240 feet or so, maybe a little less.

Six hours after low tide, however, the moon would be high in the sky, the bulge of water raised by the moon's once-daily passage across the heavens would pass Bouddica from east to west, and the water would be deeper.

With the water reaching a high-tide depth of perhaps 254 feet.

It was impossible to get a precise time without some fairly accurate tables at hand. High tide did not always keep lockstep with the moon, but lagged behind by as much as three hours, depending on the location. Wind and weather could raise tides higher, or knock them down. The position of the sun could amplify them into spring tides, or restrain them as neap tides.

But it was a safe guess that somewhere between two and four hours from now, the water beneath Bouddica would reach

248 feet—80 meters—and Pak's atomic bomb would detonate.

Murdock opened a channel. "This is Eagle Leader. The bomb is armed, repeat, armed. Colonel Wentworth!"

"I'm here, Eagle Leader. Go ahead."

"I suggest you start evacuation immediately. Get everyone off the complex and at least ten miles away."

"Roger that."

"I don't know how long we have . . . but I'm going to find out. Somebody track down some deep-diving gear for me, fast!"

Roselli touched his shoulder. "Make that two sets, L-T."

"This'll be a solo dive, Razor."

"Like fuck it will! What's the first rule of BUD/S?"

Swim buddies. You never hit the water without a partner.

"Besides," Roselli added, "it's gonna be dark down there. You'll need an extra set of eyes . . . and hands."

Murdock thought about it, then nodded. There was no denying Roselli's logic. In any case, he'd be no safer up here than he would 240 feet down.

"Okay, Razor. Looks like we're dive buddies. Let's get rigged out."

2225 hours GMT
Second level
Bouddica Bravo

Skeeter Johnson had been listening in over the tactical channel. "Hey, Skipper?" he called on the SEALs' channel. "This is Skeeter! Wait for me! You're gonna need a bus to get you down!"

"Negative Skeeter," Murdock's voice shot back. "I'd be blind in the bus, and it'd take too long to get the SDV powered up and moving. Besides, the life support won't be compatible. I'm using some of the diving gear here on the platform. You can bring our dry suits across, though."

Johnson scowled. He was being left out of this op, and he didn't like that one bit. Sure, sure, everyone had a job to do, but he and Jaybird had been parked with the satellite gear, while Murdock, Mac, and Razor pulled the actual sneak-and-peek on

Alpha. And it was a good thing they'd been posted here too. At one point during the battle, two tangos had come charging across the bridge. Whether they'd been fleeing the battle or coming over to secure Bravo for some other purpose was unknown; Sterling and Johnson had opened up on them from ambush, knocking both off the catwalk and into the sea. If the radio gear had been left unguarded . . .

But the battle was over now, with little chance of wandering tangos coming this way. Damn it, he wanted to get in on this!

He was pretty sure that the choice of personnel had been deliberate on Murdock's part; Murdock, Mac, and Razor were all long-time members of Third Platoon's Blue Squad, while he and Jaybird were relative newcomers. Murdock had probably arranged things so that the men who knew each other, their moves, their habits in combat would all be working together. It was safer that way, with less likelihood of someone getting pegged by friendly fire.

But this was different. Murdock needed him.

"Do you read me, Skeeter?" Murdock's voice came. "Send Jaybird across with our dry suits. You stay put!"

"Uh . . . roger that. I copy."

He exchanged a dark glance with Sterling, who was already gathering up the SEALs' gear, then sat down to wait.

2232 hours GMT
Diver's bay
Bouddica Alpha

Bouddica was almost embarrassingly well stocked with diving gear. There were suits of every possible kind—wet suits, dry suits, hot-water suits, even a few of the bulky, heavily armored "Jim suits" that looked like a cross between an old-fashioned hard-hat diving rig, medieval suits of armor, and the suits worn by astronauts on the surface of the Moon.

Murdock and Roselli, however, would wear their dry suits. They wouldn't provide perfect protection against the bitter cold of the North Sea depths, but they wouldn't require as much preparation and fitting out as the high-tech hot-water suits that Bouddica's BGA deep divers normally used when they were servicing the bottom pipelines and installations.

The main reason Murdock had elected not to use his SEAL gear, which should still be floating in the tethered swim bladder beneath Alpha, was that it was rebreather gear, rated for use only to a depth of about thirty feet. Pure oxygen from a rebreather became toxic at the pressure of greater depths.

They couldn't even rely on normal SCUBA gear at 240 feet. SCUBA used standard oxygen-nitrogen gas mix, the same as normal air, but at depths much below one hundred feet, the standard mix became dangerous as well. Nitrogen narcosis, sometimes called "rapture of the deep," was an affliction every diver developed to one degree or another when breathing nitrogen at greater than about three atmospheres' pressure. The best medical evidence was that at depths beyond one hundred feet, the nitrogen actually began interfering to a greater or lesser degree with the impulses passing from neuron to neuron in the brain. Concentrating on the task at hand, training, and experience could overcome nitrogen narcosis to a certain degree . . . but cold water and fear could increase a man's susceptibility.

The other danger, of course, was decompression sickness. Diving on straight air meant that as the pressure went up, nitrogen in their bodies would be forced into their body tissues. If they surfaced too fast, nitrogen bubbles could form in a man's bloodstream—fizzing up just like the carbon dioxide in a shaken soda can when the pop top was pulled. The bubbles would collect in his joints and cause an exquisite agony; some might clog vital arteries in brain or heart or lung. The condition was called "the bends," and it was both crippling and deadly.

Murdock and Roselli would be diving on heliox, a gas mixture that substituted helium for nitrogen. Helium would completely eliminate the dangers of nitrogen narcosis. While it wasn't impossible to get the bends on heliox—helium bubbles could form the same as nitrogen bubbles—the danger of decompression sickness was much reduced on a deep dive when the divers breathed helium, and at extreme depth breathing was easier too.

Of course, both men would sound like Donald Duck when they spoke.

Their headgear consisted of full-face masks, with built-in

radios. Radio signals didn't travel far underwater—no more than a few yards, in fact—but the mask transmitters would enable Murdock and Roselli to communicate as long as they stayed close to one another. There were also pickups on the pylons supporting Bouddica Alpha, so listeners on the surface would be able to hear them once they were within range. Helium, however, changed a diver's voice, pitching it much higher and giving it a squeaky, cracking effect that grew worse the deeper he went. The distortion was literally known as the "Donald Duck Effect."

More serious was the fact that helium was a far better conductor of heat than nitrogen. Breathing heliox, the divers would be far more susceptible to the intense cold.

But they would face that when they had to.

"Okay," Murdock told the others in the room as Bouddica's senior dive master buckled on an extra set of weights, investing him like a squire assisting a knight with his armor before a medieval tourney. "Roselli and I will go first. The rest of the SEALs get their chance as soon as you can get gear together for them, but this will be volunteers only. Don't dive until something happens to us . . . or until we call you down. Everybody else, except absolutely necessary personnel—and volunteers only—get the hell out." He glanced at his watch. "We probably still have two hours or so. But we can't count on much more. Everybody understand?"

There were nods and muttered agreements from the others in the room. Murdock exchanged nods with Roselli, then slipped the mask down over his face. A quick radio check—all okay—and he and Roselli flip-flopped their way across to the open wall. Murdock clung to a nylon line with his right hand, a line that led back to a winch mounted on the diver bay close by the door. The shackle on the free end would let him hook onto the eye on the end of the atomic bomb; they'd be able to hoist it up from here once he signaled the hookup complete.

As long as there were no booby traps Pak hadn't told them about, the bomb could be easily disarmed then.

All they had to do was get the rope and shackle to the bomb.

There was an elevator in the nearest pylon that should have whisked them down to the bottom, but it had never worked right. Squire Murphy, once again. Most BGA divers used a complex elevator arrangement that lowered them down the outside, but it would take too long to break that out now. Instead, they would jump from the lowest level, a drop of about forty feet, then swim for the bottom, some forty times a man's height below. Roselli went first, stepping off the edge of the door and vanishing as he fell.

"Lieutenant!" Wentworth called. Murdock paused in the open door, a step away from the night. "Luck, Yank," the SAS colonel called. "We'll be waiting for you. Right here."

Murdock gave him a thumbs-up, then stepped after Roselli into darkness.

2249 hours GMT
Anchor tug *Celtic Maiden*
Alongside Bouddica Alpha

Chun heard the first splash as something heavy landed in the sea less than twenty meters from where she was hiding. She turned in time to see a dark shape—obviously a fully suited diver—plummet out of the sky and land in the water, close by the boiling foam left the first entry.

Divers . . . two of them. It wasn't hard to guess what they were after.

It was time for her to execute her plan.

She'd been hiding here behind the massive winch on the tug's after deck, shivering, trying to stay warm, trying to stay hidden, wondering what to do. The submarine resting on the cradle nearby offered her a possible escape, but she wasn't eager to take that route. The minisub had a top speed of only a few knots; it wouldn't be hard to track the machine and destroy it.

Besides, she knew that Chong Yong would not have dropped the bomb without arming it, knew that he would have set the pressure switch to detonate within a few hours. It was her duty to stay behind, to make sure no attempts were made to retrieve it.

One SAS trooper stood guard by the minisub. He was standing with his back to Chun, watching the spot in the water where the two divers had vanished. Rising smoothly from her hiding place, Chun fired into the man's back from a range of five meters, the sound-suppressed burst from her stolen H&K snapping his spine and propelling him forward into the water.

Then she was running for the sub. The tarpaulin had been removed earlier, the hatch on top open. In seconds, she'd vaulted up to the craft's top deck, scrambled into the hip-snug conning tower, banged the circular hatch shut and dogged it, then dropped into a control room so tiny she could touch opposite bulkheads without even stretching.

The cradle was equipped with hydraulics, controlled from inside the cabin. Chun went down the line of memorized switches . . . power on, lights on, cabin pressure on, batteries on, diving planes to manual, blowers on, steering enabled, hydraulics on. . . .

With a whine and the creak of shifting mass, the stern of the little sub began elevating. Chun lay on her belly at the pilot's station, her entire world narrowed to banks of switches and controls, and a line of three small portholes giving her a view forward and slightly to either side. The water was coming up as the Squid's nose tipped down. The stern was tipping higher . . . higher . . .

Chun hit the shackle release holding the Squid astern. Smoothly, the six-meter craft slid forward; bubbles and foam exploded about the portholes . . . and then were replaced by black water.

As the sub's electric motors come up to speed, Chun hit the ballast flood controls. Water gurgled into the tanks, and as the surge of the North Sea caught her with a heavy, rolling thump, the Squid settled lower into the sea.

She started her dive.

27

Friday, May 4

2315 hours
Murdock, 100 feet down
Bouddica Alpha

Murdock was descending through Night Absolute.

The crash of landing, the surge and jolt of the waves close to the surface, all were behind them now as the two SEALs drove downward on strong, steady kicks of their borrowed BGA fins. Both men held underwater lights, but the water was so laden with silt that the beams, dazzling bright where they were reflected by the countless drifting particles, could not penetrate more than about ten feet. No matter. The massive southeastern pylon of Bouddica Alpha was vaguely sensed as a massive cliff face rising slowly past on their right, and the A-bomb, traveling more or less straight down, would have landed about thirty yards southeast of the pylon's base. They would dive to the bottom, take their bearings, and then begin a simple search pattern, working out southeast from the pylon.

Passing 125 feet. Almost halfway down. The pressure was up to almost four atmospheres now.

At sea level, in the open air, the atmosphere exerts a steady pressure of just over fourteen pounds per square inch, a condition, referred to as "one atmosphere," caused by the sheer weight of all of the air extending from that square inch of skin clear to the top of the Earth's atmosphere.

For every thirty-three feet of depth beneath the surface,

another one atmosphere of pressure is added, thanks to the
extra weight of the water overhead. At 125 feet, the pressure
was equal to 3.8 atmospheres—or fifty-three pounds of
pressure against each square inch of Murdock's body.

No wonder even the double steel hulls of submarines quickly
reached a point vividly referred to as their crush depths after
they'd descended to a depth of a scant few thousand feet.

One hundred eighty feet, and a pressure of 5.7 atmospheres—eighty pounds per square inch. Murdock felt no
differently, of course, since the external pressure was balanced
from within; his regulator was feeding him heliox at higher and
higher pressures to compensate.

Any uneasiness, any queasiness he felt was purely psychological.

It was cold too. His neoprene dry suit was designed to keep
a warming layer of air between inner and outer layers, but no
system is perfect. He suspected that water was working its way
through to the inside.

No problem. He'd endured much worse than this in training.
He kept going down. "Razor? You still with me?" His voice
sounded *exactly* like the quacking of a duck, and he had to
suppress a laugh.

"I'm here, L-T," Roselli chirped and quacked. "Great voice."

"Yeah. We should sing soprano."

Two hundred ten feet. Over ninety-three pounds per square
inch. Getting close now. Must be. The chill was fierce,
threatening to set him to trembling. He checked his watch and
was surprised to see that they'd only been in the water about
four minutes. A descent rate of fifty-and-some feet per minute?
A foot a second. Yeah. That wasn't bad.

Two hundred thirty feet. The bottom appeared like a fuzzy
white wall anchored in the round shaft of his light. Roselli's
light flashed across the mud to the left as Murdock swung his
feet beneath him and touched down in a tiny, silent explosion
of silt.

"Falcon, Falcon," he chirped. "Do you read me? Over."

No reply. They must not be close enough to the radio
pickups. Or else pressure or cold or a million other things that
could go wrong had sabotaged the radio. Never mind. Where

was the pylon? There . . . a looming, moss-covered pillar, a fuzzy cliff in the night. Rising, he swam closer. That wasn't moss after all, but fine tendrils of silt. Matter acted in strange ways at extreme depth. Carefully, Murdock gave the line he was still clutching in his left hand a tug, freeing up some more play. From here, there was no sign at all of the surface, no sign of anything at all save the two divers and their tiny bubble of light. There were no fish, no sign of any other life at all.

Murdock checked his compass. "That way."

"Roger."

Together, they started swimming toward where the bomb ought to be, each stroke of their flippers stirring up a fresh swirl of silt. Murdock was aware of strange objects looming out of the darkness all around, however, and was beginning to wonder if this search would be as easy as he'd thought it might be while he'd still been relatively safe and warm on the surface. Pipelines ran across the bottom in every direction, while storage tanks and less identifiable pieces of gear were scattered across the sea floor like a child giant's toys. Before the dive he'd been wondering if a metal detector or a hand-held sonar might be useful, but had decided against them for reasons of time. Now he realized he'd made the right choice; both would have been useless here.

The question was whether even a careful search by Mark I eyeball would be any better.

Odd. It was growing lighter.

At first, Murdock thought he was suffering from nitrogen narcosis . . . but that shouldn't be possible on heliox. *Something* was affecting his brain, however, because suddenly the entire landscape was lit as brightly as day, no matter which way he pointed his light.

He looked up . . .

. . . and stared into the dazzle of a ring of spotlights. Murdock's first thought was that he was looking at some strange kind of sea monster; there were extraordinary creatures in the deeps, creatures that could produce their own light . . . but then reality reasserted itself and he realized he was looking at the North Korean minisub. It was shaped something like a blunt-nosed, stubby torpedo, with the underside of its nose recessed beneath a massive snout. Powerful spotlights circled a row of three windows. To either side, a manipulator arm was extended as though to reach out and snatch, each tipped with grasping, titanium claws.

"Watch it, Razor!" he called. "Minisub, twelve o'clock!"

They broke left and right and the claws missed them, the submarine rushing past just overhead, buffeting them in its wake and prop wash. The noise of its twin screws was a high-pitched chirring, audible above the whine of its motors.

The sub swung to port, chasing Roselli. Murdock's mind was racing. A weapon! He needed a weapon! But there was nothing but his diver's knife, useless against . . .

Or was it? He also had the length of nylon line, still trailing down from the surface. Like every man in love with the sea, Murdock had spent his share of time in small boats. He'd once spent a very unhappy afternoon adrift on a lake, trying to cut away a length of fishing line that had become snarled around the shaft of his speedboat's propeller.

Jerking his diver's knife from its sheath, he measured off several arms' lengths of line, then cut it. He was also cutting off the shackle, of course, but there was no time to worry about that now. Leaving the main line adrift, he took his ten-foot length and advanced on the submarine, the hunter in pursuit of his prey.

He could see Roselli a few yards ahead of the monster, backing away. "Watch it, Razor!" he called. "Watch your back."

He didn't think Roselli heard him. The other SEAL backed squarely into the unyielding wall of a large undersea storage tank, his heliox tanks giving a metallic ring easily heard through the water. He tried to turn, tried to swim clear . . . and the submarine's arms descended. One claw clasped around his arm; the other groped for his face.

Murdock reached the minisub's stern a moment later, straddling the horizontal wing that mounted two propeller cowls, one to the left, the other to the right. He fed the end of the line through the starboard cowling. For a moment, the prop wasn't turning, and he kept stuffing the line through the narrow space at the front of the shroud.

Then the engine switched on, the line was reeled in . . . and with a grating squeak, the propeller stopped.

The port-side prop spun furiously, spinning the sub like a top. Murdock was knocked clear. Roselli, he saw, was free of the thing's grasp, but hurt, clutching his arm as a cloud of dark blood spilled into the water. The sub kept turning, swinging about to face Murdock, arms descending. Whoever was piloting that thing—it had to be Chun—was good. Even on one screw, she was keeping the sub trim and balanced, pivoting the bow left and right as she pursued her next victim. The sub, Murdock saw, was equipped with small, high-pressure thrusters. Even with one prop out, she could still maneuver that thing.

Damn!

He ducked left, avoiding a stroke from one snapping claw. If he could foul the second propeller . . . but he would have to swing back and find the dangling line again, and he didn't think that Chun was going to give him the luxury of time. He backpedaled, and the sub advanced. The lights were blinding, almost mesmerizing. Each time Murdock tried to shift left or right, up or down, the sub matched him, coming closer. Possibly he could get inside the reach of its arms and cling to the hull, but then what? A fast ascent might kill him; at least it would keep him away from the nuke, which had to be Chun's plan.

The lady was going to stay here, taking on all comers, until the damned thing exploded.

Murdock was just about out of options. If he could find something lying in the mud, a piece of chain, a length of pipe, anything, he might have a chance. As it was . . .

The whale shape came in from the left, arrowing straight toward the submarine's starboard side. Its blunt nose struck just below the conning tower, a ringing crack that seemed to echo off the seafloor and the BGA bottom structures nearby.

The bus! Johnson and the bus! The crazy idiot had disobeyed orders and brought the bus down, swinging in at top speed and ramming the North Korean sub.

He felt weak.

Somehow, he managed to stay focused. The submarine was

in trouble; he could hear a thin, high wailing coming from it, could see the stream of bubbles trailing from a nasty-looking dent beneath the conning tower. The pressure hull had cracked; water must be blasting into the interior, propelled by a pressure of 120 pounds per square inch. The bubble stream grew bigger, more insistent. The sub's interior space would be filling with water now, squeezing the air inside to a fraction of its former volume.

As the sub slowly settled toward the bottom, motors and thrusters silent now, he wondered if Chun was still alive.

No. She couldn't be. Not after the near-explosive compression of the tiny sub's cabin.

It took nearly ten more minutes to find the bomb, half buried in the silt about where they'd expected to find it. It took another ten minutes to find the cut-off length of line; by that time, the cold was penetrating Murdock's dry suit so badly that he was shaking violently. It was all he could do to drag himself onto the blunt, upper end of the bomb, thread the nylon through the shackle eye, and tie a knot. His first attempts failed . . . but he kept at it, and at it. . . . It would have been impossible without Johnson, who held the SDV steady to keep its forward light on the job; Murdock could never have tied that knot in total darkness.

He was having trouble breathing, and the ends of the knot kept slipping from numb and unresponsive fingers. "Damn it, Johnson, let's have some light here."

"I've got the light full on you, L-T." The squeaking voice was almost impossible to understand.

"Say . . . again. Say . . . again. You're breaking up." Damn! He almost had it that time! Angrily, he stopped and pulled off his gloves, feeling the icy water flood up his arms. If he could finish the knot before he lost all sensation in his fingers entirely . . .

It took him a long time to realize that the problem was not with Johnson's light . . . but with his brain.

Somehow, he managed not to pass out until after the knot was tied, a good sturdy fisherman's bend that any Navy boatswain's mate would have been proud of.

EPILOGUE

Recompression chamber
Bouddica Alpha

"So what happened after I passed out?"

His voice still sounded funny, chirping like the voice of a cartoon chipmunk. The recompression chamber had been charged with heliox, to avoid the complications of high-pressure nitrogen.

He looked around, taking in his surroundings. Johnson and Roselli stared back from bunks on the other side of the claustrophobic chamber, grinning like maniacs. A Navy corpsman, wearing a mask so that he could come and go in the high-pressure environment without having to decompress himself, was taking a blood pressure reading on Johnson. Roselli's arm was swathed in bandages. Murdock was still feeling groggy after the effects of nearly drowning. His chest hurt; his throat felt raw and dry. The last thing he remembered was his vision going, just as he'd tied off the knot.

He'd awakened here.

"Here" was one of several recompression chambers in service aboard the BGA oil platform, kept ready for just such emergencies with the commercial divers on the facility.

MacKenzie was peering in through the porthole at him. "You can thank Skeeter for saving your ass. He parked the bus, climbed out, double-checked on your boatswain's mate skills, you'll be glad to hear, and then dragged you back to the sub.

Stuffed you in the cargo compartment and drove you straight to the surface."

"The bomb?"

MacKenzie jerked a thumb upward. "Already safe on board. The NEST and EOD guys are giving it the fine-tooth treatment. Unless one of them sneezes or something, I think we're going to be okay."

"Ha ha."

"Don't sweat it, L-T. They told me it was a very simple detonator, easily disarmed just by jamming a piece of wood through the firing device. You might be interested, though, to know that the water depth when they started hauling it up was two hundred forty-six feet. I'm *real* glad you remembered your knot-tying lessons from boot camp."

"I didn't go to boot camp."

"OCS then."

Murdock didn't even want to think about what would have happened if the line had parted.

"So how long have I been out?"

"About twenty-four. It was touch and go there for a while. Cold water, though, can keep a man's brain on ice. They say you were probably clinically dead for several minutes. Any memories of heaven?"

"Nothing. I must've been out and missed it all. *Damn.*"

"Maybe next time."

"What about Roselli?"

"Aw, enlisted men don't rate a chauffeur, L-T. You know that."

"Sterling and I were already on our way down," MacKenzie said. "Met him at about eighty feet and brought him the rest of the way up."

"His arm'll be fine," the corpsman said, his voice muffled by the mask. "But I do recommend against his trying to arm-wrestle submarines in the future."

"Hey, I've sworn that off," Roselli said. "From now on, I'm sticking to mermaids."

"Them you might be able to handle," Murdock said, grinning.

"Speaking of which," MacKenzie said, "there's someone

here who wants to talk to you. In fact, she threatened to shoot anyone who got in her way. . . ."

A familiar face framed in blond hair filled the porthole.

"Inge!"

"Hello, SEAL," she said. "I thought you said they drown-proofed you guys."

"They do." He patted his bare shoulders and chest experimentally. "I'm still here, right?"

"I'm glad you are," she told him. "I just wish I could be in there with you."

"Are you okay? What happened?"

She grimaced. "They say the bullet went right through. I'm all bandaged up now, and they put five quarts of blood in me, but they say I'll be okay. I . . . wouldn't let them medevac me."

"She's right, L-T," MacKenzie's voice added. "This lady's dangerous. Hell, she shouldn't even be *up*! The doc here's been trying to keep her in bed, but she threatened to bring the place down if they didn't let her in to see you."

"I'll show you dangerous." Her head turned in the window; Murdock heard a thump and MacKenzie's loud "Ouch!"

Inge . . . she was okay!

And Murdock was just beginning to realize that he was in love.

He'd never been able to picture himself as being able to love anybody else, since Susan.

"Anyway," Inge told him, her face appearing once more in the porthole, "I wish I could join you in there, but they won't let me."

Murdock glanced again at Roselli and Johnson. Their grins, if anything, were larger, and Roselli waggled his eyebrows meaningfully. "Hey, don't mind us, L-T. If you want to party, we won't get in the way."

"Sure," Johnson said. "But we'd love to watch."

"That's right. SEALs do everything together!"

Murdock groaned. "Doc? How long am I stuck in here with these assholes?"

"About a week, Lieutenant."

"A *week*! Damn it, whatever happened to bachelor officers quarters? I want a room of my own!"

"Of *our* own," Inge added.

Johnson and Roselli laughed and, after a moment, Murdock joined in. "You just wait, lady," he told Inge. "When I get out of here, I'm going to teach you a lesson. I thought I told you to stay in your quarters."

"You forgot," she said primly, "to leave an army behind to guard me."

"I'd say, L-T," Roselli said, "that you've got a real armful there."

"Not yet," Murdock said, laughing. "Not yet! But in about one week I *will*!"